LORI WICK

White Chocolate Moments

HARVEST HOUSE PUBLISHERS

EUGENE, OREGON

Cover by Terry Dugan Design, Minneapolis, Minnesota

Cover photo © Jordan Chesbrough / iStockphoto

WHITE CHOCOLATE MOMENTS
Copyright © 2007 by Lori Wick
Published by Harvest House Publishers
Eugene, Oregon 97402
www.harvesthousepublishers.com

Library of Congress Cataloging-in-Publication Data
  Wick, Lori.
    White chocolate moments / Lori Wick.
        p. cm.
    ISBN-13: 978-0-7369-1780-3 (pbk.)
    ISBN-10: 0-7369-1780-2 (pbk.)
    1. Young women—Fiction. 2. Grandfathers—Fiction. I. Title.
    PS3573.I237W489 2007
    813.'54—dc22   2006029965

Printed in the United States of America

07 08 09 10 11 12 13 14 15 / BP-CF / 10 9 8 7 6 5 4 3 2 1

For Joyce Graves
and the memory of
Pastor Robert Graves.
Your lives have touched mine
in immeasurable ways.
I thank God for you.

ACKNOWLEDGMENTS

This page is supposed to get easier to write, but each time my heart is so full—and with some books the days have meted out challenges and times of stretching that I did not expect. Each of you have touched me in your own special way and encouraged me on my path to holiness.

—Betty Fletcher, how precious to have grown up with you. Your friendship is marvelous. Thanks for being there in such a loving, kind, and supportive way.

—Bob and Beth Hawkins, how delightful to call you friends. Your warmth, hospitality, loving spirits, and giving hearts have been our blessing again and again. Bob and I do not know what we would do without you.

—Jane Kolstad, so much more than a sister-in-law. Thanks for all you do, for your good thoughts and ideas, and for loving me so generously.

—Emilie Marie Barnes, thank you, not just for the use of your name but for the precious friend that you are. You and Bob are a highlight for us each summer, and we treasure you.

—Luke Sefton, Gage Sefton, Chad Hummel, Sarah Knepper, Jalaina King, and Jill Ciofani. I wish to thank you dear folks for the use of your wonderful names. My heart appreciates you so very much.

—Phil Caminiti, thank you for the song. I love the words and melodies you put down. Thank you for keeping on, for being a student of the Book, and passing on all you've learned.

—Bob Wick, who does not like white chocolate, but is still amazingly sweet. Thank you for the love and laughter. Thank you for your wonderful, fun heart, and also for the heart that takes God seriously. My heart would be nothing without you.

Prologue

CHICAGO, ILLINOIS
APRIL 1992

"Will Quinn and Austin be at Grandpa's?" eleven-year-old Arcineh Bryant asked about her cousins from the backseat of the car.

"Not today," her mother answered. "Quinn has a competition."

"With her horse?"

"Yes."

The silence in the backseat was telling. Trevor and Isabella Bryant exchanged a swift look. They had forced their daughter to give up a dance performance for this event at her grandfather's. Dance was very important to Arcineh, but she loved her grandfather, and it *was* his sixtieth birthday. That was what had motived Arcineh to come peacefully, only to learn that the standard had not been so high with every member of the family.

"Will they be there at all?" Arcineh asked after a moment more.

"Not tonight. They might come late tomorrow night so they can visit with Dad on Sunday."

"Might?" Arcineh's voice dripped with disapproval.

"Well," her father began, "it's quite a distance away, and Quinn doesn't compete until morning."

Low muttering could be heard from the backseat, but neither parent commented. They had shared a similar conversation on this very topic. Both agreed with their daughter's disapproval but knew better than to admit that to her.

"What are you studying right now in dance?" Trevor asked, his eyes on his daughter's face in the rearview mirror.

"Ballroom," Arcineh told him, her eyes meeting his.

"I've done some ballroom dancing myself," Trevor told her, his eyes lighting with a smile.

"That sounds a bit scary," Arcineh teased.

"Not at all," Isabella put in. "Your father is very good."

Arcineh laughed a little.

"I'll tell you what," Trevor said. "We'll go dancing next weekend—big band and all that."

"Where?" Arcineh was instantly taken, her eyes studying her father in the mirror.

"Suite 19 has big band sound."

Trevor's gaze flicked to Arcineh's. Catching his smile in the mirror, Arcineh couldn't resist saying, "I don't know if I can be seen dancing with a man your age. It might ruin my reputation."

Her parents found this hugely amusing and were still chuckling about it when they pulled into the circular driveway at Samuel Bryant's large home. This was not just Trevor's father but his boss. However, Trevor knew that the evening would be all fun. If Sam Bryant was good at anything—and he was actually good at many things—it was separating the office from the home. He worked very long hours but was very good at leaving the office behind.

"There you are!" Sam said the moment he set eyes on his youngest grandchild. Arcineh's smile matched his own. They exchanged a hug before Sam kissed Isabella's cheek and smiled at his son's birthday greetings. Arcineh was the one to hand him his gift.

"Open it now," she ordered, excitement filling her dark brown eyes.

"Very well," Sam agreed, grabbing a seat because the present was large and a bit awkward. He knew before tearing back the paper that it must be a picture frame, but he was not prepared for the photo itself.

Trevor, Isabella, and Arcineh smiled out at him from a formal studio setting, each looking wonderful. Sam felt his throat close a little and took a moment to look up and smile at them.

"For the man who has everything, Sam," Isabella teased him. "Family pictures always do the trick."

"This is beautiful," Sam said, standing to kiss her again. "And you," he continued, looking down at Arcineh, "look fabulous."

"It almost didn't come in on time to get framed," Arcineh said, not having heard the compliment, "but Mom talked them into hurrying it."

"She's good at that," Sam said with a wink for his daughter-in-law. Moments later, more guests arrived and the four were separated.

Without her cousins there, Arcineh mingled for only a short time before making her way to the kitchen. As she expected, Violet, who cooked and managed the house for her grandfather, was there. They were fast friends.

"Look at you in that dress," Violet said, laying out more hors d'oeuvres for the guests.

"I just got it." Arcineh hopped onto the counter, smoothed the skirt of the black velvet dress, and reached for some cheese. "It's all adults out there."

"No Quinn today?"

Arcineh made a face. "She's got a horse thing."

"Well, you know you're always welcome in here," Violet said, smiling at her. "I might even put you to work."

"In this dress? My mom would faint."

"And speaking of Mom," Isabella said from the doorway. "Hello, Violet."

"Hello, Isabella. You look beautiful."

"Thank you. And since we're exchanging compliments, I'll tell you the food is wonderful. Arcie," her mother continued, shifting her attention. "I have some people I want you to meet."

"I'm eating," Arcineh said, stuffing food in her mouth just to make it true.

Violet turned so as not to be caught laughing, and Isabella gave her daughter a pointed look, one that had her moving out the door just moments later. She met some work associates of her father, but just as soon as she was able, she escaped back to the kitchen. Not until music was put on and the dancing began did Arcineh make another appearance. And because she loved music and dancing, the evening suddenly grew very short. Long before she was ready, her father was telling her it was time to go.

"Great party, Dad," Trevor complimented, thanking his father as they took their coats from the waiting maid. As a rule Sam's only staff was Violet, but for his sixtieth birthday, he'd gone all out.

"It was a great time, wasn't it?" Sam agreed, feeling content that his family had stayed until the end, well past midnight. "Why don't you stay over?" Sam suggested when the front door was finally opened and they all saw the rain that had begun to pour.

"Thanks, Dad," Trevor wasted no time in saying, "but I think we want our own beds tonight."

"All right. I'll see you Monday" were Sam's last words before he hugged his daughter-in-law and Arcineh again.

The Bryant family moved to get into the car that had been driven under the canopy by the hired valet, everyone wearing a smile.

"That was fun," Arcineh said, settling in the backseat. "Quinn really missed out."

Trevor and Isabella, who loved their daughter to distraction, were kind enough to agree, and also to remain quiet about the fact that Arcie hadn't wanted to go in the first place.

CHAPTER *One*

Sam knew the moment Arcineh awoke because he'd been watching her face intently. Her eyes shifted around the hospital room before finding him.

"How are you?" Sam asked.

"ICU?" Arcineh whispered.

"No," Sam answered quietly, wondering if he should be worried that she hadn't remembered. "They moved you yesterday."

Arcineh nodded a little before staring into her grandfather's eyes, questions filling her gaze—not questions about the accident that only she survived, but about what would happen next. Sam, not always astute, read her thoughts this time.

"I don't want you to worry about the future. We'll be together," he said, his voice breaking a little. "We'll get through this."

"I can stay with you?"

"Forever."

She cried then for the first time, her face crumpling as the tears came. Sam got as close as he was able, whispering words of encouragement and comfort through his own tears.

Arcineh had had lots of visitors, most of whom she didn't even know were there, but for the moment, they were on their own sharing in this grief.

⟨⟨⟩⟩

The funeral and graveside services for Trevor and Isabella Bryant were over. Arcineh, growing more proficient on her crutches, made her way through Sam's front door and into the spacious foyer, her older cousin, Quinn, close by.

"Where are you going to sit?" Quinn asked. "I'll bring you something to drink."

"The family room," Arcineh answered, only because she was already facing in that direction. She made her way there and carefully lowered herself onto one of the sofas. She felt cold and was crossing her arms when her Aunt Tiffany, her father's only sibling, entered the room. She saw Arcineh shiver and covered her with a blanket.

Neither one spoke, but Tiffany sat close. They were joined by the others at a slow pace. Quinn came with Arcineh's drink, and then Sam, and eventually Tiffany's husband, Jeremy, and their son and Quinn's older brother, Austin.

"Violet is making something to eat," Sam said to Arcineh. "Are you hungry?"

"A little," she said, having learned in the hospital that if a caregiver got you to eat, he felt he'd done his job.

"Are you up to the dining room, or do you want to eat in here?"

"In here," Arcineh answered without thinking. The hip that had been broken in the accident had begun to ache. The doctor said the surgery had gone very well, but feeling normal again would take time. Right now Arcineh was just glad to be out of the hospital. For a moment her mind went to home, her own home, and she felt the shivering again.

"Here you go," Violet said as she appeared with a tray in her hands.

"This smells good," Arcineh replied, taking in the soup, bread, and her favorite pudding, and at the same time trying not to let anyone see her shake. She didn't know if it worked or not, but soon each person had his own plate and they sat around the room to eat. Their visiting was quiet and somewhat on the practical side, so Arcineh didn't fully attend. Violet's supper was very good, the best Arcineh had tasted in days, but given a choice, she would have chosen to sleep at the moment.

〜

"Are you a light sleeper, Grandpa?" Arcineh asked at bedtime, her voice husky with fatigue. Her uncle, aunt, and cousins were all still there, but Sam had gone to Arcineh's room to see her settled. It was the first night in the house for her since leaving the hospital.

"I am," Sam said, not admitting how little sleep he was getting these days. "I'm planning to sleep with my door open. Should I open yours when I go to bed?"

"Maybe you should," Arcineh agreed. "Will things be noisy for a while?"

"Probably not. I could just leave it open now."

Arcineh nodded against the pillow and studied her grandfather's face. The fine lines around his eyes seemed more pronounced in the light from the nightstand, and he looked as weary as she felt.

"What will you do with my dad's office?"

"The one in our building?"

Again she nodded against the pillow.

"For a while, nothing. Beyond that I don't know."

Arcineh didn't reply.

"Was there something you wanted?" Sam asked her.

"I don't know." She sounded a little lost and confused. "I guess I just want to visit and see it like it was."

"I'll remember that. Before I make any changes, I'll make sure you get there."

The eyes that had been watching everything so carefully now began to droop. Sam sat very still, and in spite of someone calling his name from the hallway, Arcineh dropped off to sleep. Sam sat with her for a few minutes, the light on, his heart numb. Not until his daughter came to the door looking for him did he rise, switch off the light, and exit. However, he remembered his word and left Arcineh's door open.

❧

"Are you sure Arcineh can't live with us?" Tiffany asked her father again.

"Yes. Arcineh stays here."

"Quinn cried herself to sleep just now, sure you would say no."

"She's right," Sam said without remorse. "I am saying no. Arcie can visit you this summer for as long as she likes, but I want her back in school as soon as she's able, and I want life to return to as close to normal as I can manage it. I can't do that if she moves 350 miles out of Chicago."

"Oh, Dad." Tiffany was distressed but not crying, and Sam was relieved. The grieving grandfather had spent days at the side of Arcineh's hospital bed with nothing to do but work out a plan to make life less painful for his youngest grandchild. Sending her away from him was not part of the plan.

Sam Bryant's marriage had broken up when his own children were 9 and 12. Not only did his wife walk away from him, but she also deserted their children. Trevor, the younger one, had drawn close to him and faired well. Tiffany's life had gone in the opposite direction. It had taken years for her world to look somewhat normal, and even at that, she did not have a perfect marriage or the greatest relationship with her two children.

Now Arcineh had lost not only her mother but also her father, and she had been equally close to both. Sam was not trying to maintain control for control's sake. He truly believed that sending Arcineh away from him and her familiar surroundings would be the worst thing he could do.

"You may not agree with me, Tiff, but I want your support on this."

"But you could ask her."

"She's not in a position right now to be making decisions, and if we did ask her and she didn't want to go, she'd feel bad about hurting Quinn. I don't wish to do that to either girl. I'll happily be the bad guy this time."

Tiffany had not seen it that way, but she was not quite done.

"How about this summer? We could ask her once she's finished her school year here, and then she could move in with us in the fall."

"Not even then, Tiffany. It's not time for such plans, and may never be."

Jeremy chose that moment to join them in Sam's home office and asked what they were talking about.

"Quinn and I want Arcie to move in with us," his wife explained briefly.

The surprise on his son-in-law's face told Sam he'd known nothing about this.

"You weren't in on these plans, Jeremy?" Sam asked, knowing his daughter had not meant to exclude him but wondering why it never occurred to her that Jeremy might want some say over what went on in the home they shared.

"No, but it would be fine, I guess."

"He said no," Tiffany said, her voice quivering a little, bringing her father's stern eyes to her.

"Don't start, Tiffany," Sam said.

Tiffany knew he meant it. She wasn't happy with her father right now, but she knew this was not the time and place to push the point. She hated telling her children no, and even though her father was the one who had denied Quinn's request, Tiffany knew the 12-year-old would take it out on her.

"She is welcome," Jeremy offered, "but I wonder if moving her out of Chicago is a good idea."

"It's a terrible idea," Sam said bluntly, emotions and exhaustion playing a part in his mood. "As much as I don't want you to have to deal with this fire, Jeremy, I'm not going to let Tiffany and Quinn keep this on the table. I don't care how much they complain to you, my answer is no, and that's that."

"Don't talk about me like I'm not here," Tiffany interjected, sounding petulant. "She's my brother's only child," she continued, lobbying for some sympathy and gaining none. Both men looked at her in a way that made her shut her mouth.

"I'm going to bed," Sam said quietly, knowing he was close to losing his temper. "I'll see you in the morning."

Husband and wife said goodnight but didn't move. Jeremy stared at his wife, still amazed that this had happened to all of them but also knowing that, grief or not, the idea of moving Arcineh had to be dealt with swiftly. He was not in the habit of getting into any of the battles Austin and Quinn had with their mother, but this time he was willing.

"Was this Quinn's idea?"

"Yes."

"That was sweet of her, but I agree with Sam that we're not going to pursue it."

"Do you know what she'll be like?" Tiffany let her head fall back against the chair, her weary eyes on the ceiling.

"No, she won't."

Tiffany's head came up. This was a voice she didn't often hear from her spouse.

"I'll talk to her," Jeremy said shortly. Tiffany opened her mouth to question him, but Jeremy shook his head. "Not now, Tiff. We need to go to bed."

Like her children Tiffany Rowan did not like to be told no, but this time she did not argue. When Jeremy stood and headed for the door, she was right behind him. They put out the lights on their way to the stairs and retired in an effort to find some sleep.

∽

"Are you glad she's gone?" Sam asked Arcineh when her cousin had left with her family.

"Not glad, but maybe relieved."

"Was it the tears?"

Arcineh shook her head in confusion. "She can't stop, and I don't know how to help her."

"She asked for you to come and live with them. Did she mention it?"

Arcineh looked as shocked as she felt.

"What did you say?" she whispered.

"No."

Arcineh's relief was visible. She sagged on her crutches, and Sam's heart clenched at the sight.

"I can't leave you and Chicago, Grandpa. You understand, don't you?"

"Absolutely. I would never send you away."

Arcineh stared at the floor for a long time, still trying to take it in but not succeeding. Her parents had come back to mind, and all she felt was loss. "I'm going to watch television," she finally said, turning to the family room.

"I'll be in my office if you need me."

"All right."

They went their separate ways, but not for long. Sam couldn't concentrate on a thing and soon went to check on Arcineh. He found her sound asleep, which turned out to be a good thing. Visitors began arriving the next day, and there seemed to be no end of them.

⮾

"I've got a bit of work for you," Arcineh's teacher, Mr. Sutter, said kindly. "There's no hurry, but when I spoke with your grandfather, he said you'd talked about it."

Arcineh nodded. "Thank you, Mr. Sutter. I'll get it done as fast as I can."

"There's no hurry, Arcie. You're so far ahead in almost every subject that you could miss the rest of the year, but we're still working on that World Lit project, and I want you to get going on it again."

Arcineh nodded, but she didn't feel as calm as she looked. All the work she'd done on it was at her old home.

"Is there something I can get you? Library books or anything else?"

"I don't think so. I'm going to try to get back to class next week. Grandpa wants the doctor to approve."

"There's no hurry, Arcie. We miss you, but your grades are not going to suffer."

Arcineh thanked Mr. Sutter again and walked him to the door when he left. He had been with Fetterman Academy, a small private school that Arcineh had been attending since she was seven, for ten years. He had been her teacher for two years.

Fetterman Academy was run very much like a homeschool, with a low student-teacher ratio and more than one age-group in a class. All subjects were covered, and covered thoroughly, but great amounts of time were also spent in subjects of interest to each child. Arcineh learned best when subjects were taught in solid blocks, and much of her schoolwork had been tailored with that in mind. In the fall, she had spent weeks and weeks on math and almost nothing else. Following math was science, with refresher tests for math, and after that social studies and history, again, accompanied by regular refresher tests in each subject.

But afternoons were much more open. Whatever a child wanted to study could be accommodated. Reports and papers were expected—it was not a time when a child could be idle—but the very nature of allowing the students to choose their own topic was unique. One year Arcineh had spent the entire first semester researching the life of Lewis Carroll. Another year, she had done four projects in the same amount of time.

"Is your teacher gone?" Sam asked, suddenly beside her, causing Arcineh to realize she was still standing by the front door.

"Yes. He left some work."

Sam studied her face and knew something was wrong.

"If you're not ready, Arcie, just say so."

"That's not it." Her voice was flat. "I'll need some papers from home."

Sam was now just as quiet. It might have surprised his granddaughter to know that he was not looking forward to that trip any more than she was.

⟢

More visitors arrived over the next few days, including kids from both school and dance class, as well as her closest friend, Daisy Cordell. They had been in school together for the past three years and were very close. Both were children of privilege and only children.

"I brought you a flower," Daisy said; it was a daisy. "Your grandfather's house is far enough away from ours that I don't know how often I'll get here. It's to remind you of me."

"Thanks, Dais," Arcineh said sincerely. She really was a very good friend, and Arcineh loved her.

"So how is it?" Daisy did not believe in mincing words.

"It's horrible if I think about it, so I try not to."

"Have you been home?"

"No, but I have to go soon. I need some schoolwork."

"Can't someone else go?"

Arcineh shrugged, and Daisy dropped that line of questioning. As a rule she would have told Arcineh exactly what to do and how to think, but things were not normal anymore. Her friend looked pale and thin. And Daisy knew better than anyone how much Arcineh loved dance, making her cringe at the sight of Arcineh's crutches.

"How is school?" Arcineh asked.

"You won't believe it," Daisy replied, swiftly becoming her animated self. "Miss Moore is getting married!"

"Moore the Bore?"

"Yes! She's floating in and out of rooms like a fairy, and all she does is look at her ring."

Arcineh giggled. She loved Daisy's descriptions and could so easily see the school's librarian and secretary acting just that way. She was a mousy woman in a school full of wealthy, gifted, and highly confident students who could at times be ruthless.

"When's the big day?" Arcineh asked.

"This summer. Rumor is she won't be back in the fall. Good riddance!"

For some reason the last comment bothered both girls. Their eyes caught, and Daisy looked ashamed.

"Promise me something, Dais," Arcineh almost whispered.

"Anything."

"That you won't stare at me when I get back to school."

"Not only will I not stare," Daisy said fiercely, "I'll pinch anyone who does."

Arcineh relaxed again. As long as everyone else was acting normal, she could give herself permission to do the same.

⟆

Mason Beck, Sam's assistant and right-hand man for at least 20 years, sat across from him in his home office, taking copious notes on the words his employer was firing at him. He had been doing this for years and found it routine. The only problem he ran into was Sam's habit of thinking that once he'd given an order, the job was somehow magically done.

"Is Trevor's house ready?" Sam asked.

"Yes," Mason was able to reply, although the order to make sure all was in readiness was just 24 hours old. Mason had gone himself—taking Violet and a few others with him—to Trevor and Isabella's home in anticipation of Sam and Arcineh's visit.

"You saw to it yourself?"

"I did."

Sam grew quiet and thoughtful then, something Mason rarely saw.

"How did it seem?" Sam eventually asked.

"Just normal. We opened things up so the house could air out. Violet cleaned out the fridge and left everything smelling fresh. She even brought back the dirty clothing we found in the bedrooms and plans to wash and box them."

"Where are the boxes?"

"Somewhere here, I imagine. Out of sight," Mason added, wanting to be sensitive. In all the years he'd worked for Sam, he hadn't seen him like this, a bit soft-spoken and unsure. Sam Bryant was an exacting man, expecting his orders to be carried out with precision and demanding only the best from those who worked for him. He paid each person well, and they saw bonuses on a regular basis, but he didn't always remember that his employees had families and lives of their own.

The marble that Sam provided to companies all over the United States was without equal, but to accomplish that Sam was married to his business and expected his employees to be as well. Mason got the worst of it. He was paid a small fortune for his trouble, but truth be told, had his family not become so accustomed to the life he provided for them, he would have quit on the spot.

"Why are you still here?" Sam asked Mason in a way that was all too familiar.

"I wasn't aware we were done," Mason answered with quiet dignity, never allowing his feelings to show.

"We're done," Sam said dismissively.

Mason didn't bother to say goodbye—there would be nothing in return—but simply exited. He hoped to see Arcineh so he could greet her, but she was not in sight. Instead he exited through the kitchen and confirmed with Violet that the clothing was in fact stored in an out-of-the-way place.

Sam and Arcineh sat in the car in the driveway of the place that had always been her home, neither one speaking for a time. Everything looked normal, but nothing was right and they both knew it.

"You don't have to do this," Sam said, repeating the statement he'd made when they'd left his house. "Just give me directions."

"That's just it, I don't know exactly where my papers are."

"I'll just gather everything I find and bring it out."

Arcineh still refused. She didn't want to go into the house, but something inside of her told her it would only be worse if she waited. When she'd left her grandfather's birthday party nearly four weeks ago, she had never dreamed she would not be back here in all these days.

"But then that's the way it always is, isn't it?" Arcineh spoke her thoughts out loud.

"What's that?" Sam asked.

"No one ever thinks this will happen."

Sam certainly agreed with that. He was still in shock and felt as though he always would be.

"Well," Arcineh said with a hand on the door. "I just want to get in and get out."

Easier said than done, Arcineh found as soon as they'd let themselves in. The feel of her parents was everywhere, and she felt as if she couldn't breathe. Actually feeling dizzy, she sat on the bottom of the stairs, all color draining from her face. Sam felt just as bad but made himself concentrate on the child.

"Where shall I look first?" Sam asked, and Arcineh gave in.

"Try the desk in my room."

Sam took the stairs on swift feet and was back in a very short time. Arcineh saw that he'd grabbed nearly everything and thought that might be the end of it.

"Did you see a schoolbag?"

"What color is it?"

"Blue."

Sam was gone again in a hurry, but this time he came back empty. Arcineh had taken time to look through the papers and saw that everything was there.

"No blue bag," he apologized.

Arcineh frowned but couldn't remember where it might be. She also realized she didn't care.

"Do you have something I can use?"

"I'm sure I do, and if not, we'll stop at Marshall Fields and find something."

Arcineh nodded, and they both headed toward the door, just needing to get out. They had been logical and controlled, but that lasted only until they gained the front porch. Arcineh's tears burst forth without warning, and Sam's head bowed on his own. They didn't go to the car but sat on the heavy stone benches that Isabella had used to make the front porch a welcome place. It was a bit humid, although still cool, but neither one noticed. Too few tears had passed between them, and now they came in a torrent. For almost an hour they cried off and on, saying little.

However, it helped. When Arcineh had no more tears, she wanted to go back inside. With her grandfather's help, she gathered some of the things she'd not been able to describe to Violet. Feeling drained, she still made herself look for the blue bag. They left as soon as she'd found it.

CHAPTER *Two*

"We're coming up this weekend," Tiffany told her father on the phone that evening.

Sam met this news with silence, his head still hurting.

"Dad?"

"I'm here."

"Is something wrong?"

"It's just been a rough week, Tiffany, and I don't know if that's such a good idea."

Tiffany could not believe her ears. Her father never denied her a visit. It was rather unsettling after all these years, and she knew Quinn would feel the same way.

"Did Arcie say something about not wanting to see us?"

"Of course not, Tiffany. It's nothing like that."

"Well, ask her. I'm sure she wants to see Quinn."

Sam realized for the first time why his daughter's relationships with her children were so argumentative. She expected them to have opinions and be able to reason and think like adults. When they didn't agree with her, however, a fight usually broke out.

"I'll make sure life stays calmer next week," Sam offered, "and we'll plan on next weekend."

"But Quinn has a show next weekend!"

The strident sound of Tiffany's voice told her father she had become very emotional. He didn't want to argue with her, but neither did he want to give in.

"School will be out in less than a month, Tiffany, and then we'll get the girls together as often as possible."

"Well, that's no help at the moment, is it?"

Their conversation did not end well. Sam got his way, but at great expense. His daughter had fallen to tears and recriminations and then hung up in his ear. He was still thinking about it when Arcineh came to the door.

"Are you busy this weekend?" she asked.

"No, why?"

"Could we go to the Shedd? Just for a little while?"

"Certainly. Which day?"

"Saturday morning, right when they open."

"We'll plan on it."

Sam's heart lightened a bit. He knew Tiffany and Quinn did not agree with him, but for the moment, he was going to handle this his own way.

⟨⟩

The Shedd Aquarium was one of Arcineh Bryant's favorite places in the world. It had been a Chicago landmark for more than 60 years, and she loved everything about it. The architecture and layout of the building captivated her, and that was even before she began to roam from level to level and room to room to take in the thousands of sea creatures, amphibians, and reptiles.

The Pacific white-sided dolphins and beluga whales delighted her, and she could stand for an hour at the penguin display. Time became no more when she watched the antics of the Alaska sea otters.

The crutches inhibited some of her normal activities, and it was fairly crowded even at this early hour, but that didn't change Arcineh's pleasure. The last time she had come was with her father, and she had to push that memory from her mind, but for Arcineh the Shedd had a calming effect, and that was true this time as well.

"I'm going to try walking a bit," she said to Sam about an hour after they arrived.

"Don't, Arcie," he begged. "The floor is cobbled here. Why don't you wait?"

But Arcineh had a stubborn look on her face and only handed him the crutches. Sam wanted to argue with her but held his tongue. His body gripped with tension as he watched her, a tension that didn't leave until she grew weary and wanted the crutches back.

"Let's head to the Oceanarium," Arcineh suggested tiredly.

Sam agreed, hoping the dolphin show was over. They found the seating area nearly empty, and Arcineh went down about halfway to the water, sat down, and just stared.

The Oceanarium was where the dolphins lived and performed. Long roof trusses eliminated the need for support columns, and thanks to the floor-to-ceiling windows, the two million gallons of water in Whale Harbor appeared to flow directly into Lake Michigan.

This was Arcineh's favorite place at the Shedd. She enjoyed the dolphin show, but more than that she enjoyed sitting in the large room, watching the dolphins race around on their own and looking out over Lake Michigan.

Sam sat beside her, more concerned with her hip than the view of the lake, but trying to stay calm. He wanted to ask if she was all right but decided to let the matter rest. He was determined, however, not to hold her crutches when he didn't feel it was safe.

∽⚬∽

"I thought I heard you," Violet said, suddenly at the kitchen door and finding Arcineh looking into the refrigerator at about 1:00 in the morning.

"I'm sorry I woke you."

"What can I get you?" Violet asked, ignoring the apology.

"I don't know." Arcineh continued to stand, the cold air hitting her, not sure what she was hungry for.

"I can heat up that soup you like."

Arcineh shook her head. "I think I'd just like a peanut butter sandwich."

"With or without jam?"

"I can make it," Arcineh offered, but Violet was already on the move. Arcineh gave up and sat on one of the counter stools. She didn't talk, and Violet didn't ask any more questions. She prepared the sandwich, sliced it just the way Arcineh liked, and placed it in front of her. Arcineh thanked her and began to eat.

Violet did not try to engage her in conversation. She was very concerned for the little girl who seemed too old for her body and experiences and didn't seem to cry enough. Such a thing didn't seem natural to her.

"I think I can sleep now," Arcineh said when the sandwich was gone. Violet was pleased to see that she'd drunk the milk she poured for her as well.

"I'll walk you to your bed."

Arcineh was relieved. Every once in a while her grandfather's house felt huge and scary, and right now most of the lights were off. Violet walked behind Arcineh, letting the little girl set the pace, before tucking her into bed.

Violet bent and kissed her check, something she'd done only since the accident, but something to which Arcineh did not object. She then switched out the light and exited the room. Not until she was back in her own bed did the housekeeper shed her own tears.

∽

Arcineh's first day back to school, a few days later than they planned, was an event in more than one way. She moved slowly but without crutches. On the Monday after their visit to the Shedd, the doctor had given her leave to walk without them, albeit with a warning about her activity level. Sam wanted her to have a day around the house without the crutches, so she started back to school on Wednesday of that week.

Having been dropped off by Violet—her grandfather had an early meeting on his schedule—Arcineh stood quietly in the elevator, a conveyance she'd never needed before, and hoped she would be treated normally. When the doors whooshed softly open, Arcineh walked carefully out and turned for her classroom. Relief filled her when Mr. Sutter suddenly stepped into the hallway.

"I was wondering if I might see you today."

"I made it," Arcineh said with a smile.

Mr. Sutter's pleasure in her appearance and his matter-of-fact way put her at ease. It was a good start back to normal.

❦

"How did she seem?" Sam asked Violet. His meeting was done and he'd called as soon as he was free.

"A little tense."

"Did you walk in with her?"

"She didn't want that."

"You should have anyway."

Violet was dead silent after that, and Sam knew he'd overstepped. Violet had told him early in her employment that she would do everything in her power to do things as he liked, but when it came to judgment calls, she expected him to trust her and even be forgiving if she erred. She was the only one of his employees to ever stand up to him in this way. And she had never let him down.

Sam backtracked.

"What made you decide not to walk her in?"

"She has her own way of handling this, Sam. I'm not going to push in where I'm not wanted. She knows I'll do anything she wants."

"All right," he agreed, but still wished he knew more. He thanked Violet and got off the phone, turning immediately in his calendar to see if he could get home before 3:00.

When Arcineh got home, she found her desk had arrived, and more of the things from her bedroom. She had lived upstairs only a few days at her grandfather's—the climb had been too hard on crutches—and even though it seemed strange to have these things here, she appreciated Violet's efforts.

Little by little that woman had been bringing Arcineh's possessions to Sam's house. Her clothing was all there, and everthing else Violet thought she might want. Now the desk was there, the one from her bedroom. Arcineh touched it and felt emotion flood through her.

She remembered the day her mother bought it for her. For a long time it had sat on the screen porch, a place where Arcineh loved to do her homework in good weather. Only recently had she moved it to her bedroom.

Without warning, tears filled her eyes. The enormity of what she'd lost and how life was never going to be the same crushed down on her like a huge boulder. She stood very still and cried, sobbing into her hands and desperately wanting her mother.

Violet had come up to check on her and was almost at the door when Arcineh broke down. That woman did not intrude but stood outside in the wide hallway and felt her own tears run unchecked down her face.

This was the way Sam found them. He had meant to be home already, but the streets had been clogged. He watched Violet's slim shoulders shake and could hear Arcineh from the top of the stairs. He moved a little, and his housekeeper heard him.

"How long?" he asked her.

"Just a few minutes," Violet managed.

Sam nodded but stood still. He didn't know if he should leave Arcineh alone or not. She had not been overly teary—she never was—making him think she might need this. She might feel squelched if she knew he and Violet were listening.

Sam touched Violet's shoulder and motioned her to follow him downstairs. The two went to the kitchen, hoping Arcineh would come there when she was ready.

∽

"Your dance teacher called today," Violet said to Arcineh when she came to the kitchen some 30 minutes later. She found her grandfather eating a snack. He gave her a muffled greeting around a mouthful of food.

"What did Geneva want?" Arcineh asked, taking a few crackers from the package Sam had opened.

"She wanted to know if you were coming back anytime soon."

Arcineh only nodded. Geneva Sperry had not even mentioned her returning when she had visited in the hospital.

"What will you do?" Sam asked, having watched her closely the whole time.

"I don't think I want to dance anymore." Arcineh's voice was quiet. "But I don't know how to tell Geneva that."

Sam wanted to tell her not to give it up, but he remembered what Violet had said. Arcineh seemed to know what she needed at times, and Sam saw no reason to push her in this.

"How was school?" he asked next.

Arcineh's sigh was huge—a sigh of relief. "It was okay. People stopped staring by lunchtime, and only one person made a crack about your money."

"What was said?" Sam asked in genuine curiosity.

"Just that you have even more than my folks did, and something stupid like my situation could have been worse."

The anger on Sam's face was unmistakable. He'd never heard of such nonsense, and his opinion of the school that Arcineh attended, never having favored it, sank even lower.

"What did you say?" he asked in a voice tight with irritation.

"I ignored it," Arcineh said offhandedly, reaching for more crackers and adding cheese. "You know what rich kids are like."

"I think I do, but what do you mean?" Sam was calming in the wake of her nonchalant attitude.

"They believe their money defines them and makes them special. It's pitiful."

"You don't think you're special?"

"I'm very special, but it has nothing to do with money. Only an idiot would believe that."

Sam was so struck by the fact that he and Arcineh had never talked this way before that for a moment he couldn't speak. Arcineh took his silence as negative.

"Do you think money makes you special, Grandpa?"

"No, I don't. I think you have the right idea."

"Is this person a friend of yours?" Violet asked, unable to let it drop.

"Not at all." Arcineh made a face. "He's older and completely full of himself."

The adults fell silent then, their eyes meeting for just a moment. Arcineh was going to town on the crackers. At another time Violet might have reminded her of dinner, but these days any food she ate seemed to be a bonus.

And Violet was pleased she stayed quiet. By the time she served dinner, Arcineh was hungry again. Violet took this as a good sign. Things seemed to be finding a routine. Arcineh was starting to sound and act more like the girl she had been, and even though "normal" meant that Sam worked too much, it still had a *right* feel to it.

Right up to the moment Geneva Sperry paid Arcineh another visit.

∞

Violet and Arcineh had been home from school for an hour when the front doorbell rang. Sam Bryant did not get many visitors, and they were not expecting anyone, but Violet still answered the door. She didn't know this woman by sight but somehow knew who she was.

"Hello," Geneva said softly. "Is Arcie home?"

"Yes, she is," Violet answered, moving back to allow her entrance. "May I tell her who's calling?"

"I think we must have talked on the phone. I'm Geneva Sperry, her dance teacher."

"Please come in and sit down," Violet invited. While Geneva headed into the family room, Violet took the stairs to Arcineh's room. Arcineh heard her coming and came into the hall.

"Your dance teacher is here."

Arcineh looked nervous, a look that brought Violet's chin in the air. "What's wrong?" Violet wished to know.

"I don't want to tell her. She won't like it."

"That's her problem, not yours."

Arcineh looked the housekeeper in the eye and knew why she'd always liked her. Violet Kray was no one's fool. Arcineh went toward the stairs. She smiled at the sight of Geneva in a bright pink and orange outfit, her hair a shade of purple this week, and realized for the first time she was as flamboyant a dresser outside the studio as in.

"Hello, Arcie," the older woman greeted, hugging the child in genuine affection.

"Hello, Geneva."

"May I talk to you?"

"Yes."

It was not lost on Geneva that Arcineh sat as far from her as politeness would allow. The old Arcineh would have taken the other end of the plush leather sofa, but not today.

"I was wondering, how are you doing?" Geneva forced herself to ask this question when all she wanted to do was tell Arcineh to return to her studio that week.

"I'm doing fine."

Geneva nodded, sure that was all the more she would say. "How is your hip?"

"It's not too bad. It still hurts some."

"Well, I want your doctor to give you permission to come back, but even when he does, we'll take it very slow for a while."

"I'm not coming back," Arcineh said quietly, and then waited.

Geneva did not miss the stubborn, albeit guarded, look in the child's eyes. As passionate as she was about Arcineh's talent, the teacher knew better than to argue with her.

"When did you decide this?"

"Just a few days ago. I don't want to dance anymore."

"Can you tell me why?"

Arcineh shrugged. She wasn't keeping a secret. She truly didn't know.

"Well, I'll miss you," Geneva said working to keep her voice calm. "And if you change your mind—" She deliberately let the sentence hang and then changed the subject. Geneva asked Arcineh about school and how she liked living with her grandfather, but the subject of dance did not come up again.

Arcineh enjoyed seeing Geneva but was relieved when she left and she realized her teacher had not pressed her. She had not been playing games. At the moment Arcineh had no desire to ever dance again.

"How are you?" Quinn asked Arcineh the moment they were alone.

"Most days all right," Arcineh told her, unbelievably glad to see her cousin acting normal and with not a hint of tears.

It had taken several tries, but this weekend had finally worked—no horse shows, not too busy or tired, and Tiffany itching to come to Chicago. She had brought Austin as well.

"Have you been back to your house?"

"Just once."

Quinn shuddered a little, but Arcineh didn't notice. The thought of having her parents die was horrifying to Quinn. She was sure that she would die as well. "Do you remember anything about the accident?" she suddenly asked.

Arcineh slowly shook her head no. "I remember feeling sleepy in the backseat, and then I woke up in the hospital. I must have fallen asleep."

Quinn nodded, still regretting not being at the party that night. She'd told herself that there would be no tears this weekend, but at the moment that command was taking all she had.

"Are you going cry?" Arcineh looked upset at the thought.

"No!" Quinn denied with a face that said Arcineh was overreacting. And it worked. Arcineh nodded and changed the subject, just what Quinn needed.

∽

"How's it going?" Tiffany asked her father, determined not to ask if Arcineh could live with them but hoping her father would mention it.

"I think all right. We're settling in well."

"That's good. What have you done with the house?"

"Personally, nothing. Violet arranged to have Arcineh's desk delivered, and she's been continually bringing her clothing and effects. We'll have to tackle the whole house this summer."

"I can help if you'd like," Tiffany offered, a part of her still believing that Trevor and Isabella were there.

"I'll plan on that."

Tiffany began to feel better. She had not seen her father protective of Arcineh before. Their last visit, the weekend of the funeral, was still heavy on her mind. For just a little time, she had thought that Quinn might have slipped from his mind. Everyone in the family knew that Quinn was the favorite grandchild, and that fact was as important to Tiffany as it was to Quinn—perhaps more.

"I'd like to eat at the Rotisserie tonight," Tiffany suggested. "Are you and Arcie up for it?"

"That sounds good."

Tiffany relaxed a little more. Her father enjoyed eating amazing ribs at the 12-story restaurant that overlooked the lake, and he'd not been swift to say that he'd have to check with Arcineh. Even on the drive up, Tiffany had feared too many changes at once but realized she was wrong. She was suddenly very glad she had come.

❧

"Are you going to counseling?" Austin asked of Arcineh when he found the girls in Arcineh's room.

"Get out of here, Austin," Quinn took no time in saying. "We didn't say you could come in."

Austin ignored his sister and came as far as the footboard on the bed.

"Well, Arcie, are you?"

"No," she frowned at him. "What for?"

Austin shrugged. He'd been quiet and withdrawn since his uncle and aunt died, and he'd heard his mother mention counseling to his father. He figured if he might be going, Arcineh would certainly be on someone's couch.

"Will you *please* leave?" Quinn said, using a tone that made a mockery of the word.

"I'm going, I'm going. You're probably talking about stupid stuff anyhow."

Quinn and Arcineh just rolled eyes at each other, and when Austin left, Arcineh got up and locked the door.

"No privacy at all! And in my own room," she muttered on the way back to the bed, not noticing Quinn's face. Something about that statement stung the older girl, and she wasn't exactly sure why.

"So tell me," Arcineh commanded, starting where they'd left off, "Do you still like that guy at the stables?"

"Yes, but he likes the owner's daughter."

"How old is she?"

"His age—16."

"I thought he was only 14."

"No, that was the other one," Quinn answered as a matter of course. She fell in and out of love on a regular basis.

"You'll be 13 in just a month," Arcineh tried to encourage her. "You never know when he might notice."

Quinn couldn't help but smile. She knew she was pretty, but it was more than that. Arcineh had sounded like her old self: confident, upbeat, and willing to encourage.

"I am thinking about changing my hair," Quinn offered.

"Show me!" Arcineh exclaimed, instantly into that, and the day was swallowed up. The two girls worked on each other's hair until it was time to leave for the restaurant.

CHAPTER *Three*

"Do I hear music?" Sam asked of Violet when he came to the kitchen on Monday. For all the years she'd worked for him, Sam had gone directly to the kitchen when he arrived home to check with her and have a snack.

Violet smiled before saying, "She's been in the family room with the stereo on for about an hour."

"Is she dancing?"

"I didn't check."

Sam was already working on an apple, so he didn't comment on what he was thinking, but he wondered if maybe Arcineh and Quinn had talked about her dancing. Austin had been quiet and moody all weekend, but the girls had visited for hours, never seeming to grow sad or weary of the other's company.

Sam had had very little time with Quinn, not the norm when she visited, but Quinn hadn't seemed to mind. Sam had missed his usual visit with his older granddaughter, who was sensitive like her mother, but knew Arcineh needed her more.

Sam finished the apple and headed in his granddaughter's direction.

She was not dancing, but the look on her face told him she was enjoying the music.

"How does my stereo compare to yours?" he asked, taking a seat across from her.

Arcineh smiled. "I think I like yours better."

Sam grinned at her, and for a moment let the music wash over him. He knew Arcineh had been studying ballroom dancing and suspected that this rendition of "You Made Me Love You" was something she'd danced to. Sam's eyes drifted to her face often. She looked thoughtful but not as though she was yearning to be on her feet. He was starkly reminded of the accident.

"How is your hip feeling?"

"Good."

"Not stiff?"

"A little in the mornings sometimes."

Arcineh's eyes stayed on him, and she knew he had something on his mind.

"What's wrong?" She minced no words.

"I was just wondering if you want to go to your father's office tomorrow?"

"When?"

"Whenever you want."

"I have a math test in the morning, but then I think I could leave."

"Do I call or send a note that I'm coming for you?"

"Could I maybe just go and take the test and leave?"

"Will they allow that?"

"Sure," Arcineh answered easily, knowing that kids left for far less significant reasons. "Will we go to the cemetery too?" Arcineh suddenly asked.

"I wasn't planning on it, but we can," Sam said, though he didn't want to.

Arcineh swiftly shook her head no, and Sam knew that on this matter they agreed. The following day's events did not come up again, but they proceeded just as Arcineh had predicted. Sam took her to school long enough to take her test and then took her to see her father's office.

———

"How did it go?" Violet asked Sam when they returned. Arcineh had gone directly to her room.

Sam shrugged a little. "She didn't say much, but I think we'll bring all of his effects here. That way if she wants to see them or have them, they'll be available."

Sam could still see her in his mind. Her face horribly pale, Arcineh slowly lowered herself into her father's desk chair and shivered as though she were freezing. Sam didn't speak; his own heart felt frozen in his chest. His son was gone. He couldn't remember the last time he'd told Trevor that he loved him or was proud of him, but he'd felt all of that and more. And now he was gone.

"Should I check on her?" Violet asked, cutting into Sam's reverie.

"I'll do it," Sam told her, starting that way, but Arcineh beat him to it. She was already coming down the stairs.

"Can I have my dad's desk chair?" she blurted as soon as she saw her grandfather.

"Certainly."

Sam didn't know what she had expected him to say, but he could see that she was fighting tears. In his opinion, everything in the office already belonged to her.

"When can I have it?" she choked out.

"Today. I'll put it in my car and bring it to you."

Arcineh nodded, but the trembling was back.

"It's all right," Sam soothed as he went to her. "I didn't take you there so I could start getting rid of things. We'll bring it all here and tuck it away for you."

Arcineh clung to her grandfather, so desperate to hug her father that she didn't think she would make it. Her little body trembled with the intensity of her feelings, and Sam closed his eyes in equal pain.

Violet came from the kitchen just then to check on them both, spotted their embrace, and backed away. At the moment she felt as they both did: Life would never feel normal again.

✆

"Mr. Bryant?" his secretary, Carlee, said, ringing him in his office midmorning the next day. "There is a Ms. Geneva Sperry here to see you. She says she's Arcie's dance teacher."

"Please tell me you're joking," Sam said in a voice that told his secretary that he was in no mood for laughter.

"What do you want me to do?"

Carlee heard her employer sigh and waited.

"Send her in, but beep me with something in about 20 minutes."

"Will do."

Carlee put the phone down and smiled at the interesting woman at her desk.

"You can go right in."

"Thank you," Geneva said sincerely, not having realized until she was in the building just how unlikely it was that Sam Bryant would agree to see her. Bryant Marble was on the top three floors of a huge office building, and Sam Bryant's own office was immense. The woman in the lobby had been hard enough to get past, but when Geneva spotted Sam's own secretary, she had all but given up.

"Come in," Sam greeted, suddenly at the door. "I'm Sam Bryant."

"Geneva Sperry. Thank you for seeing me."

"Have a seat," Sam invited without returning the compliment. He barely waited for Geneva to get settled in the sitting area of his office before saying, "What can I do for you?"

"I'm here about Arcie. She told me she doesn't want to dance anymore, but I must admit that I rather hoped she wasn't serious."

"And so you came to see me?" Sam asked, not rudely but with no enthusiasm.

"Yes. I don't know if you realize Arcie's talent. She just can't give it up."

"You speak as though you've forgotten what she's lost."

"I haven't." Geneva's voice and face were most sincere. "But I feel that dance is very therapeutic, and when someone with Arcie's natural gift understands that, it's also healing."

"Would it be just as healing if she were forced?"

Geneva, as sure and polished as she was, did not expect this question. However, she answered honestly. "No, it wouldn't be healing at all. I guess I just wanted to be heard." She stopped for a moment, but made no sign of leaving. "I've been dancing since I was three, and teaching for almost 30 years. Arcie's talent is remarkable."

Sam had heard the same from his son and believed it to be so, but he also knew dancing had to be his granddaughter's choice.

"If you want my honest opinion, I think Arcineh will dance again, but I don't think she'll make a living with it as I suspect you are hoping."

Geneva nodded. He had read her very well. But Sam was not done.

"I would wish for her to return to your studio, Ms. Sperry, but I need to know from you that whether it be next week or two years from now, she'll be welcome."

"What makes you think she'd be anything but?"

Sam smiled a little. "The more time that goes by, the more she loses. Indeed her hip might have made that decision for her. If she doesn't return to you soon, I do not want her greeted with guilt or regret that she didn't come back sooner. Or passed over out of malice."

Geneva was impressed, and nodded her head a little. "I'm glad you've made that very clear, and I'm also glad to tell you that's not who I am. It's true that in some schools in Chicago she would never be allowed in again, truly allowed," Geneva qualified. "But not with me. Arcie will always be welcome at my school and given parts that match her skill." She shrugged a little. "You are correct in your assessment that she may have lost or will lose something with this absence, and her parts in performances will reflect that, but there will be no malice. Not from me, and not from anyone on my staff."

Sam nodded, pleased that he'd been understood. A moment later, the intercom on his telephone beeped.

"That will be my secretary getting me out of this meeting as I asked her to do," Sam said, one corner of his mouth lifting. "As it was, I did not need to be rescued, Ms. Sperry, but if we've covered everything, I do have work."

"Certainly, Mr. Bryant. Thank you for seeing me."

"Thank you for your care of Arcineh. May I tell her you stopped?"

"Absolutely. I would want her to know."

Sam saw Geneva to the door, had a word with Carlee, and went back to work. He planned to tell Arcineh all about the visit, but a call came in at the end of the day that sent the dance instructor's visit from his mind.

✌

"Tonight?" Arcineh question again. "You have to leave tonight?"

"Yes, but I should be home on Friday," he said, packing all the while. "Violet will be here."

Arcineh did not look comforted. She knew her grandfather's work took him far and wide, but it never once occurred to her that he would leave her.

Sam saw Arcineh's pale face at that moment and stopped what he was doing. He sat on the bed, his gentle hands on her shoulders as he brought her to stand in front of him.

"If I could send Mason, I would, but I've got unhappy people in Italy, and I've got to handle this myself."

"What if something happens? What if you don't come back?"

"I'm going to come back," Sam said with extreme confidence. "I'll call you when I get there. I'll call you with my hotel number, and Violet will have all my flight information. I'll be home before you can miss me."

Arcineh did not look convinced.

"Why don't you ask your friend over? What was her name—Daisy?"

"She lives far away from here."

"I'll call before I leave and see if she can come home from school with you tomorrow and, just this once, spend the night on a school night."

"Really?" Arcineh perked up a bit.

"Really."

Arcineh nodded. Her face was still pale, but her heart was willing to take the proffered olive branch.

"I don't have to leave for an hour, so as soon as I'm done packing I'll call Daisy's house, and then you and I can sit and talk."

Arcineh nodded again, seeing that he *was* going to leave. She would have preferred him even to Daisy, a fact that was confirmed by the way she remained within inches of his side until he exited for the airport.

⸎

CREVE COEUR, MISSOURI

Quinn snapped at Austin during dinner, an occurrence that wasn't all that strange, but she was short even with her father. Tiffany took all of this in stride, but when it didn't stop and bedtime neared, she decided to confront her daughter.

"Who is it?" Quinn barked when Tiffany knocked on her door.

Tiffany opened the door, feeling a headache coming on.

"I've come to talk to you. What's going on?"

"I don't know what you mean," Quinn said obstinately, not meeting her mother's eyes.

"Yes, you do. Now, let's have it."

Quinn was not silent for long. Holding her feelings in had never been a strong point of her personality, and she was simply too frustrated to even try.

"I don't want to show my horse this weekend. I want to see Grandpa. We haven't talked in months."

This was not true, but Tiffany was used to such exaggerations from her children.

"You can't miss this performance," Tiffany reasoned. "I wish you'd said something earlier. We could have called."

"It's not the same by phone, and he's probably doing something with Arcie."

Tiffany heard a tone in her daughter that not even she could ignore.

"I won't have that attitude, Quinn. That's nothing but selfishness."

Quinn did not take the rebuke well, but Tiffany didn't care. She told her daughter in clear terms that they would get her to Chicago as soon as possible, but that no one was going to live with her attitude.

Tiffany did not wait to see what Quinn had to say. She went to her own room to find something for her headache. She then readied for bed but became wide awake when Jeremy made an appearance. She told him all about Quinn's attitude, wondering all the while where her daughter learned such self-centered tendencies.

CHICAGO

"We're going to Europe this summer," Daisy told Arcineh when the hour was very late.

"When?"

"Not until July. It'll be beastly hot, my mom says, but that's when Dad has business and that's when we'll go."

"For how long?"

"I think for two weeks."

"Where exactly?"

"I don't know."

"My grandpa's in Italy right now."

"Have you been?"

"No."

Arcineh felt lonely for Sam just then, but Daisy didn't notice. She was also starting to feel sleepy and said, "We're going to be so tired tomorrow," her voice scratchy with the late hour.

"Yes, and my mom will say, 'Never again.'"

"Moms always say that."

The comment was not all that funny, but both girls laughed until they were red in the face. It seemed to be just what they needed. Not even bothering with the light, they both drifted off to sleep. Only after Violet checked on them some 30 minutes later was the room left in darkness.

∞

CREVE COEUR

"Oh, Grandpa!" Quinn pulled the emerald necklace from the box, just about squealing in delight. "I love it."

Sam smiled with love at her, never letting on about his little secret. Violet had been buying the gifts for his children and grandchildren for more years than he could recall. Certainly the credit card was in his name, but Violet did all the work while he took the praise.

Looking on, Arcineh smiled from her place in the room, but in her heart she knew something was wrong. She had not seen Quinn since her last visit to Chicago several weeks earlier. They had tried to arrange a visit but could manage nothing but phone calls, and all the calls had been to her grandfather. Nevertheless Arcineh had been sure that they would pick up where they ended, but from the moment she arrived, Quinn had been a bit cool with her. Arcineh had never seen her like this, and she was nothing short of crushed with how often Quinn wanted to do things with just their grandfather. They were both finally done with school, and Arcineh assumed that they would be making every sort of plan to be together in the next few months, but Quinn said not one word about wanting to see Arcineh.

"Who's ready for cake?" Tiffany offered when the pile of expensive presents had been opened. For the moment Arcineh's uncertainties were shelved.

◠◠

"Hey," Austin spoke quietly when Arcineh joined him on the wide porch a few hours later.

"Oh, hi, Austin. I didn't see you."

Austin sighed with ill humor and said, "There's only so much *Quinn* I can take when she's made herself queen for the day."

"Is that it?"

"Is that what?"

Arcineh stopped. If Austin didn't know what she was talking about, she was not going to fill him in.

"You noticed it too, didn't you?" Austin continued, his look smug. "She's having to share Grandpa for the first time and finding out what the rest of us live with all the time. It makes her next to impossible to be around, and she's close to being that the entire rest of the year."

Again Arcineh didn't answer, but the look on her face told Austin she was not going to argue with him. The two didn't talk anymore, and that suited Arcineh fine. Much as she wanted to play with Quinn, she did not see Austin as a substitute. Unfortunately it made the weekend move at a snail's pace.

⟋⟋

"We'll be up in a few weeks," Quinn finally said to Arcineh as Arcineh and Sam were preparing to leave. They were in the driveway. "I can't wait."

"Me either," Arcineh agreed, comforted by Quinn's familiar tone. "We can do whatever you like."

Quinn looked thrilled at the thought, and they were more than halfway back to Chicago before Arcineh thought to ask her grandfather if Quinn was all right.

"What do you mean?" he asked, his brow creasing a bit.

"I don't know. She just seemed different."

Sam shrugged. "I didn't notice anything, but keep in mind that she's now a teenager. I think mood swings are to be expected."

Arcineh took him at his word, glad to know it was nothing serious. She wasn't telling Sam and Violet everything she was thinking, but lately in Arcineh's mind, everyone she loved was dying. With Quinn, Arcineh had imagined some sort of illness, but now she knew her grandfather would have told her about that.

Arcineh settled in for the remainder of the ride home, completely forgetting what Austin had said. Her young heart believed it was just as her grandfather said: Quinn was entering the moody teen years.

⟋⟋

"Do I have to go?" Arcineh asked Sam when it was time to head to her parents' house. Sam stared at her. He didn't know if it was wise to allow Arcineh to completely avoid the task of choosing what she wanted from home so it could be cleared and sold. She had been so reticent about the whole thing that it was already August. School would be starting in just under four weeks.

The summer had gone fairly well, even though Tiffany had not been able to come and help with the house. Arcineh had spent time in Missouri and Quinn had twice come to Chicago for weekend visits. Sometimes the girls got along and sometimes they didn't. Sam took it in stride. But each time the subject of clearing Trevor and Isabella's house came up, Arcineh retreated in a hurry. Sam was unwilling to push the point, and now weeks had gone by. The house was being watched over for safety and taken care of, the flowers and lawn watered, but difficult as it was, something had to be done.

"What are we going to do, Arcie?"

"I don't know."

"We can't keep putting it off."

"You could go. I could stay here."

Sam sat down. He thought she was past this.

"It's like this," he explained patiently. "Everything in the house is yours. If Violet, Mason, and I go through it without you, we might get rid of something you want."

"Well, just keep all the pictures and stuff."

Sam, knowing it wasn't that simple, shook his head.

"You're coming. Bring a book, some music, whatever you like. You'll sit on the sunporch and hang out, and when we have questions, we'll come to you."

Arcineh began to open her mouth, but Sam put his hand up. "If you need to cry, you cry. If you need a break, we'll take one, but we have to get started on this, and today is the day."

Arcineh was clearly not happy with the decision. However, she said no more and she did just as she was told. Loaded with books, music, and everything else she could get her hands on, Arcineh climbed in the back of Sam's car, resigning herself to being miserable.

⦿

"Oh, I remember this." Arcineh laughed at the picture of herself as a baby, and Violet laughed with her.

She had started on the sunporch, slumped down in a chair and angry at the world, but that hadn't lasted long. Violet had found her baby plate, cup, bowl, and tiny silverware. She'd gone out to ask Arcineh if she wanted to keep them, and minutes later Arcineh had followed her back to the kitchen. And that was just the start.

Her grandfather was going through papers in her father's study, and Mason was making a detailed list of every item upstairs. In the kitchen, Arcineh had not been interested in anything more than her dishes and her mother's favorite coffee cup, but then she and Violet had moved to the family room, a room that was filled with photos, framed and in albums.

For the first hour they stopped and looked often, but then Violet got busy. With only the occasional lingering look, she put pictures and albums into boxes, packing them neatly and labeling the outside so Arcineh would know where to look. At times Arcineh sat in the furniture and looked around. At other times she had to work not to cry. If Violet caught her, she told her not to hold back, but Arcineh only listened once.

Nevertheless they kept on and by lunchtime had accomplished a great deal. Mason had sent for food, and it was delivered on time. The four sat around the kitchen table to eat. Arcineh listened to Mason's report to Sam concerning the upstairs items and realized she was not attached to anything more than her bedroom furniture. The family room furniture was also special to her, as was the wicker from the sunporch, but nothing else.

When they were done eating, Arcineh shared this with her grandfather, who took it in stride. They weren't going to do anything drastic in the next few months, but Sam didn't share this. He simply made a mental note to keep his ears open and to not do anything until he'd checked with Arcineh at least one more time.

CHAPTER *Four*

Sam was usually home on Sundays, but today he was flying in from another business trip, this one to India. Arcineh had been in the family room listening to music, but suddenly all was quiet. Violet didn't search her out, not wanting to treat her like a baby, but began to wonder if she was all right.

For most hours of the day, life had fallen into an easy pattern. It was true that Arcineh's parents were gone and she was living with and being raised by her grandfather and his housekeeper, but for the most part, things seemed normal. However, it was never far from Violet's mind that this little girl was motherless, and it wasn't very often that you could tell. She lived life at Sam's house as though it were her own, voiced her opinion at will, and acted like a typical preteen.

But in truth, they were still working on her parent's house, and it had taken an emotional toll on all of them. Violet didn't know what Sam noticed, but she could see the chinks in Arcineh's armor and the occasional looks of vulnerability, and she wondered how the child inside was faring. Violet didn't baby the girl—it wasn't her way—but she also didn't think anything would surprise her. If Arcineh were to fall apart, she was sure she would take it in stride.

"Violet?" Arcineh found her in the laundry room. "Are we going to shop for school sometime soon?"

"How much time do we have?" Violet asked, giving herself time to catch up.

"Maybe about two weeks. I don't have any new clothes or school supplies."

"How do we know what to buy for supplies?"

"I have a list. They gave it out at the end of the school year."

"That was a good idea. Your grandfather will be home in about three hours, and we'll check with him. If he doesn't want to take you, you and I will make a day of it."

Violet suddenly found young, thin arms around her.

"Thanks, Violet!"

Violet stood, a load of damp towels in her arms, and stared at the place where Arcineh had been. She learned something about herself in that instant. The house had grown quiet and she'd expected the worst. She was not beyond surprises after all.

⁂

"You're taking Arcie shopping on Tuesday?" Sam asked of Violet after all had been explained.

"Yes."

"I thought that was going to be your new day off."

"It still is. Using your money to shop for Arcie isn't work."

Sam couldn't hold his smile. He would never fire Violet—there would never be a need—and she knew it.

"Where are you going?" he finally asked.

"Where do you think?"

"Michigan Avenue," Sam said dryly. "And I suppose I'm paying for lunch too?"

Violet only smiled at him, and this time he didn't try to hold back. His head went back as he laughed, knowing that if his housekeeper asked for the moon, especially concerning Arcineh, he would rope it and hand it to her.

∽∾

Not for the first time, Violet noticed that Arcineh had great style. She enjoyed the new trends of the day, but the clothing that fit her best was that of classic styling and lines. Isabella had been just that way, and Violet wasn't surprised to find Arcineh in the same mode.

"Do you like this color?" Arcineh asked about halfway through the morning, her hand on a dark gray-blue blouse.

"It's not the best one for you. Do you like it?"

"I was thinking of you."

"Me?" Violet blinked. "We're not shopping for me."

"But we could."

Violet eyed her. "Is that your subtle way of telling me my wardrobe needs help?"

"No," Arcineh answered honestly. "But you have a date on Friday night, and I wondered if you might want something new."

"How do you know about Friday night?"

"I know a lot of things," Arcineh said evasively.

Violet shook her head in wonder. "I am going out Friday night, but he's an old friend, and I have no desire to turn his head."

Arcineh smiled at her tone, but Violet wouldn't look at her for fear of laughing and encouraging her.

"Now," the older woman said as she tried to take back some control, "are you done shopping?"

"Not even close."

"Well, then, let's put my dating life aside and get back to business."

Arcineh did not argue. She wanted to know more about this friend of Violet's, but knew it was going to have to wait. She still had scores of ideas on her mind for shopping.

⬯

"What did you find?"

Sam had made his way to Arcineh's room after work, knowing that if he didn't distract himself, he was going to need a drink. He'd missed his son that day in the most painful way. While most of Trevor's business dealings had been passed on to other managers, Trevor's account with the Faribault Corporation had needed Sam's personal attention. All day Sam had been forced to read his son's handwriting and business notes. Trevor had even recorded some things on his small tape player, and hearing his voice was almost more than Sam could take. Right now he was willing to do anything to block out the pain. The only thing that kept him from the liquor cabinet was his granddaughter's presence in the house.

"Almost everything I need! Do you want to see?"

"Yes, I do." Sam sat on the bed, and Arcineh ran for the spacious walk-in closet. When the eleven-year-old emerged, she was utterly charming in baggy jeans, a deceptively simple top, and Keds tennis shoes in navy canvas.

Sam enjoyed the fashion show, and his praise to Arcineh was genuine. She had looked great in everything, and so much like Isabella that Sam wondered if he was going to survive.

"Are you all right?" Arcineh asked before she changed from her last outfit.

"Yes," Sam lied convincingly. "Why?"

"You look a little sad."

Arcineh had sat next to him, and Sam put an arm around her. She leaned against him, and it struck her how little they hugged. Her parents had hugged and kissed her every day, but Sam usually only hugged her when she was upset. Arcineh wished for it to be different and, in a mature moment, knew she could make an effort to change it.

This decided, she suddenly hugged him. Sam seemed a bit surprised, but just for a moment. The grandfather hugged her right back, and they remained this way until Violet called them to dinner.

⤫

The Rowan family visited on the weekend before Labor Day. Traffic on Labor Day weekend was predictably horrific, so they came up early for one last trip before settling into a new school year. Austin was entering his freshman year in high school, and Quinn was going into grade eight. Arcineh was a seventh grader.

Arcineh was looking forward to the weekend visit, but since Quinn's birthday she had held back just a bit. Quinn had become mercurial at times, and Arcineh was weary of being burned. However, Quinn showed up in fine spirits and didn't even try to gain Sam's attention.

Arcineh watched her throughout the weekend, not knowing what to think beyond deciding that becoming a teen was not worth it. Trevor and Isabella had not been moody people, and neither was Daisy. Arcineh found the behavior odd and trying. So much so, in fact, that when Quinn mentioned her reserve, she was ready to say what was on her mind.

"Are you all right?" Quinn asked late in the visit—the Rowans would be leaving in an hour and the girls were having a quiet moment in Arcineh's room.

"Yes," Arcineh said, not intending to elaborate.

"You've been acting a little funny all weekend."

Arcineh weighed her options and plunged in. "I'm trying not to get you upset."

"Why would I be upset?" Quinn frowned.

"That's what I've asked myself the last few times we've been together, and since I don't have an answer, I don't know how to avoid it."

"What is that supposed to mean?"

Arcineh sighed and didn't try to answer. Quinn demanded an answer, but Arcineh was already in trouble and opted for silence. Quinn left the room in tears, and Arcineh didn't bother to follow.

What Arcineh didn't bank on was her aunt's presence just moments later. She was already red in the face, and Arcineh had no idea what she'd done.

"What did you say to Quinn?" Tiffany demanded.

Arcineh stared at her, wishing she'd kept her mouth shut.

"Answer me, Arcineh!"

"What's going on?" Jeremy said, coming on them suddenly. Unbeknownst to Arcineh, her eyes pleaded with those of her uncle.

"I'm trying to find out why Quinn is crying," Tiffany snapped. "I know Arcineh said something."

"Tiffany," Jeremy began, and his wife turned on him.

"Don't you take that tone with me!"

Arcineh watched in amazement as the two began to fight. From the side of her bed, Arcineh stared at their flushed faces and listened to their angry words. She caught movement at the door but couldn't take her eyes from the arguing couple. Not until her grandfather walked into the room did Arcineh shift her gaze.

"Jeremy, Tiffany," he said quietly. "Stop."

These words had a unique effect on each person. Jeremy stopped altogether and exited the room, but Tiffany only shifted her attack to her father.

"He always takes Arcie's side!"

"Arcie's side against whom?" her father asked.

"Arcie said something to upset Quinn, and all Jeremy can do is defend her."

This was the last thing Sam wanted right now, but he made himself turn to Arcineh.

"What did you say to Quinn?"

"Only that I don't know what I do that upsets her," the child whispered, "and that's why I've been a little quiet."

The face that accompanied this announcement was so pale that not even Tiffany could ignore it. The little girl had curled into a protective ball near the footboard of her bed.

All Tiffany's anger drained away then, and she left without speaking. Sam continued to look at Arcineh, not sure what to say. The silence seemed to stretch between them for a long time when only seconds had passed.

"They're leaving soon," Sam eventually said.

Arcineh only nodded.

"Quinn is sensitive," he added as an afterthought, and then because he felt a need to rescue the little girl who lived with him, he said, "You don't have to come down if you don't want to."

Again Arcineh only nodded and stayed on her bed when he left. She hoped it would be a long time before they visited again.

⁓

The start of school was welcome. Arcineh had had regular physical therapy over the summer and some visits from friends, but as a whole, it had been long and a bit lonely. Violet's nearness was a great comfort, and when her grandfather wasn't working, they enjoyed one another's company, but for the first time ever, Arcineh was happy to have the school year begin.

She became even happier when a boy, just a year older than her, moved into her class. His name was Landon Rybeck III; he was from New York state; and his father had moved to Chicago for business. He was, in Arcineh's and Daisy's opinions, the cutest boy in the school, and he seemed to have eyes for Arcineh.

"What if he sits by you at lunch?" Daisy asked at the end of the week.

"He won't."

"Why not?"

"He just won't."

"Arcie, he's from New York," Daisy said knowingly. "East Coast boys are different."

The comment made Arcineh laugh. When Daisy joined her, they got shushed in the library, but at lunchtime, Daisy proved to be right. Even though Arcineh was sitting with both Daisy and Bryn, Landon sought her out and asked if he could sit down.

"Sure," Arcineh agreed, hoping he couldn't see how hard her heart was pounding.

"R.C., right?"

"Yes."

"What do the R and C stand for?"

Arcineh was opening her mouth to answer when he cut in. "Don't tell me—let me guess. Rachel Catherine?"

Arcineh laughed, and he knew he was wrong.

"Okay, how about Renee Crystal?"

Arcineh was still giggling, and Landon was in his element. Rena, Rita, and Rose came out of his mouth, as did Callie, Corrie, and Connie. Not until he threw his hands in the air, did Arcineh find enough air to stop laughing and speak.

"They're not initials," she explained. "Arcie is short for Arcineh."

"Arcineh?" he repeated.

"It's Armenian. My mother was Armenian."

"What's your full name?" Landon asked with such charm that Arcineh almost told him, but she remembered just in time that she didn't like the sound of her full name.

"What's *your* full name?" she countered.

"You probably already know." Landon's voice was dry.

"I know you're a third."

"Then you also know that my family has a complete lack of imagination. Three generations and that's the best they can do."

Again Arcineh laughed. Daisy and Bryn had done their own share of laughing, and Landon was clearly entertaining them all. But his eyes continued to stray back to Arcineh's face.

Lunch ended much too swiftly by Arcineh's standards. With Daisy and Bryn trailing them, talking behind their hands all the while, Arcineh and Landon walked together back to class. By the end of the school day they had decided to work on a project together, and Arcineh's heart was over the moon.

∽

"What have you found out?" Sam asked of Mason, long after both men should have left the office downtown.

"The houses in that neighborhood are not selling very well just now. It would probably be best to wait until spring," Mason answered. What he wanted to say was that it was too soon. He didn't feel that selling Arcineh's home should happen this close to her loss, but he knew better than to add this.

Silence fell over the room. Mason was weary and wanted to go home. He'd come into the office at 6:30 that morning, and it was now after 9:00. His commute was only 20 minutes, but he still wanted to leave now and climb into bed. It had been a long week.

"Let's leave it for now," Sam said, standing. He didn't speak on the subject again, leaving Mason to surmise that he was done for the day, but gathered his effects and started toward the elevator.

By the time Sam got home, it was closing in on 10:00. The house was dark and quiet. Coming in at this hour was not all that unusual for Sam—he was married to his work—but since Trevor and Isabella's death, he'd curtailed some of his regular habits. He realized he should have at least called and talked to Arcineh, but he hadn't thought about it until just this moment.

He was climbing the stairs, more than ready for bed, when he realized he needed to give Violet a raise. He'd asked her to take on a great responsibility with Arcineh in the house and had yet to compensate her. Sam was still running numbers in his head when he entered his bedroom, turned on the light, and found Arcineh smack in the middle of his king-sized bed. She didn't so much as move a muscle, not even with the light on, and Sam laughed a bit. Not until he'd gone into the bathroom and made some noise did Arcineh stir.

"Hey, you," Sam spoke softly when he came back to the bed and found her trying to sit up. "Did you have a bad dream?"

"No." Her voice was croaky with sleep. "I just missed you."

"Why didn't you go down and see Violet?"

"She had a date," Arcineh said around a huge yawn. All fatigue fell away from Sam. He watched in silence as Arcineh crawled from the bed and began moving toward the door. Her "Goodnight, Grandpa," was soft, but Sam heard it because he was right on her trail.

He saw her into bed and then sat down on the edge of the queen-sized mattress. Arcineh was back asleep in seconds, but Sam sat still and tried to remember the evening. He thought he had talked to Violet but then realized he'd planned on it but not called. However, it still surprised Sam that Violet would leave before he'd made an appearance.

Sam eventually left Arcineh's room and headed down to see if Violet was home. Her car was not there and her apartment off the kitchen was dark and quiet. From a dating standpoint, it was still early, and Sam did not want to stay up. He took himself off to bed, knowing he'd dropped the ball on this one and was fully to blame, but also knowing that not overreacting would be easier after some sleep.

❧

"You got home when?" Violet asked for the second time.

"Nearly 10:00."

"But I left at 7:00."

"Why did you?"

"We had tickets for a show. We had to be there at seven-thirty. Carlee assured me you'd get the message—which you did," Violet answered, repeating what Sam had told her. "But then Arcie was so positive you'd be home on time that I left." The older woman stopped, still horrified by what had happened. "I can't believe it. What if there had been a fire or a break-in?"

Sam visibly shuddered at the idea and knew it was time to talk to his granddaughter. He was on the verge of going for her when she made an appearance in the kitchen. She was not at her best in the morning, and she looked as she always did, fuzzy and adorable.

"Are you awake?" Sam said, just holding back from his interrogation.

"A little."

"We need to talk about last night."

"What about it?" Arcineh said, her voice sounding utterly normal.

"Didn't you find it odd, Arcie, that you'd been left alone?" Violet asked, her voice already tense.

"Well," Arcineh paused, thinking about this. "I did think Grandpa would be home sooner, but then he wasn't, so I just hung out."

"Why didn't you call me?" Sam asked.

"I don't have your number."

The adults looked at each other, wondering if this could be possible, and realized with fresh guilt and surprise that it was completely true.

"What did you do all evening?" Violet, who was the first to find her voice, asked.

Arcineh shrugged before saying, "I listened to music and watched TV."

"Weren't you scared?" This came from Sam.

"A little. That's why I got in your bed."

Suddenly desperate to touch her, Sam went and put his arms around her.

"I'm sorry," he said quietly. "I got the message that Vi would be gone and then forgot. I'm very sorry, Arcie."

"It's okay." She smiled up at him, hugging him back. "I got to eat anything I wanted."

The adults laughed a little, and Arcineh thought all was well, but she missed the look that passed between Sam and Violet, the one that said this would never happen again.

Sam woke up four nights later to screams down the hall. It had been in his mind to shut his door again, but something held him off. He now sprang from his bed and ran to Arcineh's room to find her sobbing uncontrollably.

Sam touched her and called her name, but Arcineh continued to yell "No, no," and cry into her arms. Sam rubbed her back until she calmed, turning the light on at some point and finding Arcineh's eyes open, her body still shuddering from the images in her mind.

"Do you want something to drink?" Sam asked.

"Maybe some water."

Sam went to Arcineh's bathroom and came back with a full glass. Arcineh sat up enough to sip it and then lay looking up at Sam.

"Can you talk about it?"

"It was so real."

"What was real?"

"My parents were alive, and the house was on fire. I couldn't do anything."

Sam rubbed her arm a little, just waiting for her to talk if she wanted.

"And Landon was there," Arcineh said with wonder. "He didn't even know my parents."

"Do I know Landon?"

"He's a boy at school that I like."

"Does he like you too?"

Arcineh's head moved on the pillow. "We're doing a project together."

"On what?"

Arcineh's mouth quirked before saying, "The Great Chicago Fire."

Sam's smile was very gentle as he reached to stroke down her smooth cheek.

"Grandpa, are my parents in heaven?"

"What did they teach you about that, Arcie?" Sam asked, having wondered when this question would surface.

"We never talked much about God and all of that. I'm not sure there is a God."

"Neither am I, honey. I think all the heaven and hell we have is right here, and I know that the love your parents had for you and for each other made this heaven for them."

Arcineh smiled in such relief that Sam's heartbeat became even again. He didn't believe in God, and even though it was hard to imagine his son lying dead in the grave, it was easier than trying to believe in some fairyland where a superior being ruled at his whim.

"Can you sleep now?" Sam asked, hoping she would not want to talk about God again. He might not be able to hide his cynicism, and he wanted her to decide for herself what she believed.

"I think so. Can you stay a little bit?"

"Sure. I'll turn off the light, and you just go to sleep."

"Your door's open?"

"Yes, it is."

Arcineh's sigh when she heard that was audible, but Sam's was very quiet. This wasn't what he'd bargained for, but at least he had this precious girl. He missed Trevor and Isabella more every day, but Arcineh was his, and she was here to stay.

CHAPTER *Five*

"Okay, I found some good information at the library last night," Landon told Arcineh as soon as the afternoon session began. "Look at this book."

"Oh, wow." Arcineh's eyes widened when Landon put a thick book full of photos and articles concerning the fire on the library table. Landon's job was facts and details. Arcineh was concentrating on the people and the more personal stories.

"There isn't as much in here for you, but there are some names you might want to check on."

Arcineh took notes when Landon turned pages and pointed or read out loud. Her grandfather had wanted to know more about Landon over breakfast, and for a moment, Arcineh's mind went back to that conversation.

"How old is he?"

"Just a year ahead of me."

"Did you decide to do this project together, or were you assigned?"

"We decided."

"And you're allowed to do that?"

"Sure. I always do well on my projects, so Mr. Sutter trusts me to do it my way."

"And does Mr. Sutter trust Landon?"

"Landon just got here from New York, so Mr. Sutter doesn't really know him yet."

"And you feel like you do?"

"Grandpa," she had said impatiently, "I'm not marrying the guy. We just like each other and decided to do this project."

"What does like mean exactly?"

Arcineh rolled her eyes. "You know."

"No, I don't. Explain it to me, please."

"Tonight, Sam," Violet cut in. "Arcie is going to be late."

Sam had not looked thrilled, but he'd let her go. Arcineh knew, however, that the topic would return to the table that evening.

"Are you listening?" Landon's voice came to her.

"Oh, sorry," Arcineh said. "I was thinking about something."

"What?" Landon smiled, hoping it was him.

"My grandfather wanted to know all about you," she explained with a small shake of her head. "He's so funny."

"You told your grandfather that we like each other?"

"Sure."

It was Landon's turn to shake his head.

"What's the matter?" Arcineh asked.

"Just that: You tell parents something and they want to know everything."

Arcineh made herself ignore the word parents and even laughed a little. And it was funny in this case because it was proving to be very true.

∽

"How much do you know about boys?" Sam had barely taken a seat at the dinner table before he asked.

"I don't know." Arcineh felt confused, not having expected this. "What's to know?"

"How old is he, this Landon?"

"He'll be 13 in two weeks."

"Oh, Arcineh." Sam's voice was pained.

"What's the matter?" Arcineh's eyes had grown a little, and she looked tense.

The upset in Arcineh's face stopped Sam. He had been on the verge of telling her how young men thought, not knowing any other way to handle it. Tiffany had been promiscuous from the moment she turned 12. For a moment Sam had forgotten that Arcineh was nothing like her aunt.

"Nothing's the matter," he tried again, "except that boys sometimes have different thoughts than girls. I don't know this boy personally, and I want to know that *you're* going to be careful."

"Okay," Arcineh agreed, sounding a bit at sea.

"Can you tell me a little about him?" Sam asked.

"Like what?"

"Maybe his full name for starters."

"Landon Rybeck III," Arcineh said with a small laugh. "He likes cars and he misses New York sometimes."

"Why did he move here?"

"His father's job changed. I don't know what he does."

"Landon Rybeck III, huh?" Sam worked to keep his voice light. Arcineh laughed again before answering.

"He says his family has no imagination when it comes to names."

"And why do you like him?" Sam asked, feeling calmer now.

"Well, he's cute and nice, and he liked me first."

"Of course he liked you." Sam's voice was utterly sincere. "You're smart and fun and beautiful."

"You think I'm beautiful?"

"I know you're beautiful."

Arcineh smiled at him, a shy smile that told him she appreciated hearing that.

Did your dad ever talk to you about boys?"

"I don't think so."

"Well, their minds move faster. You might like it if he holds your hand, but he might want to kiss you."

"I don't think Landon does," Arcineh said innocently.

"I'm not talking about Landon right now," Sam answered, knowing she would not accept any criticism of this young man. "I'm talking about boys and men in general."

Arcineh nodded. She looked accepting, but Sam was not quite done.

"Has he held your hand?"

"No, it's not like that."

"What will you do if he wants to?"

Arcineh made a face. "I think I'd be embarrassed."

Sam had to smile. She was so mature at times and utterly child-like at others. She was only about a month from her twelfth birthday, and somehow he thought she'd be more interested in hand-holding and such.

"Are we done with Landon now?" Arcineh asked.

"I think so, why?"

"I don't know. It just seems like a lot of talk over nothing."

"It might seem like nothing at the moment, but if you could remember this conversation for future reference, I think that would be wise."

Arcineh looked at him, her face intent.

"The nerds kiss sometimes."

"Who are the nerds?"

"A pair of seniors at our school. All they did was study until last year—now they study and kiss."

For the first time Sam thought that Arcineh's school might not be so bad. Had she been in a public school, or even a larger private one, she would have witnessed kissing all along.

"Do you do much kissing?" Arcineh asked, and Sam knew that he'd not cut off soon enough.

"As a matter of fact, I don't."

"Who do you kiss when you do?" Arcineh asked, her face as open as though they were discussing the weather.

"No one you would know."

"How about Vi? Do you think she kisses much?"

"I don't ask her, and you're not going to ask her either."

Arcineh leaned back in her seat, her smile slow and mischievous. Sam caught the look and threw back his head as he laughed. She'd been having him on, and until the smile peeked out, he'd not caught it. It was something her father would have done to him and also gotten away with.

"Eat your dinner, you little monster," Sam growled at her as he speared a piece of now-cold potato.

Arcineh picked up her fork and began to eat, but a satisfied smile lurked in the depths of her eyes.

⁂

"We're leaving for Creve Coeur on the Wednesday before Thanksgiving," Sam informed Arcineh a week ahead of time. She'd come to his office and found him working on his home computer.

"We're having Thanksgiving at the Rowens'?"

"Yes. Where did you think?"

"I don't know," she answered quietly, still glad the family hadn't come up for her birthday. "I guess I thought we'd be here."

"What does it matter?"

Arcineh didn't answer out loud but knew it did matter. Here she could disappear in many different directions. At Quinn's house, the locations to escape her moody cousin were much more limited.

"Are you still thinking about the last time they were here?"

"Yes," Arcineh answered, deciding to be up-front.

"I don't know what's happened between the two of you. You used to get along so well."

"Do you really not know?" Arcineh asked, having finally figured it out.

"Do you?" Sam stopped studying the computer screen and looked at Arcineh.

"Yes. Quinn's never had to share you."

"What are you talking about?"

"She's the favorite. She knows it. We all do. She's always had you all to herself. Now I live here, and I'm with you every time you go there, and she hates it."

Sam was so stunned he couldn't move. Quinn *was* his favorite, but he didn't think anyone knew that. He studied Arcineh's face to see if this bothered her and realized she'd known all along. He also knew in that instant that Austin knew too.

Sam Bryant, not normally a fool, realized he had been just that. Quinn had always been special in his heart. She was his first female grandchild. He would never forget the day she was born, and all the memories that came flooding back of how he'd failed her mother. In his mind, Arcineh had never seemed as needy as Quinn, and neither had Austin.

Sam almost started when he realized Arcineh was still standing there watching him.

"Do we have to go?" she asked.

"Yes."

"Can we come home on Friday?"

"Arcineh," Sam said patiently. "You could try getting along with her."

"I'm not the problem," Arcineh replied, her voice becoming tight with anger.

"It takes two to tango," Sam said, causing Arcineh to roll her eyes and walk away. Sam watched her, thinking he might do some eye rolling of his own. He wondered if any of them would survive Quinn and Arcineh's adolescent years.

∽

"I missed you," Arcineh told Violet when she arrived home the Saturday after Thanksgiving.

"I missed you too. How did it go?"

"It was good," Arcineh said, still surprised. "Quinn and I had a lot of fun. Even Austin wasn't too much of a jerk."

Violet wanted to laugh at this description. She'd seen Austin in action more than one time, and the name *jerk* usually came to her mind as well.

"Did you eat a lot of turkey?"

"And gravy!" Arcineh said, one of her favorite foods.

"Stuffing and mashed potatoes?"

"Of course, but I like your stuffing better."

"When have you had my stuffing?"

"Last Thanksgiving. Did you go with Ed and his family?"

"He doesn't have family, Miss Nosy. And if you must know, we ate out."

Arcineh looked into Violet's eyes, her own becoming serious.

"Will you marry Ed?"

"No," Violet said without hesitation, serious as well. "I've been married, and I'm not doing it again."

Arcineh stayed very close, and Violet suddenly saw tears in the little girl's eyes.

"What is it, honey?"

"I miss my mom," she whispered as words came pouring out. "We always ate gravy together. She loved it too, and Aunt Tiffany kept talking about Christmas, and I don't even want Christmas this year. Not without my dad and mom. I don't want to shop or even have a tree. It won't ever be the same, and I just don't want it at all."

Arcineh would have run from the room then, but Violet's arms were around her. The older woman thought that life was cruel just then. Arcineh had enjoyed her holiday, only to remember that Christmas was less than a month away. Sam had never wanted Violet to go overboard with decorations of any kind, so this house would probably not even remind Arcineh of Christmas at her own home, but it would still be painful.

Sam came to the kitchen just then to tell them that he was headed to the office. He changed his plans, however, when he found Arcineh upset. He had been pleased with how well the girls had done over the weekend, but he had wondered how Arcineh was doing inside.

Against his own heart's desire, Sam canceled his visit to the office and suggested they see a movie. Violet declined, but Sam and Arcineh spent a wonderful afternoon and evening together, making life feel normal again for the 12-year-old.

∞

"Where does the money go?" Arcineh asked of Sam when he explained that it was time to put her family home up for sale.

"Where all your money is, into special accounts."

"Don't you use some of Dad's money to pay for me living here?"

"No, I don't."

"Not even with the lawyer and everything you had to do to become my guardian?"

"Not even then."

"How about the hospital bills and all my physical therapy?"

"There's insurance to pay for most of that."

"What does my dad's money do, just sit in the bank?"

"Until you're ready for it, yes."

"I don't want it," Arcineh said, not for the first time, her look becoming guarded.

"That's fine," Sam said, also repeating himself but still not knowing why it bothered her so much.

"You can sell the house, but I don't want the money."

Again Sam agreed, not going into details about the fact that it was hers, like it or not.

"Do you want to see the house again?"

"Not if it's empty."

Sam watched her shiver a little and knew it had nothing to do with the frigid February day. She weathered things at the most amazing times and in the most amazing ways. She and Quinn had fought through Christmas—even Sam had seen that Quinn was impossible to please—but now that it was time to sell her parents' last possession, she was all right as long as she didn't have to deal with the money.

"What are you thinking right now?" Sam asked.

"That I want hot chocolate."

Sam nodded, not even attempting to probe deeper. He took Arcineh at her word, reminding himself that she had always been up-front with him in the past.

"Do you want some?" she asked.

"Ask Violet to make mine coffee, and I'll have to drink it in here if I'm going to get my papers in order for my trip."

Arcineh only nodded and made her way from the office. She didn't like it when he traveled, but it had become more normal to her. His travel, for some reason, was always the greatest reminder that her parents were gone.

All the way to the kitchen Arcineh thought about them. If you had asked her how long her parents had been dead, she could have told you, but part of her heart didn't believe that it had been almost a year. Less than two months would mark the one-year date, but for Arcineh it had been much longer.

She could no longer remember her mother's laugh. She had tried hard to hang on to that wonderful sound, but it had slipped away. As had her father's imitation of Mickey Mouse. It had never sounded just like Mickey, but Arcineh had liked it better.

"Vi," Arcineh called to that lady when she reached the kitchen, but she wasn't around. Arcineh was headed to look for her when she realized she never did anything for herself in the kitchen. Not sure how to make coffee and knowing she'd need Violet for that, Arcineh did go ahead and make herself a cup of hot chocolate. It didn't taste just like Violet's, but Arcineh—proud of her own efforts—thought it was good. And when Violet came and praised her, she felt even better, thoughts of her parents slipping momentarily from her mind.

⌘

Violet caught Sam at the door as he came in. She looked almost secretive as she motioned to him with one hand. Sam followed his housekeeper to the closed glass doors of the family room. The furniture was pushed back, the rug rolled up, and the music blasted from within.

Arcineh Bryant, showing her grandfather what Geneva Sperry had seen all along, danced in the middle of the floor to one of the latest pop songs. As if she'd written the music herself, her body moved in perfect rhythm, her face relaxed with pleasure. For several long minutes Sam could only stare.

"When?" he finally asked.

"Just today."

Again the adults continued to watch, moving for a better view. As they stared, the music changed, and so did the dance. The beat a little slower this time, Arcineh danced as though she had a partner. Sam and Violet continued to watch until the beat picked up again and Arcineh made the transition so smoothly that Sam slowly shook his head. Not until the fastest song ended did Arcineh seem to need a break, and that's when she spotted them.

"Hi," she said as she came out to greet her grandfather, her face moist. "You're back," she said, kissing his cheek and smiling.

"And you were dancing," Sam said in quiet amazement.

"Yeah," Arcineh shrugged a little. "I was in the mood."

"Did your hip hurt?" Violet asked.

"No." Arcineh looked surprised. "In fact I was wondering if Geneva would let me come back."

"Yes." Sam's voice was definite.

"How do you know?"

"She came to see me."

Arcineh's mouth opened a little.

"When was this?"

"Last year. I forgot to tell you. She wanted me to order you back but understood why I couldn't do that. She did make it very clear to me that you could come back anytime you wanted."

Arcineh looked as pleased as she felt and even went back to the family room to dance a little more.

The next day was Sunday, and Geneva's studio was not open. However, the moment school ended on Monday, Sam was there. He'd left the office early to pick up Arcineh. He drove her to the studio and learned that Geneva was good on her word: The dance instructor welcomed Arcineh back with open arms.

❦

The first weekend in March brought a surprise visit from the Rowan family. They arrived late on Friday night, just as Sam and Arcineh were talking about going to bed.

"Quinn has one performance after another coming up, and we thought we'd better come while we can," Tiffany explained, clearly pleased with herself. Arcineh was not thrilled. She and Quinn had not enjoyed the visit at Christmas, but there was more to it than that. Arcineh waited only ten minutes before catching her grandfather's ear to remind him.

"I have a special practice at Geneva's tomorrow."

"Do you have to go?" Sam made the mistake of asking.

Arcineh's look was telling. "She gave me a lead part," she said, her voice tight with irritation. "I can't miss this."

Sam wanted to argue but remembered that his daughter hadn't warned them they were coming and that Arcineh could hardly be blamed. However, Quinn did not take it that way. She sulked through Saturday because Arcineh was gone for hours, and wouldn't talk to her when she got home that evening or on Sunday at all. Arcineh ended up just as angry, coming from her bedroom to see them off only because her grandfather ordered her to do so. The house was very quiet after their car drove away, right up to the moment Sam tried to fix things.

"You don't understand," Sam began without warning. "Quinn is sensitive."

"What has she got to be sensitive about?" Arcineh argued.

Not expecting her angry tone with him, Sam stared at her in some surprise, but Arcineh was not done.

"Both her parents are alive!"

Sam's look became patient before he said, "She's just like her mother in that regard. Tiff is sensitive too."

"And why should she be?" Arcineh spat, feeling rage now. "Aunt Tiffany has a husband and two children and lives like a queen. You call it sensitive—I call it ungrateful!"

Sam did not know what to say. In truth Arcineh had an excellent point, but he felt dreadfully disloyal to Quinn and Tiffany by agreeing with her. As it was, Arcineh didn't give him a chance. She turned and walked toward her room, saying she wanted to be left alone.

Sam covered his own hurt with anger and took her at her word, not even allowing Violet to call her for supper. She would have gone without if she'd not made an appearance before the meal ended. By then, both Sam and Arcineh had calmed down. They talked about various things, but the subject of the family did not come up. It wouldn't have done any good. It was not a topic they would agree upon.

CHAPTER *Six*

"Hey," Landon spoke as he sat down next to Arcineh in the library. "What are you working on?"

"Not much," Arcineh said, not happy to see him for the first time. She didn't want to see anyone right then but knew she couldn't explain.

"Big plans for the weekend?" he asked.

"I have a dance thing," Arcineh told him, not mentioning that her dance performance in the children's wing at a hospital was coming two days before the one-year death of her parents, partnered with the fact that she'd never danced without her mother before. She felt sick at the thought and suddenly knew she wanted to go home.

"Do you get nervous?" Landon asked. He noticed her demeanor but didn't understand it. They had become more friends than anything else. Landon had wanted more but never said that to Arcineh. He could tell that she didn't see him that way, and when he'd found out about the death of her parents, he didn't have the heart to demand more of her.

She was the first girl he'd been sensitive with. The girls in New York had liked his looks and money and wanted to be with him. Arcineh was different, and Landon had not been willing to lose her friendship over his own ego—a mature act for his normally selfish behavior.

"I think I'm going to go home," Arcineh said, hoping she wouldn't be sick on the spot. "I don't feel too well."

"Okay," Landon replied, noticing that she looked white, but he didn't say that. He didn't offer to walk her to the office either—he wasn't *that* sensitive—but when he saw Daisy, he reported to her, feeling as though he'd done his part.

⊂⊃

"Better?" Violet asked Arcineh after she'd had a brief nap.

"I think so."

"Did you get sick?"

"No."

Violet touched her forehead. "No fever."

"I don't think I'm sick," she said.

"What's going on?" the housekeeper asked, well aware what day was approaching—not Arcineh's dance performance, but the death of her parents.

"Geneva gave me the lead. I can't just back out."

"Why do you want to?"

"I can't do it, Violet. My mom's not here. I've gone on with my life. She would be so hurt."

"You haven't gone on with your life," Violet argued, wishing Sam were there. "Your little heart has been turned upside down over this, Arcie. You didn't even want to dance until a month ago. And even if you had, your mother loved you more than her own life. She would want you to do whatever makes you happy. If you want to dance, she would want that for you."

"But she's not here!" The tears and anger finally arrived. "How could she leave like that? I need her here."

Violet just sat on the edge of the bed and let the child cry and vent. Arcie alternated between grief and rage and then guilt that she would accuse her parents of dying on purpose, and for the first time she tried to remember what had happened.

"You fell asleep, Arcie," Violet reasoned. "You can't remember something that's not in your mind."

"But what if they needed me? What if they cried out to me for help?"

The tears came again, and Violet was glad. Trevor's and Isabella's deaths were swift and violent. Mercifully Arcineh's parents had no time to call on their daughter for help. Violet would tell Sam what Arcineh had said, but she would not be the one to explain these details. She hoped that Arcineh would fall asleep after crying so hard, but the girl finally calmed and lay awake. Violet offered both food and drink, and just about everything else she could think of, but Arcineh declined it all. Not until Sam came home from work did Arcineh want to get up. She didn't discuss her parents with her grandfather, but she stayed very close to him the rest of the evening.

∽

Saturday morning found Violet and Sam at the hospital, lingering in the hallway outside the children's wing, waiting for the dance to begin. The troupe was scheduled to do what Geneva would call a mini-musical. She enjoyed taking portions of musical productions or a medley of dances from just one show and putting together a 20- to 30-minute performance that seemed to be just right for the children.

There were no singers in the group—the music was all on tape—but the dancers performed the steps in costumes as close to the original as they could find. Today's performance was from both *The Sound of Music* and *Oklahoma!* There were no lead dancers for *Oklahoma!* but Arcineh played Maria's role from the *The Sound of Music,* and her performance was perfect. Smaller children played the parts of the von Trapp family children. The patients confined to beds and wheelchairs were delighted, and the staff could not thank the dancers enough.

Sam's and Violet's hearts were near to bursting as they watched Arcineh in her element, and Arcie came away smiling and proud of how well the troupe had done. In fact she didn't stop smiling until they were back home and she remembered that the following day was her grandfather's sixty-first birthday. She found Violet in her apartment, and the older woman could see that she was ready to panic.

"I didn't shop for him!" Arcineh said twice before Violet could get a word in. "Grandpa's birthday is tomorrow."

Violet tried again. "I shopped for you," she said, and was finally heard.

"You did?"

"Yes, do you want to see it?"

Arcineh nodded in relief, and Violet produced a box. The shirt and tie inside were exactly the type her grandfather loved, and a great color for gray-and-black hair. Violet had even added a tiny bottle of expensive cologne. She knew that Sam would never wear it, but Arcineh would have a great time giving it to him.

"Oh, Violet, these are perfect, but how will I pay you?"

Violet smiled. "I just used your grandfather's credit card. He doesn't need to know."

The two laughed together before sharing a hug and then spent the next hour wrapping the packages, giggling like girls and acting completely innocent when Sam came looking for Violet. He was hungry and wanted to know what she'd planned for dinner.

⁂

"I have something to tell you," Sam said the morning after his birthday. They had spent a good birthday together—he'd enjoyed his gifts and the call from the Rowans—but this morning, the day of Trevor and Isabella's deaths, had not been far from Sam's mind.

"What is it?" Arcineh asked. She was ready for school, but it was the last place she wanted to go.

"I've bought myself a birthday present that I think you'll enjoy."

Arcineh looked at him. "Are you going to tell me what it is?"

"I think you should guess."

Arcineh laughed a little. She was all ready to be sad, but his playful mood was infectious. "It's for you?" she clarified.

"Yes."

"But I'll like it?"

"Yes!"

Arcineh laughed a little again. "Something to do with dance or music?"

"Nope."

Arcineh chuckled at his tone but really had no idea what he was talking about. She glanced at Violet, who was frying bacon at the stove, but that lady only smiled. By the time Arcineh looked back at her grandfather, Sam had sneaked a pair of swim goggles onto the table. Arcineh spotted them and stood.

"A pool? Are you buying a pool?"

"Yep."

Sam thought she would strangle him. Her arms were around his neck, and she was squeezing with all her might. Her home—on which he'd already accepted an offer to purchase—had a pool, and she'd loved it. She'd never uttered a word of complaint about not having a pool here, not so much as a hint, but Sam had known how much she missed it.

"When?" she finally let go to ask.

"They start today. That's why I had to tell you."

For some reason Arcineh wanted to cry. Tears filled her eyes, and she could not speak.

"I think," Sam said slowly, "that you should just stay here and watch them start. I'll let your school know, and you can look at the plans and even say if you want some changes."

"You'll be here?"

Sam nodded because tears were clogging his own throat. He held out his arm, and Arcineh moved close to sit in Sam's lap and be held. Sam couldn't speak for a long time. When he did, all he could manage was, "We'll get through this."

Arcineh only nodded against his shoulder, glad that she didn't have to answer. She might have gone on sitting there for a long time, but just five minutes later they heard the trucks arrive. Like conspiratorial children, they went to the front door. It was the perfect remedy for this painful day.

CREVE COEUR

"Dad's putting in a pool," Tiffany told Jeremy when she got off the phone.

"Is he?" Jeremy sounded as distracted as he felt.

"Hot tub and all."

Jeremy heard her sarcastic tone. He didn't want to ask what was bothering her but forced himself.

"Why is that a problem?"

"Do you know what Quinn will say? She's been wanting a pool for years, and you always say no. Now Arcie will have one."

"Tiffany, you've got to stop this."

"Stop what?"

"Seeing Arcie as the competition. No wonder Quinn fights with her."

"I don't do that."

"You do it constantly!" Jeremy said in a tone that always bothered Tiffany and silenced her in the bargain. Jeremy was normally a mild-mannered person. When he grew truly angry, his tone became tense and quiet, and he sounded like that now. And on top of all of that, Tiffany knew he was right.

"Even if I stop right now, Quinn will still feel the same way."

"I've heard that excuse for the last time. We're going to start expecting Quinn to treat Arcineh better. You've both forgotten how alone she is and turned Sam into some type of prize. I'm sick of it and I want it to stop now."

"Are you guys fighting?" Austin asked, suddenly at the edge of the room.

"No," Tiffany said, giving her standard answer. "I was just telling your father that Grandpa's putting in a pool."

"Oh, man!" Austin shouted without warning. "That'll put another burr under Quinn's saddle!"

Tiffany looked at her husband, her brows raised to remind him she'd been right, but Jeremy was on his feet, calling his son's name and rushing from the room in an attempt to stop Austin from finding his sister and cruelly breaking the news.

～

CHICAGO

"A pool?" Daisy said with delight the next time she and Arcineh had a chance to talk. "When will it be done?"

"By the time school's out. We even get a hot tub."

"Your grandpa is so cool," Daisy said, having only met the man twice. "I've never known an old person to get a pool."

"He's not old," Arcineh said, defending him.

"I didn't mean it that way," Daisy protested. "Don't be so touchy."

Arcineh was ready to do some defending on her own account but stopped. She *was* a little touchy about things Daisy said. She used to join in on cruel comments and jokes without a second thought. And she knew Daisy was aware of the change in her but didn't care.

She regretted every angry thought she'd ever had about her parents, every cross word they'd shared. Saying mean things about others only reminded her of that regret.

Without warning Quinn came to mind. She didn't want to have regret where Quinn was involved either. The Rowans were coming for a visit as soon as school was out. She was willing to live in peace with Quinn, but she wasn't going to compete with her, not on any level. Quinn wanted Sam's full attention, and Arcineh wasn't going to fight her. Quinn would also want the pool and the hot tub while she was there, and again, Arcineh was going to let her have them. She comforted herself with the knowledge that it was just for the weekend. When the family left, she could have her life back.

∽∽

"What happened here?" Sam asked of his granddaughters when he arrived at the edge of the hot tub. Jeremy and Tiffany had gone shopping, and Austin was in the pool. Sam had come home from work to find a bottle of baby oil spilled on the pavement.

"Arcie did it," Quinn said. "I told her to clean it up."

"I did not, Quinn," Arcineh wasted no time saying. "You bumped it over five minutes ago and left it."

"I wasn't anywhere near there."

"Enough!" Sam said sharply, sick of the way the girls had been acting for the better part of the week. "Austin, what happened here?"

"I didn't see it," Austin lied, watching Arcineh's face behind his sunglasses.

Sam turned back to his youngest grandchild. "Clean this up, Arcie."

Arcineh's gaze was murderous as she looked at Austin and then shifted her eyes to Quinn across the hot tub. Quinn would not meet her gaze, and Arcineh got out to do as she was told. There had been a cold war between the girls for most of the day, but now Quinn had crossed that line. Arcineh had been willing to at least be in the pool and hot tub with her cousin, not responding to the rude comments she made under her breath or reacting to the way Quinn sometimes treated her possessions, but this time she'd gone too far.

Cleaning up the oil and then retreating to the only person who always was on her side, Arcineh hung around the kitchen with Violet for the rest of the day.

✐

"What is going on with that child?" Sam asked of Violet early the next morning. The Rowans would be leaving that day.

"It's hard with Quinn here. You know that, Sam."

"It doesn't have to be. Arcie could choose to get along."

Violet didn't reply. She continued to work on the egg dish and coffee cake she'd be serving and kept her opinion to herself.

"Out with it!" Sam ordered. "I can hear you thinking from here."

"Then there's no need for me to say it."

Sam sighed in irritation. "Why does everyone expect me to take sides between my own granddaughters?"

"Who expects that?"

"Everyone," Sam muttered angrily before stalking from the room.

Violet stared at the place where her employer had been. If she'd spoken up, he'd have only accused her of taking Arcineh's side. He was going to have to find out for himself who his granddaughters really were.

✐

Arcineh had never known a summer to fly by so quickly. She danced every week, spent hours in the pool, had friends over, had to contend with only one more visit from her cousins, and basically had the time of her life. In no way was she ready for the school year to start, especially considering the fact that she wouldn't have Mr. Sutter this year.

She was now in the eighth grade in some subjects, and in the ninth grade for the rest. Miss Knepper would be her new teacher, and although she'd heard nothing but good things about her, Arcineh wanted to be back with Daisy and the other girls her age.

She also wasn't sure she was ready to be with high schoolers all day, but in all of these thoughts, Arcineh missed how her new classmates might feel about her. She was just six weeks from her thirteenth birthday, and changes had happened over the summer. Curves had begun to appear, and since she was dancing again, her legs took on the long, lean look that drew attention from the first day of class.

With her dark hair shining with perfect health, tanned, and dressed in the latest fashions, Arcie turned male and female heads when she walked into the room. Landon had gotten into a serious relationship over the summer with a girl who didn't attend their school, but even his eyes strayed when the *new* Arcineh walked in. By lunchtime she'd been approached by kids as old as the junior class, and although she didn't have a lot to say, there was much running through her mind.

One girl even asked her to go shopping that weekend, wanting to know the exact spot she'd found her Cole-Haan shoes.

"We can just go together," Hillary Littman suggested. "I've got the car all weekend."

"I'd have to ask," Arcineh ventured quietly, sure she would be laughed at.

"Sure." Hillary acted as if she'd heard this before. "If your folks need to meet me, I can come early."

"I live with my grandfather."

"No problem. I'm good with old people."

Arcineh only nodded, a little surprised at the older girl's flippant attitude but also rather captivated. Hillary was one of the most popular kids in school. And coming from a school where popular was the norm, that was saying something. Arcineh quietly watched her the rest of the day, wondering what her grandfather would say about a shopping trip with Hillary.

Arcineh was not to know. He'd been called away on business, and Violet was not willing to give permission for such an outing. Arcineh hoped Sam would check in before she went to bed, but that didn't happen. She went to sleep hoping he'd be home long before Saturday.

❧

"Arcie," Miss Knepper called, motioning her to her desk on Thursday of that first week. "Will you please come here?"

Arcineh, hoping she wasn't in trouble, left the table where she was seated at the back of the room and went up front. She felt eyes following her and wondered what it meant.

"Bring a chair," Miss Knepper instructed before Arcineh could get to her and she grabbed the closest one.

"I want to talk to you about this algebra test from yesterday," Miss Knepper spoke gravely as soon as Arcineh was settled close by.

"All right."

"Are you used to scores like this?" the teacher asked, holding the test so they could both read the "100%" at the top.

"Yes," Arcineh answered, but she didn't look happy about it. She certainly hoped Miss Knepper did not think she cheated.

"Just in math, or in all subjects?"

"All subjects." Arcineh's voice had grown even quieter.

"Do you know what?"

Arcineh only shook her head no.

"I knew that," Miss Knepper confessed, her voice dropping a little. "I checked your records. You're an amazing student. I just wanted an excuse to call you up here and tell you that."

Arcineh couldn't stop her smile.

"Ah, so she does smile." The teacher's voice had turned warm with gentle teasing, and Arcineh laughed a little. "You don't have anything to fear in this room," Miss Knepper said next. "It's going to be a fabulous year."

The smile Arcineh gave her this time was full wattage. Miss Knepper smiled right back, handed Arcineh her test, and told her she could go back to her work. Arcineh didn't miss Mr. Sutter for the rest of the week.

"Who is this girl?" Sam asked, having been met at the door on Friday night with a long, not-even-pausing-for-breath story.

"Her name is Hillary Littman, and she's a junior. She likes my shoes and wants me to shop with her. She asked me! We're in the same class."

Sam couldn't contain his smile. She was so excited about this, and this was the first time he hadn't come home to find her aching for him.

"You can't just tell her where you found the shoes?" Sam teased gently.

"Well, she didn't ask that." Arcineh was utterly serious. "She asked me to shop with her."

"And I suppose you need something too?"

"Well, I never did find all the sweaters I needed. Vi and I looked for ages."

Sam nodded and studied this girl that had become his own. It was no surprise that this Hillary person wanted something Arcineh had. Yes, she dressed in the latest styles from the most upscale stores Chicago had to offer, but it was more than that—Arcineh had a style of her own that was captivating. Isabella had been the same way. Like a young Jackie O, the woman who had married his son had been amazingly classy.

"I would want to meet her," Sam said, yanking his mind back to the present. "And if after she arrives, I'm not comfortable with this, you won't be going in her car. I could drop you off maybe, but I want some sense that she's not going to get you both killed."

"Grandpa," Arcineh replied, looking horrified. "Do you know how embarrassing that would be? Please just say I can ride with her—please."

"Those are the terms, Arcie. Take it or leave it."

Looking as though the weight of the world had just landed on her shoulders, Arcineh's shoulders slumped. She stared at her grandfather and shook her head in dismay.

"Are we agreed, Arcineh?" he pressed her.

"We're agreed, *Samuel*." She stressed his name and brought a reluctant smile to his face.

Seeing that he wanted to laugh, she tried one more tactic, but Sam held his ground. He also laughed, but he waited until Arcineh had left the room, wondering how many more surprises she would bring, considering the school year had just begun.

Seven

Arcineh climbed into Hillary's gleaming black Mercedes, buckled up, and sat ready to go. It took a moment for her to realize that Hillary had climbed in behind the wheel but just sat staring at her.

"What's the matter?"

"You live here?" Hillary checked.

"No," Arcineh replied, having learned she could tease her. "I live next door. I just hang out here."

Hillary laughed a little but still didn't start the engine.

"What's the matter?" Arcineh asked, starting to frown.

"That house is amazing."

"Okay," Arcineh said, her voice saying she didn't get it. "I'm sure you live in a nice house too."

"Until today I thought I lived in a *mansion,* but my house is not in this class. What does your grandfather do?"

"He owns his own company."

"What company?"

"Bryant Marble."

"I've never heard of it," Hillary admitted.

"Do you have marble or stone at your house?"

"All over."

"Your house has heard of it," Arcineh said dryly, making Hillary laugh and admire Arcineh all the more. She was so collected for an *almost* 13-year-old. True, Hillary was only 16, but she considered herself quite mature.

Still working on what it was about Arcineh Bryant that she wanted to emulate, she started the car. It was time to shop.

❦

CREVE COEUR

"Why would we go to Chicago?" Jeremy argued with his wife. "It's Arcineh's birthday. Why would we take Quinn anywhere near the girl?"

Tiffany didn't know when she'd been so hurt. Her husband had made it sound as though it was all Quinn's fault, and Tiffany was sure that could not be the case. Yes, Quinn could be difficult, but it was just a stage.

"We didn't go last year either," Tiffany pointed out, hoping another tactic would work. "What is she going to think of us?"

Jeremy stared at his wife, wondering if she was in reality at all. Arcineh never even saw them off these days unless Sam sought her out and forced her to come down. And even when he'd ordered Quinn to say goodbye, she'd ignored her own father and stomped to the car. He well remembered his thirteenth birthday. He'd had a great time of celebration surrounded by people who loved him. Why would he try to ruin Arcineh's day by adding Quinn to the mix?

"We're not going," Jeremy said flatly, his voice final.

Tiffany, however, was not done. She cried and cajoled for the next hour, but to no avail.

❦

The changes in Arcineh just two months after the school year started were noticeable to all. It wasn't so much her attitude, although that had slipped into occasional arrogance, but the confidence with which she did things. The phone rang from the moment she arrived home from school, both male and female voices asking to speak to Arcineh.

Sam had to put a moratorium on the phone during the dinner hour because the sound of it was driving him crazy. He was married to his work—he was willing to admit that—but his workers knew he did not want to be bothered at home, so he was simply not used to the phone ringing constantly.

On top of that, his traveling schedule had increased. It seemed he was on a plane somewhere every other week—he was traveling that very day—and even though he hated to admit it, he could feel a distancing between him and his granddaughter. The last time they had done more than share a few words at a meal had been her thirteenth birthday three weeks past. They'd gone to the Shedd after school and then out to dinner and had a marvelous time. Sam asked himself why he worked as hard as he did. He'd run out of things to spend money on, but then it had never been about the money. He'd always just loved to work, as his wife had pointed out to him many years past. It had cost him his marriage.

"Grandpa—" Arcineh began talking from the moment she entered the kitchen.

"Arcineh." Her grandfather stopped her. "Why don't you come in and sit down before you start the conversation?"

"Oh." She looked surprised but amenable and took a seat. "A bunch of kids are going shopping on Saturday. Do you think I could go?"

Sam thought about this. A bunch of kids was a little harder. Sam had approved of Hillary—he genuinely liked her—but unbeknownst to Arcineh after she had asked permission that first time, Sam had been on the phone to Mason, having Hillary's family checked out.

Had all not been in order, Arcineh would not have been allowed to ride with the girl.

"Are you thinking about it?" Arcineh cut in.

"Yes, Arcie."

"Well, hurry, Sam," she teased. "I have school."

"And you have to know today?" he asked pointedly, secretly thinking it funny when she called him Sam.

"Well, it would be nice. I'm sure I could be in Hillary's car if that's what you prefer."

"And is anyone else even close to your age?"

"Landon just turned 15, and he'll be going," Arcineh said carelessly, flipping her hair over one shoulder and reaching for the toast rack.

"What is that?" Sam suddenly asked, leaning toward her.

"What's what?"

"On your ear?" Sam was no longer having fun.

"Oh, yeah!" Arcineh held her hair away from her ears to show the extra piercing she'd gotten on both sides. "Do you like 'em?"

"Where was I when you did this?" Sam asked, his voice growing agitated.

Arcineh caught his tone and reacted in kind. "Belgium or France," she said with mild sarcasm. "I've lost track."

Sam didn't know when he'd last been so angry.

"Pack your things," he said quietly, pushing away from the table. "You'll be going to Italy with me this afternoon."

"*What?*" Arcineh could not believe her ears. "I have school!"

"Oh, you'll be in school all right," Sam muttered and stormed from the room, his breakfast forgotten.

Arcineh turned in horror to Violet. That lady's brows rose before she spoke.

"What did I tell you about those ears?"

"I know," Arcineh had to agree, "but I forgot."

Violet's brows only rose a little more, reminding Arcineh of the housekeeper's reaction the day she'd come home with Hillary and showed them off. Violet had warned her that she was on dangerous ground to do such a thing when Sam was out of the country, but Arcineh had not been worried, assuring the older woman that he would love the new look. Arcineh had then forgotten to tell her grandfather she'd had them done.

Arcineh realized she had only one choice: apologize to Sam and plead her case. She exited the kitchen intent on doing that and headed to his office. Too late. He was already on the phone, giving terse orders to someone on the other end, booking a second seat on his flight. When he hung up, she still tried to lobby concerning school, but he'd taken care of that as well. They would be stopping on the way to O'Hare and getting her assignments for the next week.

✺

ROME, ITALY

"This is Sarafina," Sam said quietly to Arcineh the morning after they arrived. "She's here to teach you."

"Teach me?" Arcineh asked, having not said much to her grandfather since they left Illinois. The girl's eyes darted between her grandfather and the 30-something Italian woman he'd just let into their suite.

"Italian," Sam answered. "Your lessons begin the moment I leave."

"What about my schoolwork?"

Sam's look said he wasn't falling for it.

"We both know that the work Miss Knepper sent will take you only about two hours to complete."

"But I didn't know I'd have to learn Italian," Arcineh protested, panic setting in.

"If you recall," Sam responded firmly, "you complained about not being in school, and I said you would be."

Arcineh knew he meant it. She told herself she was not going to cry in front of this strange woman, but it was going to be an effort. Sam saw the fear on her face and hardened his heart. He was not going to let Arcineh get away from him, and if drastic measures like sweeping her out of the country without warning was what it took to remind her he was in charge, he would do it.

"I'll be back this evening," Sam said quietly, watching Arcineh's fear turn to anger. Her chin lifted as their eyes met. Sam had to keep himself from laughing when he said, "Goodbye, Arcie."

"Goodbye, Sam," she spoke just as cordially, but her eyes were shooting sparks.

"Shall we start?" Sarafina asked in gently accented English when the door closed on Sam's heels.

"I guess so," Arcineh said none-too-graciously, but Sarafina ignored the tone. She began by pointing to every object in the suite and having Arcineh repeat the Italian word. Carpet, bed, lamp, dresser, pen, paper, sheet, curtain, window, pillow, shower, towel, and on and on it went. Arcineh thought she would lose her mind, but this woman, for all her gentle ways, had a will of iron. Until Arcineh could say every word by memory and to Sarafina's satisfaction, they did not move on.

Arcineh, as with every area of learning, was a quick study. By noon she was saying simple sentences with a charming accent and gaining approval from Sarafina when that woman would suddenly point to something in the room and Arcineh remembered what it was from two hours past. Not until her head was pounding and her insides rumbled did Arcineh begin to resist.

"What's the word in Italian for 'I'm starving'?"

Sarafina studied her student for a moment. Sam's child had taken it very well, and Sarafina was impressed, but she remembered his warning not to go easy on her.

"We will go downstairs and eat in the small restaurant here in the hotel, but from the moment we leave this room, you will not speak a word of English."

"How am I to order my food?"

"You will have a menu. You will read it and figure it out."

"Where did Sam find you?" Arcineh asked, speaking her thoughts.

"Right here. My father owns this hotel."

Arcineh took time to put on makeup and fix her hair, but Sarafina would not allow a change of clothing.

"You're eye-catching enough," that lady said quietly while ushering her charge out the door.

Arcineh considered the fact that she was in Italy. The morning before she'd woken up in her own bed. All the way down on the elevator Arcineh told herself she must be dreaming.

ᏽ

By 4:45 Arcineh's head was pounding and she could not go on. However, Sam was nowhere in sight. Sarafina was reticent to leave Arcineh alone, but Arcie sincerely assured her she didn't want to go anywhere.

As soon as Sarafina left, Arcineh lay on the sofa and stared into space, but that only lasted for ten minutes. She was sure that her grandfather would be back by 5:00, and when the clock crawled on to 5:30, Arcineh's temper began to rise. By the time he opened the door at 6:15, she was in full-blown rage.

"Do you know what time it is?" Arcineh shot, immediately on the attack.

"I'm sorry it's so late, Arcie. I got held up."

"You're sorry!" Arcineh flopped into a chair, not sure why she was so put out save the fact that she hadn't wanted to come along in the first place.

"I've got something for you."

"No, thank you, Sam," she responded, using his name and hoping to irritate him.

Sam still came to her chair and held out a small gold box.

"What is it?"

"Take it," Sam urged. "Try some."

Arcineh wasn't happy with him, but she took the gift. She found small white blocks of candy inside and picked one up.

"What is it?"

"Just try one."

Arcineh bit in unwillingly, a frown still on her face. But that soon changed. She sat very still as the confection melted in her mouth. She took another bite and let it melt again. Only then did she look at Sam.

"What is this?" Her voice had softened.

"White chocolate."

"I don't think I've heard of it."

"They make it in Turin, in northern Italy."

Arcineh finished the piece, her whole body melting with pleasure. Not until it was completely gone did she look up into Sam's eyes.

"Thanks, Grandpa."

"You're welcome." He smiled at her. "How did the lesson go?"

Arcineh answered him in Italian, and Sam stared at her.

"Now that didn't occur to me."

"What's that?"

"That you would learn to speak Italian better than I do."

While Arcineh was still smiling over this, Sam asked, "How about some dinner?"

"Can we leave the hotel?"

"Yes."

Arcineh was out of her chair in a flash and headed to change. She would give him no time to change his mind.

❧

Given the choice, she would have stayed home, Arcineh realized, but four days later, sitting on a plane bound for Chicago, Arcineh knew she would never forget her time in Rome. Starting on the second day, Sam allowed Sarafina to take Arcineh from the hotel. Sarafina demanded she speak in Italian at all times. Arcineh was often tempted to scream at the woman and run away, but in truth she'd come away with a fine education on the language as well as the city.

Sarafina had even taken her to her home, a lovely villa not far from the hotel, where she could relax in comfort, all the time working her brain for her exacting teacher. She learned that Sarafina was not a teacher by trade, but a retired model. She was to be married in the spring, and Arcineh had even met her handsome fiancé.

Arcineh realized right then that she'd actually enjoyed herself. It also occurred to her quite suddenly that she hadn't thanked her grandfather for taking her along. She turned to do just that but held her tongue. Sam Bryant was sound asleep in his seat and looked as though he would stay that way all the journey home.

∞

"We'll plan on Christmas," Sam said to Jeremy on the phone the week of Thanksgiving.

"Yes," Jeremy agreed. "I can't seem to lick this cold, and with the kids not getting along, I'm just not up to it, Sam."

"I understand, and that will give me a whole month to make it clear to Arcineh that she's to get along with Quinn."

"I appreciate that, Sam, but Quinn isn't getting along with anyone right now."

"What's that about?"

"Some of it is her age, but it's also not having you without Arcie. I wouldn't want Arcie to be anywhere else, but Quinn is threatened by it."

"Tell her when she's here, we'll go to breakfast—just the two of us, like old times."

"I'll tell her, and you have a good holiday up there."

"Thanks, Jeremy. You too."

The men got off, and Sam sat thinking about Quinn for a long time. In truth, he didn't see any less of her than he ever had, but Jeremy was correct: Arcineh had not been around in the past, not nearly so much anyway, and Sam still believed with all his heart that Quinn was a sensitive person.

"Just like her mother," Sam said quietly in the office, wanting to do a better job with the next generation.

∽

"This is what I'm talking about." Sam spoke patiently into Arcineh's upturned face, remembering his breakfast with Quinn that morning and determined to gain Arcineh's cooperation on this. "Getting along at this moment means taking Quinn with you."

"She doesn't even know my friends," Arcineh replied, managing to stay calm. "I don't think she'll even want to go."

"But we're going to ask her, and if she wants to, it's a done deal."

Somehow Arcineh knew she would not win this one. Sam had made up his mind that she was the problem, and Arcineh was still holding to her vow to never compete with Quinn. However, where her friends were concerned, she knew that boundary lines were needed.

She waited patiently while Sam asked Quinn if she wanted to go to the mall with Arcineh and her friends, and to Arcineh's surprise, her cousin said yes. Arcineh stayed calm in the face of all of this, but while she and Quinn walked out to Hillary's waiting car, Arcineh made herself heard.

"I put up with enough with Grandpa when you're here, Quinn, but I draw the line at my friends."

"I don't know what you mean," Quinn made the mistake of saying.

Arcineh stopped at the bottom of the steps and looked her cousin in the eyes. Quinn had a hard time meeting Arcineh's gaze.

"We both know exactly what I mean. No games and no lies tonight. If you even attempt it, I'll humiliate you so badly in front of my friends you'll never want to show your face in Chicago again."

For once all arrogance and defensiveness drained away from Quinn. She nodded in sincerity and climbed in the back when one of the guys jumped out to let her in.

Arcineh made the introductions, and Quinn, rising to the occasion, blended right in. In fact, they had a marvelous time. They shopped in the pre-Christmas throngs and then went to a restaurant for huge slices of cheesecake.

For the whole evening, Arcineh had the old Quinn back. She was fun and bright and looked happy. Jordan, one of the guys along, seemed quite taken with her. And Arcineh could see why. She'd bleached her hair since the last time they'd seen each other, and it looked good. In Arcineh's opinion, her makeup was too dramatic, but somehow it suited her. Quinn even thanked Arcineh as they climbed the steps back to the house.

"It was fun," Arcineh said. "I'm glad you came."

"Jordan is sure cute."

"Yes, and he couldn't take his eyes off you."

"Does he have a girlfriend?"

"No. Did he ask for your number?"

"He started to and then remembered that I would be here."

"Did he invite you for the day after Christmas?"

"He did."

The girls were at the door now, but Quinn stopped Arcineh with a hand to her sleeve.

"Are you all right with that?"

"Sure," Arcineh said, wanting to add that Quinn would have to remember what she expected, but she left that alone.

The two slipped inside and found everyone in the family room. They joined them and talked about their evening. Arcineh didn't miss the fact that her grandfather looked extremely pleased. She was glad for him but still wished there was a way to make him understand.

∽

"What time today?" Sam asked of Arcineh concerning her dance performance.

"Two o'clock at the studio, and then we'll go to the community center."

"All right. Make sure Geneva doesn't schedule anything big for you next week. I want you to go with me to Paris."

"Why?" Arcineh asked, her voice telling him she thought she was in trouble again.

"It's almost April, and I've not seen much of you since Christmas. I want you to go."

"You could stay home more," she muttered, and got *the look*. Arcineh lowered her eyes, knowing she'd been out of line.

"Plan on the trip." Sam was done being kind. "I thought you'd appreciate a bit of notice, but evidently not."

"Why am I going exactly? More languages?"

"I hadn't thought of that," Sam said, hiding his hurt that she didn't want to go. "But it's a fine idea. I'll make the arrangements."

Arcineh didn't reply. She was just rebellious enough not to admit that she'd enjoyed learning Italian and was still working on it in her mind. She didn't think leaving next week would be that much of an issue, but something inside of her didn't feel like going.

Sam didn't check with her again. Her performance went well that afternoon, but she felt a bit off-step and was glad she was in the back row.

And then on Tuesday, just as he'd said they would, they flew to Paris. Arcineh sat in a hotel room for three days with a French teacher who was nowhere near as congenial as Sarafina had been, but she did learn some French and found she liked it almost as much as Italian.

Sam was even busier than he had been in Rome, but he made up for it at the end of their trip by allowing Arcineh to shop. She did her level best to buy everything Paris had to offer, and Sam teased her all the way home about not taking her again, saying he just couldn't afford it.

Arcineh took the teasing in stride and enjoyed the attention when she arrived back at school and every girl she knew had something to say about her new clothes. When Sam got home that evening, Arcineh actually remembered to thank him for the trip and the shopping.

CHAPTER

Eight

"Are you busy?" Arcineh asked of Sam on Mother's Day 1995.

"No, why?"

"Can we go to the cemetery?"

Not in the three years since Isabella's death had Arcineh requested such a thing. The years had somehow flown by. Arcineh was halfway to her fifteenth birthday, and Sam could not have said where the time had gone. For a moment he looked into eyes that reminded him so much of his son that he ached to see them.

"Grandpa?" Arcineh questioned softly, not calling him Sam this time.

"Yes," he said simply, drawing his mind back. "Right now?"

"I just need to grab a jacket." Arcineh began to turn away and then stopped. "And can we make a stop on the way home?"

"Where?"

"I want to get flowers for Vi."

"She would like that."

"I should have done that last year. I thought of it but didn't."

Sam nodded.

"Oh," Arcineh stopped, remembering something more. "I spent my allowance on a purse, so I'll need to borrow some money."

"Your entire allowance on one purse?" Sam clarified.

"And some shoes."

Sam stared at his granddaughter, knowing he'd created this monster but still not willing to live with her.

"We'll go to the cemetery," he said, his voice holding no rebuke. "And we'll get Violet whatever you like, but sometime very soon we'll visit the subject of your spending."

Arcineh had known he would say this and did not argue. All she wanted to do right now was get to the cemetery. For the first time in her life it was important, and yet she was scared. She just wanted to go before she could change her mind.

⌒⌒⌒

"Did you order this?" Arcineh asked as she looked at the large ornate headstone that held her parents' names. Dark gray marble with a beautifully etched picture of a river and trees, and then their names in lovely script with the dates they were born and died. Between them rested a heart, their wedding date carved inside.

Arcineh touched it all very gently, not noticing that her grandfather hadn't answered. Sam was so choked up at the sight of this, remembering the day they'd been buried, that he thought his throat would burst.

Not until Arcineh turned to him with swimming eyes did he feel as if he could openly cry. He broke down, hugging Arcineh close when she came to him, both of them awash with fresh grief.

Arcineh didn't know why she had wanted to come. It hadn't helped at all. Mother's Day had not meant anything to her the last few years, and she wished she hadn't tried to change that.

"I want to go," she sobbed. "I just want to get flowers for Violet and hug her."

Sam did not argue. The lovely lawn and spring flowers that bloomed all around were lost on Sam Bryant. This was a place of death. A place of hopelessness and of no return. He sincerely wished that Arcineh would never want to come again.

❦

"Sam," Arcineh said in the car after nearly an hour. Traffic was awful, and it had taken a long time for Arcineh to stop crying.

"Yeah?"

"What happened to Grandma Bryant?"

"She left," he said simply.

"Why?"

"A lot of reasons, I suppose, but mostly because I worked all the time and she was alone."

"But what about my dad and Aunt Tiffany?"

"Your grandmother wanted a new life. She couldn't do that with two children."

Arcineh looked over at her grandfather's profile. He was still a handsome man. He never seemed lonely, but Arcineh now wondered.

"I have no idea where she is," Sam went on thoughtfully. "I couldn't even tell her about Trevor's death."

This never occurred to Arcineh's young heart. She felt cold with the thought that someone she loved could die and she wouldn't even know.

"Are you all right?" Sam asked.

"I think so. Are we almost there?"

"Yes, there's a place that will have just what you want."

And he was right. Even on Sunday, Arcineh found a beautiful bouquet for Violet. That lady was surprised speechless when Arcineh walked into the kitchen with it. Arcineh didn't care. Violet's loving arms around her were all the thanks she wanted.

⟨∞⟩

"Starting the second week of your summer, you're going to come to my office three days a week and work."

Arcineh was so stunned by Sam's words that she couldn't say a thing.

"You'll be filing, typing, and anything else Carlee wants you to do. You'll be quiet, and work hard, and I'll pay you well."

"Why?" Arcineh finally managed.

"You've got too much time on your hands during the summer, and you need to understand that money doesn't grow on trees."

"I was going to keep working on my Italian and French," she argued. She had gone overseas twice more with him in the last year, and her languages improved each time.

"You can't do both?"

"What kind of summer is that?"

"The kind you're going to have."

And that, Arcineh learned, was the end of that. She had one week off to do as she pleased, but on Monday morning, June 12, feeling as though she was still asleep, she climbed into her grandfather's Bentley and went with him to start her first day of work.

⟨∞⟩

Sam watched the male interns waiting to get on the elevator and had enough heart for them to feel sorry. They knew he was standing nearby, but not looking at Arcineh was nearly killing them. And she was worth a second glance. She didn't go overboard with her makeup or wear the high heels that she loved, but her hair, face, and clothing always looked together. And she was beautiful, all biases aside.

Sam had not considered her effect on the office when he suggested that she work with him. At times it amused him, and at other times he felt concern. For the first few weeks, he kept a very close watch on Arcineh, but she seemed preoccupied with doing her job. This pleased Sam—it pleased him very much—but it was a curiosity to him as well.

He was under the impression that most young ladies were looking to hook a man, or at least practice their flirting skills, but Arcineh didn't seem to fit his mold. She would deliver packages or files to some of the best-looking men in his office and not seem to give them a second glance.

Arcineh, on the other hand, affected them very much. Sam had been forced to turn a laugh into a cough when one of the newer men poured coffee on his pants simply because Arcineh walked by the break room.

The elevator arrived, and Sam pulled his mind back to the business at hand—not just the marble business, but also the one of keeping an eye on Arcineh.

∽

Arcineh loved Carlee. She was bright and fun and she treated Arcineh like an adult. She included her for breaks and lunch, and when Arcie got to work with Carlee, the time flew.

"I've got some advice for you," Carlee said when August was half over.

"What is it?"

"If you ever go searching outside of this office for work, you'll have to remember some things if you want to get hired for the right reason."

Hanging on every word, Arcineh listened carefully.

"You're a very beautiful girl, which means if you dress as nicely as you do, in clothing that accentuates that, some men may hire you so they can look at you or try to get away with something.

"At the same time," Carlee went on, "many women won't hire someone who looks like you because they'll see you as competition."

"Is that all true?" Arcineh asked, finding it hard to believe.

"Yes. The best secretaries and office workers blend into the background. Sometimes it's the safest way."

Arcineh looked into Carlee's large blue eyes and saw that she didn't have a bit of makeup on. Arcineh realized at the moment that more than one time that summer she had wished Carlee would do a little more with herself. Suddenly she knew this was just the way Carlee wanted it.

"What if you meet a man and you want to catch his attention?" Arcineh asked.

Carlee smiled, thinking this one was much too bright for her own good.

"You're 15, Arcie." The secretary's voice was gentle. "I'm not about to tell you that. If by 20 you don't have it figured out, come back and see me."

Arcineh smiled at her. "You promise?"

"Yes, but I don't think it's a promise I'm going to have to keep."

Arcineh didn't press Carlee, but her own question stayed on her mind for a long time that evening. Indeed she fell asleep still thinking about it.

ᘓᕽᕽᕽᘓ

Sam took Arcineh to her first day of tenth grade, hoping that he'd done the right thing. He'd decided he could fit in one more trip to Paris before Labor Day, and Arcineh had asked to go along. Sam was so pleased by her willingness, he didn't see what followed next. She hit every shop she could find, including a hairdresser who taught Arcineh how to straighten her naturally wavy hair. The look was stunningly different, and even Sam had not been able to stop staring at her.

"Do me a favor," Sam said when she moved to get out of the car. "Let them down easy."

"Let who down easy?"

"The boys who ask you out."

"Sam," she said with a smile, "I've been going to school with these guys for years. There's no one new."

"Only you."

Their eyes met, and Arcineh saw what he meant.

"Lean over here so I can kiss you," Sam told her. Arcineh added a hug to the kiss Sam put on her cheek and then slipped from the car. She thought a few people might look at her hair and new clothes, but all but dismissed what her grandfather had said. Arcineh swiftly learned she'd been naive. Nothing could have prepared her for what the next few days would bring.

∽

"It makes me so angry, Vi. What am I supposed to do about it?"

"Go over it with me one more time," Violet requested. "Slowly this time."

"Okay, it's like this. Brody Hammel came back for his junior year looking amazing—tan, skin cleared up, tall, and muscular."

"Okay."

"Both Hillary and Daisy have mad crushes on him, but he asked me out."

"And they're both mad at you?"

"Exactly."

"What did you say?"

"About what?"

"To him when he asked you out?"

"I said no! I don't want all my friends mad at me."

Violet looked at her lovely familiar face and wished there was a way for the girls to know that their friendships with each other were important. It was a sad fact that most boys came and went.

"Did you want to say yes?" Violet asked next.

Arcineh frowned. She hadn't even thought about it.

"I don't know. I've known Brody for a long time, and all we've ever been is friends. I don't think he really wanted to ask me out—I think he just thought we'd look good together."

"How do you know that?"

"Oh, something Bryn said. Maybe she doesn't know, but it sounded like something that might happen. The boys at school can be so shallow."

"How much do you wish you had a boyfriend?" Violet asked.

"A little bit. Usually I don't feel I have time for one."

Violet couldn't argue with that. Arcineh's summer had been full and had gone by very swiftly. The school year would be even worse.

"So what will you do?" Violet asked in her wonderfully practical way.

"For the moment, be glad it's Friday."

Arcineh grabbed an apple from the always-available fruit bowl and left the kitchen. Not many minutes passed before Violet heard the beat of music.

"Be glad it's Friday and get a little dancing in too," the housekeeper said to herself, continuing her work on dinner and wondering what the rest of the school year would bring.

❦

Quinn had not planned on fighting with Arcineh. In fact, the last few times they'd been together, she had been fairly content, but when the family visited in October for Arcineh's fifteenth birthday, Quinn took one look at her cousin and thought she might actually hate her.

She didn't care that Arcineh's parents were dead; Quinn wished hers were dead all too often. All Quinn could see was the perfect person Arcie was—smart and beautiful, with all the money any girl could want.

Quinn found it easy to forget that Arcineh had worked all summer and hadn't complained. She knew her cousin got good grades but never believed she had to work for them.

Quinn's tortured thoughts set the entire weekend on edge. Even Sam noticed her quietness, thought she might be struggling with her self-image again, and decided not to give Arcineh her gift until the family had left after the weekend.

However, this drove Quinn and Austin crazy, and in turn, they nearly drove Arcineh out of her mind.

"Just tell me," Austin said for the fifth time on Saturday morning.

"Are you deaf, Austin?" Arcineh asked. "I don't have it yet. If I knew what I was getting, I'd tell you."

Austin clearly didn't believe her, and Arcineh had had enough.

"You only want to know so you can taunt Quinn. You're so pathetic, Austin."

Austin turned and left, his face showing how angry he was and also how close Arcineh had come to the mark.

Arcineh didn't care what he thought. She just wanted peace. Unfortunately Quinn had other ideas. She was at her door just minutes later.

"What did Grandpa give you?"

"He hasn't given me anything yet," Arcineh said, thinking this might be the longest birthday of her life. Her cousins, the least favorite people in her life, were in town, making the hours drag.

"You're lying."

"Why would I lie about that?"

Quinn didn't have a good answer for that, so she turned and left. Arcineh sat down on her bed and tried not to think about the disappointments of this school year. Things still weren't completely ironed out with Hillary and Daisy. Brody had stopped asking her out, but because he hadn't sought either of them out, they didn't believe her.

What is it about me that makes people think I lie? she suddenly asked herself. *My cousins think I'm hiding my gift from Sam, and Hillary thinks I'm secretly seeing Brody.*

Arcineh sat and brooded over this for a time and then got mad at herself. She realized she didn't care what the others thought. Violet would have said it wasn't her problem. She *wasn't* seeing Brody, and if her grandfather wanted to give her the moon for her fifteenth birthday, that was his choice!

Arcineh eventually got into her swimsuit and went down to the pool. It was just plain cold outside, but since the pool had gone in, her grandfather had agreed to leave it heated until her birthday each year.

The family heard her splashing around, and it wasn't long before they joined her. Tiffany, Austin, and Quinn took up residence in the hot tub, but Jeremy challenged Arcineh to a water volleyball game and even took the deep end. Violet served German chocolate cake that night, Arcineh's favorite kind, and in the morning, the Rowan family left right after breakfast.

As soon as they departed, Sam, looking mischievous and much too pleased with himself, took Arcineh to the garage. Parked next to his car was a brand new BMW 5 Series.

"Happy birthday, honey," Sam said quietly.

"But I'm 15," Arcineh pointed out when her mouth would work.

"You'll be starting Driver's Ed in just a few months and need this. Besides, everyone expects it at 16. This way it's really a surprise."

Sam found his neck in a stranglehold, and Arcineh could not stop laughing.

"Was it a good birthday?" Sam whispered in her ear, still hugging her tight.

"The best," Arcineh said with a laugh, knowing she would never be able to explain.

"Tiffany called," Sam said a few days later. He'd found Arcie in the family room and caught her between songs. "It seems Quinn is pretty upset with you."

Her grandfather never told her what her aunt said during their phone calls, so this took her by surprise. She turned the stereo off and sat on one of the sofas. Sam took a chair.

"Did she say why she was upset?"

"She says she tried to discuss something with you, and you wouldn't talk about it."

Arcineh nodded, her face turning impassive.

"Do you know what it was?" Sam asked.

"Yes."

"Are you going to tell me?"

"There's no point. When Quinn is involved, you never believe me."

"That's not true."

Arcineh only stared at him, and Sam heard himself. Sam's hand went to the back of his neck, and he rubbed at the ache there. He knew men who deliberately had children at his age, but in his view, being a father to a teenager at this stage in his life was almost impossible.

"I'm sorry you don't think I believe you," Sam apologized lamely. "I didn't mean to do that."

Arcineh shrugged but still knew it was no use trying to explain. On an impulse she took another tact.

"You're something of a prize these days, Sam."

Sam stared at her, wondering where she was going.

"It wasn't like that when my parents were alive, but now that I'm here, you're the prize and Quinn has to have you. That might not be news to you, but this will be. I'm not in the competition. I'm not going to vie for your attention or anyone else's. Either you want me or you don't.

"There's a boy at school right now that all my friends like, but he likes me. They're all mad at me about that. I don't know what I'm

supposed to do. I can't control his feelings. I look forward to the
weekend when I can come home and just be here with you and Violet.
It's hard when there are others because everyone wants to compete
with me, and I don't know where to go."

Sam felt his heart clench. He hadn't known that she felt this way,
and he hadn't known about her friends.

"I'm sorry about your friends, Arcineh. I didn't know."

"I think I told Violet all about it, and that got it out of my
system."

"But I still don't understand." Sam could not let go of Tiffany's call.
"Why couldn't you just discuss what Quinn wanted to talk about?"

"Because I didn't know what you were getting me for my birthday
until after they left."

Sam's mouth opened. "That's what she wanted to know?"

"She and Austin both. They didn't believe me when I said you
hadn't given me my gift yet."

Sam did not know what he was expecting, but this wasn't it.

Arcineh was expecting some type of apology, and when it didn't
come, she stood to cover her hurt.

"I'm going to finish my workout now."

"All right," Sam said, his head in a complete muddle.

Not waiting for him to leave, Arcineh went back to the stereo
and turned the music up loud. She kept her back to the door after
the music fired up. By the time the dance turned her around, her
grandfather was gone.

❧

"Hi," Daisy said quietly, coming to stand at Arcineh's table in the
library at the beginning of November.

"Hi," Arcineh said in return.

"Can I sit down?"

"Sure."

Daisy sat, but she looked upset. Arcineh waited for her to talk, sure that if she said anything it would only get her into more trouble.

"So it's like this," Daisy began, glancing at Arcineh from time to time but not holding her gaze. "I just had a long talk with Brody this morning, and he told me what you said."

"What was that?"

"That you wouldn't go out with him and lose all your friends, and then I realized because we didn't believe you, you lost us anyhow."

Daisy was crying now, and Arcineh just listened.

"I'm so sorry, Arcie. Do you remember when we both liked Richard? And we promised never to let a guy split us up? And then I broke my promise."

Daisy put her hands over her face to cover her tears, but her whole body shook with the intensity of it all.

"It's all right," Arcineh said, not sure it really was but wanting Daisy back in her life so much that it hurt. "You don't have to cry anymore."

Daisy looked at her, her makeup having gone on the run. Arcineh dug in her purse and handed her a mirror.

"And to think my shrink has been working on me for days," Daisy muttered into the mirror, "trying to get me to a good place for when you didn't forgive me."

"Your shrink?" Arcineh didn't bother to hold her surprise.

"Yes! I've been so sad about all of this, my mother made me go."

"Has it helped?" Arcineh asked, glad that her grandfather had never forced her to talk to a stranger.

"A little," Daisy sniffed as she tried to fix her face, "but I missed your birthday."

"That's all right," Arcineh said and meant it this time. "Sam more than made up for everyone."

"Jewelry?" Daisy guessed, handing back the mirror.

"A car."

"But you're 15!"

"That's what I said, but he says everyone gets one at 16, and what's the surprise in that?"

Daisy cried again, this time with laughter. Before the teacher in charge that day could come and tell them to hush, they had made plans for the weekend. The girls would spend one night at Arcineh's, the next night at Daisy's, and fill every minute in between.

CHAPTER Nine

"I'm going to die," Arcineh said for the tenth time. "You know that, don't you?"

"You're going to be fine," Sam lied, telling himself again that he was too old for this. He well remembered teaching Trevor to drive. It went smoothly. He was a natural. Arcineh on the other hand was more like Tiffany. The creative side of her did not allow for something as basic as the gas on one side and the brake on the other.

"I don't think I want to learn to drive. I don't mind walking."

"You're doing fine," Sam lied again, thinking that if she braked hard one more time, his head was going to go through the windshield.

"Did you have trouble like this when you started?"

"It was so long ago, I can't remember."

His tone was so dry Arcineh began to laugh, and because she was scared, it was nervous and high pitched.

"All right, Arcie," Sam said, trying to sound firm, thinking she sounded slightly hysterical. But he ended up laughing with her.

The lessons continued, and Sam's words actually ended being true. When all was said and done, Arcineh did fine. Those first few days out were a bit rough—they did almost die—but within two weeks, Arcineh was gaining competence and confidence. Sam kept her in what he called *her world,* simply having her drive to the school, the dance studio, Daisy's house, and home. There were no trips downtown or onto the interstate unless they were driving to Creve Coeur, and then he didn't let her take the wheel until they were well away from Chicago. Thankfully it was April so the snow and ice had abated and there was little of that to contend with.

It would be October before she could test for her license, and Sam believed she would pass. For the moment, however, Sam was certain he heard Chicago, and possibly the state of Illinois, give a collective sigh of relief.

⁂

A beginning-of-summer trip to Missouri was unlike anything Arcineh had ever known. Sam wanted to visit Creve Coeur, and although Arcineh dreaded it, she found that life had altered. Both of her cousins had met people and gotten into relationships that changed the dynamic for her.

Austin was in his junior year, and Quinn was a sophomore. Austin's girlfriend was Lexa, and Arcineh genuinely liked her. It was a mystery as to what Lexa saw in her cousin, but at least she was nice.

Tayte, Quinn's boyfriend, was another matter. He was more in love with himself than Quinn, but the eyes of adoration that Quinn turned on him were blind to all else. Tayte never said or did anything inappropriate toward Arcineh—indeed he barely looked at her—but Quinn imagined that Arcineh was out to get him.

It made for some heated moments near the end of their visit. Arcineh simply avoided her cousin the rest of the time, and if the adults noticed, they kept their mouths shut. As usual, when Arcineh was able to drive away from the Rowan house, a peace filled her inside.

∞

"Have you noticed that we don't go on vacations?" Arcineh asked of Sam. Working again at Bryant Marble during the summer, Sam's granddaughter had learned from Carlee that no one was in his office and had gone in and made herself at home.

"Come in and get comfortable, Arcie," Sam said dryly as he watched her sprawl into a chair.

"Thanks, Sam, I will."

"Now, what were you saying?"

"Just that we never go on vacation."

"This coming from a girl who's crossed the Big Pond at least eight times."

"That was always business, and you know it."

Sam looked at her, thinking she had a good point but not willing to admit it.

"Where did you want to go?"

"Anywhere?"

"*Anywhere?*" Sam pressed her.

"Not Chicago or Creve Coeur."

"So you're not thinking about something out of the country?"

"It doesn't matter, as long as I don't have school and you don't have business."

"I'll think about it."

"And I want Violet to come."

Sam stared at her again. He was going to keep teasing her, but it occurred to him how few demands she made on him. Why had he never seen that before now?

"Anything else, my lady?" Sam asked to cover what he was really feeling.

Arcineh grinned. "I'll let you know."

"Go on, get out of here." Sam shooed her away, but she had made him think. By the end of the day he'd booked three flights for Hawaii, something he did not share with Arcineh. He called Violet so she could get the dates on her calendar, and he even told her the biggest surprise of all: They would be going in October to celebrate Arcineh's sixteenth birthday.

⤶

"Brody!" Arcineh started when she walked into the break room to check on the coffeepot. "Do you work here?"

"I just started."

Arcineh nodded.

"How long have you worked here?" Brody asked, trying not to stare. Arcineh always looked so good.

"This is my second summer."

"Wow, you started when you were 14?"

"Well, my grandfather—" Arcineh began, but Brody cut back in.

"Bryant." He looked as amazed as he felt. "I never made the connection."

Arcineh smiled at him before asking, "What do they have you doing?"

"For now I'm shadowing Mr. Nelson."

"How did you get the job?"

"Mason is my grandfather's neighbor."

"Mason is so nice."

"Yes, he is," Brody agreed, thinking he could sit here all day and talk to Arcineh. He hadn't been thrilled when his father talked to his grandfather and arranged this, but things were suddenly looking up.

⤶

"How do you feel about Brody these days?" Arcineh asked Daisy on the weekend. The two were on air mattresses in the pool, bikinis and sunglasses in place.

"I'm over him. I mean, I would have liked to see if it could work, but who wants a guy who isn't crazy about her? Not me."

Arcineh listened for notes of sincerity and heard plenty before saying, "He's working at Bryant."

"You've seen him?"

"I talked to him twice this week."

Daisy sighed. "He's so good-looking."

"He is nice-looking, but I'm not into blonds."

"You like dark hair? I didn't know that."

"That's because I don't fall in and out of love every nine-and-a-half minutes."

"I don't do that anymore."

"You just told me you were over Brody, and then you sighed about his looks."

"But I'm still over him. I just think he's gorgeous."

The conversation swayed away from Brody for a moment, but Daisy suddenly jumped back without warning.

"Listen, Arcie! If Brody asks you out and you want to go, go!"

"He's not going to," Arcineh assured her.

"You don't know that."

"I know what it's like at work. Everyone fears my grandfather. The last thing they would do is show interest in me."

"So you don't get to flirt or anything?"

"Except for Brody, they're all too old. But they look."

"I'll bet they do," Daisy said sincerely.

Arcineh looked over to find Daisy peering at her over the top of her sunglasses. Arcineh flicked water at her, and they both laughed. That settled, they went back to the topic of boys and then clothing and shoes for the rest of the afternoon.

❧

"So how about a movie this weekend?" Brody finally got up the nerve to ask as the summer sped by.

Arcineh turned to look at the young man behind her, emotions flooding her brain. She had never been on a date and wasn't sure she wanted her first to be with Brody, but she found herself wanting to say yes.

"What movie?" Arcineh asked, making herself move cautiously.

"Well, I'd like to see *Independence Day* or *Mission Impossible*, but if your grandfather objects to those, there's also *The Nutty Professor*."

"If that was supposed to be charming," Arcineh told him, "you missed the door by a long shot."

"What did I say?" Brody laughed a little over the way her arms crossed and her head tipped in irritation.

"You think I'm a baby."

"Not a baby," Brody countered swiftly. "Let's just say—" he hesitated, trying to find a word that wouldn't get him in trouble. "Let's just say you're protected."

Arcineh opened her mouth to object and closed it again. Brody tried not to even smile, but it didn't work. A low laugh escaped him.

"I am protected," Arcineh said with a small laugh of her own, confident enough to just admit it. "But my grandfather's not unreasonable."

"So you'll go?"

"Sure. I think *Independence Day* looks interesting."

"Friday night?"

"All right."

"I'll check the times and get back to you."

"I have a dance performance on Saturday, so early works better than later for me."

"So home by..." Brody let the sentence hang.

"Probably 10:30—11:00 at the latest."

"Okay," Brody heard himself agreeing. He'd not been home before

1:00 A.M. on a Friday night in the last year, but this was a date with Arcineh Bryant, and in circumstances like that, you just didn't argue.

"I have a date on Friday night," Arcineh told Sam in the car on the way home.

"A date?"

"Yeah. Brody asked me to a movie."

"The kid that works with Nelson?"

"Yes."

The car got very quiet after that. Arcineh didn't notice. She was hungry and trying to find a radio station that her grandfather wouldn't object to.

"What if I say no?" Sam asked.

"About what?"

"The date."

"Oh, that. I don't know. I guess I didn't think you'd mind." Arcineh turned her head to look at him. "Brody and I talked about the fact that you're protective, but I told him you're not unreasonable."

"Maybe I am," Sam said in a tone that made Arcineh smile. He clearly didn't like the idea, but unless he told her she couldn't go, Arcineh planned to be on that date.

"I won't be out late," she said, as though this settled the idea.

Sam turned to look at her, and Arcineh just smiled into his eyes.

Sam's gaze went back over the wheel as he said, "I'm too old for this."

Arcineh simply laughed without mercy.

"How was it?" Violet was the one to ask the next morning.

"It was a good movie. We had fun."

"Did he try anything?"

"No," Arcineh answered on an incredulous laugh.

Even Sam was looking at Violet by now, but he didn't try to stop her.

"Don't you give me that look, Arcineh Isabel Bryant," Violet warned. "Boys don't ask girls out if they're not attracted to them, and I don't know this boy."

"Well, I'm sure he is attracted to me, but he knows I don't have time for a boyfriend."

"Did he ask you out for next weekend?" Violet asked with a knowing voice.

Arcineh's lack of answer was answer enough.

"He might have heard you say you don't want a boyfriend," Violet said, "but he wasn't listening."

Violet went back to work, and Arcineh looked at her grandfather. That man winked at Arcineh, causing her to hide her laugh behind a quickly grabbed napkin.

❧

It had taken a great deal of restraint, but Brody didn't kiss Arcineh until their third date. They'd seen yet another movie, adding dessert afterward, and Brody was now parked in front of Arcineh's house. The car was shadowy, even with the lights from the front door, and the time just seemed right.

Arcineh's eyes opened slowly. She'd never been kissed before and hadn't realized what a pleasurable experience it could be.

When she didn't draw immediately away, Brody kissed her again, his arms going slowly around her to pull her close. Arcineh kissed him right back, not sure what she was doing but enjoying it with every fiber of her being.

"I don't have time for a boyfriend," she pulled back enough to say.

"Okay," Brody agreed, a hand going to the back of her head so he could kiss her again.

It was another 15 minutes before Arcineh got out of the car. Brody walked her to the door and asked her if he could call the next day. Arcineh heard herself agreeing before she slipped inside.

∞

"I'm 64 years old," Sam said to Violet late in the evening on Labor Day, his face lined with fatigue. "I'm too old to be surrounded by that many hormones."

Violet laughed, but she knew just what he meant. The Rowans had just left, including Tayte and Lexa. Brody had been a part of the weekend's activities as well. Somewhere along the line, Arcineh had forgotten she didn't have room in her life for a boyfriend and was certainly making time for one.

Having young people around was always fun, but Tiffany and Jeremy were rather distracted, and the responsibility that went with having a bunch of teenagers in swimsuits was more than a little stressful on both Sam and Violet.

They had nearly lived in the backyard for the weekend, grilling, sunning, and swimming, but Sam—and even Violet—could not be on call that many hours. For that reason alone, it was something of a relief to have Monday arrive. Arcineh hadn't wanted Brody to go home, but Sam had been firm.

Now all was quiet. Arcineh was not even on the phone, and as far as Sam was concerned, it was going to be an early night.

∞

Arcineh had never even considered what it would be like to have a boyfriend in school. Part of the time she liked it, but at times it only added stress. Brody was not the student Arcineh worked to be. He was easily distracted when she was near and grew impatient when Arcineh wanted to study more than hide in the library stacks and kiss.

She was leaving in ten days for Hawaii, a trip that was like a dream come true for her, and all Brody could say was how much he would miss her. His moping made Arcineh wonder what she really felt for him. She liked being with him and they had great fun together, but she was confident they could pick right back up when she returned in nine days. The whole issue bothered her so much, she talked to Violet about it.

"He's smitten," that lady reasoned, "and your feelings aren't as strong. A little like Tayte and Quinn, only in reverse."

"Do I act like Tayte?" Arcineh looked as horrified as she felt.

"Not at all, but Quinn and Brody are in the same boat. They're in love with people who just care for them."

Arcineh looked thoughtful, and Violet saw her chance. Something had been on her mind for a time, and she was ready to be heard.

"Do you and Brody kiss a lot?"

"Sometimes," Arcineh said. Violet was so easy to talk to.

"Does he press you for more?"

"He wants more."

"He tells you this or tries to show you."

"Both."

"Do you give him more?"

"No," Arcineh answered, and Violet knew she was telling the truth.

The older woman came away from the stove. It was where she was the most comfortable; in her mind it made her invincible. But right now she left the stove, came around the island, and took the stool next to Arcineh. She turned both stools until their knees almost touched, and holding Arcineh's eyes with her own, she began.

"If you never hear another word I say, hear this. Don't do anything you don't want to do. I won't tell you how much I hate the thought of someone your age in a sexual relationship because it won't do any good. A step like that has to be your idea and your belief, but until it is..." Violet stopped and made sure Arcineh was listening. "You say no!"

"Thanks, Violet," Arcineh said, and meant it. She didn't know if she would be that strong when the time came, but Violet had certainly given her some things to think about.

∽

"What was that all about?" Arcineh asked Daisy the next week in school. She had just watched Brody and Landon down the hall, laughing and talking about something before a teacher told them to break it up.

"Oh, guys are such freaks. Landon was teasing Brody about going without because you leave for Hawaii tomorrow."

"Going without?" Arcineh's repeated, her voice dangerously soft.

"Yeah, you know."

Arcineh did know, and it made her sick to her stomach.

"What did Brody say?" Arcineh asked, and Daisy finally caught her friend's glittering eyes.

"What's wrong, Arcie? Guys always talk like that. It's not as though Brody will be unfaithful to you. He'll wait until you get back."

"Wait for what?" Arcineh's teeth nearly clenched in her jaw.

Daisy's mouth opened. "You mean, you haven't?"

"No, we haven't. Is Brody telling people we have?"

Daisy nodded miserably and watched Arcineh turn and walk away. Her friend went into the women's bathroom and Daisy followed, but Arcineh wanted to be left alone. Daisy had just assumed that Brody was telling the truth. She felt terrible for having believed him, but not as bad as Brody was going to feel when Arcineh got done with him.

⬿

HONOLULU, HAWAII

Vacationing with her grandfather and Violet was more fun than Arcineh could have dreamed. Brody came to mind, certainly, but not because she missed him. At the moment, she was so angry that she didn't think she ever would.

Arcineh laid on the beach, tried to talk Violet into a bikini, tasted mahi-mahi, learned to surf, ate shave ice until her tongue began to peel, and vowed she wanted fresh pineapple every day for the rest of her life.

Sam's head was buried in a magazine most of the time, but Arcineh couldn't remember the last time she'd seen him so relaxed. Violet said she was naked without her stove, but she grew tan and even joined Arcineh in the surf and in looking for shells.

Flying back to Chicago on the red eye—much too soon in Arcineh's opinion—the 16-year-old hoped they would go every year.

⬿

Arcineh wasn't the only one in the family to have boy trouble during the 1996–97 school year. By Christmastime Quinn and Tayte had broken up, and all the older girl wanted to do was sit in her pajamas and watch television.

Austin and Lexa were doing better than ever, but Lexa was with her family and not in Chicago, so all Austin did was mope. And to top it off, Tiffany got it into her head that everyone should go to church on Christmas Eve. Sam hated the idea and didn't hesitate to say so. Tiffany's tears would not be stopped, and as usual, Arcineh retreated to the kitchen.

But Violet wasn't feeling well and had gone to her rooms to lie down. Arcineh ended up slipping quietly out of the house and driving herself to Geneva's studio. She knew she shouldn't do it—hiding behind her dancing was not healthy—but at the moment she was desperate.

Two hours later she got home to find her grandfather irate over her leaving, and the two of them argued. Arcineh never before remembered wanting the new year to start so much or even caring if she opened her gifts.

❦

"She can finish with high school in December?" Sam clarified with the two people sitting in his office at the end of January.

"That's right," Miss Knepper said. "She's already in college courses."

"But she's only in her sophomore year," Sam felt a need to point out. "She'd be done halfway through her junior year."

Both Miss Knepper and Mr. Stocco, the principal, nodded.

"Does Arcineh know this?"

"No." Mr. Stocco took this one. "It's entirely up to you as to how you want us to handle this. We can tell Arcie, or you can tell her, or we can keep her in school and advance the work, but to tell you the truth, it would be a shame to keep her from college if she wants to go."

College two months after her seventeenth birthday, Sam thought with a good deal of shock. He knew she was bright and a devoted student, but such a thing had never occurred to him. He didn't want her away from home that soon, and he wasn't sure she'd be willing to go.

"I hope I have time to think about this."

"Of course. That's why we've contacted you so far in advance."

The three of them talked for another 30 minutes. Sam had several more questions, and in the course of that time he decided he would tell Arcineh himself. He left the office planning to discuss it with her that very night.

CHAPTER *Ten*

"They didn't think I knew?" Arcineh asked after her grandfather explained.

"I guess not." Sam smiled at the amused look in her eyes. "What do you think of all of it?"

"Being done at the end of this year? Great. Going to college? No, thank you."

"Never?"

"I don't know. I'm so tired of homework and deadlines, Sam. I want to *really* be done and not ending each year knowing that it starts all over again in three months."

"What would you do?"

"Work full-time with Carlee," Arcineh said, as though it was the most obvious thing in the world.

Sam thought about this. His staff loved having her around, and she was good at everything she did, but there was a tension in him when she was in the building, and it was all about the men in his office. He didn't trust some of them, certainly not their eyes or mouths, and his desire to protect Arcineh was very keen.

"What are you thinking about?"

Sam thought about it for a moment and then told her. Arcineh's eyes showed her surprise, but then she gathered her thoughts and told her grandfather exactly what she thought.

"I think your wanting to protect me is special. I would be disappointed in anything else. But I also think your opinion of me needs to change."

"How is that?"

"I'm not going to put up with lewd comments or spend any more time than I have to around men who try to look down my shirt. The men in your office already know that. They might fear you, but they're also learning from me how I expect to be treated."

"Where did you learn this?"

"Violet."

"I'm not paying her enough," Sam said dryly, bringing a laugh from his granddaughter.

"So what do you think? Can I start full-time at Bryant next year?"

"I don't see why not. Are you sure you want to stay an assistant to Carlee? She adores you, but there's quite a bit more to the business."

"I like working with Carlee."

"All right, but if you change your mind, you know who to talk to."

Arcineh thanked him but didn't linger in his office. She was going to be done with high school in two semesters. She had to tell Violet and then Daisy, in that order.

❧

April 4, 1997, fell on a Friday, a perfect day for Sam Bryant to turn 65. A party, much like the one they'd had for his sixtieth, was planned. At least 80 people had been invited, mostly business associates; and Violet, along with her regular cleaning crew, did a yeoman's service to get ready for the big day. The only blip on the horizon was that this weekend marked the five-year anniversary of the death of Arcineh's parents.

It was not something that Arcineh could ever forget, and much as she wanted to join in the fun, another party was a stark reminder of her last night with her folks. Nevertheless she put her best face forward, even with the Rowans coming to town, and joined in the celebration.

❧

"How are you?" Mason Beck caught Arcineh at the back of the room about halfway through the evening.

"I'm doing well, Mason. Thank you. How about you?"

"I'm fine," Mason said quietly. "Are you enjoying the party?"

"It's nice," Arcineh said, trying to sound sincere. She looked up to find Mason's eyes on her.

"Five years tomorrow, isn't it?"

"Yes," Arcineh said, sighing a little. She had been getting a few pitying looks through the evening and was glad Mason was simply willing to say it. "It's a little unreal."

"It certainly is. Do you think about your home much?"

"Not very often," she admitted. "Right after I got my license, I drove over there, just to look."

"How was it?"

"The same. A different car was in the drive, but no big changes."

"Was that a comfort or did it hurt more?"

"It was a comfort," Arcineh realized just as she answered.

"I'm glad," Mason said, and then changed the subject. "I heard the good news about your graduating early."

"I'm so excited to be done. And I love working with Carlee."

"The two of you make quite a team."

Arcineh smiled at the compliment and then noticed Mason's wife headed their way. She had a headache and wanted to leave. Arcineh saw them out, a little sorry to see Mason go. Violet was being run off her feet, and most of the people she knew from the office had already had quite a bit to drink.

Arcineh glanced at the clock. It was almost 10:30. With a little luck, they'd all be cleared out by 1:00.

愀℞愀

"You can't be serious," Quinn screamed at her mother from behind the closed family room doors that did nothing to contain the sound.

"Calm down, Quinn," Tiffany said, trying to reason with her on Saturday morning.

"I won't! I can't believe she's graduating ahead of me."

"It's not important, Quinn," Tiffany tried again. "Think of all you have that she doesn't."

"Like what?" Quinn demanded, on the verge of hysterical tears.

"Like Tayte!" Tiffany was able to say. The two were seeing each other again. "And you're far prettier."

"I'm smarter too."

"Of course you are," Tiffany agreed sincerely. "You know Arcie goes to one of those special schools. It's probably not even real."

Standing out of view outside the glass-paneled family room doors, Arcineh felt as though she'd been slapped. She hadn't wanted to stay and listen, but somehow her feet would not move.

Noise behind her made her turn. It was Sam. She didn't know how long he'd been there or how much he'd heard, but Arcineh didn't want to talk to him or anyone else. She turned and headed toward the backyard. It was still a little cool for the patio in April, but that was perfect. No one would come outside and bother her.

∽

"I wondered where you'd gone off to." Sam's voice came to Arcineh where she was settled on a lounger, a thick quilt swaddling her.

"I don't feel like talking right now."

"All right," Sam agreed, but still sat in the lounger next to her. He let a minute or two of silence fall between them. He knew she didn't want to talk, but he felt he had to say something.

"Quinn didn't mean any of that, I'm sure. She's just insecure and upset."

"She meant every word," Arcineh said, doing nothing to hide her anger. "And so did Aunt Tiffany."

"If you could just try to understand," Sam began, but Arcineh bit back in.

"I understand plenty!"

"That's enough!" Sam rebuked her, albeit softly.

"You can tell me that's enough after listening to Quinn and Tiffany just now?" Tears she hated filled her eyes. "And is that what you all think? That Fetterman isn't real and my diploma is some sort of sham?"

"No, Arcie, not at all," Sam said with some force. "I've known about your intelligence level since the time you were a child. Your diploma is real and worth every moment you worked for it."

More silence fell now, a cold silence, even worse because they'd shared angry words. Sam debated his next move and decided not to over think. Reaching over, he placed a small box on the quilt that covered her.

Arcineh eyed it before asking quietly, "Is that what I think it is?"

"Open it and see."

Arcineh found white chocolate hearts inside. She put a whole one into her mouth and just let it sit there. She didn't speak until it had melted.

"Why don't I ever remember that I love this stuff?" She said aloud, her voice completely calm.

"Shall I have Vi stock some?" Sam offered.

"I don't think that's a good idea. I'd be in it all the time and wouldn't fit into my clothes."

Arcineh put another piece in her mouth.

"As good as last time?" Sam asked.

"Better, I think. Last time I was just mad at you. This time I'm mad at you and missing my dad."

This time Sam didn't try to answer or fix anything. He let Arcineh enjoy her chocolate, his mind dwelling on his son. He missed Trevor to the soul of his being and only wished that something as simple as white chocolate could heal some of the hurt.

"Quinn just isn't as mature as Arcineh is," Austin told his grand-father. "Quinn knows it too, and that's always made her jealous."

How the two of them had ended up alone in the kitchen early Sunday morning and talking about Quinn, no less, Sam couldn't say. However, he heard his grandson out. He didn't agree with him, but he was glad they were able to talk. Austin's natural bias would be to take Arcineh's side against his sister. He knew the siblings had never been very close.

"And Quinn isn't always impossible," Austin went on. "When Tayte is in her life, she's over the moon with happiness."

"What about Lexa?" Sam asked. "Is she still around?"

"I'm going to marry her," Austin said confidently. "I haven't told her that, but it's true."

"She's a sweet girl," Sam said sincerely, "and she'd be lucky to have you."

Austin looked inordinately pleased, and Sam knew a moment of disquiet. He really didn't seek the boy out enough—he suddenly knew that—but found it easy to blame on Austin. He'd been a little odd as a child and a rather strange teen, but Sam now admitted to himself that college life seemed to agree with him.

Indeed Sam asked Austin about his schooling a moment later, and that young man had plenty to say on that subject as well. They enjoyed the best visit of their relationship before Tiffany arrived, looking for coffee.

ᏯᎦ

What had seemed like a long-ago plan was finally in front of them. Arcineh finished her finals on December 19 and became an official graduate of Fetterman Academy. There was no ceremony for December grads—she would come back in June to walk with her class—but when she got home, she was greeted by Violet and a cake.

"And this is just the start," Violet said cryptically.

Arcineh soon found out that her grandfather had been very busy. The cake was not to be eaten until she, Violet, and Daisy dressed up and were taken to the Shedd for a lovely meal at the Soundings Restaurant.

Arcineh floated on a cloud the whole evening. She felt as though she'd waited her whole life for this moment, and that wasn't all: In just three weeks, she would be back at Bryant Marble.

ᏯᎦ

Arcineh climbed from Sam's car in front of the Bryant warehouse and followed him inside. Taking notes on what he said and trying to look around at the same time, Arcineh was surprised when Sam suddenly stopped.

"You're not wearing safety glasses."

"I didn't know I had to."

"Have you not been in the warehouse before?" Sam asked as he took her arm and marched her back to the door where they came in.

"I guess not," Arcineh answered, not having thought of it.

Sam plucked a pair of safety glasses from the bin and handed them to her. Arcineh put them on and stared at him.

"Let me guess," she said dryly, "I've never looked better."

"You look like a bug."

"So do you, now that you mention it."

The two continued their work right up to the moment Arcineh spotted something.

"Is this the tile you have in your bathroom?"

"Good eye," Sam complimented her. "It's a bit rare and hard to find."

"Where's the marble from the kitchen?"

"Over here."

And with that the two of them were off. Arcineh had never thought about seeing these goods in their raw form. Sam had come to check on a few items, but Arcineh was not running out of questions. They didn't get out of the warehouse for almost two hours.

❦

CREVE COEUR

"I can't take the drama anymore," Jeremy told his wife and daughter. "Quinn, you're going to be done with Tayte. He's hurt you for the last time."

"No, Daddy, please," begged the sobbing 18-year-old.

"Stop," Jeremy commanded. "I tell you, I just saw him with a blonde plastered to his side in the front seat of his car. It's over, Quinn."

"How can it be, Jeremy?" Tiffany chimed in, fighting her own rage and tears. "She sees him everywhere she goes."

"Then we'll get her out of Creve Coeur, out of Missouri if we have to. But he's not going to hurt my girl again."

Quinn dissolved into full-blown hysterics, but Jeremy's mind was made up. He would do whatever had to be done to get Quinn away from Tayte Urbik.

⟡

CHICAGO

"Something has come up." Sam opted to tell both Violet and Arcineh the news at the same time. He found them in the kitchen.

"What's wrong?" Violet asked, not liking the look on his face.

"Quinn will be coming to live here for a while."

Arcineh couldn't keep the shock from her face. Violet flicked a glance at her and then back to Sam, whose jaw had tightened. He was clearly preparing for battle.

"How long?" Arcineh managed after a moment of silence.

"That's indefinite."

"What happened, Sam?" Violet asked.

"Something with Tayte. Jeremy wants her out of the area for a while."

"What about school?" Arcineh asked.

"She'll come as soon as the year ends."

Arcineh could hardly believe what she was hearing. Quinn coming. And not just a visit but to stay. Arcineh had vowed never to compete on this, but she could not stay quiet this time.

"What happens to me?" she asked.

"Nothing," Sam answered shortly. "You'll live here as usual."

Arcineh could only stare at him. She could see that there was no use in trying to argue, but in her heart she knew she couldn't do it. She could not share a home, not even one this large, with her cousin.

Arcineh left the room without another word, but her mind was already at work. Her eighteenth birthday was still six months away, but one way or another she would get out of the house. Right now she didn't know how to do that, but she knew that if Quinn was coming, she could not possibly stay.

"How can you do that to Arcie?" Violet asked the moment she and Sam were alone.

"What exactly am I doing to Arcie?" Sam snapped, ready to do battle with Violet as well.

"This is her home."

"And it's large enough to include Quinn."

"You know how she feels about Quinn!"

"She doesn't have to feel that way about Quinn. If she would just be a little kind and compassionate."

Violet considered walking out on the spot but knew she couldn't leave Arcineh. She also knew that it would do no good. Where Quinn was concerned, Sam had only one view. She just hoped it wouldn't cost him his younger granddaughter.

"Were you in my jewelry?" Arcineh asked of her cousin two weeks after she arrived.

"I needed some pearls," Quinn nearly whined. "I can't believe you would miss them."

"I wouldn't have," Arcineh replied, her voice rising, "but you left my jewelry spilled all over my closet."

"Sorry," Quinn muttered.

"You sound sorry." Arcineh's voice dripped with sarcasm.

"Please tell me you're not arguing," Sam said from the door. "Because if you are, I'm going to lose my mind."

Both girls turned and looked at their grandfather. Arcineh was about to explain, but as usual, Quinn beat her to it.

"I just wanted to borrow some jewelry from Arcineh, and she's throwing a fit."

The look Sam gave his younger granddaughter mirrored all his frustration, but he turned back to Quinn.

"Did you ask?"

"No, I forgot."

"Next time, ask."

Quinn nodded in complete agreement before Sam's eyes swung back to Arcineh.

"And can you please just share?"

"I'll do that," Arcineh said quietly as she slipped from the room, grabbed her purse, and headed to the kitchen. Arcineh almost left the house without speaking to Violet, but she stopped.

"I'm going out," she told her.

"Where to?"

"Just out."

"Arcie." Violet's voice caught her before she could go. Arcineh stopped but didn't turn around until Violet touched her. "It's not too late to apply for college."

Arcineh slowly shook her head. "College won't solve a thing, and I can't take it here much longer," she whispered when their eyes met. "I don't want to be separated from you, but I can't stay here with Quinn."

"I know," Violet agreed, tears filling her eyes.

"I'll be back in a little while."

"Okay."

Violet stood very still when the teenager left. She had tried to talk to Sam twice more, but nothing had changed. In her heart she felt sorry for Quinn but knew that all her troubles were of her own doing. Violet just hoped that someday Sam would come to the same conclusion.

Sam didn't move from his bed, but he knew the exact moment

Arcineh arrived home. His bedside clock said 2:00. He had been ready to go to sleep for more than three hours but had not been able to put her from his mind.

She had missed several days of work in the last month, simply asking Carlee for the day off and not telling anyone where she was going. Sam knew that Quinn was the reason, but he couldn't send Quinn back to Creve Coeur to fend for herself. Life had handed his older granddaughter a bad hand, and he had to be there for her until she sorted it out.

Arcineh's footsteps in the hallway and then the closing of her bedroom door finally let Sam relax. He thought about going and talking to her but knew they would only argue. Sam drifted off, telling himself it was a stage they would all have to get through and trying not to think about how old he would be by the time all his grandchildren were in their twenties.

⟨⟩

Arcineh had seen more of Chicago since Quinn moved in than she had in all of her 17 years in that city. Arcineh used any excuse to be out of the house, picking new spots and places where she would not know anyone.

The café she settled on near the end of August was eclectic and interesting. Finding a table on the patio, Arcineh ordered coffee and a sandwich. She had brought a paperback to read, but couldn't get into the story and ended up watching people go by. Her food had just arrived when she heard conversation from the table behind her.

"You'll never leave me," a man's voice said. "I own you."

"You don't own a thing—" a woman answered back, "not your own pathetic choices and certainly not me."

The next sound was a slap, flesh hitting flesh. Arcineh turned in time to see the man grab the woman's arm, and she moved without thinking. Taking her purse, she hit the man over the back of the head and continued until the woman's voice got through.

"A play! A play!" The woman was waving a small book at her. "We're just rehearsing. It wasn't real."

The man had scrambled away from her in fear and now stood looking at her with huge eyes. The woman's eyes were large as well, and Arcineh wished the ground would swallow her whole.

"I'm sorry," she whispered. "I'm so sorry."

Ducking her head, Arcineh sat back down. She looked unseeingly at her food, wishing she'd never ventured out. Staying home with Quinn was preferable to making a fool of herself in front of these complete strangers.

The other two chairs at her table suddenly moved, and the actors sat down. Arcineh, blushing from chin to hairline, forced herself to look at them.

"Anyone who comes to my aid in this day and age is a person I have to know," the woman said, holding her hand out. "Jalaina Ciofani."

Arcineh shook the hand.

"Arcie Bryant."

"And I'm Mic Abbott," the man said, also offering his hand. "Were we really that convincing?" He leaned forward in his excitement.

"You were," Arcineh admitted. "I'm so sorry I hit you, but I heard that slap, and when I turned, you were grabbing her."

Both the actors looked very pleased over this, and Arcineh had to laugh a little.

"I've gotta go," the man suddenly said as he stood. "It was nice meeting you." He kissed Jalaina on the cheek and told her he would see her in the morning. Arcineh watched him walk away before looking back to find the woman studying her.

"So you're an actress?" Arcineh ventured uncertainly.

"At the moment," Jalaina said, her voice perky and matter-of-fact at the same time. "I like to try different things."

Arcineh nodded, not sure what to say. She realized she was hungry but didn't want to eat in front of this woman who had no food.

"Go ahead," Jalaina said. "I'll order something the next time the waiter comes by."

"How did you know I wanted to eat?"

Jalaina looked again as though she'd been given a compliment.

"I pride myself on reading other people. It's the creative side of me."

Arcineh did eat. It was a little odd having Jalaina watch her, but she was well and truly hungry.

"Where are you from?" Jalaina asked.

"Chicago."

"What side?"

"Near the lake."

"I knew you couldn't be from around here."

"Why?" Arcineh felt a bit defensive. If Jalaina noticed, she didn't let on.

"Your clothing and jewelry for one thing, but also the way you hold yourself and eat. You're a dancer, aren't you?"

"How did you know that?"

Jalaina looked so delighted at having guessed correctly that Arcineh began to relax and enjoy herself. She wasn't sure what she'd expected, but this wasn't it. The longer they sat together, the more Arcineh liked her. And when Jalaina suggested they go to a movie that night, Arcineh agreed. She had the time of her life.

Where the weeks went from there, Arcineh could not have said, but Jalaina's friendship was like a balm to her hurting heart. She was fun, but also levelheaded enough to be practical. Jalaina ended up being just the person Arcineh needed.

The evening before her eighteenth birthday, Arcineh called Carlee's number at the office and left a message saying she would not be back. She hugged Violet goodbye, gave her a letter for Sam since he was on a business trip, and told the housekeeper she would be staying with a friend. She also remembered to tell Violet not to expect her home anytime soon.

CHAPTER *Eleven*

Nothing in Arcineh's life could have prepared her for Jalaina Ciofani's house. She did not have an apartment but still lived with her family on Chicago's northwest side. Her family included her older brother, younger brother, and a grandmother, who at the moment was visiting her sister in Rockford.

All the way up the stairs to her room, Jalaina told Arcineh what to expect, and especially not to let Nicky bully her.

"Who's Nicky?"

"My older brother. He owns my uncle's business and thinks it makes him king of the universe. Whatever you do, stand up to him. He's never even met anyone as classy as you, and you'll intimidate the life out of him. I can hardly wait."

Arcineh wasn't sure what any of that meant, or even if she heard it all. She was too busy looking around her. Jalaina had taken her to a bedroom that would have fit into Arcineh's closet at home. It had two beds, but Arcineh had no idea how she was going to fit herself or any of her things.

"Are you really sure it's all right that I stay here, Jalaina? I mean, did you ask someone?"

"I didn't need to," Jalaina said with utter confidence. "You can stay as long as you like. Throw your stuff anywhere. We'll get organized later. Come on." Jalaina was already back at the door. "It's my turn to make dinner."

Arcineh found out in a hurry what Violet had been doing in the kitchen for years. Jalaina gave orders to both her and Marco, her younger brother, but since Arcineh had done little more than boil water, it was not as easy as it sounded.

"So tell me something, Princess," Jalaina teased after Arcineh bent too far over the pot and got a face full of steam. "What was your cook's name?"

"She wasn't *my* cook," Arcineh retorted, taking the teasing in stride. "She was my grandfather's housekeeper, and her name is Violet."

"But you didn't go near the kitchen, I can see."

"Not to cook," Arcineh said quietly, and Jalaina watched her face.

"Not even gone a day and you already miss them."

"Not them. Just Violet," Arcineh said in a tone that closed the door. Jalaina, still watching her, realized she'd never had such a gentle put-down. She could have crowed with laughter thinking about Arcineh going head-to-head with Nicky.

⣔⣔⣔

"Who is that?" Nicky demanded of his sister the moment he got in the door. He'd come inside through the kitchen door and spotted Arcineh setting the table in the compact dining room.

"A friend of mine." Jalaina worked to keep the pleasure from her voice. "She'll be living here for a while."

"Just what we need," Nicky muttered. "Another deadbeat."

"You can say that with some of the lowlifes you bring home?" his sister threw at him.

"I also bring home the money," Nicky said, giving his standard line as he went to wash for dinner.

❦

"Did you get kicked outta your place?" Nicky asked near the end of the meal. Marco had done little but stare at Arcineh all evening, but he was done eating now and in the living room watching television.

"Not exactly," Arcineh said quietly, trying to recall Jalaina's advise. "Your sister offered me a change of scenery, and I took it."

Jalaina, her eyes swinging between the two, had all she could do not to laugh. Nicky's brows had risen on this dignified reply of so few words. There wasn't anyone in their world who could have pulled that off.

"So where you from?" Nicky asked next.

"Chicago," Arcineh answered as she had to Jalaina.

"What side?"

"Near the lake."

"Let me guess." Nicky's slight Italian accent became more pronounced, his tone knowing but also a bit skeptical. "You got a Mercedes for your sixteenth birthday."

"Actually it was a BMW, and it was for my fifteenth birthday," Arcineh stated simply. "Nine days in Hawaii covered my sixteenth, and for my seventeenth birthday, sapphires and diamonds."

"You expect me to believe that you have sapphires and diamonds?"

Arcineh reached for the gold chain on her neck and pulled it free until it revealed a pendant of unmistakable wealth and beauty. Sapphires clustered around a half-carat diamond, all set in an 18-carat gold circle.

"The matching ring, bracelet, and earrings are in my bag upstairs."

Nicky's eyes went from the pendant and back to Arcineh's face several times before he turned to his sister.

"Where did you find her?"

"At Barlow's Café, and I'm keeping her."

Nicky laughed, and the mood instantly lightened. The three ended up talking for hours before Arcineh helped do dishes for the first time in her life. Not until she climbed into bed many hours later did Arcineh miss Sam and Violet. Seeing their faces in her mind, she felt as though her heart would burst. It probably would have done a world of good to cry herself to sleep, but Jalaina was in the next bed and she didn't want her to see how weak she truly was.

"You're in a good mood," Arcineh said to Jalaina a few days later. That young woman was whistling in front of the mirror, the mascara brush moving fast.

"We're going out. Didn't I tell you?"

"With whom?"

"Just ourselves, but we'll probably meet some guys."

"Where is Marco?" Arcineh asked, not sure why she wasn't excited about this.

"At the neighbor's. He just about lives there, even when Grandma's home."

"And Nicky."

"Out with his girlfriend, Libby. You'll meet her one of these days."

Arcineh didn't answer, but neither did she start getting ready. Jalaina had nearly finished her makeup and just had to get dressed.

"What's the matter?" the older girl asked, finally turning from the mirror. Arcineh looked into her beautiful face and had just one question.

"Why am I really here?"

Jalaina looked at her, her heart sinking a little.

"You have this full wonderful life," Arcineh continued, "surrounded by people who love you. Why did you want me around?"

Jalaina sat down on the bed across from Arcineh, knowing that she would have to be honest. She could do nothing else.

"You're the kind of girl that gets places. I'm not. I'm from a middle-class, working family, and nice places don't hire my kind of girl."

"Where do I come in?" Arcineh asked.

"I don't want anything, I just want to watch you do what you do."

Arcineh thought about this and realized Jalaina could do the same for her. In this world she was such a child, ignorant of nearly everything.

"Are you mad?" Jalaina asked.

"No, but it comes with a condition. I get to learn from you as well."

"Deal," the older girl said.

The two sat and stared at each other for a moment.

"Do you want to go out?" Jalaina finally asked.

"Yes, but not to look for guys."

"Okay," Jalaina said—such a thing would not have occurred to her. "A movie?"

"I was thinking it would be a nice evening to go to the Art Institute of Chicago."

"I've never been."

Arcineh smiled, and a moment later Jalaina smiled too. They were out the door 30 minutes later.

ᖗᒣᖕ

Arcineh had been at the Ciofanis' for a week when Grandma came home. She was kind to Arcineh but watched her with a touch of suspicion. Grandma didn't say too much, but her old eyes didn't miss a thing. After observing Jalaina and Arcineh staying up late, sleeping late, and playing their days away, she made an announcement at the dinner table Sunday night.

"Nicky, the girls have lain around this house long enough. I want them to go to work with you in the morning. Find something for them to do."

"Yes, ma'am," Nicky replied, methodically eating his dinner.

Jalaina didn't look too happy about this, but neither did she comment. Arcineh, on the other hand, nearly choked. Nicky laid tile for a living! Arcineh looked around the table to see if anyone would object, but everyone continued with their meal as though nothing was wrong.

By bedtime Arcineh had convinced herself that Grandma Ciofani didn't mean it. She thought differently when Jalaina's alarm went off at 5:15 Monday morning and she found herself in Nicky's truck, headed for a work site.

∞

"Chummel," Nicky said, speaking to a big man with curly, fair hair after he had walked Arcineh into a large, newly constructed office building. "This is Arcie. Have her shadow you, and keep track of her at all times.

"Arcie," Nicky continued. "You'll be safe with Chummel. He'll keep track of you and bring you to me at lunch."

Arcineh, still thinking she was dreaming the whole thing, nodded. Not until Nicky walked away without a backward glance did Arcineh look at the man standing next to her. He was a good deal larger than Nicky, but she didn't think Nicky would leave her with anyone who wasn't safe.

"So you needed a job, huh?" Chummel asked.

"I guess so," Arcineh answered, following Chummel as he began to clear the foyer area they were standing in. There was a Dumpster by the door, and Arcineh followed suit as Chummel cleared the floor and countertop and threw everything into it.

"What's your name again?" he asked after a few minutes.

"Arcie."

"I'm Chummel."

"That's a little different."

"It's a nickname for Chad Hummel."

Arcineh broke a nail at the moment, so all she did was nod. Chummel watched her jump and study her hand. He worked not to smile before saying, "You won't have any of those by the end of the day."

"I can see that," Arcineh said quietly, her mind registering the pain and having to face the fact that she wasn't in a dream.

❧

Jalaina followed Arcineh up the stairs, but Arcie was still not speaking to her. Jalaina knew she was going to leave and right now she could have killed her grandmother for having done this.

"I know you're upset," Jalaina tried again, "but if you could just let me explain."

"Come and stay as long as you like." Arcineh mocked Jalaina's voice as she dragged her cases out and began throwing things into them. *"My family won't mind at all. We can just hang out and do nothing."*

More things were thrown into the case, and Jalaina could see that Arcineh was not going to listen. Her grandmother came to the door just then, but Arcineh didn't see her. Not until Grandma said a soft word in Italian did Arcineh turn to her.

"Look at my hands!" Arcineh spat in furious Italian. "They're bleeding! What kind of hospitality is this? You didn't ask me if I wanted to work. You didn't tell me that my being here was a bother to you. You just sent me to this job." With that, Arcineh turned back and continued to throw things into her case.

When Arcineh had began her furious tirade in Italian, both Nicky and Marco had run up the stairs. The four Ciofanis stared at each other in shock. Grandma was the first to recover. She moved into the room, sat down on the bed, and reached for Arcineh's hand. Out of respect for this older woman, Arcineh let her take it.

"You're a good girl," she started, still in Italian. "I didn't mean for you to be hurt, but you cannot live your life in idleness. The job is good for you. Maybe Nicky can find something that won't make you bleed, but work is good." Grandma made sure Arcineh was listening. "And Jalaina wants you to stay."

Arcineh looked down at the old woman and saw unguarded kindness for the first time. Grandma saw the acquiescence in Arcineh's eyes and called for Nicky.

"What have you got for Arcie that will not break her hands?"

Nicky smiled, not sure Arcineh would thank him but knowing just the thing.

ᥫᦢ

"How does it look?" Arcineh asked, as she had been asking all day. She'd been working with Chummel for three weeks, learning how to grout and lay tile.

"What's this right here?" Chummel asked as he pointed.

"I didn't see that," Arcineh muttered, and attacked with a gentle hand a bit of grout that was not just perfect. She sat back when she was done and looked at him. Chummel smiled his infectious smile and told her to keep going. He walked back to where he was working, shaking his head all the while.

He didn't know where the Ciofani family unearthed this girl, but she certainly fascinated him. She'd even told him she wanted to lay tile for the rest of her life. Chummel had not argued with her, but he looked at her hands and those slim shoulders and secretly wondered if she would last two months.

∽

"Hi, Violet," Arcineh spoke into that lady's answering machine about three weeks after New Year's 1999. "I'm sorry you're not there to get this. I'm all right. I'm sorry I didn't call for all these months, but I've been working and staying busy." She paused right then, not wanting to cry but not sure she could help it. She'd never missed a single holiday with her family, and now she'd missed them all.

"I miss you," she whispered at last. "And I love you." Not able to say anything more, Arcineh hung up and stepped out of the phone booth and went back to her lunch break.

∽

Arcineh eyed her paycheck, her mind centering on the date and not the amount. Not in her wildest dreams would she have believed that she would stay away from home for more than two years. She had called home twice in the first year, and once more last year, but Quinn had answered each time. Arcineh had not tried again.

Sam Bryant was 69 years old today. Arcineh wanted to talk to him so much that she ached. Slow tears trickled down her face, though she was barely aware of the fact. Part of her didn't care who answered—Arcineh wanted to call. The other part of her felt she'd been replaced. Even the fact that Quinn was answering the phone made her seem like a beloved only child.

Tears came in a torrent then. Arcineh tried to muffle her sobs against her pillow, but Jalaina heard her from the hall. The older girl came in, sat on her bed, and looked over at her friend. She waited until Arcineh was a little more under control before she spoke.

"Do you want to talk about it?"

"It's my grandpa's birthday."

"How old is he?"

"Sixty-nine."

"You miss him?"

Arcineh could only nod, more tears coming.

"So call him," Jalaina said in her matter-of-fact way. "Just pick up the phone and dial."

"I don't want to risk someone else answering."

Jalaina felt swamped with guilt. She had brought Arcineh home because she seemed lonely and because she liked her—but also so she could learn from her, and she had. Jalaina had landed a plum job at a nice clothing store, something she had wanted for years. It wasn't Michigan Avenue, but Jalaina was thrilled.

Arcineh, who had stuck around far longer than anyone imagined, had never even hinted at going back to her world. Most weeks she worked six days. She actually gave Grandma rent money, and never, even working on construction sites, did she lose her charm and class. But deep inside Jalaina knew she was the same person, just living out of her world.

"When's the last time you danced?"

Arcineh only groaned and rolled her eyes.

"Tell me."

"I don't know, Jalaina. I'm so far out of shape I wouldn't last five minutes."

"This Saturday you're going."

"Where?"

Jalaina thought quickly. "It's a little ways from here, but there's a dance studio. It's very nice. I'll get you there and you'll dance."

"I don't know if it's that easy, Jalaina. Not all studios take walk-ins."

"We'll go and find out." Jalaina would not be swayed. "Wear some of those tight things so you look the part."

Arcineh had to laugh. It was just like Jalaina to think that way, and she appreciated her friend's desire to help. And she was good at her word. On Saturday morning, Jalaina drove her to Blankenship Dance and Aerobics and left her at the door.

⁂

"Okay, ladies," the instructor at the front of the room called as the class assembled. "Let's start our warm-up, nice and easy now."

Arcineh had been almost an hour early, but Jalaina had been right. She was able to join a large aerobics class, and just feeling the pull of her muscles and hearing the beat of the music worked wonders on Arcineh's heart. She was out of shape, but all worries and heartaches fell away in the next hour. The time flew. Before she was ready, Arcineh found herself going up to thank the teacher, something she'd practiced from the time she was little. However, not all was lost. Arcineh learned that they met again on Monday night.

⁂

"So it's like this," Jalaina said the next week—the girls were working on dinner. "I think what you need on Friday night is a date."

Arcineh looked at her roommate and wondered what had come over her. They had lived in peaceful cohabitation for two and a half years, and suddenly Jalaina seemed more aware of her.

"What is going on?"

"Nothing, I just want you to do more than work, read, and practice your Italian."

"I do," Arcineh argued.

"What?" Jalaina demanded.

Arcineh grated cheese and didn't answer. She hadn't really thought about it. Her life was full. Grandma Ciofani treasured her, and Arcineh loved her in return. Marco was the little brother she'd never had, and Jalaina was an amazing friend.

Arcineh worked hard and was good at her job, and Nicky made sure she was treated well by the men. If the truth were to be told, she would rather be in an office somewhere, but she was content and proud of her ability.

"I don't like blind dates," Arcineh finally said.

"But if I find someone, maybe someone Will knows," Jalaina replied, referring to her new boyfriend, "you could at least meet him."

"And you would stay and not leave me alone with some stranger?"

"I swear."

"And if I didn't want to go out after I meet him, you're not upset with me and he's not pouting?"

"No being left alone, no pouting," Jalaina repeated with a hand in the air, looking like a large Girl Scout. "But will you at least try?" she added.

"Yes," Arcineh heard herself agreeing, hoping she would not regret that word.

∾

"You've danced before," Pam, the aerobics instructor, said as she caught Arcineh when she went to thank her on Thursday.

Arcineh nodded, not sure what to say.

"Listen," Pam continued, lowering her voice and taking in the wary look in Arcineh's eyes, "you can take this or leave it, but you really should be in the class Tina teaches."

"What class is that?" Arcineh asked, wondering vaguely if she sounded as guarded as she felt. It had felt good to be invisible in the back row. She obviously hadn't pulled it off.

"They do aerobics, but at an advanced level. It's more about dance than getting in shape. You won't have any problems."

"When do they meet?"

"Some Sunday afternoons, but mostly Monday, Tuesday, and Thursday evenings."

Arcineh studied the other woman before asking, "Would I have to call someone?"

"No, I'll just let Tina know that someone new might be by."

"Thanks," Arcineh said and turned to go, honestly not sure what she would do.

She would have bolted and never returned if she'd known that Pam had already told Tina all about her.

CHAPTER *Twelve*

"You do not have aces!" Arcineh said to Marco on Friday night. "I know you're bluffing."

"You'll have to put some pennies on the table to find out," the 12-year-old said, looking smug. Arcineh looked away from his beautiful face, knowing she would smile if she didn't. His black eyes and hair, coupled with his olive skin, made him very eye-catching. Her own skin tanned very dark in the summer, but Marco managed to stay dark year round.

"Are you playing for money?" Grandma came to the dining room just then, trying to look outraged.

"Just pennies," her grandson told her, and proceeded to put a winning hand down on the table.

Arcineh said something in Italian that made Grandma laugh.

"What did she say?" Marco demanded, but his grandmother had no sympathy.

"You should work as hard on your Italian as Arcie does, and you would know."

Marco was ready to argue, but the front door opened just then.

Jalaina led the way, followed by Will, and behind him a stranger. A tall good-looking stranger.

"Arcie, this is Kevin," Jalaina wasted no time in saying. "Kevin, this is Arcie."

"Hello." Arcineh stood to shake the man's hand and tried not to stare. This was not the kind of person she pictured Will and Jalaina bringing home.

Will had the presence of mind to introduce Grandma and Marco as well, but Jalaina was too busy watching Arcineh's face. When their eyes met, Jalaina saw approval and suggested that everyone head into the living room to get better acquainted.

❦

"Are you busy tomorrow night?" Kevin asked Arcineh when she walked him to his car several hours later.

"No," Arcineh answered, feeling breathless and hoping he couldn't tell.

"I was thinking dinner would be nice, and maybe a movie."

"I'd like that."

For the moment they just stared at each other.

"Jalaina said you were an angel," Kevin said with a smile. "I was silly not to believe her."

Arcineh smiled, and Kevin's eyes went to her mouth. Had she not been so attracted to him and impressed with what she'd seen all evening, she would have been scared to death.

"Tomorrow night. Six-thirty," Kevin said.

"I'll be ready."

Arcineh stayed on the walk until he drove out of sight. She almost ran back to the house to tell Jalaina she had a date.

❦

"I was born in Maine," Kevin told Arcineh over dinner. "I didn't come to Chicago until I was ten. How about you?"

"Born and raised here. Very boring."

"And do you really lay tile with Jalaina's brother?" Kevin suddenly asked. It was a question that intrigued him.

Arcineh laughed before saying, "I have the hands to prove it."

Kevin laughed with her, but he was very impressed. She hadn't tried to hide her hands, and she wasn't embarrassed. He couldn't picture her doing anything but sitting elegantly in fine clothing, but when he did notice her hands, they were a little rough-looking, and her nails were short.

"I'm glad you enjoy it," Kevin said, hoping she hadn't seen him looking. "But I'll be honest and tell you that I see you in an office building."

"I wouldn't mind working in an office, but I just haven't taken the time to pursue it."

"There are openings in my building."

"At Brockton Printing?"

"Yes. Do you have any experience?"

"A little," Arcineh hedged, not willing to talk about her past.

"Filing and such?"

"Yes."

"That's all you need to get in the door. From there you can study the job board and maybe move around."

Arcineh had more questions for Kevin, and he had answers for each one. It ended up being a fabulous evening. Not only did she enjoy her time with this handsome man, she began—for the first time in two years—to seriously consider a job change.

❧

"Are you Tina?" Arcineh asked the woman who seemed to be in charge on Monday night.

"I am. Are you from Pam's class?"

"Yes. Pam told me she thought I might like your class."

"I hope you do," Tina spoke sincerely. "Can I get your name?"

"Arcie."

"Darcy?"

"No, there's no *D*, just Arcie."

"Okay," Tina said with a smile. "We'll be starting in about five minutes."

Arcineh nodded and asked herself why she'd come. She couldn't believe how nervous she was. Nerves and dancing were a new combination for her. Dancing had always relaxed her, but right now she was tight as a knot.

"Okay, ladies." Tina announced from the front. "Let's get this music going and get to work."

Arcineh was glad that this class was fairly large. She stayed near the door with about 30 women in front of her, realizing the other class must have had at least 50. Trying not to worry about how she did, Arcineh concentrated on the music and Tina's moves and directions.

She learned inside of ten minutes that Pam had been right. This was no problem for Arcineh. She changed moves and tempo without effort, and when it seemed that no one was even aware of her, she relaxed.

The class was at least 30 minutes longer than aerobics had been, but Arcineh went the distance. She was dripping and tired when Tina called a halt, but she was also hooked. At the moment, she couldn't remember why she'd ever stopped.

∽

"Are you setting the alarm?" Arcineh asked Jalaina from her bed on Saturday night. The other girl was making a racket.

"Yes, I'm going to church in the morning."

Arcineh sighed loudly. It was always the same. Jalaina believed that sleeping with a man before she was married was a sin. She and Will had not done that, but they did kiss and Jalaina was tempted toward more. Whenever one of their dates got a little heated, Jalaina felt guilty and went to church.

"I don't know why you do this," Arcineh said. "Why do you bother with a religion that makes you feel guilty for being in love?"

"It's not that simple. God wants me pure on my wedding day."

Arcineh sighed again.

"And before you say it," Jalaina cut back in. "Unlike you, I do believe in God, even one who makes me feel guilty."

Arcineh didn't comment further. They had had this talk more times than she could count. It was no use going over it again.

⮿

"Can I talk to you, Nicky?" Arcineh asked on a quiet Sunday afternoon. She had had a date with Kevin the night before, and he'd given her three possible positions to apply for at Brockton.

"Sure."

"I'm thinking about getting another job," Arcineh didn't know how to be anything but up front. "I don't want to leave you in the lurch or seem ungrateful for the way you trained and paid me, but I'd like to try office work again."

Nicky had leaned back in his seat, his eyes inscrutable as he watched her.

Arcineh could not tell what he was thinking, and when the silence continued, she expected the worst.

"Are you upset, Nicky? I don't have to quit," she said, beginning to recant. "I don't want to leave you in a bind."

"Listen to me, baby girl," he said in the accent she loved. "You don't belong in this business. Sure Chummel trained you, and you turned out to be a perfectionist with very fine hands, but this job is not for you."

Arcineh's mouth opened.

"I'm just surprised that it took you this long to see that."

For some reason, his words made her want to cry. She'd been so afraid of seeming ungrateful.

"Now don't go getting all watery on me," Nicky said, but Arcineh knew he didn't mean it. "Come here," he said, standing. They met in the middle of the living room, and Nicky's hug was warm and comforting.

"Thanks, Nicky," Arcineh barely managed.

This was the way Jalaina found them.

"What's up? Why is Arcie crying?"

"I just fired her," Nicky teased, but his sister just waved a hand at him in disbelief. She didn't take more than a minute to get the story from Arcineh, and then she took over.

"You need to take this week off, Arcie. Your hands and nails need to heal, and you need some new clothes. Come to the shop in the morning, and we'll get you all set."

"I can't do that, Jalaina. I just gave notice to Nicky."

Both women looked at that man.

"I do need you tomorrow, Arcie, but the rest of the week is fine."

"I was going to work two more weeks for you."

"We'll be fine."

Arcineh thanked him again, trying to take it all in. It was no easy task. Jalaina was talking at her usual pace, making plans for Arcineh's life as she went.

⟿

"It says here that you graduated in 1997 but that you were born in October of 1980. Are these dates correct?"

"Yes, I was actually done in the middle of my junior year."

"Why was that?"

"Well, I'd completed everything and there was no reason to stay."

"Did you not start college?" Mrs. Feldman asked, moving her eyes back to the application.

"No."

Arcineh felt herself begin to sweat. Kevin had made it sound as though she was a shoo-in, but this lady was tough. The woman's eyes came back to her face a few times, but nervous as she was, Arcineh simply sat in dignified silence.

That was Arcineh's undoing. Mrs. Feldman didn't like what she believed to be missing years on the application, and she didn't like how controlled and pretty Arcineh was.

"We'll call you if there's an opening" was all she was willing to say.

Arcineh left the building, thinking that tiling wasn't looking so bad after all.

⟨⟨⟩⟩

"We won't give up," Kevin said on their date Friday night. "I'll keep asking around."

"She was tough, Kevin," Arcineh said. "I wish you had warned me."

"She didn't interview me, so I didn't know," he said regretfully, as the line to get in the theater moved slowly along.

"I feel like I did something wrong. I just don't know what."

Kevin put an arm around her. "You can't beat yourself up. It might not have been anything you did."

Arcineh looked up at him, and Kevin bent his head just enough to brush her lips with his own.

"Not where I would have chosen for our first kiss," he said, his mouth in a crooked smile.

"But it was nice," Arcineh said.

Kevin took that to heart. They sat near the back of the theater and kissed a few more times before the movie began.

∽

"How long did you dance at Geneva's?" Tina asked in a soft voice on Monday night. Arcineh had been planning to put on her street shoes but turned to find the other woman behind her. They were alike in height and build, and for a moment, Arcineh only stared into Tina's eyes.

"How did you know?" she finally asked.

"It's written all over your moves. At least it is for me, but then I've been a fan of Geneva's for a very long time."

"She's good," Arcineh agreed.

"So are you," Tina said.

"Thank you," Arcineh's responded graciously. "I've enjoyed your class."

"I do have one other class you might want to try."

Arcineh waited.

"We meet after the Tuesday and Thursday sessions, and more when we have something special coming up. We'll be starting in a few minutes if you want to check us out."

"How many people?"

"Eight to twelve, depending on the time of year."

Arcineh was too curious not to stay. She followed Tina into a part of the studio that she didn't know existed and knew instantly that this dance class was by invitation only. Geneva had a similar setup.

The darkness of the room was completely controlled with lights. There were no windows to the outside world. Up one side was a small balcony area with folding chairs. A small sound booth was on the opposite wall, and the front and back walls were all mirrored.

Arcineh didn't say a word, and neither did Tina. Seven women from the class she'd just been in trickled in, and one who had just arrived. Arcineh got a smile from Penny and Barb and a wink from Joanne before the music fired up and the women took their places. Tina was at the front of the room, calling changes to the women and the person in the sound booth. She also tended to hurl insults that made the women laugh.

Arcineh was easily the youngest one in the group, but she had nothing on these women. Watching them intently, she was greatly impressed with the hours they had so clearly put in. Moving in perfect rhythm to choreographed routines, Arcineh realized she had seen some of the moves before. Without being asked, and when she thought she understood, she joined in. She thought she'd been hooked in the advanced aerobics class, but she was about to understand true addiction.

∾

Nicky and Libby were getting married, and changes were happening all over the house. Grandma and Marco would be going to live with Grandma's sister, something they were both thrilled over. Jalaina and Arcineh would be getting their own place. Arcineh was still looking for office work, and Jalaina had taken it upon herself to find their apartment. Arcineh nearly choked when she said she'd found the perfect one.

"It's where?" Arcineh asked, thinking she must have heard wrong.

"Near the financial district. Start looking for work there."

"What about your job and how far we'll be from everyone?"

"We can see them whenever we want, and I've got a new job. I'm telling you, this is a good thing."

Jalaina had to do some talking, but Arcineh listened. She thought about everything she knew concerning the financial district, even the fact that Bryant Marble was not too far from there. Jalaina knew all about her past, but she'd never seen the location of her grandfather's company.

"What's the matter?" Jalaina suddenly asked.

"Just thinking," Arcineh said truthfully, her mind having gone back to her days working for Carlee. Unbidden, she remembered the advice Carlee had given her about finding work outside of Bryant. In her mind, a light had come on.

"The apartment's fine," Arcineh suddenly said, things falling together all at once.

"Really? You mean that?" Jalaina was overjoyed.

"Yes. I'll be headed down there in the morning to find work."

∽

Breakfast was a normal part of the day for the Ciofani family, and so Arcineh's new family was the first to see her next plan. She arrived at the dining room table when everyone was eating, but after one look at her, they stopped.

Her hair pulled back as tightly as she could manage into a plain, nondescript bun and a pair of thick-framed glasses on her face were only the beginning. Arcineh had found a woman's suit in a pale blue. It wasn't completely out of fashion, but almost. The skirt stopped just below her knees, and the shoes she'd found were just shy of orthopedic.

"What have you done?" Grandma was the first to find her voice.

"I've gotten desperate. This will get me a job."

"Arcie," Jalaina began, "those glasses—and what did you do with your breasts?"

Arcineh did a small turn. "Isn't it the most dreadful suit? It completely covers my figure."

"Not completely," Jalaina said dryly, having teased Arcineh about her curvy dancer's derriere in the past.

"What do you think?" Arcineh asked with a huge smile, having ignored Jalaina.

"Don't smile with those beautiful teeth, Arcie," was Nicky's only warning. "It ruins the whole effect."

The table laughed before continuing with the meal. Arcineh wasn't overly hungry. She was excited, and it was a bit of a commute, so she wanted to get on the move.

⟍⟋

Arcineh would never know that she was hired at Rugby Shades, a high-end manufacturer of sunglasses, out of pity. The woman who did the first interview thought she was perfect for filing, a low-profile job for such a young mouse of a woman whose presentation of herself needed work.

"Can you start tomorrow?" the woman in charge of hiring asked.

"Yes, I can," Arcineh said, trying to keep from jumping in the air.

"Be here at 8:00 tomorrow morning, and I'll show you where to go. You'll be on your feet most of the day, so be sure your shoes are comfortable."

"Thank you."

"You're welcome, Arcie. I hope you enjoy the work."

At the moment Arcineh didn't care. She was back in an office. Just the smell of the building delighted her. She had to force herself not to think of Bryant, just four blocks away, because that only brought thoughts of Sam, and that would have her in tears. For the moment she would concentrate on work, and that started in the morning.

∞

"Okay, Arcie," Vanessa, her boss, explained when they arrived in the filing office. "Our system is simple, but it might take a little getting used to."

Vanessa began to explain, and Arcineh followed along. Her job *was* simple. Requests would come from all over the building. The files were to be pulled and taken to the person who requested them. They had to be signed for. At times someone else would deliver them or pick them up, but usually Arcineh would be expected to make the delivery herself. It would be slow some days and utterly harrowing at others times.

Arcineh was left on her own by lunchtime, and even though she had some questions, by the end of the day, she knew she would land on her feet.

∞

The girls carried the last of the boxes into their first-floor apartment, sat down on the sofa, and sighed.

"We did it," Jalaina said.

Arcineh looked around. "Why was it so tiring when we have so little?"

"I don't know. At least we got to bring our beds."

"Did we remember sheets?" Arcineh suddenly asked.

"I don't think so," Jalaina said, and her face was so funny to Arcineh that she began to giggle. Hearing the sound, Jalaina joined her. Too little sleep and too much work made everything too funny. The two laughed until they couldn't move, but it didn't change their contentment. They had their own place.

∞

"You call this dancing?" Tina shouted from the front of the room, bringing a smile to everyone's face. "We've got a performance in two weeks. Are we going to be ready?"

The beat of a song vibrated around the room, and although the ladies had smiled, no one had lost time. The music switched to another song, this one with a more pronounced beat, and the ladies moved with the ease of breathing. A moment or two of a pounding march, and the music cut. The ladies froze until Tina shouted.

"Yes! That was perfect. Woo hoo, ladies!" Tina clapped like a one-man audience. A few women from the earlier class had gained permission to sit in the balcony, and they clapped as well.

"All right, that's a wrap. Be at the care center on Saturday at 10:30. Have a safe drive home, ladies."

"Tina?" Arcineh caught her as soon as they broke. "I don't have a way to get to the care center. Is there someone I can ride with?"

Tina studied her. Arcineh was a fascinating woman in Tina's view, a mystery and remarkably talented in the studio, but there was something almost sad about her. Much as Tina wanted to know about her, she knew it was not her place to ask questions.

"I can take you. Where do you live?'

"Not too far from here, but I can get myself here if you want me to meet you."

"Ten o'clock?"

"I'll be here."

The women said goodnight, but Tina was still thinking about her. Curious as she was, she would never probe and run the risk of having Arcineh quit.

⟆⟆

Arcineh pushed a cart of files into the elevator and pushed the fourth-floor button. She knew that was where the owner's office was, but she'd never been up there. Historically they sent someone down from that floor, but not today.

The doors of the elevator opened quietly, and Arcineh found herself in a beautiful lobby, not unlike her grandfather's. A woman sat at a corner desk, and Arcineh went that way.

"Hello," Arcineh greeted and was greeted in return. "I have files for Patrice Bradshaw."

"I'll ring that you're coming. It's right through that door."

Arcineh headed the way she was pointed and found an office with greater color and comfort but no waiting room.

"Are you from files?" Arcineh was asked.

"Yes. Patrice Bradshaw?"

"That's right."

"Please sign here."

The paperwork done, Arcineh unloaded the files where she was told and went away with her cart. Not until she returned to file storage and found Nita, a woman who sometimes worked with her, waiting to go to lunch did she find out what she'd missed.

"Did you see him?" Nita asked as soon as Arcineh explained where she'd been.

"Who?"

"Gage Sefton, the owner."

"I don't think so."

Nita laughed and said, "There will be no *think* about it—when you see him you'll know."

CHAPTER
Thirteen

Nicky Ciofani's wedding day was July 14. The day was warm and lovely, and the entire Ciofani family was out to celebrate. Nicky looked over the moon as he smiled down into Libby's face, and after the reception began, the celebration went on for hours.

It looked nothing like Arcineh's old world, but all the family, friends, and happy celebrators sent her thoughts home. Kevin was beside her, and she laughed at all his jokes and joined in all the fun, but deep in her heart, she yearned for Violet and her grandfather. She felt herself growing maudlin and didn't want that.

"Let's dance," she said to Kevin, touching his arm.

"I hate dancing when it's like this, Arcie," he said.

"Okay." Arcineh was surprised, but not daunted. She left him to find Jalaina, who let her have Will.

"Are you having fun?" he shouted over the music.

"Yes. How about you?"

"I am, but the music is too loud."

Arcineh only laughed, and when Jalaina joined them, the three continued to dance in a tight triangle and have the time of their lives.

It took some doing on Arcineh's part, but eventually Sam and Violet faded to the back of her mind.

∽

"Arcie, we've been dating for almost four months," Kevin said quietly. "When is the time going to be right?"

"I don't know."

The two were alone in the apartment after getting home from a show. They had just started out talking, but that swiftly turned to kissing. Kevin was ready to do more than kiss, but Arcineh had called a halt to things before they could venture far at all.

"I love you," Kevin said. "I want to make love to you."

Arcineh didn't answer. She had never been able to tell Kevin that she loved him, and in her opinion, without that element, sex was out of the question. But it was more than that. They had talked about many things, but she'd never told him who she was. She didn't know why, but she feared his response.

Not until dating Kevin, whose world was much closer to Bryant Marble than the Ciofanis had ever been, did she realize just how far from home she was. She wasn't a snob. She wasn't even impressed with money. But a lot of people were.

She was very proud of what she had done. She'd left with only two cases of clothes, her passport, birth certificate, and the money she'd earned at Bryant. She had more money than most since she'd lived at home and had few expenses, but it was still money she'd earned.

She felt guilty for not giving Kevin more of a chance, but something stopped her. Jalaina knew she was Sam Bryant's granddaughter, a statement to which Jalaina had said, "Who's Sam Bryant?" Somehow in Arcineh's heart she knew Kevin would be amazed. And some voice inside wondered if that might not make her all the more desirable. True, he'd already told her that he loved her, but there was never a mention of marriage, just love and lovemaking.

"I care for you, Kevin," Arcineh finally said. "And I want you in my life. But unless I know I am in love, truly know, sex is not a part of the plan."

"You don't know if you love me?"

"No," Arcineh admitted, even when his tone said he was not happy.

"How can you not know?"

"I could ask you the same question. How can you know in four months?"

Kevin's face held all the frustration he felt. This girl was special—he knew that—but she never let him get as close as he wanted. Not only physically, although he certainly wanted that, but with herself. She always seemed to hold a little something back.

"What do I have to do to prove it?" Kevin finally asked.

"I don't need you to prove anything. That's not what this is about." Arcineh said the half-truth, knowing that she was waiting to know more about him. "This is a serious thing we're talking about, and I want to be sure. Marriage is a big step."

"Who said anything about marriage?" Kevin asked quietly.

Arcineh froze. She hadn't meant to say that, but wasn't that the very thing she wondered? If a man said he loved a woman, why was he not talking about marriage?

"I'm sorry." Arcineh said stiffly, and she stood from her place on the sofa. "I misunderstood you."

"I'm not ready for marriage right now," Kevin, backtracking, said quietly, standing as well.

"My mistake," Arcineh said, her voice a bit cool.

Kevin didn't know exactly what had gone wrong, but it was a mess. He stared at Arcineh, completely confused by who she was. They usually had such fun. He didn't know why she needed to be so serious about this one issue and have everything settled.

"I wonder if we might need a little time apart," Kevin ventured, hoping Arcineh would argue.

"Or a lot of time," Arcineh said, keeping her distance.

Her stance and tone, and the glittering anger in her eyes, made Kevin angry as well. He left without another word. Arcineh, ready to throw something, thought she would kill for some white chocolate. Instead she attacked the ice cream in the freezer and didn't cry until Jalaina came home.

❦

September 11, 2001, rocked Chicago as it did the rest of the world. Arcineh and Jalaina, who had both started off to work, got to one another and then to Nicky's as fast as they could. Nicky drove them to be with Grandma and her sister. There the family crowded around the television to watch in horror and sorrow.

"I have to call home," Arcineh said at one point, and Grandma stood with her when she dialed. The phone lines were jammed. Not until Friday was Arcineh able to talk to Violet.

"Vi," she said quietly, only to sit and listen helplessly when that lady began to cry.

"Tell me you're all right," Violet finally managed.

"I am. Are you?"

"Yes."

"And Sam. Is he all right?"

"Yes. He's been stuck in Milan, but he'll be home tonight."

"Okay," Arcineh said, knowing she was going to die from the pain in her heart. She missed this woman and her grandfather so much.

"Please come home," Violet suddenly said.

"Quinn?"

"Yes," Violet answered, her voice dropping a little. "She's still living here."

Arcineh didn't know what to say. She didn't even want to stay on the line, but Violet was speaking again.

"Are you all right? Do you have enough money and a place to live?"

"I'm fine. I have a job and an apartment with a friend."

"Are you married or anything like that?"

"No, nothing like that."

Things got quiet then. Arcineh didn't know what to say, and Violet just wanted to sob.

"I'd better go," Arcineh finally said.

"Please be safe," Violet begged her.

"I will. You and Sam too."

After Arcineh hung up, she realized she had a horrible headache. She knew it was from the tears—not just the tears over missing her family, but those shed for the loss and the hurting hearts of 9/11 families everywhere.

❧

Little by little, life went back to normal. Rugby Shades had let people go home to be with families as they felt they needed, but in time, things slowly fell back into place. Production was down as businesses were hit hard, but those people who had jobs with Rugby were able to keep them.

Arcineh enjoyed her work with the files, but now that she had the system and office down pat, she found herself doing her job too fast and having nothing left to do. Shortly before Thanksgiving she began reading the inner office memo board and checking out the jobs available.

In February of 2002, she spotted the first one that intrigued her because it sounded so much like what she'd done for Carlee. The pay was significantly more than she was making in files. She didn't need more money now, but she worried about when Jalaina would marry Will and leave her to carry the apartment on her own salary.

Arcineh, still wearing her dowdy clothes, pulled-back hair, and thick black glasses, debated if she should fix herself up or not but decided against it. She let Vanessa know what she wanted to do, and that woman, who had come to appreciate Arcineh's hard work, sent her through the proper channels.

Two days later Arcineh found herself sitting with Patrice Bradshaw. Arcineh had not seen her more than a few times in the eight months she'd worked for Rugby, but she looked just the same: beautiful, very professional, and a little cold. Arcineh missed Carlee in an amazing way just then but did her best not to think about it.

"It's not exactly an assistant to the assistant," Patrice explained. "We need someone to do small jobs and assist where needed. How are you with a computer? Do you know your way around Word?"

"Yes," Arcineh was glad to be able to say.

"But it's not all computers," Patrice was swift to add. "The executive conference room is on this floor, and during meetings I would expect you to be in the room, not looking bored, keeping an eye on me for anything I might need, and keeping everyone's water pitcher full."

Put like that, Arcineh thought it sounded dreadful, but the pay was not to be ignored. She also wondered where it might lead. Would a job in the top office of this building lead to something better or look good on a resume?

"I'd be willing to try," Arcineh heard herself say, knowing that it sounded lame, her scrabbled brain not able to come up with anything else at the moment.

"I have your information here. Files, yes?"

"Yes."

"I'll be calling you if you get the job."

"Thank you," Arcineh said, sure that it would never happen. She went back to the file room, glad to see Nita around.

"How'd it go?"

"Not great. I'm not sure I'm right for the job, and it doesn't sound like much fun."

"Well, at least you tried, and it's almost Friday," Nita said comfortingly.

The day was winding down, and at last the women walked together from the building. They were about to go their separate ways when Arcineh spotted a good-looking man.

"Who is that?" she asked of Nita, who seemed to know everyone.

Nita's smile was huge when she said, "Gage Sefton."

Arcineh looked at the other woman.

"Are you serious?"

"Yep."

"He's gorgeous."

"I told you."

Arcineh stared at him as he walked toward the parking garage. He was tall, slim, and dark, a lethal combination for her.

"Maybe you could see yourself on the fourth floor after all," Nita teased. Arcineh only laughed and told her she'd see her in the morning.

Arcineh did more than see Nita in the morning. When she arrived, both Vanessa and Nita were waiting for her. Congratulations were in order—Patrice had hired her.

ᙣᕊᕓ

"Welcome aboard," Mallory said the moment they were alone. She was one of Arcineh's new coworkers. "You'll do fine if you remember one thing: It's all about the money."

"What do you mean?"

"I mean, we all put up with Patrice for the money."

"That bad?"

"Worse. Gage is hers. You must never forget that. And if you have an idea, she'll tell him it was hers."

Arcineh nodded. This she could deal with. She wasn't going to compete with Patrice for anything. And no matter how good-looking Gage Sefton was, she wouldn't compete for him either.

Mallory looked as if she was going to say something else, but Patrice came in to see how they were doing. The women had been in the break room, readying coffee for the morning and making sure all was in order. This was, she was told, a morning ritual. They were in the midst of it when Gage entered the room.

"Gage," Patrice said warmly, "meet our new recruit, Arcie."

"Hello," Gage greeted Arcineh, who greeted him in return and shook his hand.

Arcineh kept her greeting quiet and looked at him only long enough to be polite. It was long enough. In that instant, she saw that Gage Sefton had the most beautiful gray eyes she'd ever seen.

⟨⟩

"How was it?" Jalaina asked the moment the two were home together that night.

"Oh, boy," Arcineh said, dropping into a kitchen chair. "Everyone is wonderful except Patrice."

"Well, can you avoid her?"

"She's in charge of all of us."

"How many?"

"Victoria is at the desk in the lobby. Mallory is what I am, only with more responsibilities, and I haven't figured out what Felicity is, but she's all over the place, fixing this and changing that. I even met some of the executive officers, including the owner."

"What was he like?'

"Younger than I expected and very good-looking."

Jalaina suddenly looked disgruntled.

"What's the matter?"

"He's good-looking, and you have to go looking like an old maid. There's no justice."

"It wouldn't matter. Patrice has claimed him, and you know how I feel about competition."

Jalaina shrugged in her prosaic way and told her the pizza was almost out of the oven.

A week passed before Arcineh saw Gage again, this time waiting for the freight elevator on the first floor. Arcineh had had to take boxes downstairs, and she'd been told not to go through the downstairs lobby. She had her eyes on the numbers over the door when he came up.

Arcineh glanced and said, "Hello, Mr. Sefton."

"Gage is fine," he wasted no time in saying, working to remember her name. "Darcy, is it?"

"No, it's Arcie, no *D*."

"Is it short for something?"

"Yes, it is," Arcineh said, her mouth going silent and her eyes back to the numbers.

Gage stared at her profile. He was surprised but also a little amused that she didn't elaborate. Gage turned just enough to study her without being caught, finding her oddly curious but also familiar.

The elevator arrived, and Arcineh stood back.

"I can wait," Arcineh said when he didn't move.

"There's no need," Gage said, his hand going out.

Arcineh went in, pushed the number she needed and stood as far in the corner as she could manage.

"Have we met somewhere else?" Gage asked.

"I don't think so," Arcineh said, careful to look at him only as long as she had to. However, she did wonder if he'd ever been to Bryant or to some social gathering her grandfather had carted her off to. There hadn't been that many, and right now they were all a blur.

Thankfully the doors opened onto the floor where she had to return the cart, and she had an excuse to leave.

"Goodbye," Arcineh said, not trying to maintain eye contact or anything else. He really was too good-looking. She had to get away before she started to gawk.

❧

February turned into March, and March faded into April. Arcineh found that the job was filled with a lot of grunt work and insignificant little tasks, but it was also different every day. And in the process, Arcineh was learning something about the sunglass trade. Rugby had several different lines—sport, bike, and ski among them—and then the new frames they came out with each year and sold for a pretty penny in the finest department stores all over the world.

And if rumor could be trusted, a new Italian line was being talked about. Arcineh had only overheard some of this and knew better than to ask, but the idea fascinated her. She would have enjoyed seeing pictures of what they had in mind.

The only fly in all of this was Patrice. Some days she was a little kind, but most days she was demanding and cold. If Gage was in the room, she watched the women like a hawk. Arcineh had no plans to do anything with Gage Sefton, but just knowing that Patrice suspected her made her look and act guilty.

For a time she feared she could lose her job, but then Patrice seemed to relax a little. Arcie had never so much as been in Gage's office, and then one day Patrice needed her to find backup documentation and had her work on a stack of files in his empty office.

Arcineh kept to the task at hand, not allowing herself to even glance around. And the office was worth a second look. Once again, she was reminded of Sam Bryant, who enjoyed open spaces. Gage's desk was huge, but so was his office, paneled in dark mahogany, with windows that had a stunning view of the lake.

Reading in files for specific wording, Arcineh worked steadily along on Gage's long sofa until close to the end of the day. With only 30 minutes left to closing, Gage and Patrice came into the room.

"Arcie," Patrice began, "we have a huge favor to ask of you. We have to have that file you're looking for tomorrow. Is there any way you could work late?"

"Sure," Arcineh agreed, mentally planning to call Jalaina.

"Great."

Arcineh watched the two of them go back to talking and even leave the room. Gage then came back on his own.

"Okay, do you have a car we have to see to?" he asked her.

"A car?"

"Yes. Security won't want it left in the lot."

"Are we going somewhere?" Arcineh asked.

"Oh." He was momentarily nonplussed. "Didn't Patrice tell you? I have an apartment just a few blocks away that we use. We'll go there and work."

Arcineh had never heard of such a thing, but she had no reason to say no, and not even a car to take care of. Less than 15 minutes later, she found herself in Gage's car. He navigated traffic, pulled into the underground parking of a posh apartment building, and took her to the penthouse. Again Arcineh wanted to look around, but Gage had put the files onto the coffee table, and Arcineh knew she was to go right back to work. She did, at the last minute, remember Jalaina.

"May I use your phone?"

"Of course," Gage said, telling her where it was in the kitchen. "I'll just head out and find us some food. What do you like?"

"Anything is fine."

Arcineh made her call, not allowing Jalaina to ask too many questions, and then went back to the files. She read carefully, but she'd been reading all day, and her eyes were growing weary. It was good to have Gage return with food—huge burgers and fries, and chocolate shakes. He tucked into his like a man starving, and Arcineh read and ate at the same time. Not until Gage had finished his food did he speak.

"Are you sure we haven't met?"

"Yes," Arcineh said as she glanced up just briefly and then went back to the paper.

"How old are you?"

"Twenty-one." Again just a glance and back to work.

"Are you from Chicago?"

Arcineh set the page down and looked at him. Gage saw the move and smiled.

"I'm interrupting."

"Just a little."

"But you work for me," Gage said lightly, wanting to tease a smile from this woman, although he didn't know why.

"Be that as it may, I'll probably be the one who will have to explain to Patrice why I couldn't find the file. You won't be in trouble, but I will."

"Good point," Gage agreed, and Arcineh almost laughed. She stopped herself by picking up another file. From her periphery, she watched Gage reach for a file as well. They worked along for three hours like this but came up with nothing. They took another break at 8:30. Gage found some Oreos in the kitchen, and even some fresh milk. At close to 9:00, Gage changed chairs, taking a more comfortable position. He was asleep before 10:00. Arcineh was tired, very much so, but since she had no way to get anywhere, she continued to read.

She had no idea what time it was, but Gage was suddenly waking her.

"Arcie," he said softly. "Here, get up."

Arcineh did as she was told, completely disoriented.

"Come this way." Gage was leading her down a hall. "Here," he stopped at a door, reached around the corner, and put on the light. "Climb into bed and get some sleep."

"I'd better go," a very disoriented Arcineh said.

"It's all right. No one will disturb you here."

Arcineh felt his hand on her back, and then the door was being shut behind her. Arcineh's brain was so fuzzy she barely knew what to think, but that bed looked amazing. She had the presence of mind to lock the door. From there she undressed, climbed into bed in her underwear, and fell into a dead sleep.

∞

The clock read 6:26 when Arcineh woke up. For a moment she couldn't believe she'd spent the night there, but only for a moment. Not caring if it would land her in trouble or not, Arcineh took a quick shower in the bathroom that adjoined the room and climbed back into her clothes. She hated not having a toothbrush and putting dirty clothes on a clean body, but on the chance she was headed back to the office for the day, she knew she had to be clean.

Momentarily forgetting her hair and glasses, Arcineh headed out to the living room and found all quiet. Sitting down on the sofa, she began to read again. It was going smoothly when Gage came in through the front door.

"I was being so quiet, and you're already up," he said congenially, breakfast obviously in the bag in his hand. "How about some coffee?"

"Thank you," Arcineh said, taking the offered cup and going back to her reading. Gage sat back in his place, but it took some time for Arcineh to realize he wasn't doing anything more than staring at her.

"Did you say there was breakfast?" Arcineh tried, suddenly realizing what a position she'd landed herself in.

"Yes!" Gage began to unpack the sack he'd brought in. He'd no more finished this when the phone rang.

Working like a magician, Arcineh got her hair and glasses into place in record time. She was eating and reading when he came back, looking as she always did.

Gage said nothing else, and Arcineh didn't find him watching her again. An hour later, she located the documentation they were looking for.

CHAPTER

Fourteen

Arcineh didn't see much of Gage on a regular basis. He seemed very busy, and Arcineh wasn't even sure he came to the office each day. But as the time drew closer for the July meeting with Siena Designs, Arcineh became more interested in the business. She finished her lunch early one day and was sitting in the lobby reading a brochure on Rugby Shades. She hadn't realized that the name came from Gage's love of the sport. Arcineh was completely into the brochure when Gage sat down next to her.

"What do you think of the new line?" he asked.

"Are these just out?"

"Hitting the stores next week."

"I think they're beautiful."

"What's your favorite?"

Arcineh studied the frames and chose a classy pair that the old Arcineh could have afforded.

"We have similar taste," Gage said, still wondering what it was about this woman, who quietly did her work and didn't bother anyone but who seemed needy to him. She was just short of mousy in her manner, and he knew she could look better with a different hairstyle. But even as she was, Gage found her interesting. He could also tell she was intelligent and wondered where she'd gone to school.

Arcineh had a few more questions about the glasses in the brochure, and Gage answered them, clearly excited about his work. It was then that she noticed him staring again. She knew that Patrice was somewhere around and didn't want her to gain the wrong idea.

"I think you're trying to place me again," she said quietly, "but I really don't think we've met. I'm sure I would remember."

"Let me see you without your glasses again. What do you look like?"

"I think the same," Arcineh said with a shrug, hoping she was convincing and knowing she could never take them off. She was not stuck on herself, but having Patrice know she was more attractive than she appeared would make for a miserable time in the workplace.

Arcineh suddenly looked at the clock.

"I've got to get back to work."

Gage nodded, not sure what he'd seen on her face and wishing she would meet his eyes more. Arcineh wasn't thinking about Gage. Patrice had come upon them, and she did not look happy at all.

❧

"You have done nothing but sit all evening," Jalaina charged Arcineh. "You didn't even go to dance."

"I can miss a night," Arcineh said, knowing it was a weak excuse.

"What's going on?"

Arcineh told her about what happened with Gage and Patrice—a short version, but she got the point.

"Can you believe it?" Arcineh added. "I think he might be a little interested even when I'm not dressed up, and I can't get near the man."

"And you want to?"

Arcineh's eyes closed. "I have a crush on my boss. Is that the stupidest thing you've ever heard or what?"

"What if you saw him outside of the office?" Jalaina asked, wanting to find a way to help. "Maybe we could find out where he grocery shops and *run into* him."

Arcineh laughed at her friend's wide eyes and exaggerated voice, but funny as she found it, she knew it was the last thing she would do. The crush would have to remain a secret because Gage Sefton was a closed door.

⌒

"What did you do to get on Patrice's wrong side?" Mallory asked five days later.

"I think she saw Gage talking to me and took it the wrong way."

"Just ride it out," that lady said sympathetically. "It happened to me when I first got here. It helped when I got a boyfriend and she saw that I had no designs on Gage."

"Thanks, Mallory," Arcineh said and meant it.

Patrice had been nothing short of rude to Arcineh for the last several days. Arcineh thought she could take it but suddenly found herself comparing Patrice and Quinn. It crossed her mind to try and talk to Patrice, but that had never worked with Quinn and she wasn't willing to try.

She also needed this job. Will had finally popped the question, and Jalaina was to be married by the end of the year. Arcineh was thrilled for her friend, but it put a new weight on her that hadn't been there before. And it wasn't as easy as finding another roommate. Arcineh liked the one she had and had no desire to replace her.

Taking Mallory's advice, Arcineh began the process of *riding it out* and hoped she would survive.

ᙡ

The big day had finally come. The conference room was ready, and Patrice was strung as tight as a bow. Arcineh was in trouble for everything, but she knew she wasn't making mistakes. She was only thankful she'd sat through some other meetings and knew just how Patrice wanted things done.

It took everything Arcineh had inside not to turn and talk to these five Italian men when they arrived in the large conference room. There was a translator—they had brought their own—and some had decent English skills, but Arcineh understood every word they said and naturally wanted to talk to them in Italian. She also knew it would be the very last thing she could do.

When the meeting finally got underway, Arcineh forced herself not to attend, but to keep an eye on Patrice and the physical needs of those present—pens, pads of paper, glasses, and water pitchers. And it hadn't turned out to be so painful. When Patrice had described this part of the job, Arcineh had not been thrilled, but she liked taking care of small details.

Arcineh was thinking about that when something registered in her mind. The translator had just gotten something wrong. Arcineh began to listen. At first she wondered if it was her not paying attention but soon knew better.

Moving as quietly as she could manage, Arcineh found a small scrap of paper and wrote a note to Patrice. She did not mince words. The note said, *Something is wrong.* Moving subtly, she folded it and put it in front of Patrice, who read it and then turned to frown at Arcineh. Arcineh kept her face impassive, but her brows rose when Patrice looked at her.

The meeting moved on. Arcineh had to go and collect something from Gage's office, but when she returned, she caught more talk of deceit. Arcineh began to watch the translator and knew in an instant that he was not comfortable with what he was doing. The man was sweating.

Feeling she had no choice, Arcineh wrote another note: *They are planning to cheat Rugby Shades.* Again she watched Patrice read the note, but this time that lady didn't even turn. For a time her back was stiff with rage, but she did not look in Arcineh's direction. Not until they took a break did Arcineh know how poorly she had failed.

"What do you think you're doing?" Patrice asked in the now-empty meeting room, her face looking as though she was going to have a stroke.

"Patrice, I'm sorry, but they are not telling the truth."

"And how could you possibly know that?"

"Well, I—" Arcineh began, but Patrice cut her off.

"Do you have any idea how quickly I could have you fired? Gage does whatever I say, and you had better remember that."

Arcineh stood helpless. Like being swept back into some cruel time warp, Arcineh looked at Patrice but saw Quinn's face. The words were different, but the intent was all the same.

"I'm sorry" was all Arcineh said, remembering Mallory's words about the money.

"See that you are," Patrice gritted out, turned, and stalked away.

The meetings went back into session, and Arcineh heard more subtle half-truths and lies, but she kept her mouth shut and sent no more notes. This was one battle she was not going to fight.

❧

Things went from bad to worse in the weeks that followed. Patrice did everything in her power to make Arcineh miserable, and it worked. Arcineh dreaded work each day and tried to find times to study the job board when no one would be around to notice.

However, she never had a chance to apply for another position.

The final straw came in the form of a four-year-old boy, whose mother had a meeting with Gage. Arcineh was flabbergasted that this woman would bring a child to a business meeting, and even more so when she was asked by Patrice to babysit the child in the conference room. Arcineh acquiesced, but only out of fear of losing her job.

Christopher was a handful from the first moment. He tried to get out the door repeatedly, and the longer Arcineh spurned his efforts, the more agitated he got. Her attempts to have him draw or look out the window were all rebuffed, and the first time he kicked her, Arcineh was so stunned she could barely move.

And that was just the beginning. Before Christopher's mother returned for him, Arcineh's face had been hit several times, her leg was bleeding, and she had two bite marks on her arm.

The child's mother thanked her in a distracted way, never really looking at her, and took her son away. Arcineh stood alone in the conference room for a long time and weighed her options.

❧

The office was large enough that it was unusual for everyone to be in the same place at the same time. But when Arcineh came from the conference room, slipping into the break room to get her purse, everyone was in Patrice's office. Arcineh got her purse and began to walk past them.

"Arcie?" Mallory was the first to spot her face.

Arcineh did not so much as look at the other woman. She was out the door and halfway to the elevator when Gage caught up.

"Arcie," he said, stopping her with a hand to her arm.

Arcineh paused only long enough to tell Gage not to touch her. The moment he let go, she went right back to walking. She was at the elevator in just seconds, the button pushed, when he stepped in front of her.

"You can't leave. You're hurt."

"Get out of the way," Arcineh said, even though the elevator had not arrived.

"Please listen to me," Gage was saying when Arcineh began to step around him. He made the mistake of reaching for her arm again.

"Step off!" Arcineh spat at him, her voice low with rage.

Gage looked into dark, furious eyes and did just as she said. Keeping his hands to himself, he tried asking her to stay, but Arcineh wouldn't even look at him. Gage made a move to join her in the elevator, but the look she gave him was so hateful he stopped.

The rest of the office had come to the middle of the lobby to witness all of this, their eyes large with surprise and upset. Had she known it, it might have been a comfort to Arcineh to know that even Patrice was shaking, realizing this time she'd gone too far.

∾

Gage watched Patrice hang up the phone again.

"Same thing," the woman said. "That number has been disconnected, and there's no posted change."

"Get me her address and directions to the place," Gage said, heading to his office to gather some things. "And keep working on the number. Call the phone company."

More than two hours later, Gage sat outside of Nicky Ciofani's house, having gotten lost twice. Gage climbed from his car and went to the front door. He had prepared so many things to say that he felt let down when no one was home. He knocked for 10 minutes and even sat for another 15 in his car, hoping she would show up.

Eventually Gage gave up and returned to the office, thinking there was nothing else he could do.

∾

Arcineh took a day to lick her wounds, but when work ended for Nicky the next evening, he arrived home to find Arcineh sitting in the living room, talking to Libby.

"Arcie!" he shouted with delight, coming to hug her, but he stopped short when he saw the bruises around her eye. All pleasure drained away, and Nicky's face became stern.

"What happened to you, baby girl?"

"It's a long story."

"Who is he? I swear I'll kill him. I swear I will."

"Nicky." His wife's voice finally got through. "It wasn't a man. Arcie knows better than that. Sit down and she'll tell you."

Arcineh didn't start at the beginning but gave enough details to satisfy Jalaina's brother. "So the truth of the matter is, I'm out of a job, Nicky. Any chance you can use me?" she finished.

"As a matter of fact," Nicky started, looking very pleased over what he was thinking. "I've got a special job starting after Labor Day. I could use your perfectionist little hands."

Arcineh was pleased and even laughed at his description, but the date he'd named was a month away, which meant no paycheck for six weeks. She would not go back and get what Rugby owed her, no matter how bad things got. She settled her mind for a lean month to come, and when Libby invited her for dinner, she accepted.

⟳

"Do you want more salad?" Jalaina Schafer asked of Arcineh when she had her friend over for lunch. Will and Jalaina were back from their honeymoon and settled into a spacious apartment.

"I think I do. This shrimp is amazing."

Jalaina smiled, but then she had done little but smile since marrying Will a few weeks earlier. They had honeymooned in a cabin on a lake in Wisconsin and had the time of their lives.

"When do you start for Nicky?" Jalaina asked, dishing up their dessert.

"Not until after Labor Day."

"Well, if you run out of food, come and see us."

Arcineh laughed, but after she got home, she sat down and looked at her checking and savings accounts. She had some money set aside. However, she thought if she was careful, she might make it without getting into it. She had wanted to buy furniture with the money—Jalaina had taken several of her own pieces with her—but that might have to wait.

Arcineh sat on her one living room chair and looked at the end of the kitchen. Jalaina had taken the kitchen table and four chairs. Arcineh thought she might miss those more than the sofa.

Feeling lonely all of a sudden, Arcineh knew she didn't want to sit around by herself and wondered why she'd left Jalaina's so soon. Changing into workout gear, she caught a bus to the studio, hoping there would be a class in session.

⟨⟨⟩⟩

One delay after another turned Nicky's Labor Day job into a mid-November one. An old house was being restored, and Arcineh was to lay the mosaic tile in the kitchen. It was a delicate, painstaking task, and Nicky told her not to rush.

She loved it. She missed working with her hands in this way, and the reproduction tile was beautiful—tiny squares in a amazing array of colors that Arcineh would not have thought available at the time.

The house was built in about 1872 and was grand for the day. Everything was being ripped up and replaced. Crews had to move carefully to avoid injury. The kitchen floor was one of the few rooms where the floor was safe. Arcineh would start work early and still be there at 5:00, tiling away and trying not to think about how lonely her life had become.

At the same time, she liked being alone when she worked. Chummel was always welcome, but she didn't like being around a bunch of men who had nothing to talk about but women and alcohol. She also didn't like being introduced to the strangers that came through, something Nicky was aware of and compassionate about when he was on the job site.

There were few visitors at the beginning—the job site was too un-predictable—but after the first of the year, more visitors came. When they arrived, Arcineh simply stood out of the way while Nicky or Bud, the man in charge of everything, gave a quick tour or explanation.

It was a snowy day in early February when Nicky brought in two men. Arcineh set her tools aside and stood across the room. Some-times she didn't even look at the guests, very much wanting to be left on her own, but this time she had no choice.

Sam Bryant was in the kitchen with her, and the other man was Gage Sefton. Arcineh knew she did not look the same. She was wearing an ancient sweatshirt and jeans and had stuffed her hair under an old White Sox baseball cap. If she could have chosen a day to look her worst, this was it.

"It's slow work," Arcineh finally heard Nicky saying. "We would love to talk to whoever did the original and ask him what he was thinking, but the plan is to have it look the same, and all those curves and angles go together very slowly."

The room suddenly grew quiet. Arcineh had tried to just listen to Nicky, but her eyes would not stay away from her grandfather. He was looking at her as well. Arcineh spoke.

"Hello, Sam."

"Hello, Arcineh."

The other two men watched this exchange and stayed quiet.

"Is this actually what you do for a living?" Sam asked. A small smile bent the corners of his mouth, and his voice did not give away the pounding of his heart.

Arcineh had to smile as well. "For the moment, yes."

The words died between them then, and she looked over to see Gage studying her.

"How did things end up with Siena Designs?" she asked him.

"That's who you are," Gage said in wonder. "Do you remember much about that meeting?'

"I remember everything about that meeting."

Gage's entire stance changed. He came to full attention and demanded without thinking, "I need you to tell me exactly what you know!"

Arcineh's brows rose in a way that both Sam and Nicky knew as dangerous, but she addressed herself to her grandfather. And in Italian.

"Mr. Sefton has forgotten himself. I don't work for him anymore."

"What did she say?" Gage asked quietly of Sam, knowing he'd blundered.

"I'll tell you later."

"But if she can help," Gage began.

Sam turned his full body to the younger man.

"I don't know what's going on between the two of you, but right now you need to trust me when I tell you that now is not the time. I will get back to you on this."

Gage looked into the older man's eyes and nodded, a tough thing to do when he was up to his ears in litigation with the design firm from Italy and suddenly saw Arcineh as a potential lifeline.

Sam walked to Arcineh next, reminding himself not to hug her.

"Will you have dinner with me tonight?" he asked.

Arcineh looked surprised but still asked, "Just the two of us?"

"Yes."

"I would enjoy that."

"Let's dress up," Sam said next.

Arcineh laughed a little. "My hands are pretty rough these days."

"You'll look beautiful," he said sincerely, his eyes on her face.

Arcineh smiled at him, not sure how she was keeping from falling apart.

"I'll pick you up," Sam said next. "Just give me the address, and I'll find it."

Arcineh told him, but suddenly grabbed his arm.

"How is Violet?"

"She's fine. She just left for a six-week trip to Europe."

Arcineh's mouth opened, and Sam laughed.

"How did you talk her into that?"

"It wasn't easy," Sam said, his smile lighting his whole face.

Arcineh studied him, thinking he was the same and yet very different. She wondered how she seemed to him.

"What time can I pick you up?"

"Well, I get home about 5:30. I could be ready by 6:15."

"I'll be there."

Sam didn't stay around. He could feel the emotion welling up inside of him and knew that Arcineh was close to tears. With a word of thanks, Sam exited, Gage close behind him.

"Do you want to tell me who that is?" Nicky asked of Arcineh when they had the old kitchen to themselves.

"My grandfather, Sam Bryant."

"Arcineh Bryant. I never made the connection," Nicky said, thinking out loud. "And he knows Gage Sefton?"

"He must. How do you know Gage Sefton?"

"This was his great-grandfather's house. He's the main benefactor on this project."

Not at any point had Arcineh heard this, and she wondered if it hadn't been talked about or if she was spending too much time lost in her own little world. She eventually went back to work, her head full of what had just happened and trying to make sense of it.

"Your granddaughter?" Gage questioned Sam as he drove them both back toward the financial district.

"Yes."

"Why was she working for me?"

"I don't know. We've been estranged. Today was the first time I've seen her in more than four years."

Gage didn't know what to say. He wanted to jump right back to the issue with Siena Designs but knew how insensitive that would be. And indeed he was sensitive right then. Sam's face was thoughtful, but he didn't have much to say. If he hadn't seen his granddaughter for four years, he was probably in a little bit of shock.

Gage was happy to make the drive back in silence.

Fifteen

"This is nice," Arcineh said, looking around the restaurant but not seeing many people. Her grandfather had clearly asked for a private table. She was glad. She had already cried at work, and then in the shower after work, and she knew it would happen again.

"I picked it for a special reason."

"Why was that?"

"They have a white chocolate dessert that I think someone will love."

Arcineh had to look away. He remembered the white chocolate. She knew if she looked into his smiling eyes any longer, she was going to burst into uncontrollable tears.

"We can cry later," Sam teased her gently. "Why don't we order?"

Arcineh nodded, and sure enough a waiter was headed their way. It took a little doing—the menu was diverse—but when he left they went back to talking.

"How is Quinn?" Arcineh asked. Somewhere along the line she'd run out of anger. She didn't want to live with her cousin, but she did care.

"She has a baby."

"A baby? Did she ever get married?"

"Yes, and she's already in the midst of a divorce."

Arcineh looked stunned.

"The marriage was not a good thing. The same day she learned she was pregnant, she also realized Tayte was cheating on her."

"Tayte? She married Tayte?"

"I'm afraid so."

"That's sad."

"She's doing well now," Sam added. "I bought a house in Schaumburg, and she lives there with the baby. When the divorce is through, I'll gift it to her."

"And everyone else?"

"About the same," Sam said. "Jeremy and Tiffany are still in Creve Coeur. Austin and Lexa are married and have a child."

"Wow. You're a great-grandfather," Arcineh said, watching when he didn't smile.

"I know you didn't mean it this way, but it's got to be said, Arcie. I haven't been a great grandfather, and if you don't want anything to do with me, I'll understand. But I hope you'll allow me to apologize."

Their salads arrived just then, and that was good. Arcineh needed a moment to regroup. It was such a shock to hear him say that. But there was still something she needed to make clear.

"It was never you," Arcineh said softly. "I just couldn't live with Quinn."

"I know that now. She confessed everything to me, all the lies and manipulation. I was a blind fool where she was concerned."

"She told you?"

"Everything she could remember. She's a different person now."

Arcineh didn't know what to say. This was the last thing she expected. All this time she pictured Quinn and her grandfather in the same place, but that image had been all wrong.

"How is your salad?"

"It's very good. I was hungry."

"You look very nice, by the way."

"Thank you. I noticed your suit. You're still classy," Arcineh said, thinking that his hair was almost all white these days. It made him very distinguished. His face on the other hand, had no more seams in it than the last time she saw him.

"I was nervous before you picked me up," Arcineh admitted, "and drank a bunch of water. Will you please excuse me?"

"Of course. I would stand up, but then I'd have to slide back into this booth."

This made Arcineh laugh before she scooted off to take care of matters. Sam continued to eat, but it wasn't long before he looked up and saw Gage walking by. The younger man just happened to glance that way, and Sam waved.

"Hello," Gage said, taking the edge of the booth. "I didn't expect to see you out."

"I'm here with Arcie."

"I'm glad, Sam. I won't stick around."

"Why don't I call you tomorrow?"

"Sounds good," Gage agreed, and moved to go. He changed his mind when Arcineh chose that moment to return.

She was dressed in a little black dress that, although not overly tight, showed Arcineh's true figure to him for the first time. It was simply cut and not at all revealing in the neckline, and stopped midway down her thighs to show those dancer's legs. Gage could only stare. Her hair was dark and thick around her face and shoulders, and so were the lashes around large, dark eyes. Her skin looked creamy, and just in time, Gage pulled his mind back from studying her mouth.

At last he looked at Sam, who was watching him in confusion.

"I'll call you tomorrow," Sam repeated.

"Yes, I'll plan on it."

Sam waited only until Gage was out of sight to turn to Arcineh, but she had the first question.

"Why was he here?"

"Just a coincidence, I assure you," Sam answered before asking, "What happened just now? He looked at you like he'd never seen you before."

"He hasn't. At least, not like this."

Sam looked completely confused but waited.

"I had to dress down to get a job. Carlee advised me about that a long time ago, and not until I'd been turned away by everyone in the financial district did I remember. I dressed down, and Rugby hired me on my first interview."

"How did you look?" Sam asked, finding himself completely fascinated.

"Oh, hair pulled back as tight as I could get it, terrible glasses, and clothing large enough to hide everything."

Sam had it in his heart to feel sorry for Gage. Arcineh was a beautiful woman, and up to a few minutes ago he hadn't had a clue.

"How do you know Gage Sefton?" Arcineh asked.

"He's my neighbor."

"Whose house did he buy?" Arcineh asked, picturing the houses all around where they'd lived.

"Actually, I moved into his neighborhood."

Nothing could have prepared Arcineh for this. She felt as though the wind had been snatched from her.

"How long?" she finally asked.

"Only about seven months."

"Why?"

"I was ready for something smaller, and it seemed a nice fit."

Arcineh stared at him. She couldn't picture him anywhere else but his old home. She went back to her meal, hoping she wouldn't cry.

"Next thing you'll be telling me you're retired," she said, her voice saying he never would. When Sam didn't reply, she looked at him, her eyes growing large.

"I sold Bryant," he told her.

"Why?" she asked again.

"Ready to be done. Weary of the travel."

Arcineh had expected to hear remorse in his voice over this, but he was remarkably upbeat. She couldn't picture this any more than she could him selling the house, but then she hadn't pictured her grandfather like this either. Something was very different, and Arcineh couldn't put her finger on what it was.

While she was still thinking about it, Sam's finger went in the air. The hovering waiter came over.

"One of those white chocolate desserts, please. And more coffee."

"Yes, sir."

Arcineh waited only until his eyes came back to her before saying, "Thanks, Grandpa."

∽

Gage slipped in behind the wheel of his car but didn't bother to use the key. He didn't notice the cold. Like a man in a dream, he realized he *had* seen Arcineh Bryant before she joined his staff at Rugby Shades. Letting his mind drift back, he remembered exactly where it had been.

"All set?" Luke asked Erika when he and Gage picked her up from aerobics class.

"Are you in a hurry?" Erika asked.

"I don't think so. What's up?"

"Just a little something special I've been invited to. Come this way."

The men—Erika's husband, Luke, and her brother, Gage—moved to the stairway she was headed toward, slipped into a small balcony, and sat down.

"You're going to watch another dance class?" Luke asked.

"Just for a little bit."

The men sat down good-naturedly, waiting until the music started up. A slow song started the set, and Luke leaned toward his wife.

"You've got to be kidding me," he whispered.

"Just wait," she said, turing to him with entreating eyes and adding, "Please."

Luke rolled his eyes at her, and she smiled when she knew she had him. However, she did not forget her brother who had landed on her other side.

"Do you mind?"

"No, but if you rescind your offer of pie, I won't be so forgiving."

Before Erika could even say it was a deal, the music changed. All three pairs of eyes swung to the women on the floor, moving in perfect rhythm to a rock song from the '70s. The moves looked spontaneous, but no one missed a beat.

Gage watched in fascination as the bodies moved as one until his eyes found a dark-haired woman whose face was relaxed and not intense. Gage could not stop watching her. She was small but nicely shaped and didn't even appear to be trying.

"Pick it up, Brooklyn," the teacher said to someone, and Gage noticed the sound booth for the first time. "Here comes the new part," she said next. "Do what you can."

The tempo changed, and mistakes began to happen. Only the dark-haired woman and two others were able to stay with the instructor. The others backed away and watched the four moving as one. Gage didn't know the last time he'd been so transfixed.

A horn honked in the cold parking lot, and Gage came back to the present, wishing he could somehow replay the memory again. Arcineh Bryant had been the dark-haired woman. She was also the mousy little woman who had worked in his office and the woman laying tile in his great-grandfather's kitchen. To top it off, she was also the beautiful granddaughter of Sam Bryant, and she wanted nothing to do with him.

Gage finally started the car and took himself home. He didn't know what to do about any of this, and right at the moment he was too tired to care.

∽

Sam and Arcineh talked until almost 11:00, the restaurant patiently bringing them more water and coffee as they wanted. Arcineh knew she would be tired in the morning, but it was one of the most wonderful times she'd had in years.

Sam drove her home, and because he could park where he could see the door, she told him not to get out.

"When am I going to see you again?" Sam asked before she could exit.

"I don't know. I mean, my schedule is pretty free."

"Okay," Sam said, not wanting to press. "I know where you're working, and I know where you live. How about a phone number?"

"I don't have a phone right now."

"Did something happen or can you not afford one?"

"I can't afford one."

Sam's emotions, which had been close all evening, almost got the best of him then.

"Please let me buy you a phone, Arcie," he requested quietly.

Arcineh smiled at him. "I'm all right, but thanks for the offer."

"What do you do if something happens?"

"Go to the neighbors'. They're very nice."

Sam gave her a long-suffering look, but Arcineh could see the smile in his eyes.

"I'll see you later," she said, finally bidding him goodnight and scurrying in out of the cold.

Sam drove himself home, his heart so full he didn't know how he would stand it. He had taken his granddaughter to dinner. She was safe, and they had talked. And although she was different, she was still his Arcineh.

And a few times she had looked at him. He hoped she was seeing how different he was. Indeed he had prayed for that very thing all evening. Now he must wait for just the right time to tell her how profound the change had been.

⤖

Arcineh did not hear the door. She was working along, her mind intent on the grout, when the most wonderful smell assailed her nose. She turned her head to find it and saw Sam.

"Did I miss lunch?" he asked.

"No." Arcineh laughed a little. "What have you got there?"

"Oh, just a little something I picked up."

Arcineh came toward him. He was utterly out of place in his elegant coat, hat, and gloves, but a most welcome sight. He even had a tall thermos that Arcineh assumed held something hot to drink.

"Can you eat now?" he asked.

"Yes," she said, so pleased to see him. Arcineh looked into his face and realized the time they'd lost.

"It's all right," Sam said, seeing the tears in her eyes; his eyes filled too.

"I missed you," she whispered.

Sam held out his arms, and Arcineh walked into them. She cried against his chest like a lost child.

"I'm so sorry I drove you out of our home," Sam said, his throat thick. "I can't tell you how I've regretted it."

It was a while before they got to the picnic hamper, but worth it because Sam had outdone himself. Chicago pizza was inside, along with salads and bread. The thermos held hot coffee with cream and sugar. They sat together in that dirty workplace, taking the teasing of men who smelled the food and came looking, but mostly lost in catching up, both secretly deciding they never wanted to be separated again.

∽

"Do me a favor?" Sam had asked just before leaving Arcineh to her work.

"What?" Arcineh had returned, wary of his tone.

"Talk to Gage."

Arcineh made a face at the time, but Sam still had a smooth way about him. Inside of ten minutes, he'd talked her around. Now on Saturday she sat in a restaurant booth with both men and tried to tell her story.

"You gave notes to Patrice and she ignored them?" Gage repeated in disbelief. "She wouldn't do that."

Without warning, Arcineh was on her feet, gathering her coat to leave. She didn't know how she would get home, but she wasn't going to stay any longer. Arcineh stood on the street, trying to figure out where to go. Sam was suddenly beside her.

"Here, take my keys."

"What will you do?"

"Gage can give me a lift."

Arcineh didn't take the keys. She looked across the street at nothing, frustration filling her. To be called a liar by someone who didn't even know her was hard to take.

"You could also come back in, and I'll explain things to Gage. I've been there. I can make him understand."

Arcineh didn't know why she agreed to go back, but when she did, her grandfather took charge.

"You have to understand," he began, "Arcie would not lie to you about this. She has better things to do than play games with people's lives. If she tells you this happened, you can believe her. What you do with it is your choice, but don't accuse Arcineh of making this up. I made that mistake a long time ago, and the cost has been enormous. I don't want to see you do the same."

Gage had not expected this, but his respect for Sam Bryant won out. He turned back to Arcineh, whose face was not open, but he was ready to try again.

"Will you do me a favor and tell me about your employment with Rugby?"

"From my start in the file department?"

"Yes—how you came to have that job, and how you got to the fourth floor."

Arcineh did as he asked, keeping it brief and to the point.

"When you left on the day of the babysitting debacle," Gage asked next, "why was none of your personal information correct? The number we had on file was no longer in use, and I tracked down the house but no one was home. Did you actually commute from that neighborhood?"

"Just for the first month I worked here. The folks who lived there changed their number sometime after I moved out."

"But why didn't we have updated information on you when you moved to my office?"

Arcineh shrugged. "No one asked, and I didn't think to mention it."

Gage shook his head. "That was highly unprofessional."

"That's not all that was unprofessional," Arcineh said, and Gage looked at her.

"I'm going to want to know what that means, but will you first tell me everything you remember about that meeting? I won't interrupt you."

Arcineh began again, and Gage couldn't keep the amazement from his face. To hear that deception was discussed while they all sat there unaware was astounding to him. He had researched Siena Designs for a long time and thought it couldn't be a better match for Rugby Shades.

"Did you and Patrice talk about it after the meeting?" Gage wanted to know next.

"Mr. Sefton," Arcineh began.

"Gage," he corrected her, his eyes never leaving her face.

"Gage," Arcineh started again. "I don't know if I'm the best person to tell you this."

"Why wouldn't you be?"

Arcineh looked at Sam.

"Are you afraid of what Gage's relationship might be with this woman?" her grandfather guessed.

Arcineh nodded. "I think there was a serious error in judgment, but I'm not trying to get anyone in trouble or fired."

"You can tell me," Gage said, and waited for Arcineh to do just that. The waitress brought more coffee, and when Arcineh had added cream and tasted it, she started.

"Nothing else I could tell you will make sense if you don't know how Patrice views you."

"How she *views* me?"

Arcineh saw no help for it. She took a breath and plunged in.

"My first conversation with Mallory was her telling me to remember that she and the other women put up with Patrice only for the money."

Gage looked stunned over this, and Arcineh waited. She wasn't sure if he was hurt by the statement or wanted to argue.

"Why did she say that?"

"Because Patrice had laid claim to you. I feared speaking to you or looking at you for fear of losing my job."

"Did you really believe that would happen, Arcie?"

"You probably don't remember this, but one day I was in the lobby looking at the new brochure and you sat down with me."

"I remember," Gage put in softly.

"Well, Patrice saw us, and that's when the job changed for me. None of us were allowed to get close to you. After that she criticized everything I did, so that when I sent her those notes, she wouldn't even consider that I might know what I was talking about."

Arcineh was warming to the topic now and went on without

mercy. "I've never heard of an employee who was expected to work at the boss' apartment after business hours and then spend the night. Some women might have got it into their heads to accuse you of something, and you'd be in a sexual harassment lawsuit right now. But then, I suspect that Patrice thought me safe enough to not do that or to even tempt you.

"And I also assume the babysitting job was her idea. You should have looked at that woman who showed up, bringing her child to a business meeting, like she'd grown another head. And then done the same thing to Patrice when she suggested that someone on your staff babysit!"

Arcineh was a little red in the face now with emotion. She was not shouting—her voice was level—but she was going to have her say.

"I can see that you have a growing, thriving company, but don't ask me how. You have some business practices that I highly question, and you allow your assistant to run things so you don't have to think about them."

Gage was so flooded with emotion that he knew it would take some time to sort it all out. He looked down at the table, his mind trying to take it all in.

"Thank you," he said at last, and Arcineh stared at him. It was the very last thing she expected.

"What will you do?" Sam asked the younger man.

"First of all, I'll talk to my people. I don't expect them to lie to me, but I certainly won't tell them what I now know."

Gage looked at Arcineh.

"We go to court in about six weeks. Would you consider testifying?"

"What does that look like?"

Gage's mouth tightened a bit. "It could get pretty ugly. Siena has denied all charges. But we would try to keep you as informed as possible. Surprises are sometimes the worst part."

"Who's *we?*"

"My lawyers and I."

"I don't wish to be difficult," Arcineh knew she had to add, "but I hate competition. I won't do it."

Gage stared at her, not sure what she was saying.

"Do you mean with Patrice?" Sam asked.

"Yes. If my helping at the trial means putting me back on her radar as someone out to steal you, I'd rather not put myself through that."

"Did you know that Patrice is engaged to be married?"

Arcineh gawked at him, more confused than ever. "I have no desire to vilify this woman, but her need to be needed by you caused her to have a serious lapse in judgment, and now you're up to your ears in litigation.

"Patrice runs that office with amazing efficiency, but she also had some issues. I hope everything works out for the best, and I don't want to see Patrice fired, but you did ask me what I thought."

Again Gage thanked her. She had been a huge help, but he also got more than he bargained for.

Sixteen

"Your granddaughter is a beautiful woman," Gage said to Sam in the older man's family room much later that day.

"Yes, she is," Sam could not help but agree.

Gage was about to ask a question about her, but he looked at the older man's face. His head was tipped back, his mind far away.

"My son was a good-looking man," he said after a minute of quiet. "But Isabella, Arcineh's mother, was stunning. She drew eyes, male and female, everywhere she went. And classy—Arcineh has her style."

"What happened to them?"

"They died in an auto accident. Arcie was eleven. She came to live with me."

"I take it the two of you didn't get along."

"As a matter of fact, we did very well together until I let my other granddaughter move in. Arcie was 17 at the time and moved out as soon as she could. I thought Arcie was being unreasonable. I was totally blind to who Quinn really was at that time."

The things Sam said that afternoon helped everything come into focus for Gage. He found himself more fascinated than ever. Gage wrestled with what he was thinking for a time and then just spit it out.

"Do you think Arcie will ever let me anywhere near her?"

Sam smiled, not surprised he would feel that way.

"Tell me something, Gage. Do you dance?"

"A little. Mostly ballroom."

Sam smiled at him, and Gage laughed.

"If that's the prerequisite, I probably don't stand a chance."

"I was just teasing you, but do take my advice on this. Don't ever make her compete for you. She'll walk away without a backward glance."

Gage felt compassion for the man but took each word to heart.

∽

"I'm still in shock," Sam told Pastor Simon Orr when the morning service ended. "I've seen her every day, I think just to convince myself that she's really back in my life."

"Will you see her today?"

"I'm headed there now," Sam said with a smile.

Simon clapped him on the shoulder and said, "I'll be praying."

Sam thanked him and headed to his car.

∽

"Hi," Sam said quietly, causing Arcineh to start.

"I didn't hear you," she said, shutting her front door behind her. The hallway was always a bit cool.

"I didn't mean to startle you. Did I catch you at a bad time?"

"No, I'm just putting the trash out."

Sam took the sack from her hand and said, "I thought you might want to come over for lunch."

"At your house?"

"At my house."

Arcineh bit her lip. She loved the idea, but found it a little scary too.

"Just the two of us?"

"Yes."

"Okay," Arcineh agreed, though she was not sure why. "Let me grab my coat."

Arcineh shot inside the building but came right back out.

"Do you think it would be all right if I did my laundry?"

"Of course," Sam said, wondering why she wasn't inviting him in.

"My stuff gets pretty dirty on the job," she apologized.

"Get your laundry, Arcie," Sam said, and Arcineh smiled at him. Sam found the Dumpster and then went in to wait by her door. Arcineh came out with a large sack and shut the door rather swiftly.

"Have you got a man in there you don't want me to see?" Sam teased her.

"No, things are just messy," Arcineh said. It was true, but not the full truth.

"I'm sure I'd be horrified," Sam remarked dryly.

Arcineh laughed but was glad he'd not pushed the point. If he struggled with her not having a phone, he would have been really upset to see that Jalaina had taken most of the furniture.

"Where do you usually do your laundry?" Sam asked when they were headed down the road.

"There's a small laundry room at the apartments. I don't mind, but I got behind, and Sundays are pretty busy in there."

"And this will save you a little money," Sam mentioned, no censure in his voice.

"I suppose you think I'm crazy. My parents' money is sitting in your bank, and I don't touch it."

"You've never wanted it, Arcie, so that's nothing new, but it is hard for me not to just hand you everything."

"I guess it would be. I've never thought about it before." Arcineh looked over at him, realizing now that his face looked younger than the last time she'd seen him.

"Is anything wrong?" Sam asked with a glance at her.

"I'm just looking at you."

"I missed you too." Sam said the words.

"Did you look for me?"

Sam laughed a little. "About a thousand times I hired an investigator to track you down, only to call him back in five minutes and cancel. I knew you'd come home when you wanted to."

"When did all this begin?"

"Not right away. I was too angry. But when I realized that you'd gathered your birth certificate and passport, I got scared. I was glad you at least called Vi."

"I called you too, but Quinn always picked up."

"Did you talk to her?"

"No, I just hung up."

They were at the house now, and Sam hit the garage door opener. Arcineh looked around, thinking she would never see him in something this small but also understanding that in some parts of Chicago, this would be a mansion.

"Come on in," Sam invited, climbing from the car and retrieving the sack of dirty clothes. "I'll show you around the downstairs."

Arcineh followed him, hardly able to believe her eyes. It was like a scaled-down version of his old house. Nothing was quite so large or grand, but it was almost all there.

"The backyard is big!" Arcineh commented when they stopped before the patio doors.

"Yes it is, and just to the right," Sam pointed, "will be the pool."

"You're getting a pool?" Arcineh couldn't hide her pleasure.

"I am. I told myself when I moved here that when my girl came home, I'd put in a pool."

Arcineh put a hand over her mouth, thinking she'd not cried this much in the four years she'd been gone. She had hardened her heart and forced herself not to. Now all the walls were tumbling down.

But she didn't want to cry again, and thankfully Sam rescued her.

"Why don't I show you where the machines are."

"All right."

"Then I'll start lunch."

"Can you actually cook these days?" Arcineh asked simply to distract herself.

"I'll have you know that I can heat a can of soup to perfection."

"Is that what we're having?" Arcineh had to laugh.

"Not just that," Sam said, managing to sound offended.

"What else?"

"Crackers and milk."

Arcineh chuckled all the way to the laundry room.

∞

Lunch eaten, they had not been settled in the family room for more than five minutes when Arcineh noticed a Bible on one of the tables.

"Do you read the Bible these days?" she asked Sam.

"I do. I thought I knew what was in it, but I couldn't have been more wrong."

From far away, Arcineh heard the washing machine beep and excused herself. Almost as soon as she left, Sam was swept back in time to when his views began to change.

Sam stood in the stark hospital room, tense and agitated, and watched Mason's eyes open slowly. He blinked a few times before focusing on his boss.

"Oh, Sam. I'm glad you came."

"How are you feeling?" Sam made himself ask. It was the last place he wanted to be.

"As good as can be expected for a dying man," Mason said, his voice pragmatic.

"Don't joke." Sam's voice was a little harsh, and for the first time Mason didn't take it.

"You never stop, do you? Always the boss," the man in the bed said.

Sam had the good grace to look ashamed.

"I've got some things to tell you, Sam, and this time I have nothing to lose."

Sam had no reply to that, but Mason didn't need one. He wasted no time on politeness or pleasantries.

"You're going to hell," Mason said, his voice firm, ignoring the angry tightening of Sam's jaw. "I was headed there too, but thankfully I got cancer and made myself stop and face the music."

"I don't know what you're talking about."

"Then I'll tell you. I've been reading my Bible. I hadn't touched it since I was a kid. It says that men like us will perish forever. We do nothing but live for ourselves—you know we do.

"Did you know," Mason asked, his voice filled with fascination, "all the comics and cartoons are wrong? There is no angel waiting to dialog with us at some great gateway. By the time we die, eternity is settled. I found Jesus' words and works are known too. Believe in Him, you're saved. Don't believe, you're condemned already. It's black and white in John 3, Sam."

"And now you're telling me you're saved?" Sam asked, doing nothing to hide his contempt.

"Amazing, isn't it?" Mason didn't respond to the scorn. "At this late hour, God still allowed me in."

"In where?" Sam heard himself ask, not sure why he wasn't storming from the room.

And Mason answered. He answered in plain terms, and Sam's life had not been the same since.

Arcineh came back with a load of clothing to fold. She sat on the sofa just where she'd been and began the methodical work. She hadn't even folded two shirts when she picked up where they'd left off.

"I don't understand. You just suddenly started reading the Bible?"

"It wasn't sudden, but it would seem that way to you."

Arcineh looked tense now, and Sam knew he would have to tell her something.

"Did I tell you that Mason Beck died?"

Arcineh put her hand to her head. It was all so much to think about.

"What happened?"

"Cancer."

"Oh, Sam," Arcineh began. "I don't know how much more I can take."

"I'm sorry I didn't tell you before."

"But it has something to do with your Bible reading, doesn't it?"

"Yes. Mason set me straight on some things. It's been a big help."

"So what? You've had some sort of religious experience?"

"You make it sound pretty disgusting."

"I didn't mean to," Arcineh immediately recanted. "I have a friend who's very religious, and she goes to church, and she's very sincere. It just all sounds so hard that I can't imagine wanting that. There was a time when you didn't."

"That's very true. I'm thankful that people can change."

Arcineh could only look at him. He was changed. Remarkably so. The old Sam would have blamed her, to some extent, for leaving. He would have said she could have tried harder to tell him or thrown it onto Violet. This humble, almost gentle, man took a little getting used to.

"Did you have enough lunch?" Sam said, not ever planning to shove his beliefs down her throat.

"I did, thank you. Can I ask you one more thing?"

"Sure."

The phone rang before Sam could say anything. He got up swiftly, checked the caller ID, and came back.

"Go ahead," Sam said.

"Why didn't you pick up?"

"Because it wasn't Vi. She's the only person I'd pick up for right now—so you could talk to her."

Arcineh could only stare at him. "You're so changed."

"Yes, I am."

"I think I don't want to ask any questions," Arcineh decided. "I just want you to tell me exactly what happened."

∽

"She speaks Italian?" Patrice all but whispered.

She was sitting in Gage's office, and he had just learned that Patrice did remember the notes from Arcineh.

"This is all my fault," Patrice went on. "I ignored her, and now we're in this terrible mess."

"Why did you ignore her?" Gage asked.

"I—" Patrice began, but stopped. How did she tell this man that she must protect him? She saw the adoring looks he got but knew that none of those women were good enough. When one came along that met the standard, she would know, but it hadn't happened yet.

"Patrice?"

"I'm rather protective of you," Patrice said, finding the words. "But I've failed miserably, and I see no choice but to resign."

"I don't want you to resign. I have no plans to fire you, but before this is over, you'll be dragged over the coals. Arcie will sit on the witness stand and say she tried to warn you. The main focus will be on the lying translator and whoever hired him, but the light will definitely hit you as well."

Patrice nodded, thinking she deserved nothing less, but Gage wasn't done.

"And there will be some changes around here. I find it hard to believe we can't get our jobs done unless you fill each woman with fear."

Patrice licked her lips. "Arcie did quite a bit of talking."

"She got some things off her chest," Gage said, putting it mildly. "And she was right. My head's been in the sand. I don't want these hardworking women to stay because the pay is good. I want them to enjoy each day, be productive, and not fear your reprisal."

Patrice was not so humble now. It wasn't like that, she was sure. The women enjoyed working on this floor. Arcineh hadn't been around long enough to know anything.

"What exactly did she tell you?"

"Many things, but mostly that your need to be needed by me clouded your judgment. She was very surprised to learn you were going to be married. She was sure you were protecting me for yourself."

"Well, I'm not."

"But you do protect me," Gage said, glad to have it on the table for the first time. He'd been aware of this in the back of his mind but never let himself think about it.

"You don't see the looks!" Patrice snapped. "The women mooning over you—one of these days one is going to get her hooks in you and make you miserable."

"And you thought Arcie was the next candidate?"

"I guess I did," the assistant admitted, calming down some and sitting back in her chair.

"What exactly did you object to?"

"She's such a mousy little thing, without a lick of style! She's all wrong for you."

"You need to trust me when I tell you that there is nothing mousy about her."

Patrice looked at him but kept quiet. She watched while he picked up the phone, dialed, and spoke into it.

"Mallory, I need everyone in here as soon as you can manage it. All right. Thank you."

Gage replaced the phone, his eyes going back to the woman in front of his desk.

"I've been checked out for too long, Patrice. We're going to have a brief meeting. I'm not out to humiliate you, but the changes begin now."

∽

"Hello," Arcineh said when Gage suddenly appeared in his great-grandfather's kitchen.

"Hi, how are you?"

"Fine. Yourself?"

"Doing fine."

"Will I be in the way in here?" Gage asked, wishing he didn't feel so nervous.

"No," Arcineh said, not sure why he was there.

"How is it coming?"

"A little faster right now," Arcineh answered, seeing that her hand was not so steady at the moment. "It's nice to hit a straightaway and make some progress."

The room grew quiet. Arcineh did her best to keep working. It felt as though the silence lasted an hour, but Gage spoke after a minute.

"I've always heard about people who looked good no matter what, but I never met one before you."

"Did you have breakfast?" Arcineh asked. "Are you feeling a little dizzy?"

Gage laughed, but added, "You even looked good in those low shoes and frumpy skirts and blouses you wore to the office."

Arcineh looked up at him from her place on a stool.

"It was an interesting experience to become invisible. I'd never known that before," she said without conceit. "You were very kind during that time, and I appreciated that."

Their eyes held for a few seconds before Arcineh made herself turn back to the tiles.

"It's pretty, isn't it?" Gage said, coming close to inspect a part she had finished.

"Yes. I didn't think of colors this vibrant for the time, but obviously I was wrong."

"Have you seen the carpet that just came?"

"No."

"Come on. I'll show you."

Arcineh followed him, feeling this wasn't quite real. She had had a crush on this man at one time, and even though she'd been ready to hit him on her last day at the office, she was still very drawn.

"This is the carpet?" Arcineh asked, looking to where Gage had turned back the roll.

"That's it."

Arcineh looked down at an amazing pattern of colors. Blues, reds, yellows—every color she could imagine—drawn into an intricate pattern Arcineh would have pegged as modern.

"It's so pretty."

"Evidently my great-grandmother liked lots of color."

"And your great-grandfather let her have it."

"She was the love of his life," Gage said. Arcineh didn't know why, but it made her look at him. He was looking right back. Arcineh wondered how long they would have stayed like that had Bud not wandered onto the scene.

He snagged Gage's attention, who, after telling Arcineh goodbye, went on his way. Arcineh went back to work and would not admit to herself that the kitchen seemed lonely.

❦

"So talk some sense into me," Arcineh demanded when she'd told Jalaina and Will the whole story. "I should hate this man, right?"

The husband and wife exchanged a smiling look.

"What does that mean?" Arcineh asked, feeling uncertain.

"He's sounds perfect for you," Will answered.

"How can you say that?"

"Do you remember how it was with Kevin?" Jalaina asked. "His not knowing about who you were held you back. Gage Sefton knows exactly who you are. He's seen you in every way, and he's still coming around."

"I'm probably reading something into it. He's probably not interested at all."

Both Jalaina and Will laughed hysterically over this.

"Oh, no," Jalaina struggled to get up, her very pregnant abdomen making it a challenge. "Every time I laugh, I have to excuse myself."

Jalaina waddled from the room, and Arcineh looked at Will.

"I didn't think you two would feel this way."

Will smiled and said, "Let me get this straight. You recently sat in a restaurant, raked this man over the coals, and he thanked you."

"Yes." Arcineh's voice was quiet.

"And is this not the same man who was very nice to you when you wore those horrible shoes to the office?"

"Yes."

"That's not normal," Will told her. "No one likes to be told how badly he's failed, and men don't have a tendency to look below the surface. This man has to be a little bit special, Arcie."

Arcineh had not looked at it this way. In a few short sentences, Will had given her a lot to think about.

∽

"Gage, have you heard anything I said?" his sister asked.

"I think so." He looked at her, trying desperately to catch up.

"If I didn't know better," she muttered, "I'd swear you were in love. You've been in a fog all night."

This said, Erika walked from the living room. Luke, on the other hand, noticed Gage's thoughtful face.

"What's her name?"

"Arcie."

"That's different."

"She's different."

"Special or peculiar?"

"Special."

"How does she feel about you?"

"I wish I knew."

"Who is she?"

"Sam's granddaughter."

"The one who just had a baby?"

"No. Arcie hasn't been around for a few years. I get the impression they're going to need to get to know each other all over again."

Both men heard Erika coming back from the kitchen. Luke had more questions but kept them to himself. Gage didn't bring it up again.

CHAPTER
Seventeen

Help me to trust You, Sam prayed early one morning. *I want Arcineh to know You. I want her to accept Your salvation, but I must trust Your timing on this. I know You can change her heart, but she's not been able to trust all the people in her life, and I fear that will spread to You.*

Help me to believe Your Word and Your promises. Help me to be the example she needs, but mostly be the grandfather she needs. She might not want to see the family, but she seems to be all right with me. Please, Lord, please save both of us. Save me today, Father, and save Arcie for eternity. I ask You, Father, in Your Son's name and with all my heart. Amen.

Sam eventually climbed from bed, but his heart continued to pray, not just for Arcineh, but that he would learn a deeper trust and gain a deeper faith through all of this.

"Quinn has invited us over," Sam told Arcineh when he saw her at the old house a few days later. "A week from this Saturday. Jeremy and Tiffany will also be in town."

Sam had brought lunch again, so the two had been visiting, but the tiler had not expected this. She was not thrilled. Her look spoke volumes but she didn't say no.

"Are you going to tell me what you're thinking?" Sam asked.

"I'm trying to think what Quinn might be thinking."

"She wants to see you but knows it's more complicated than that. She'll understand if it will hurt you too much."

Those words coming from Quinn, ones that said she was putting others ahead of herself, made Arcineh curious. Arcineh wished she could see her cousin without having to talk to her—watch her in action from a distance with no opportunity to be hurt by her—but knew this was impossible.

She also knew the invitation would only come up again. Arcineh took a moment to say that she would go, but she agreed only to get it over with.

∞

"So how is it going?" Gage asked Mallory in a private meeting.

"It's fine," she said—this is what she always said—and Gage stared at her.

Mallory began to look uncomfortable, thinking this was worse than trying to figure out Patrice.

"You can speak freely," Gage said after a moment. "Patrice is trying to change. Don't worry about being made miserable."

"Miserable on this job has become normal," Mallory finally admitted, barely believing those words had come from her mouth.

Gage shook his head a little. He'd been foolishly unaware. But he was trying to change as well.

"What was your impression of the meeting with Siena, Mallory? Were you in there at all?"

"I wasn't in the room, but it's been my job to type the notes, and I've seen inconsistencies. I didn't think that was what I was reading, but when all of this came up, I went back and looked." She looked frightened for a moment but still admitted, "I even took a copy of the notes home with me so I could study them. It's subtle, but it's there."

"Were you going to tell me?"

"I have about five pages left to read. I was going to talk to you once I'd marked everything. And I was afraid of what you'd say when you found out I'd taken them from the office."

"It's all right, but as soon as you have them done, I'd like you to show me what you're seeing."

Mallory agreed, and when the room became quiet, she mentioned, "It seems Arcie told you a lot."

"What was your impression of her?" Gage asked, not bothering with Mallory's question.

"Quiet, but amazingly capable. There wasn't any job she couldn't do. I've wondered if that's why Patrice saw her as a threat. And Victoria knew!" Mallory grew animated. "We talked after your meeting with us, and she said she knew there was more to Arcie than met the eye."

"She told me that also," Gage said. He had a few more questions for her, thanked her for her time, and then went to find Patrice. He wanted all of this to simply smooth out so he could go back to the business of making sunglasses, but he couldn't do what he'd done before and let others handle things without being aware. It was not a good time, but he was not going to let the changes get the better of him or his business.

❦

"What do you do at church?" Arcineh asked. It was the next Sunday afternoon, and Sam had picked her up again.

"We have a sermon, and then we split off into groups for Sunday school."

"Do you go to Sunday school?" Arcineh asked, feeling drawn and somewhat horrified at the same time.

"Yes, we meet as families. I go with the group whose children are grown. Most have spouses, so I'm different in that way."

"What do you do?"

"We've been studying on the topic of fearing God for a while. The teacher talks for most of the time, but there's lots of sharing from people in the room."

Arcineh thought about this for a while and then asked, "What's 'fearing God'?"

"It's recognizing who He is so I think and act like Him," Sam said, trying to keep it simple.

"Why do you believe in God after all this time? I mean, just believing in God doesn't suddenly make Him there. It makes no sense to me."

"I had come to a time in my life that was pretty painful. You were gone; all Quinn did was sit around and cry for Tayte; and your aunt called every two minutes to check on her. Then I went to see Mason in the hospital, and he told me I was condemned. I don't mind telling you that I didn't take that very well.

"All the way back to my car, I talked to God and told Him He wasn't there. I then sat behind the wheel and said, 'If You're not there, who am I talking to?' It was a defining moment for me since I was thinking differently than I had. I'd never read the Bible, but what did I have to lose? If I was so sure that God didn't exist, why not look in the book? I thought it might be a good fantasy read."

Sam suddenly smiled. "I was captivated. I knew that people believed in creation, but I'd never looked at the order in which it happened or considered Satan's part in the garden. I could not stop reading.

"Mason didn't live much longer, but he did live long enough for me to go back and ask him some questions. He couldn't answer much—his own faith was fairly new—but he sent me to my present church. I've not missed a Sunday in more than two years."

His own faith was fairly new. Arcineh didn't know what to do with that statement. She had longed for a renewed relationship with Sam for so many months and years, and now he was not the man she remembered. There wasn't anything she could object to, but there was comfort in sameness—even when the sameness had been far from perfect.

"What bothers you about it the most?" Sam asked with tremendous kindness. His heart was so full of love for this woman that he barely held his emotions when she was with him.

"I don't know," Arcineh said. She thought it was the change in him but suddenly wasn't sure. "I guess," Arcineh tried to begin, "we have such history together, but not like this. I've been content without that, and your needing God surprises me."

"I can see how that would be true. I just hope you'll ask me questions if you have them."

"Why is that important?"

"I hope we can be closer than ever, and if you find me odd or inconsistent, I think that will put distance between us."

This was definitely not the grandfather she knew, but for the first time she was comforted by his words.

Sam, watching her face and seeing something different, did not have a chance to question her. The phone rang, and this Sunday it was Violet. When she learned that Arcineh was back in Sam's life, all she could do was cry. When the tears abated, Sam had to talk her into staying where she was. Arcineh tried as well, and Violet agreed, but both Bryants had the impression they would see her very soon.

∽∾

That night Sam read in Deuteronomy 10:12-13, "Now, Israel, what does the LORD your God require from you, but to fear the LORD your

God, to walk in all His ways and love Him, and to serve the LORD your God with all your heart and with all your soul, and to keep the LORD's commandments and His statutes which I am commanding you today for your good?"

Thank You for Your words, Lord, Sam prayed. *I have to remember that my job is to trust You while You work Your plan. I asked You to bring Arcineh back to me, and You did this. I need to trust You for her salvation. I am foreign to her, and she doesn't know what to do with me. Please don't let me stand in the way of her knowing You. Please give her a hunger to know more and to understand that You are there.*

Sam was out of words then, remembering the day that God had changed his mind toward Him. Before he slept, he cried. He cried in grief and thanksgiving, awe and fear, his heart a jumble of emotions but mostly wanting to be obedient. Reminding himself of how much God loved him, Sam finally drifted off to sleep.

⟨⟩

"Is that Gage?" Arcineh asked Sam when they exited her apartment building midmorning on Saturday. Someone was already sitting in the passenger's seat of Sam's Maybach.

"Yes. I thought we needed an impartial party."

Arcineh had to smile. She would not have thought of such a thing, but it wasn't such a bad idea. However, she would not have considered Gage. She was still working out his presence when they neared the car and Gage opened his door.

"Actually," she said to him, "I think I'll be more comfortable in the back, but thank you."

"Are you certain?"

"Yes," Arcineh said, proving her point by opening the door and slipping in behind the front passenger's seat.

Gage, with only a glance at Sam, got back in the front. He had not intended to take Arcineh's place, but outside of blocking her way, there was nothing he could do.

Once again he hadn't counted on being nervous but got back into the car feeling slightly rattled. He didn't know what this woman had that put him on edge, but she had it in spades. It also didn't help that she looked fabulous in simple jeans and a light pink sweater that only worked to accentuate her dark hair and eyes.

"Do you have a specific time you need to be back?" Sam asked his granddaughter after they were underway.

"I think I have an hour," she joked, bringing a smile to Sam's mouth as he began to navigate the city.

The men fell to talking, initiated by Sam, with Arcineh only half listening. Her mind had drifted back to times with Quinn, times of hurt and confusion. She had thought she was over those, but they had come back to haunt her. Somewhere in her mind, she realized Sam was talking to her.

"Are you asleep back there?"

"No, just wandering. How close are we?"

"About ten minutes."

"Ten minutes?" Arcineh's voice betrayed her panic.

"Yes. Are you all right?"

"I need to stop!"

Sam did not argue. He pulled off the road as soon as it was safe, and Arcineh opened her door. She swung her feet out to rest on the cold curb and attempted some deep breaths.

"Arcie?" Sam was in front of her—he'd even hunkered down on his haunches to be at her level.

"I don't know if I can do this," she said breathlessly.

"I know it's a lot to ask, but try to trust me on this."

"You don't know, Sam," Arcineh whispered. "It was awful."

"Yes, it was, but unlike before, I'll believe everything you tell me." Sam looked into her face and knew that she was ready to back out. He had to try something. "Try to think back as far as you can to the old Quinn, the Quinn that was fun and not mean. That's the Quinn she is now."

"What happened?" Arcineh asked with a good deal of doubt.

"She believes differently."

"Like you?"

"Yes," Sam said briefly, not explaining how recent a decision Quinn had made for Christ, but still knowing she was a woman at peace for the first time.

Because she was still sorting out her feelings concerning Sam, Arcineh wasn't sure it was much of a comfort, but she did eventually nod and close the door. Sam put the car back in motion, and Gage had all he could do not to turn and speak to Arcineh. He hadn't turned around once, but missing the conversation was impossible. Sam had brought him as an impartial party, but he found himself not trusting this Quinn person for the simple reason that she'd hurt Arcineh.

∾

The two-story house was lovely. Arcineh could see that Quinn had decorated with good taste, and it felt like a home. For some reason this helped Arcineh. And Quinn helped too. She didn't attempt to hug Arcineh or act overly excited and sickening about seeing her. Indeed Quinn got down to business in very little time. Arcineh didn't know where her aunt and uncle were at the moment, but she was soon climbing the stairs behind her cousin in order to see the baby.

"She's only been asleep a little while," Quinn said without attempting to whisper, "or I would get her up."

"No, don't wake her," Arcineh said, hating the thought and not sure she wanted to hold the child.

"This is Megan," Quinn said, the pleasure in her voice was unmistakable. Arcineh peeked down into the crib and could not stop her smile.

A miniature Quinn lay on the soft-looking sheet, her hair dark and fluffy. Arcineh could even make out Quinn's nose and mouth.

"Oh, Quinn," Arcineh breathed, relaxing for the first time since waking that morning. "She's amazing."

"I think so," Quinn said with the shyest smile Arcineh had ever seen from her.

"Was it hard for you, being pregnant and all that?"

"At times. I was sick at the beginning, and that's not very fun. The labor is tough, but you forget all that really fast."

Arcineh looked back into the crib, trying to sort out her cousin, much the way she wanted to Sam. She could feel herself wanting to cry and looked at the walls for a distraction. There was quite a bit to see. Quinn had put baby pictures up, but not just of Megan. Next to some of the shots was her own picture, and the resemblance was startling. Arcineh was still in the midst of this when Tiffany entered the room.

"Quinn," the grandmother wasted no time in saying, "who is that fabulous-looking man in your living room?"

"He's a friend of Arcie's," Quinn explained just as her mother spotted her niece.

"I didn't see you, Arcie. Come and give me a kiss."

Arcineh complied, not attempting to speak or correct Quinn's assumption.

"A friend?" Tiffany lost no time. "If you'll listen to your aunt—although no one ever does—you'll snap him up in a hurry."

Arcie didn't comment, but Tiffany didn't notice because she was talking again, this time about an outfit she'd seen at Nordstrom's and how slimming it would be on Quinn. Not seconds later she said she needed to speak to her father about something and sailed back out the nursery room door. Not until she left did Arcie realize her aunt hadn't even peeked in the crib. She refused to believe that was normal behavior for a grandmother, and when she looked at Quinn, she knew that it bothered her as well.

Quinn's smile was sad as she met Arcineh's eyes and said, "Some people never change, Arcie."

Arcineh read the pain in her cousin's eyes and said exactly what she was thinking.

"That's certainly not true of you, Quinn. You have changed." Arcineh stared at her for a moment. "And your baby is beautiful."

"Thank you," Quinn managed, bending over the crib to hide the moisture in her eyes.

Arcie didn't linger but left the baby's room. She walked back down the stairs and followed the voices to the living room. With no idea as to what prompted her, she sat down next to Gage on the sofa when the rest of the sofa was empty. His arm had been resting along the back, and he shifted enough to look down at her but didn't move his arm. Because Sam and Jeremy were in a discussion and Tiffany was not in the room, they could talk for a moment "alone."

"Are you all right?" Gage asked quietly, bending his head just enough.

"I think so." Arcineh slanted a look at him. "My aunt tells me I'm supposed to snap you up."

Gage laughed softly before saying, "Remind me to thank her."

Arcineh looked at him for a long moment. If she doubted the interest she thought she might have noticed in his eyes, she doubted no longer. Gage did nothing to hide his attraction, his gaze taking in every detail of her face and hair before settling back on her eyes.

She looked away before saying, "I don't think you know what you'd be getting yourself into. I'm damaged goods—rather broken right now."

"All of us would have to say that," Gage countered. "But I come with extra Band-Aids."

Arcineh turned again to look at him and then couldn't pull her eyes away. It was a remarkably kind and romantic thing to say. She would have questioned him about it or just gone on looking into his eyes if Tiffany hadn't returned. That lady walked into the room, her voice alone demanding everyone's attention.

"I wasn't going to do this right now," Quinn began. She was nursing Megan and had caught Arcineh alone after lunch. "I mean, I was going to write to you and not try this in person, but you're here and I want to say I'm sorry. I treated you so badly when all you wanted was my friendship, and I'm sorry, Arcie. I can't tell you how sorry I am."

"Why did you, Quinn?" Arcineh asked. "What was it about me that you hated?"

"I think I was just jealous and insecure to begin with, and then I saw you having Grandpa to yourself all the time. It didn't have anything to do with you—there was enough of him to go around—but I didn't see it that way at the time."

"Sam told me you'd talked to him about it."

"He really didn't know," Quinn said with a small shake of her head. "He really thought that you were as much to blame as I was. I was sick when I realized what I'd done. All the lies I'd told. When you left, I never dreamed you'd stay away. Grandpa was angry at first, but then he began to miss you. For a while I was even threatened by that, but then the months went by and I missed you too. Your leaving was supposed to take care of all my problems, but it didn't come close. And then when you didn't come back for all those years, I knew I had to tell Sam how bad it had been. Did you call a few times?" Quinn suddenly asked.

"Yes."

"I knew it. At first I was glad you hung up, but then I wanted to talk to you. I tried dialing that call-back number, but I must have written the number down wrong because it never worked."

"It wouldn't have done any good," Arcineh admitted. "I was angry for a long time."

"I don't expect you to just get over it, Arcie," Quinn knew she had to add. "It's not that easy. But I did want you to know how much I regret my actions."

"Thank you," Arcineh said, not sure what the correct reply might be.

An awkward silence fell on them just then. Arcineh didn't want to talk about it anymore, but she didn't know how to change the subject.

"Do you want to hold her now?" Quinn asked, done with nursing.

Arcineh nodded, taking the one-month-old baby in her arms, glad that no other words were needed. The silence was no longer uncomfortable. Both women were content to sit and watch the baby sleep.

Arcineh actually enjoyed her day. Her Uncle Jeremy was perfectly delighted to see her and made the same assumption as Quinn had that Gage and Arcineh were a couple. Tiffany was just the same, gossiping about this and that, but unlike the past, Sam and Quinn never commented or argued with her.

And Gage was simply constant. He stayed fairly close to Arcineh but didn't act as though no one else was in the room. The ride home was much more relaxed, and the three of them talked.

"I'll walk you to your door," Gage offered when Sam pulled back up to the apartment building.

"All right. Thanks, Sam."

"You're welcome. I'll come by tomorrow and get you for lunch."

"Okay. Is it all right if I bring more laundry?"

Sam sent her off with "You don't even need to ask."

Gage opened Arcineh's door and then walked behind her to her apartment. Arcineh didn't get her key out but turned to look at the man, not sure what to say. Gage knew exactly what he wanted to say.

"Can I have your phone number?"

"I don't have a phone right now."

Gage looked completely fascinated by this and asked, "Why is that?"

"Money is a little tight since my roommate got married and moved out."

Gage had the same reaction Sam did—he wanted to jump in and take care of her.

"Just out of curiosity," the man went on, "if you had a phone number, would you give it to me?"

Arcineh studied him. Clearly there was a whole lot more to this man than she had already seen. A part of her heart was filled with doubts, but if she was forced to be honest, she wanted to know more. She smiled before saying, "Yes."

Gage smiled as well. "I'll see you later," he said, watching her all the while.

Arcineh used her key and got the door open enough so that Gage would turn and go. He moved off and she slipped inside. She didn't take advantage of her neighbors, using their phone only if there was a real need, but tonight she might have to make an exception. She thought if she couldn't talk to Jalaina, she would burst.

CHAPTER

Eighteen

"Okay, so where did you meet your friend Jalaina?" Sam asked on Sunday afternoon. For a time he had not pressed her to share her life, fearful that she would run away again, but they were both beginning to relax.

"At a café," Arcineh said, telling him the story about the way she'd hit Mic and causing her grandfather to laugh.

"And you went home to live with her, just like that?"

"It was a little more planned than that. I'm sure you figured out a long time ago that my leaving was very calculated."

"Not until I found you'd taken your personal papers from the bank. Then I knew."

"I never even told Violet that there was a person named Jalaina Ciofani. And that was deliberate. When I said I was going to stay with a friend, I assumed she would think it was Daisy or someone like that."

"That's exactly what we'd both thought," Sam confirmed, thinking of all the people he'd checked with. He was subtle about it, but he'd even gone to see Geneva Sperry, only to be told she hadn't seen Arcineh in weeks.

"And what about now, Arcie? What are the odds I'm going to come to your apartment and find it empty?"

"I'm not going to do that."

"I hope if you do move again, you'll tell me where. Even if you don't want me contacting you, it would be good to know where you are."

"I don't think that's going to be the case—why would I?"

"I don't know, but I guess we're both a little gun-shy at this time."

"I'm done running, Sam."

"Why is that, do you think?"

"Because you believe me," Arcineh said simply, and Sam's heart knew nothing but relief. Arcineh was reaching for more pizza, the most natural thing in the world. Sam next asked about her dancing, and even though he knew his heart was completely different, they visited like old times, something Sam had yearned for for a very long time.

❧

On Monday night after work, Arcineh had been out of the shower for only ten minutes when someone knocked on her door. She peeked through the hole to see Gage in the hallway and had to wipe the smile from her face before opening it. The moment she did, he held a small cell phone out to her.

"What's this?" Arcineh asked.

"Have you not seen one of these?" He was all at once solicitous, exaggeratedly so. "This is a wonderful invention. It's called a telephone, and you press numbers into it and then talk to people."

Arcineh tried not to even smile, but his tone and face had been outrageous. With a laugh, she took it from his hand.

"I can't afford this right now."

"Did I say anything about getting money from you?"

"No, but I'm not sure I get the point."

Gage leaned until his face was close to hers. "I want to call you. That's the point."

Arcineh looked into his amazing gray eyes and wanted to melt, but doubts rushed in swiftly. When Gage saw them, he straightened up. Not until that moment did he look beyond her. Without even asking for permission, he scooted past her and into the apartment. He looked in every direction before turning back to her.

"You don't have any furniture."

"I have a chair," Arcineh said, "and a mattress."

"With or without a frame?"

"Without."

Gage looked at her, his brows raised, but Arcineh didn't let him say anything.

"You have lived in luxury way too long, Gage Sefton," Arcineh told him, her chin tilted stubbornly. "It might do you good to find out what you can do without."

Gage smiled at her and turned to look around the room again. It was all very neat, but empty.

"So what's for dinner?" he suddenly asked.

"I haven't gotten that far."

"Why don't I pick something up for us? If I recall, you liked those burgers we had at the apartment that night."

"How do you remember that?"

"There's very little about you I can forget."

"Why is that?"

"I don't know. I thought you were such a shy, sad little thing at the office, and that broke my heart. I wanted to see you laugh."

"How are things at the office?" Arcineh asked, making herself ignore the personal comments.

"Getting better. I'm distracted knowing this trial is coming up, but we're still trying to do business."

"I miss talking to Mallory and Victoria."

"They liked you too."

"How do you know that?"

"Things are different now. Patrice is running things differently, and I'm talking to the other women and not leaving that all to her."

"I'm impressed," Arcineh said honestly.

"Well, a certain frumpy little employee, who happens to know quite a bit about business, informed me of a few things."

"And after the way she talked to you," Arcineh said, "you still want to spend time with her?"

Gage didn't answer. He looked at Arcineh, who looked right back.

"How about we go out?" Gage suggested.

"I'm not very dressed," Arcineh spoke, glancing down at her jeans and old sweatshirt.

"It's the burger place. Jeans are perfect."

"Is it very expensive?"

"It's not, but I'm still paying for your dinner."

Arcineh still hesitated. Gage kept watching her.

"Yes," he finally said quietly, going back to third person, "I want to spend time with her."

Arcineh relaxed a little and said, "I'll get my coat."

❧

"So tell me," Gage asked over dinner. "Why don't you find another roommate?"

"Because there will never be another Jalaina, and I don't want anyone else."

"And moving back in with Sam would be what, impossible?"

"Not at all, but he hasn't mentioned it, and I'm not going to ask. I am 22, by the way. It's not as if I shouldn't be out on my own."

"There's a difference between being out on your own and being alone with no furniture or social life."

Arcineh looked down at the table. He had managed to make her sound rather pathetic. She knew he wasn't trying to be cruel but just making an observation.

"It's just the way it is right now," Arcineh ended up saying. "And I do do things on the weekend."

"Like what?"

"See friends."

"When was the last time you saw a movie?"

Arcineh didn't answer. There wasn't a lot of extra money, but she didn't like to keep going back to that.

"Is there anything good playing these days?" she asked.

Gage smiled. "You dodged that very nicely."

Arcineh looked for the waitress, and Gage didn't push her. After their food arrived, however, he did mention going with her on a real date.

"A real date?" Arcineh asked.

"Yes." Gage did not let her distract him. "I was thinking dinner and a show."

"Are you seeing someone right now?" Arcineh asked.

Gage looked genuinely surprised.

"No, I'm not. Why would you ask that?"

"I don't know you very well. Maybe you like seeing several women at one time."

"For months now the only thing in my life has been my business."

Arcineh nodded, wishing she'd kept the question to herself. This man rattled her, and she did not know what to do about it. At the same time, she did not want to compete with other women. He said Patrice was engaged to be married, but Arcineh was not convinced that the woman was not in love with her boss. If that was possible, Gage might also love Patrice and not know it.

"I don't suppose you want to tell me what you're thinking," Gage cut into her thoughts.

"I don't mind," Arcineh answered. "I was thinking about Patrice. When will she be married?"

"This summer."

"Will she keep her job at Rugby?"

"As a matter of fact she and David recently decided to live in Indianapolis, where he's from. I would ask you to apply for her job, but I couldn't handle having you around all day every day."

"What's that suppose to mean?"

"Nothing hidden. I simply find you distracting."

"I could wear my frumpy clothes," Arcineh offered, knowing she didn't really want the job.

"I felt you could have looked better, but contrary to what you believed, you were not repulsive in those outfits. Not even close."

Arcineh knew this was the crux of the matter. She hadn't looked repulsive, but neither had she been appealing, and yet this man had still been attracted. This fact made him much too fascinating, and Arcineh feared losing her head and heart.

"What does it mean when you get quiet?" Gage asked.

"I was just thinking. You're different from any man I've known. You don't add flirting to your compliments. In fact, you make them sound very genuine. But I still don't know you, and I tend to be drawn to men who look like you, only to learn they're all wrong for me."

Gage knew it was the worst thing he could do to tell her he was *not* all wrong for her, so he merely nodded. In his heart he was sure. Having seen so many facets of Arcineh Bryant, he was sure they could have an amazing relationship. But it was obvious she wasn't ready to hear this.

"Now you can tell me what it means when you get quiet," Arcineh said.

"I'm just thinking about the fact that I'm not going anywhere. I don't plan to give you any other reasons to hate me, and I'm your grandfather's neighbor."

"I don't think I ever hated you."

"Not even the day you walked out of the office?"

"I was pretty angry, but I don't think I was hateful."

"You had every right to be," Gage was saying when their food arrived. Arcineh didn't reply. She would have agreed with him until just recently, but had suddenly realized how swiftly time slips away. She didn't want to waste any time on hating. Seeing Quinn with a baby and knowing that her grandfather was already 70 had done this to her heart.

"Is your food all right?" Gage asked. He'd been watching how slowly she ate.

"Yes, I'm sorry. My mind was wandering."

Gage wanted to know where it had gone but knew that he had pumped her enough. Hoping she would simply want to talk about herself, they both fell to eating.

∞

"What do you think of Gage?" Arcineh asked of Sam when he brought lunch on Wednesday.

"I like him. I like him a lot. Why?"

"He brought me a cell phone on Monday night, and then we went for hamburgers."

"I got the impression last Saturday that he might be interested in you."

Arcineh nodded distractedly.

"Are you all right with that?" Sam asked.

"I think so. He seems a little too good to be true."

"In what way?"

"Well, I was drawn to him when I worked for him, and now I think he's drawn to me."

"What makes that too good to be true?"

"I don't have good instincts when it comes to men. They usually turn out to be all wrong."

"So how do you decide?" Sam asked, wishing he knew about the hurts she had in the last four years.

"I don't know. I hate breaking off with someone but don't know how to avoid it without staying alone the rest of my life."

Sam stayed quiet and listened as she shared. Just that morning he'd talked with Pastor Simon about not worrying over Arcineh. Sam wanted her to believe, but there was nothing he could do about that. Simon had given him some very timely advice.

Just keep your relationship with her healthy and real. She'll see the love of Christ in you and find her way. Right now, her most important relationship is with you. You can't choose her friends or husband or where she chooses to live, work, or anything else. She'll be calling the shots on all of that, but you can love her without restraint, and eventually she'll understand.

"This roast beef is good," Arcineh noted, staring down at her sub sandwich. "Which deli did you say?"

"The Submarine Shoppe. It's my favorite these days."

Arcineh ate a chip and Sam smiled at her.

"What are you grinning about?"

"You're just so cute in that White Sox cap, shoving chips into your mouth."

Arcineh smiled before taking a drink of root beer right from the bottle, but clearly her mind was still on Gage.

"So if I began to see Gage, you wouldn't be worried?"

"No," Sam was able to say, thinking about how swiftly he and Gage had hit if off and the amount of time he'd spent with the younger man. In the months they'd lived side by side, Gage had been at his house every night of the week, even weekend evenings when the younger man might have been on a date. The topic was usually Sam's success in business. Gage was hungry to improve his business and listened attentively when asking Sam for advice.

"What do you know about him?"

"He's young to own a company that successful—only 27. He has a sister and a brother-in-law that he's close to. His parents divorced when he was young, and he's had no relationship with his mother for years. His father died just a few years ago. He loves his work and wants to succeed. He's never been in a lawsuit before and doesn't know what to expect."

"He asked me to meet with the lawyers on Friday. I asked Nicky for the afternoon off."

"I'm glad to hear that, Arcie. I think you might be the turning point in this case. Gage made a big mistake when he didn't have his own translator, but he's not unethical. Of that, I'm sure."

Arcineh listened quietly, glad of his input.

"What time do you meet?"

"Two o'clock."

"Will you try to get back to work?"

"No."

"Why don't the two of you come here for dinner?"

"Soup or pizza?" Arcineh teased.

Sam laughed before saying, "I'll have you know, I'm planning to grill steaks."

Arcineh laughed with him and said it sounded fun. She also told her grandfather that he could mention it to Gage. She wasn't ready to ask the man for a date just yet.

⁓

"He gave this to you?" Jalaina asked, holding the small cell phone.

"Yes. He said he wanted to be able to talk to me."

"Has he called?"

"Every day."

"What do you talk about?"

"Nothing serious. Just small things, mostly chitchat."

Jalaina looked at her. "I always wondered who you would marry."

"Jalaina," Arcineh began, "you haven't even met the man."

"But I can tell."

Arcineh decided not to argue with her. She was not sure of anything right now. Gage managed to confuse, delight, and scare her all at the same time.

"How are things with your grandfather?"

"Pretty good. He's religious now, and I don't know exactly what to do with that."

"What do you mean by religious?"

"He's found God, and he's different. He says his relationship with God is personal."

"Personal?" Jalaina asked, finding this interesting. "In what way?"

"He's quoted some verses to me and told me that's how God wants him to live and other verses that talk about how much God loves him."

"Does he feel God loves him personally, or along with everybody else?"

Arcineh shrugged a little but then said, "It sounds like it's all pretty intimate." She paused but then said, "I want you to meet him. When you do, you can ask him about it."

Jalaina thought that might be embarrassing, but given the chance, she knew she would ask questions.

The women talked until Will got home, and then Jalaina insisted they drive Arcineh home. Arcineh didn't want to put them out, but she did appreciate it. Since Gage had said something about her being alone, it had become quite clear to her how right he was.

∞

Arcineh did not dress up to meet with Gage's lawyers, but she still looked good. She wore navy slacks and jacket, a white shell beneath, low heels, and understated jewelry. And although she used a light hand on her makeup and kept her hair simple, she arrived at Gage's office on Friday afternoon looking vastly different than the women on the fourth floor had ever seen.

Victoria, at the first desk, took a moment to place her but then actually came around her desk to hug her.

"How are you?"

"I'm fine, Victoria. How are you?"

"Since you talked to Gage, better than ever."

Arcineh's brows raised in surprise, and she would have asked a few questions, but the door to Patrice's office opened just then. Gage came out.

"I wondered if you might not be here."

"Am I late?"

"Not at all. Come in."

To Arcineh's surprise, she passed none of the other women. Mallory, Felicity, and Patrice were not in sight. Arcineh followed Gage into his office and found three other men. Everyone was introduced and invited to get comfortable, and then questions began. They were kind, although thorough, and Arcineh did her best. The meeting lasted almost two hours and was rather intense at times, but when the men had asked every question they had, they sat back, looking satisfied.

"Very good," Stan Esser, the head lawyer stated. "I think this is just what we need to put this away."

"What are the court dates?" Arcineh asked, rather hoping she'd be done at the Lawson house by then. Stan wrote them on a piece of paper and handed it to her. The men stood, and Gage began to walk them to the door. Arcineh began to follow, but Gage turned.

"Stay here."

Arcineh stopped where she was, wondering what he was up to. Feeling free for the first time, Arcineh began to look around the office. She got close to paintings she hadn't seen before, and even stood for a long time and studied a photo of a young-looking Gage with a man Arcineh assumed to be his father. They looked alike and very happy.

"Can I help you?" a cold female voice broke in.

Arcineh only turned long enough to say, "No, thank you," and went right back to her perusal of the picture. She hadn't expected to react emotionally to seeing Patrice but suddenly knew she was in no mood to speak to the woman. Anger from her last day in this office surfaced without warning.

"I'm sorry, but you can't—" Patrice began, but stopped when Arcineh fully turned to face her.

"Gage told me to stay here," Arcineh informed the other woman. "So unless you now consider this your office, I'll just concern myself with what Gage has to say."

Patrice did not know when it hit her as to who this was, but she felt as though she were moving in slow motion. Every conversation she'd had with Gage concerning Arcineh in the last three weeks came rushing back to her. Not once did he mention that she did not look the same. The woman standing across from her was beautiful. Gage also hadn't mentioned to Patrice that Arcineh would be in the office today.

Patrice truly loved her job and cared for her boss. For these reasons alone, she turned and walked from the room, not saying another word to Gage's guest.

She wasn't two steps from Gage's door when he appeared. There was no way he could miss Patrice's angry face, so he stopped her.

"What's wrong?"

"I didn't know Arcie would be here. Why didn't you tell me?"

"Because you and Mallory had that meeting, and I wasn't sure you'd even be back. I also saw no reason for everyone to be tense about it." Gage paused. "I take it you went into the office."

"Yes," Patrice said shortly, not about to offer anything more.

Gage didn't question her when she moved to her desk. He returned to his office and found Arcineh standing at the windows, which covered two walls of the office. Her back was to him, but her stiff posture told him she was in the same state as his assistant.

"Did something go wrong?" Gage asked, joining her at the glass.

"I didn't expect Patrice to come in, and when her voice had that same tone she used to belittle me in the past, I reminded her that this was your office and you'd told me to stay."

Gage had to smile. He didn't think Arcie was by nature a touchy person, but even Gage had to admit that Patrice could bring out the worst in others.

"Are you ready to go?" Gage asked.

"To Sam's?" Arcineh welcomed the change in subject.

"Yes."

"Do you mind stopping by my place so I can change? It sounds like he's planning a barbeque."

"No, that's fine."

They both started toward the door, but Arcineh stopped.

"Where is everyone?"

"Why does that matter?"

"I'm not here to make Patrice miserable, but neither do I want to be chatty with her."

"Everyone knows I'm leaving for the day. You can say goodbye to whomever you wish, or just ignore them all and walk away."

Arcineh need not have worried. Only Mallory and Victoria were present, and she enjoyed speaking to them before stepping onto the elevator with Gage. He pushed the button, and the doors closed.

"When does Patrice leave?"

"June. Mallory has already been hired to take her place." Gage slanted a glance at her. "Thinking of coming to visit me this summer?"

"Maybe," Arcineh answered, smiling but not looking at him. "Maybe."

CHAPTER
Nineteen

"Why sunglasses?" Arcineh asked of Gage as the three began to eat in Sam's kitchen.

"My father was an ophthalmologist," Gage began. "I was always fascinated with the sunglasses. When I would visit his office, I would spend all of my time trying them on."

"What did you do in college to prepare for that?"

"I took business classes and then had a generous father who had just received an inheritance from his uncle. He lent me the money to start my company. For the first two years I worked seven days a week. Had things not caught on, I would have collapsed, but suddenly the Rugby Shades name was getting noticed, and orders began to pour in."

"And is this what you always dreamed of, working for yourself?"

"Not always, but in college I interned for a small company and learned I didn't like the way they did things. I knew I would pursue sunglasses, but not until then did I think about starting my own company."

"What is the downside?"

"The hours. I work a lot."

Arcineh nodded, wondering if he was truly sincere about seeing her. She didn't know when he would have time. For many years she had lived with a man who owned his own company. She knew first-hand how long the hours could be.

"When do you introduce your new season?" Sam asked, the busi-nessman in him coming out.

"April or May. Some companies unveil theirs earlier, but that works for us."

"What's your most popular line?" Arcineh asked.

"The sport line, and then probably the bike line. Which pair do you have, Arcie?" Gage asked.

"I don't have a pair."

Gage looked surprised and then said, "You were gone by Christmas, weren't you?"

"Do you actually give them out at Christmastime?"

"To the new employees, yes."

"You know, Gage," Arcineh knew she had to say, "I was pretty hard on you that day in the restaurant, but the other side of it is the fact that I was treated well down in files. Your people are kind and work hard, and I was impressed."

"Thank you," Gage said to her, wanting to say how much that meant coming from her but not wanting her to be embarrassed and sorry she'd said that. "I do work with a lot of great people."

For a moment their eyes held. For a moment they forgot Sam was in the room. Not until Sam stood and said he was making coffee did they remember they were not alone. To cover her slightly pink face, Arcineh got up to help her grandfather, teasing him all the while about his new skills in the kitchen.

Gage walked Arcineh to the door with no other plans but to see her safely inside. That worked right up to the moment he remembered what her apartment looked like. Much like before, he slipped past her and went inside. Arcineh shut the door and watched him.

"I have an idea," Gage said. "Why don't you move in with Sam?"

"We've already talked about this."

"But you're still here."

"He hasn't mentioned it, Gage. And I'm not going to." Arcineh had no more said this when she watched Gage's brows go up. "Let me guess," she went on. "You're going to run home and call him."

"No. I'll call from the car."

Arcineh had to put a hand over her mouth. She did not want to laugh and encourage him but thought him so funny. Nevertheless she did not want it to happen this way.

"Let it go, Gage."

"On one condition."

"Which is?"

"That we have a real date next Friday night. Just the two of us—a show and dinner after."

"How dressy are we talking?"

"I'll be in a suit, not a tux."

Arcineh thought about this. She did not have an extensive wardrobe these days and for the first time in many years wished she could go out and buy an amazing dress.

"I've seen you in a black dress that would be perfect," Gage put in when it looked as if she would say no.

Arcineh thought for a few moments longer. Her confused heart told her if she kept Gage at arm's length, she'd never be hurt. At the same time, she wanted to get closer. And each time he mentioned living with Sam, she wanted it more and more.

"That sounds fun," Arcineh heard herself saying, hoping she would not have regrets. "What time shall I be ready?"

"I'll let you know."

The silence that fell around them just then was a bit awkward, but Gage was not put off. He was confident that she would come to trust him, and just as confident in himself that he would not let her down.

When Gage left a few minutes later, Arcineh stood alone in her apartment, simply wishing she could trust her own instincts. He seemed special to her, but she'd been wrong before. Feeling as if she needed to cry, she knew it was time to go to bed.

⁓

"I've met someone," Gage told his sister Saturday morning after she'd given him coffee and started the eggs.

"Someone who isn't in love with your money?" his sister asked with a frown, remembering a woman from the past, someone who saw Gage as a ticket and not a person.

"She doesn't care about money."

"We've heard that before," Erika said, turning to Luke for support.

"How about we hear what he has to say," her husband asked, "or have you decided to hate anyone he brings home?"

Erika went back to the eggs, knowing he was right but still not able to conquer her fears on this topic.

"Is it Sam's granddaughter?" Luke asked.

"You knew about this?" Erika questioned her spouse, who ignored her.

"Arcineh Bryant," Gage supplied. "She finally agreed to go out with me on Friday night."

"What do you mean *finally*?" Erika was clearly not pleased. "What does she object to?"

Both men turned to her, but she was not going to back down on this. She knew it was not only her opinion that her brother was a fabulous catch.

"Tell me, Gage, what's wrong with this woman?"

"She's been hurt and wants to take it slow."

"And you want to…what?" Luke asked.

"As a matter of fact, I'm willing to wait."

These words scared Erika more than any others. Her brother was a driven man. When he wanted something, he went after it and could be relentless. Who was this woman he was willing to be patient for?

It took about two hours to talk it out, but Gage answered the questions of both family members. And he enjoyed it. Any excuse to think or talk about Arcineh suited him fine.

∽

"Tell me she's not run away again?" Violet said into the phone, not even telling Sam hello.

"She has not run away."

"What did she think of her room?"

"She's not living here. She has an apartment."

"Oh!" Violet was stopped by this. She thought Arcineh was home with Sam.

"How often do you see her?"

"Every Sunday, and during the week too."

"You saw her today?"

"Yes. I go get her after church and give her lunch. Sometimes she does her laundry."

Violet fell silent for half a minute. When she spoke again, her tone was desperate. "I've decided to stay the whole time, Sam, but you've got to hang on to her. Make sure she doesn't run before I get there. My heart can't take it."

"I think she'll be here, Vi. Don't worry about it. She would hate it if she spoiled your trip."

"I think that's why I'm staying. I'd rather be there, but I don't want her to feel bad about my coming home."

"You're doing the right thing. Are you having fun?"

"We saw the Louvre today," Violet told him, sounding pleased for the first time.

The two talked about everything she'd seen and done, and how much her friend, Alice, was enjoying the time away. When it was time to get off the phone, she cried as she sent her love to Arcineh, but Sam was able to reassure her, truly believing that Arcineh wasn't going anywhere.

◈

"Do you have a minute?" Mallory asked of Gage the moment he got to his office Monday morning

"Sure, come on in," he invited, surprised to see Victoria with her and Mallory shutting the door behind them.

"We want to tell you something and ask you something."

Taking a seat on the sofa and inviting the women to join him in the sitting area of his office, Gage said, "Shoot."

"We want you to know how much we appreciate what you've done for our jobs and how much we like working here now."

"You're welcome, and I'm glad you like it. That's important to me."

"But we do have a question, and we don't want to overstep."

"Go ahead," Gage said, clearly not worried.

The women looked at each other before Mallory asked, "Did you happen to notice how attractive Arcie Bryant is?"

Gage stared at them. He looked at these very professional women, who did their job well, searched their expectant eyes, and shouted with laughter.

"Well, did you?" Victoria pressed, glad he was taking it so well.

"Yes," he finally admitted. "How could I not?"

"Well, we just want to say that we got to know her a little bit, and we think she'd be perfect for you."

Coming from anyone else, this would have been impertinent, but these women were the soul of caring and discretion.

"We'll get to work now," Victoria offered, and all three stood.

"Thank you," Gage said to them. "I assume this will be our little secret?"

Both women nodded vehemently before slipping out the door and to their desks. Before they went their separate directions, however, they shared a swift conspiratorial smile.

❧

Gage, it's Arcie.

Gage, completely ready to head out the door, decided to listen to the voice mail on his cell phone before planning to shut it off for the night.

It's not going to work tonight, Arcineh's voice went on. *I'm sorry to give you such late notice. I hope you can find someone else to go with you. I'll talk to you later.*

Gage no more let the message end before he dialed Arcineh's cell phone. It rang several times before a woman picked up.

"Arcineh?"

"No, this is Jalaina."

"Is Arcineh there?"

"Yes and no. I take it this is Gage?"

"Yes."

"Well, Arcie is here at my apartment, but she's sound asleep. She's coming down with something."

"She's sick?"

"Yes. Are you still going to the play?"

"No, I'd like to see her."

"Well, that might be best because I have a prior commitment that I can't cancel. I have to leave in an hour. If you could come and take her back to her apartment or to her grandfather's, that would be great."

"Give me the address," Gage requested and wasted no time finding the place. Not sure what he thought about this cancellation, he knocked and waited.

"Well, now," Jalaina said when she opened the door, "Arcie and I never have the same taste in men, but you *are* good-looking."

"Thank you," Gage said, instantly seeing why Arcineh liked the one and only Jalaina. She was warm, beautiful, and real.

"Come in," Jalaina invited.

Gage stepped into the nice apartment, a move that put him directly into the living room. He spotted Arcineh on the sofa and went that way. He stared down at her flushed, sleeping face, wishing she had just told him what was going on.

"Do you know why she came here?" Gage asked.

"She was in a panic. She wanted to go on this date, but she said she felt a little dizzy and odd. I think she has a fever," Jalaina put in. "And then she cried and said her dress would probably be all wrong and wished she could have bought a new one. Then she said you would probably kiss her, and not like the way she kissed, and she just wished she could live with Sam."

Gage stared at the expectant woman in his presence, realizing she'd repeated the words to him just the way she'd heard them. He looked back to Arcineh and then took a seat on the coffee table. He reached out and touched her warm face. She woke a few minutes later.

"Oh, Gage," she pushed into a sitting position, her voice raspy. "How was the play? Did you find someone to go with you?"

"No," he said quietly, reading in her glassy eyes that she was indeed sick. "I got your message and came to take you to Sam's."

"Did I leave you a message?" she asked, frowning against her headache and trying to concentrate.

Gage decided not to answer this. He turned to Jalaina for a few words, made sure he had Arcineh's phone and purse, and started her toward the door.

"I don't want to go to dinner, Gage," Arcineh told him. "I have a headache."

"How about we go see Sam?"

Arcineh didn't answer, but she was afraid if she saw her grandfather she would burst into tears. She planned to tell Gage that, but once she was settled in his car, she just felt like sleeping.

∽

Arcineh woke up Saturday morning, her eyes taking in her room, sure she was dreaming. She still had a headache, but that wasn't the main problem. It was her room in every way. Just as she remembered it. Arcineh wanted to get up and look around. She wanted to find Sam and ask him so many questions, but all she could do was fall back to sleep.

∽

"I haven't said anything to you because Arcie didn't want that, but you needed to know."

Sam had heard Gage out in silence. The younger man had come over as early as he dared, and he and Sam had just had a long, en-lightening talk. Sam knew there was a reason Arcineh had not wanted him in the apartment, but he'd not guessed this.

"You also must know that it wouldn't hurt my feelings to have her living next door."

Sam's eyes twinkled over this admission. He would not say any-thing to Gage or Arcineh, but when he'd met Gage, he thought him perfect for his granddaughter. He didn't know what Arcineh felt, but a relationship between the two of them would not bother him at all.

"So how do I handle this?" Sam put himself on the younger man's mercy—at this point he might know her better. "Do I tell her you told me and ask her what she wants, or find her key and send someone to clear out the place?"

Gage laughed. "I've seen Arcie angry, so I probably wouldn't have the guts to use the key, but I don't think I would stop talking until I had her convinced."

"Maybe I should go talk to her now," Sam said lightly. "She's slightly delirious and would probably agree to anything."

Gage took that as his cue to leave. He wanted to check on Arcineh himself, but knew he couldn't do that. He left his neighbor and took himself home, his heart still next door.

～～～

"It's not that simple," Arcineh told Sam after he'd pled his case. She was still in bed on Saturday evening but had eaten a little soup. "I'm not willing to be waited on anymore. I like cooking. I like doing my own laundry." Arcineh made a sudden face. "I won't fight anyone for the privilege of cleaning the bathroom, but Violet isn't used to sharing your house in that way. I don't know if it will work."

"Violet will do whatever I ask. You know that. And don't forget, she has her own place over the garage. You won't be in her way there. It might take some adjustment here, but she'll do anything to have you back."

Arcineh thought for a moment. "I'm out of work in about two weeks."

"That's good," Sam surprised her by saying.

"Why is that?"

"You've got some things you need to take care of."

"Such as?"

"Two large storage units that are holding all of your parents' things. They don't fit on this property, but I couldn't get rid of them."

"I'd completely forgotten about that."

"And at some point we've got to talk about your money. I'm not going to live forever, and then you'll have even more to deal with."

Arcineh nodded. She knew he was right. It just felt odd to her. She was mature enough these days to admit that extra spending money would be nice, but she was also proud of how hard she'd worked. However, she'd had little time for anything but work in the last four years.

"I think some time off would be nice," she said softly. "I know that's a luxury that many can't afford, but I wouldn't mind having some time with no rent to pay."

"No rent?" Sam teased. "What do you think I am, made of money?"

For some reason tears filled her eyes.

"I missed you, Grandpa," Arcineh said. "If you think it will work, I'll come home."

Sam could not contain himself. Tears filled his eyes. He had never wanted to lose her. His anger over her leaving had eventually cooled, and all these years he'd yearned for her presence. Losing her from his life had felt like Trevor and Isabella dying all over again.

"It's done," Sam said when he could speak. "I'll go and gather whatever you need for the next few days. You live here now."

Arcineh had not had the strength to get out of bed, but when Sam came close to hug her, she clung to him, never wanting to be separated again.

ᴄᴏ

"How are you?" Gage asked when he came over on Sunday morning. Sam had gone to church but had let Gage know that the back door was unlocked.

"Better," Arcineh said. "I actually don't remember even arriving here, so I must be feeling better than Friday night. Except," Arcineh suddenly said, "I completely ruined the evening. Did you do something with the tickets?"

"No, it's not important."

Arcineh stared at him, still not feeling herself but glad to see him.

"Why don't you have a girlfriend, Gage?"

"That's a long story."

Arcineh laid her head back against the sofa and waited.

"Did you know I moved here only a year ahead of Sam?"

Arcineh's head moved against the sofa.

"When I first became a success, I bought all the trappings, the mansion and Ferrari, but then I learned that those purchases draw a lot of unwanted attention. I could never tell if a woman cared for me or my money."

"So you moved here?"

"Yes. I still live in luxury, but with less show. I've taken more time with my sunglasses in the last few years and not tried to think about having a relationship."

"Until now?" Arcineh asked, risking embarrassment.

"Until now," Gage confirmed.

"Why me? Or am I just the one who's getting you started again?"

"Wow, Arcie," Gage had to say. "You are an amazing person, with a very insecure little heart."

"I don't know about being amazing, but I am insecure," Arcineh had to agree. "It doesn't matter that my parents didn't deliberately die. I still felt abandoned. And then, I was not Sam's favorite grandchild. That didn't matter when he wasn't forced to choose between us, but he was suddenly the only parent I had, and he never took my side. He's apologized for all of that, but trust comes hard in those circumstances."

"Are you willing to try?" Gage asked. "If you aren't, I'd want to know right now."

"I am willing. I want to get to know you. I want to throw my hat in the ring, but I might be full of doubts and move rather slowly."

"Slow I can handle, never is too hard. I won't keep hanging around if your heart already knows this is never going to happen."

"What exactly?"

"A relationship with me, and whatever that looks like as time unfolds."

Arcineh could not have asked for a more direct answer. Gage was sure of himself, and she respected his putting the cards on the table. And he agreed to move slowly. She would be a fool not to follow her heart at least a little bit. In the next few minutes, and in so many words, Arcineh told him she was more than willing to give this a try.

∞

"You must be feeling better," Nicky said when he spoke to Arcineh on Tuesday.

"I do feel better, but I might have to knock off early. I get tired."

"That's not a problem. How many more days here?"

"I think only about six. Will that work for you?"

"Yeah, that's good."

Nicky had gone close and looked at some corner work.

"This looks good right here. Your work looks as good as mine."

"Why didn't you take this one, Nicky?"

"Because I'm at the new office building downtown, and that job's going to go on for about a year. This one is too short-term. I've got to make sure we don't mess up in that office."

"But you must have a contract," Arcineh began.

"That says they can cancel. It's too valuable a job for me to be across town all the time."

"How's Libby?" Arcineh asked, changing the subject.

"Sick to her stomach all the time, but just glad to be pregnant."

"Grandma is over the moon, you know." Arcineh had talked to her recently. "She can't believe she'll have two great-grandbabies in one year."

"Marco even said he would babysit, as long as his friends didn't find out."

The two shared a laugh over this before Arcineh went back to work. She was ready to be finished with this job. It was hard when she was tired. Not that she was looking forward to a walk in the park. It was time to go through her past and do some letting go.

CHAPTER
Twenty

"You're going out?" Arcineh asked Sam on Thursday night. She had made dinner, and he'd come to the table in clothing that indicated as much.

"Yes. Each week I have Bible study at Pastor Simon's. This week it's tonight. Do you feel up to coming?"

"It's at his house?" Arcineh sounded as doubtful as she felt.

"Yes," Sam answered, simply waiting.

"I was thinking I might come along on Sunday. That's in a church, right?"

"Yes, and you're welcome."

"I think I'll do that."

"Okay. I'll be home in a few hours."

"All right. If I'm not here, I'm probably at Gage's."

"I'll call you when I get in."

They finished dinner, and then Arcineh started the dishes. Sam was not gone five minutes when she wished she'd gone with him. She didn't want to be in a house full of religious people, but being near him was so important right now. Arcineh finished with the kitchen and then literally sat by the phone, hoping Gage would be home early enough to invite her over.

⟋⟍

"Do you believe in God?" Arcineh asked Gage. He had put a movie in the DVD player, but Arcineh was still thinking about Sam.

"I do believe in God. Do you?"

"I don't know. I mean, I never did, but now I'm starting to wonder."

"What made you wonder?"

"How changed Sam is. Something had to have done that, and he gives all the credit to God. I don't want to believe it, but I don't know what else to do."

"Why don't you want to believe it?"

"Because if God is up there, why did my parents die? And why didn't He do something with my grandfather before I had to spend years away from home?"

"Those are good questions."

"Why do you believe in God?"

"I just always have. My father took my sister and me to church, and I've always believed He was in charge of everything, even when my mother left us. Sam has the most personal belief in God I've ever seen—I don't think I can go that far—but that doesn't mean I don't think God is there. All of this had to come from somewhere, and I think the billions-of-years theory is ridiculous."

Arcineh had to think about that. The movie played, but she looked right through it. Gage looked at her.

"Why don't I just turn this off?"

"What's that?" Arcineh asked, not having a clue what he said.

Gage smiled and hit the off button.

"I'm sorry," she laughed a little. "I don't think I was paying attention."

"I know you weren't."

"You're not supposed to be watching me. There was a movie on."

"Yes, but the actresses in this just aren't as beautiful as you are."

"Now that was flirting."

"It was, wasn't it?"

They smiled at each other, and Arcineh was suddenly glad they had not shared the sofa. Gage on the other hand, was ready to invite her over.

"Sam will be calling soon," Arcineh said after reading his mind.

"My loss," Gage replied.

Both knew they were on thin ice. The attraction was far too strong. Without further words, Gage put the movie back on, and both pretended to be interested in the story.

❧

"Will you consider the greatness of God with me?" Pastor Simon Orr asked the congregation Sunday morning. "Listen as I read Psalm 145:3: 'Great is the Lord, and highly to be praised, and His greatness is unsearchable.' Unsearchable. This is God speaking to us here, and He's using the word 'unsearchable' to describe His greatness. There is no such thing as 'unsearchable' in His world; there is no part of Him that does not know all there is to know; but we do not, and will not, have the same insight into this great God of ours.

"That's not to say that God cannot be known. I see faces all over this room who know Him personally, but none of us will ever stop searching to know and grasp His greatness, not even in eternity. We'll be changed in eternity—so much will be clear—but the infiniteness of God's greatness will always be something we'll yearn to search out."

Arcineh was not missing a word. She had never heard anyone talk like this before. Coming that morning, she had thought she would be nervous, especially when she learned that Gage would be joining them, but she was not. She sat between the two men, taken with the pastor's words.

"But I'm going to keep trying." Simon went on. "God's greatness might be inexhaustible, but I'm going to keep at it. So now turn with me to one of my favorite verses on this subject in the first chapter of Genesis."

Gage had actually brought a Bible. Sam shifted his toward Arcineh at the appropriate time, pointed, and let her read with him.

" 'In the beginning God created the heavens and the earth.' I think it might be easy to read past this verse swiftly, but we've got to stop ourselves. Our unsearchably great God has done the miraculous here. He created heaven and earth!

"Do not yawn over this statement. Gasp in wonder and awe. In fact, do more than that, gasp all week. Come back to these seats next Sunday, amazed at the great God we have, and amazed that He wants to be a part of your life, save you, conform you, and have a relationship with you."

Pastor Simon had a few more words to end his sermon, and then they sang a new song they had worked on as the service began. Even the words of the song made Arcineh think. She didn't try to sing but stared at the words printed on the back of the bulletin, trying to take in each one.

What does my soul cry out for more than the truth?
What does my spirit thirst for more than holiness?
I long for light from the Word, and sight from the Lord.
I want to be like my Savior and God.

So work in me, and save my soul.
Oh cleanse my heart, and make me whole.
Oh make us one in righteousness.
Pour out Your power and send Your grace.

Arcineh did not let her mind wander one time, but not everything made sense. She planned to ask Sam about some of it but hadn't counted on Gage beating her to it. They were no more in the car when he began.

∽

"So Pastor Simon thinks you can have a personal relationship with God too?"

"Yes, he does," Sam answered.

"But the God he just described is immense. He's totally unattainable."

"From a human standpoint you're right, but a supernatural work went on when God sent His Son to give us a path to Him. Simon didn't go into that this morning, but it's true."

"The cross," Gage guessed.

"Yes. What do you know about it?"

"The cross itself, not very much, but Jesus is the most pivotal figure in history. I'm just not convinced that He's God."

"Then why did He die?"

"Well," Gage reasoned, "I think *He* thought He was God."

"Gage, who do you think He is?"

Gage didn't answer right away. Why did Jesus have such an effect on history? There had been many men throughout the ages who had left their mark, but not like Jesus had.

"I don't know," Gage suddenly said.

"Arcie?" Sam glanced in the back to speak to her.

"I'm here."

"Are you all right?"

"Yes, just thinking."

"Anything you want to talk about?"

"I don't know. I can't put it into words right now. I liked Pastor Simon, but I didn't understand everything he said, and I hate missing the point."

"Just think about this one thing, Arcie," Sam decided to say. "God wants to enter the life of each one of us, but He'll not shove His way in. If you're open, you can understand everything God wants from you and for you."

The three continued the ride in silence. It had been a tense morning for Sam, but at some point he knew he would have to stop trying to save his granddaughter and Gage Sefton. He didn't think there could be anything sweeter than the two of them coming to Christ and making a life together in Him, but he realized this was his plan and might never be God's.

Somewhere along the line in talking to Gage, Sam knew that he could not sit back and worry. He would have to give direct answers and ask direct questions, but the balance between not wanting to overwhelm and fear that he would offend was a hard line to walk.

For the moment he was all right with the silence, but he was going to get back to his granddaughter on all of this. She might not embrace his beliefs, but there would be no doubt in her mind as to what he believed.

❧

"Okay, I've thought about it," Gage said to Arcineh late in the day on Sunday. "Our first official date is going to be a little more low-key. Nothing fancy, no set times."

"All right," Arcineh said, not sure why having an official date was so important but thinking him very sweet and romantic. "Where are we going?"

"I'm not going to tell you."

"How will I know how to dress?"

"Casual."

"Which kind of casual? Business casual, or barbeque-in-the-park casual?"

"As casual as you want, just as long as you're comfortable from head to foot."

Arcineh laughed at him but still said, "What will you wear?"

"Jeans and a long-sleeve shirt with comfortable loafers."

Arcineh's eyes narrowed. Dressed like that they could be going any number of places. Arcineh was not an overly curious person, but this might drive her crazy.

"Well, I'd better get home," Gage said, enjoying himself a little too much.

Arcineh watched him move toward the door. Just before he went out, he turned and smiled at her. Arcineh did her best to frown, but Gage's smile only grew larger.

∽

"I'm going to try and wrap up here this week," Arcineh told Nicky on Monday morning. "I think if I work a little longer each day, I can get it done by Friday."

"It's up to you." Nicky's shrug was real. "It can go into next week, you know."

"I'll only do that if I have to. I probably would have been done for sure this week if I hadn't gotten sick."

"Grandma wants to hear from you."

"Okay. Tell her I'll call."

"No, she wants you over so she can feed you and meet this guy."

"How does she know there's a guy?"

"She has her ways."

"You mean, you talked."

"I might have."

Arcineh laughed.

"She means it," Nicky said now. "You'd better get over there."

"Yes, sir."

"Don't try that 'sir' business with me. I saw you drive up in your fancy car."

"I'll have you know that's the one I got for my fifteenth birthday. It's in great condition, but hardly new."

"Why are you driving it now?"

"Because my grandfather's been bringing me, but today he's visiting my cousin and her baby."

"How's it going with your grandfather?"

"It's going well. It feels amazing to be home."

"Where to from here?" Nicky asked, fairly certain she would not work for him again.

"My grandfather has asked me to work on some things in storage. My parents' things."

Nicky nodded. At times it was easy to forget how alone she had been. She never complained or let on.

"Don't forget us," he finally said.

"That's not possible," Arcineh said as see turned to her work, knowing if she looked at him for a moment longer, she's be tempted to cry.

"Are you feeling better?" Tina asked Arcineh before the Windy City Troopers could start on Tuesday night.

"I am, thanks. Did I miss anything big?"

"No, but I think you look pale, so do me a favor and don't faint or hurt anything."

"I never faint," Arcineh replied dryly, "and I'm pale because it's March."

Tina only smiled at her. It was time to start class and work on their number for the fundraiser for the children's wing at the hospital.

"I have a question," Arcineh said to Sam when she arrived home.

"Okay."

"Do you believe you'll go to heaven when you die? Do you believe in heaven and hell now?"

"Yes to both of those."

"Where are my parents?"

"I can't know that for sure, Arcie. We never talked about God, so I have no encouraging memories to draw on."

Arcineh's eyes closed.

"Listen to me." Sam's voice came to her. "I have chosen to trust God for this, Arcie, but it doesn't change the fact that I grieve over the choices I made, choices that surely affected the choices my son made. But I know this: God is in control and He died for your parents as He died for you and me."

"But if hell is real, it's awful."

"It is awful, Arcie, but there's nothing I can do about that. Much as I love and miss your folks, you're here and now. That's my main focus."

"But you trust a God who will cast people out."

"Yes, I do, but it doesn't have to be that way. All people have or had a chance to accept Him. Even your parents."

Arcineh fell quiet then. Sam too, his heart prayerful. He had known that Arcineh would ask this, but he could not shrink back from the truth, even when he feared it might drive her away. He begged God to give Arcineh a hunger and answers when He did.

How many times, Arcineh was asking in her heart, *am I going to be asked to be separated from the people I love? How alone do I have to be?*

"I have to think about this," Arcineh said, not wanting to think about those questions. "I just don't want it to drive us apart."

"I don't want that either. You must believe that."

Arcineh knew it was true—she could read it in his eyes. She was opening her mouth to tell him the same thing when they both heard the front door. Violet was home.

⁂

"Tell me you are not up and making coffee!" Violet said, arriving in the kitchen after Arcineh, thinking it might be the first time she'd made coffee in her life.

Arcineh laughed before saying, "I've got to get to work."

"Today?" Violet sounded as disappointed as she felt. "I come rushing back from Europe, and you're not going to be here."

"You did not rush back, and this is my last week on the job."

Violet smiled at being caught out. She had been so wound up the night before that she hadn't fallen asleep until late. Getting up had been almost impossible, and she hadn't beaten everyone to the kitchen, which was her way. Jet lag was wearing on her, but she had to see her girl.

"Why don't you go back to bed? I'm not even eating breakfast."

Violet ignored this suggestion and continued to watch Arcineh making sandwiches and then preparing a huge travel mug of coffee, adding cream and sugar.

Arcineh felt her eyes on her and wondered if she was all right with all of this. A glance to the side showed her all was fine. Violet's elbow was on the counter, her chin propped in her hand, clearly having the time of her life.

"I have to go," Arcineh said with a smile.

Violet came to hug her. "Enjoy your day," she said, just as she had when Arcineh was a child.

Arcineh left, her heart thinking about so many things and wondering at the fact that Violet hadn't changed.

⁂

Arcineh studied the work in front of her, enjoying the even rows and perfectly spaced tiles. She even looked at her own hands, knowing her grandfather would say that God created it all.

Are You really out there? Do You really determine all of this, or are we wound up and allowed to run on our own?

Somehow Arcineh knew that God was listening. She didn't have answers to her questions, but her grandfather kept rushing back to her mind. It was true that they'd only been back in each other's company for six weeks, but the person that he'd become was having a profound effect on her.

Arcineh realized she'd come to a dead stop. She made herself get back to work. Sam was back in her life and she was in his. She wanted that more than anything, and no matter who he was, she was sure he would never again give her a reason to leave.

❧

"I didn't see enough of you this week," Gage said when they left on Friday evening in his car.

"I wanted to finish your great-grandfather's kitchen."

"And did you?"

"I did. By the way, what are you doing with the house?"

"Opening it to the public. I'd like folks to be able to see one of Chicago's old residences. It's going to be as original as we can make it, furnishings and everything."

"You have the original furniture?"

"Most of it. I come from a family of pack rats."

"How much longer will it take?"

"Months," Gage told her. "I just learned that the company that is reproducing the wallpaper is way behind, so we might be looking at a year from now."

"It sounds like it will be worth it."

"I think you're right." Silence fell for a few blocks and then Gage asked, "What's next for you?"

"I have to start through the storage units that hold all my parents' possessions."

"Are you looking forward to that?"

"I don't know yet. It might be interesting, and it might be painful."

"What's there exactly?"

"Well, we went through things the summer after they died, and I knew I didn't want all their furniture, but anything that I was iffy over, Sam saved. His place was so large that he just packed a few rooms with it, but now it's sitting in storage, and it's time I decided what to keep."

"What will you do with what you keep?"

"I don't know. Maybe I won't want that much, and I can take a reasonable amount. There is room at Sam's house for quite a bit, but I need a good reason to keep things, especially since I live in a furnished home."

"Are we talking photos and such?"

"Yes."

"That might be a little hard."

"I think so too."

When Arcineh fell quiet, Gage let her be. He remembered going through his father's things and what a painful process that had been. He and Erika had waited about a year, and maybe that was too soon. Arcineh's parents had been gone for years. Maybe that would make it easier.

"The Shedd?" Arcineh suddenly asked, seeing where he was headed. "We're going to the Shedd?"

"Um hm."

"I love the Shedd."

"I think I knew that."

"Do you like it?"

"I love it—always have."

Arcineh got out of the car like a kid at Disneyland. It had been so long, and she couldn't wait to get inside.

Gage, standing by the car watching her, waited for her eyes to meet his. As soon as they did, he bent and kissed her.

"What was that?" Arcineh asked.

"Just a kiss. Now we can relax."

Arcineh studied him a moment. "Is that what it did, relax you?"

Gage studied her right back. "Not in the least."

Arcineh laughed at his face as well as his tone. But she did not hesitate when he reached for her hand and started toward the building.

Twenty-One

"Look at this fish," Gage pointed through the glass, and the two watched a neon tetra glide slowly by.

"Maybe Sam and Pastor Simon are right," Arcineh said, amazed at the color. "I'm not sure any of this could have just happened."

"Have you been thinking about our Sunday conversation all week?"

"Constantly."

Gage put an arm around her and began to walk them along. "What bothers you the most?"

"Being left alone again."

"I'm not going anywhere."

"You'd better not," Arcie said, "but I want Sam too." She looked up at him. "If heaven is there and he's going, I want to go too."

"It sounds wonderful," Gage agreed. "I wonder if there's any real way to know."

Arcineh didn't have any answers, but it felt good to talk about it. They stopped for a long time to look at the seahorses and then went to the Soundings Restaurant where Gage had already booked a table. They sat at the window and looked out over Lake Michigan.

"Tell me about your sister," Arcineh asked when they'd ordered their food.

"How did you know about Erika?"

"Sam. I asked about you."

"Ah, checking up on me."

"Guilty."

"Well, Erika is three years older than I am and married to Luke Barnett. I see them every week or two."

"Children?"

"No. That part of their lives has not gone so well. Erika has never conceived in at least six years of trying. They've just started looking into adoption, but it's too early to know how that will go."

"And you're close to them?"

"I am. My dad is gone, so it's been good to have them living in the Chicago area with me."

"Were you born here?"

"No, but both Erika and I went to Northwestern and wanted to stay. Did you go to college here?"

"I didn't go to college at all. I was so tired of school when I finished high school that I had no desire to go on. I still don't love the idea. I think if I knew what I wanted to study, I might, but not right now."

"So where did you learn Italian?"

Arcineh laughed, and Gage got ready for a good story. She told him about being whisked off to Italy with a few hours notice and then eventually living with Jalaina and her family.

"Grandma spoke Italian to me every day. I couldn't help but get good at it."

"And Nicky and Jalaina are her grandchildren?"

"And Marco. He's still in high school."

"Where are their parents?"

"Their mother never married their father, and he left when Marco was a baby. Then Jalaina's mom took off a few years later, and Grandma moved in."

"And where do they all live now?"

Arcineh explained the changes Nicky's marriage had made, where everyone lived, and when all the babies were due. She finished with, "I want you to meet them. In fact, Grandma expects it. She wants to feed me and meet you."

"Should I be afraid?"

"Not unless you're playing games with me."

"That's the last thing I would do."

"What's the first?" Arcineh flirted a little.

Gage looked at her mouth.

Arcineh reached for her water. It was suddenly very warm in the restaurant.

❦

"Have more lasagna," Grandma commanded Arcineh before she was finished with the first helping. "You too, Gage."

Before it was over, everyone had more on their plate, even Sam. It was delicious, however, and everyone's praise was genuine.

"I'm going to explode," Arcineh told the woman in Italian.

"You're skinny," she fired right back. "It's the way Nicky works you."

"What?" Nicky could not let that go, but he was speaking in English. "She's done, off to lead a life of luxury."

Jalaina threw a balled-up napkin at her brother, and Grandma scolded them all. Grandma's sister, Aunt Viola, got her words in as well, but she was mostly taken with Gage.

"He's good-looking," she told Arcineh in Italian, watching the younger man all the time.

Arcineh only smiled and agreed and then laughed out loud when she asked if Sam was single. Arcineh did not let on that Sam could understand every word.

It was hours before the three left Aunt Viola's home, and everyone had to promise to return.

"This is your other family," Sam said from the backseat. Arcineh had driven.

"Yes. It was not without challenges, but they took me in and treated me like their own. And Aunt Viola wants to treat you like family as well, Sam," Arcineh teased.

"Be that as it may, she couldn't take her eyes from Gage."

"That's hard for any woman to do," Arcineh said, loving Gage's pleased smile as she put the car into motion.

∽

"I had a man in my office this week," Simon said from the pulpit. "He lost his brother about five years ago. He had not stopped grieving for him in all this time, and he thought the answer to his hurt might be in God, so he came to see me.

"We talked about God's plan for man and the life that only God can give, but this man could not get past the fact that if his brother had not believed, he was lost. I don't know if I'll see that man again. I opened my Bible to passages that talk about God's love and His work on the cross, but he wanted me to pray for his brother. He did not want to accept the fact that his brother's decisions were made while he was alive, and there was nothing more for us to do.

"I showed him in Scripture where Jesus talks about Lazarus and the rich man, but he would not accept it when I told him that all he can do now is make sure *he's* ready to meet God. He didn't believe me when I told him that if his brother were not with God in eternity but had a chance to come back and tell him the right thing to do, I know he would say, 'Run to the cross. Run as fast as you can to the cross of Christ.'"

Pastor Simon looked out on his flock, his eyes a little moist.

"How many do I need to say it to today? How many in this room? Run to the cross. No matter who's gone before you or will come after you, understand *your* need for a Savior and the great love God is ready to show you through His Son. Be ready for eternity and run to the cross."

Sam sat and listened to this, amazed at the workings of God and asking his heavenly Father to help Arcineh hear Simon's words. She had asked this very thing of him, and he had tried to answer. He wanted to look down at her but forced his eyes to the front, right through the closing prayer.

Not until the service ended did he look at Arcineh's face, and to his gaze she looked a little pale. When she didn't want to linger, he followed her and Gage to the car. And just like the week before, Gage beat her to the punch in asking questions.

∽◈∽

"What if it's all true, Sam?" Gage asked him the moment they were in the car. "If what your pastor said today is true, my father is probably lost. There's nothing I can do about that." Gage sounded as though he was reading a list. "I've got to make sure I'm ready for eternity."

"I think that sums it up," Sam said, having just realized that he'd prayed for Arcineh during the service and forgotten Gage.

"I'm not ready," Gage said to him, Arcineh watching him from the backseat with huge eyes.

"What happened this morning, Gage?" Sam asked. "What did Simon say that has you thinking so seriously about this?"

"It just makes sense for the first time," Gage said. "I mean—" his voice broke a little but he kept on. "I don't know what my dad believed. He was a good man, but he might not have accepted the cross like Pastor Simon says we must. But if it's true, and he's lost for eternity, he would want my sister and Luke and I to all know the truth."

The younger man looked into Sam's eyes, not sure when he'd last felt so vulnerable. He wanted to cry for the first time in years, desperate to understand what had happened inside of him that morning.

Sam's own eyes grew moist, remembering how he felt when he realized that Trevor and Isabella were probably lost. He'd come to the same conclusion. He had to make sure he was ready.

"There is grief that comes with understanding that not everyone will be saved, Gage. The cross is there for the taking—God's Son died for all—but some will choose otherwise. However, you could not be more correct in realizing that you can only answer for you, and that you must not throw your life away because someone else did not make that choice."

"You must also realize that a life lived in Christ and for Christ is the most amazing experience you could possibly imagine. Knowing that God loves me, and wants to help me in every area of my life, brings indescribable peace. I didn't know what I was missing all those years."

Gage suddenly turned so he could look at Arcineh in the backseat. Her eyes were filled with tears. He shifted so he could take her hand. Neither one spoke. There were no words right then.

Sam started the car and put it into gear. It was bitterly cold and time to go home. There they could continue to talk or cry, whatever was needed.

⌘

"I can't be separated from this man again," Arcineh told Pastor Simon concerning Sam. It was later that afternoon. Sam had called him, and he'd offered to come. Gage was also in attendance. The three of them had talked for hours after arriving home. Things were making more and more sense to Gage, but Arcineh felt completely lost.

"Do you believe you sin, Arcie?"

"I don't know if I'd call it sin. I think I do wrong. Everyone does."

"That's very true. That's why Christ died for the whole world."

Arcineh nodded, desperately trying to take it in.

"You can't have salvation vicariously. You can't experience it through Sam."

Arcineh knew that he was right but somehow felt let down.

"May I make a suggestion?" Simon offered.

"Yes."

"Follow Sam's lead. If he goes to church, go with him. If he wants to tell you about a verse, listen to him. If he wants to study the Bible with you, do it."

"What will that do?"

"Well, for one thing, it will help you to see why he believes the way he does. I suspect that right now you don't even know what questions to ask, and that will help you."

"I might find what he has?"

"If you keep searching for God, Arcineh, He will be found. His Word promises just that."

"Where does it say that?"

Simon opened his Bible to Proverbs 8:17 and read, " 'I love those who love me; and those who diligently seek me will find me.' And this next verse is from Jeremiah 29:13. Listen to this, Arcie. 'You will seek Me and find Me when you search for Me with all your heart.' "

The pastor looked at her, and Arcineh could not control her tears.

"I was so afraid," she cried. "I can't be left alone anymore."

Sam was close enough to touch her and reached to put an arm around her. Sam never dreamed that Arcineh would hunger for God so quickly. He wanted to take all the hurt away, but he realized the hurt was probably the very thing that would lead her to Christ.

Gage, on a chair across the room, was ready to confess his need for Christ at that very moment but feared that Arcineh would feel devastated and betrayed.

Simon did not stay much longer. Arcineh had stopped crying and sincerely thanked him for his time, telling him she would think about everything he said.

Sam and Gage walked Simon to the door. Not afraid to have Sam hear, Gage asked Simon when he could meet with him that week. He and Simon set a time. When the men returned to the living room, Arcineh was almost asleep.

❦

"Oh, my," was all Arcineh could say when Sam unlocked the door to the first storage unit and flipped the light on so they could step inside.

Sam knew what caught her attention. It was warm inside with plenty of room to move around. Things were completely organized. Boxes were labeled and shelved. There would be no scrounging around to find what she wanted. A choice off the shelf in the year she wanted was all that was needed. Along with the fact that nothing smelled musty or old. The constant, dry temperature assured that.

"There's more furniture than I remembered."

"I think Mason feared you would change your mind and it would be gone. And don't forget, there is one more of these next door."

"With as much in it?"

"A little less."

Arcineh ran her hand over the beautiful carved mahogany dining table and chairs. They were a small shadow in her mind right now. She couldn't even recall eating at this table, but then she had always been the same in that respect, loving the kitchen most.

"God knew all along that these would be here, didn't He?" Arcineh suddenly turned and asked.

Sam nodded, not surprised to hear these thoughts. She had been talking like this since waking up from her nap the day before. Clearly new thoughts about God were popping into her head all the time.

Unbidden, Arcineh remembered Jalaina and Will's dining table. None of the chairs matched, and one leg on the table had to be propped up with an old paperback book.

"Sam, is there any reason I can't give things away?"

"None at all. Who were you thinking of?"

"Jalaina and Will. At least making the offer of this dining set."

"Are you sure you don't want it?"

Arcineh looked at it, trying to remember something significant about it.

"I'm sure," she said, and this is how it went. Arcineh was almost completely disconnected from the furniture that had been stored for her. She was on the phone off and on for an hour, offering various pieces to Jalaina, Libby, and Grandma. The conversations were humorous as each woman argued and said she must keep her things before giving in.

It was the light moment before the storm. Right after lunch, Arcineh started on the pictures and papers. Thinking to get so much done in the first day, her progress came almost to a halt. Tears she did not want to shed but would not be stopped plagued her for the next two hours. She finally gave up and let Sam take her home, hoping tomorrow would be a better day.

∞

"Unlike Arcie, I've always believed in God, but not like Sam—not in a personal God," Gage shared with Simon on Tuesday morning. "So much of what you said on Sunday makes sense to me, but I don't know what this looks like. And I'm a little afraid to find out."

"I'm glad to know you're taking it seriously, Gage. It's an awesome work that was done on the cross and not to be entered into lightly."

"But it's true, isn't it? Running to the cross—believing in Christ, repenting—will save me, won't it?"

"Yes. Your sins will be forgiven, and you'll have new life in Him."

Gage felt as though a weight had been lifted from him. Forgiveness of his sins. The sound of it alone was amazing to him. All that had been said in the last two Sundays, and everything Simon had shared in Sam's living room, was who he was—a man living for himself, not even aware of how separated he was from God and lost if he didn't do something about it.

"What should I do?"

"You should pray," Simon told him, "and confess to God that you need His saving work on the cross to take away your sins. Tell Him you believe in Him as Lord and Savior, and give your life to Him."

Gage needed no other urging. Bowing his head and praying out loud, he felt as though he could cry all over again. He had prayed before, but never in true humility, and never in such need. When he was done, he felt drained. He asked many questions that Simon answered, but eventually his heart turned to Arcineh.

"I need to tell Arcie about this, and I'm not sure how."

"Is it pretty serious between you?"

"It is for me." Gage suddenly shut his eyes. "The thought of hurting her kills me. I think she'll see this as betrayal."

"Why will she feel betrayed?"

"I think you know about the years she was separated from Sam?"

"Yes."

"She struggles with feeling abandoned. I think she'll see my belief as abandonment. We spent some weeks talking about this and even searching together, and now I've found Christ on my own."

Simon thought about this for a long time.

"I'm going to say something to you, Gage, that's not the normal.

You must hear me out, and repeat it all back to me so I know you understand."

"All right."

"A believer must never marry an unbeliever. Never, Gage."

Gage nodded, his heart heavy.

"To do so is to disobey God in a very serious way. Now, that being said, I don't want you to cut Arcineh off without a chance. You must keep your heart in check. You must want salvation for her more than you want to love her and make her your wife. Because if she doesn't accept Christ, the two of you can't even be a couple, let alone husband and wife. But her heart is bruised and searching right now."

Gage nodded, but it wasn't enough. Simon made him say it all back and then questioned him again to be sure.

"Now, listen," Simon began again. "If this is not an issue where you can keep your heart in check, you'll have to break off with her and leave her in God's and Sam's hands. Not an easy task, I know, but unless you can be careful to guard your now-believing heart, you don't have a choice."

It was too bad that Gage had another meeting scheduled that he could not miss. He was quite willing to do as Simon directed, but he had more questions about the Bible, and he desperately wanted to see Arcineh and Sam.

Thanking the pastor and trying to control his racing thoughts and emotions, he went back to the office, his decision, the morning, and Arcineh filling his mind.

⁓⁓⁓

"You can't be serious?" Jalaina said when Sam and Arcineh followed the moving truck to their apartment. Jalaina had come out to peek in the back, her mouth dropping when she saw the dining table and chairs.

"Do you like them?" Arcineh asked.

"What's not to like?"

The women embraced, and Sam could not stop smiling. He did not expect Arcineh to handle things in this way, and he was unspeakably proud of her. Jalaina and Will were taking the table and chairs, the buffet, two dressers, and a leather recliner. The sofa was going to Grandma, and Nicky and Libby were getting the rocking chair and the bedroom set.

"Arcie," Jalaina said, suddenly taking her by the shoulders, her expanded stomach nearly touching the other woman. "You might change your mind. It might feel like you've lost your parents all over again. Come back for these things if that happens. We'll take good care of these until you're really sure."

"I'm sure. Don't worry about scratching things or babying them— just enjoy these pieces."

Jalaina stared at her and said, "I don't know how to thank you."

"Since when do you run out of words?" Arcineh teased, but Jalaina had tears in her eyes.

"I love you," Jalaina said, and Arcineh said it right back. The men wanted to unload the truck, but that had to wait for just a few minutes. The women hugged in very real friendship, momentarily in a world of their own.

⟡

"My sister has invited us to dinner on Friday night." Gage had come over to see Arcineh on Tuesday night when she returned from dance. Violet had gone to her apartment, and Arcineh was already baking cookies. "Are you free?"

"I think so," she said, but sounded uncertain.

"You'll like Erika."

"Is she protective of you like Patrice?"

"She is protective, but nothing like Patrice. And you'll love Luke. He's very laid back and lovable."

"Should I dress up?"

"No, be very casual."

"Can I bring dessert or something?"

"No, Erika will have it all together."

The timer dinged just then, and Arcineh went to the oven. She put hot cookies on a plate and took them to Gage.

"Peanut butter! These are my favorite."

"Violet told me," she said with a smile.

"Thank you." He smiled back, knowing his news could wait no longer. In short sentences, working to keep his emotions at bay, he told Arcineh about his conversation with Simon.

For one long minute Arcineh said nothing. She could not identify the sensations rolling through her right then and didn't try.

"I'm happy for you, Gage."

"Thank you. I didn't want you to feel left out, but I had to tell you."

"I'm glad you did," Arcineh said over her shoulder, pulling out yet another pan of cookies and adding them to Gage's plate.

"Arcie?" he called her name when she did not look at him.

"Yeah?" Arcineh made herself look up.

Gage read the confusion in her eyes but had no idea what to do about it. Arcineh saw that Gage looked concerned about her but also excited about his news. She wished someone would tell her it was all right to cry or scream because she felt she needed to do both. Sam came into the room, and Arcineh started to breathe again.

"Oh, Gage, I didn't hear you come in," Sam greeted, taking a cookie from the tray.

"Hi, Sam." Gage had no more greeted the man when his phone rang. "Excuse me," Gage said before taking it, and then, "I've got to run home. Stan Esser needs to know about a file on my laptop."

"Okay," Arcineh agreed, mustering a smile.

"We'll see you later," Sam said, not catching anything amiss.

Not until Gage left and Arcineh stood staring into the oven did Sam question her.

"You'll be pleased," she told him quietly. "Gage talked to Pastor Simon today, and he believes like you do."

"He told you this?"

"Yes, and before I forget, I have a performance in the children's wing of the hospital on Saturday. I'll be headed there midmorning."

Sam didn't think his heart could take this. She felt utterly rejected. It was almost like looking into her face after her parents had died. Elated as he was for Gage, Sam felt his own heart die a little too.

"Some people are just supposed to be alone, Sam," Arcineh said, still not looking at him.

"I'll never leave you, Arcie. You must believe that."

Arcineh turned and gave him a sad smile. "I think you really believe that, Sam, but it's just a matter of time before Gage doesn't want me. He has Jesus now. And then I won't be able to live here, being this close when I care so much. I'll be the one to leave."

The timer sounded again, and wordlessly Arcineh took the cookies out. She put them in a container and cleaned up the mess. It felt good to put her hands in warm water as she was suddenly cold.

Her work done, she told her grandfather goodnight. She could tell he wanted to talk, but right now her heart was too confused to take anything in. She climbed into bed but didn't sleep for a long time. She lay looking at the ceiling, trying to understand what God wanted from her.

❧

Please help me, Gage prayed in his bed. *I want You in my life. I know now that I've been searching for You for a long time. Always restless, always searching, always thinking I just had to pour more of myself into*

Rugby. And Arcie, Gage broke off, his heart so hurt he didn't know if he could handle it. *Please show Yourself to her. She needs You as I do. Don't take Sam and me and leave her, please, Lord God. Please.*

Gage cried out to God until exhaustion swept over him. He didn't set the alarm, knowing he didn't have to be in early, but he still had a plan. As soon as he woke, he'd go see Arcineh. With the cell phone off, he would tell her everything Simon had said.

Twenty-Two

"How about we run away today?" Sam was in Arcineh's room before 7:00, inviting her out.

"Where to?"

"I was thinking Galena. Quinn's house is on the way. We could stop and see the baby then and take backroads that eventually land in Galena."

"You don't have anything going on?"

"No, we'll just take off and come back when we're ready."

Arcineh was not going to pass that up. She showered and put herself together, ate a quick bowl of cereal, and went out the door with her grandfather 45 minutes later. She stared at Gage's house as they drove away, unaware that he was calling to talk to her not five minutes later.

❧

"She's so much bigger," Arcineh said, looking down at Megan in her grandfather's arms.

"Eleven pounds at the doctor's office last Friday," Quinn said, her eyes filled with adoration as she looked at her daughter.

"Did she cry when they weighed her?" Sam asked, remembering a long-ago session when Tiffany was a few months old.

"Like they were trying to kill her," Quinn laughed. "Then she slept through the rest of it, completely worn out."

"Does she sleep at night?" Arcineh asked.

"Six hours is the longest she's made it. But it used to be four, so that's an improvement."

"Is she still crying before bed?" Sam asked, shifting her so Arcineh could take her.

"No. Whatever was bothering her is gone now."

"She's smiling," Arcineh said, staring down at the baby's adorable face.

"It's so fun when she does that," Quinn said, seeing it all day these days.

"How are you?" Sam suddenly asked Quinn.

"I'm all right. Tayte doesn't want much to do with either of us, and that suits me fine right now. He just makes me cry when he comes anyway."

"He doesn't want to see Megan?" Arcineh asked.

"No." Quinn's face was very sober. "His new girlfriend doesn't know about him having a baby, so he has to be careful."

"I'm sorry, Quinn. You deserve better than that."

"I wish I had known then what I know now," Quinn said.

"Which is what?"

"That God had a plan. I never even gave God a thought. I was just trapped in my own shell of misery, fueled by my mother's misery, and never thought to look up."

"When did you realize?"

"When Grandpa changed. When he began to pray out loud at meals and was a different person. By then I was engaged to Tayte, a dream come true at the time, and I would never have broken it off, but we hadn't been married a month when I knew it was a mistake. Then Megan was on the way, and I caught him cheating and fell apart.

"Grandpa bought me the house here, but he told me in plain terms that I was destined to be miserable until I humbled myself before God."

Arcineh looked at her grandfather. "Why have you never said that to me?"

"You're a different person. All Quinn could say was 'why me?' That's not the way you think or act. Your need to humble yourself to Christ is just as real, but the process is going to be different."

"What would you say to me if you could say anything?"

"I'd say let yourself be loved by God. Stop fearing His rejection and being alone, and let Him be with you forever."

Arcineh pulled the baby close and laid her cheek on Megan's tiny, soft head.

"You still love God, Quinn, even after all He's let you go through?"

"That's the reason I love Him. I was thinking about killing myself during the pregnancy—that's how much I thought I needed Tayte. I now know better."

Arcineh and Sam did not stay much longer, but something had softened in Arcineh's heart. She kissed Megan's tiny head before giving her back and even hugged her cousin goodbye. She stayed dry-eyed but would not have managed that if she'd known that Quinn sobbed over the hug the minute they were out the door.

‍◦◦◦‍

"Did God make white chocolate?" Arcineh asked when she'd let a few pieces melt in her mouth. They had found a place to lunch, and then Sam had spotted a chocolate shop.

"Well, He made whatever plant it comes from, and the minds that dreamed it up, so I think that qualifies as a yes."

"At times I think I could trust Him, and at other times I think I hate Him."

"I'm sure He's used to that."

Arcineh didn't comment, but Sam had more to say.

"I need you to know something, Arcie. This is all part of God's plan. Just like with Quinn and Tayte when the timing seemed to be all wrong, it's not a mistake that just when you and Gage were getting close, he understood his need for salvation."

Arcineh looked at him.

"I've seen the way the two of you look at each other. You're falling in love with Gage, and I think he loves you in return, but you would both be miserable together in such disunity."

Arcineh didn't comment, but she was thinking. They passed a sign for a rest stop just then, and Arcineh realized she needed to stop. Sam called home while Arcineh was inside.

"Gage has called here three times," Violet told him. "He wants to talk to both of you, but especially Arcie."

"I'll call him, and if you don't see us tonight, don't worry."

"All right, Sam. Take care of that girl."

"Will do."

Sam had Gage on the phone a moment later.

"Have you had your cell phone off?" Gage asked.

"Yes, and I don't think Arcie even brought hers. Listen, Gage, I had to do this. I want to hear your story, and I don't want to keep Arcie from you, but this girl's heart is so hurt. I have to make sure she knows I'm going to be here. You can't make that promise anymore."

"I don't know when my heart has been so torn," Gage said. "I have peace for the first time in my life, Sam, real peace, but I might have to leave Arcineh behind, and that just about kills me."

"I'm sure it does."

"Don't let her get away, Sam." Gage's voice dropped to a whisper. "Don't let her run from you again. Keep her close."

"Pray for us," Sam said, not sure the younger man even knew how to do that at this point, but he had no time for more. Arcineh was returning to the car.

❦

Arcineh woke in a hotel room she barely remembered noticing the night before. Sam was in the room next door. She lay looking around, wondering how many people had stayed in the room and how many more would stay.

"You know," she said quietly to God, wondering at this new awareness of Him. She knew she didn't understand exactly what had happened to Sam or Gage, but having God in her thoughts was turning out to be special. Pastor Simon's words slowly came back to her. "Do what Sam does. Listen to Sam."

"I'm doing that," she said to God now, not feeling hateful or angry with Him at the moment.

The phone rang in the midst of this, and of course it was Sam.

"Are you going to sleep all day?"

"I was awake," she said, but her voice still had a morning sound to it.

"Oh, you sound awake."

"Are you going to feed me?"

"I'm dressed and ready for breakfast. Well," he amended, "I'm ready for breakfast."

"I need about 30 minutes. I'll meet you in the lobby."

Arcineh asking questions all the while, they made their way slowly toward home. Sam sensed a difference in her from the day before and asked her about it as they drove.

"I don't feel so angry right now. I keep realizing God is involved in things, and it's special, not threatening like it was."

"How so?"

"Well, I know that He knows all the names of everyone who stayed in my hotel room."

"He knows their hearts and needs too," Sam added.

Arcineh looked at him. "He does, doesn't He?"

"Yes."

"So He knows mine."

"Yes."

"Then why can't I believe like you do, and Gage?"

"Who says you can't?"

Arcineh had to think about this. She had been under the impression that God was standing in her way, but maybe she was the one.

"How humble would you say you are?" Sam asked.

"I don't know. I don't think I'm completely full of pride. Does that matter?"

"It takes humility to ask for help. It takes humility to admit you sin and need a Savior. Maybe that's where you need to start, by asking God to humble you so you can see your need for Him."

To Sam's surprise, Arcineh bowed her head. His heart clenched with love and tenderness for her, his own heart praying.

"Grandpa," Arcineh suddenly said, her voice thick with tears. "I think I see what you mean."

"About what?"

"I'm not humble." She sniffed back tears. "I don't think I'm that bad, so why would I need a Savior? But I don't think God would agree with me."

Just as soon as Sam could get off the road, he did. Sitting to the side of a quiet gas station, he shut off the engine and turned to Arcineh.

"Listen to me, Arcie. You're heart is overwhelmed right now. I will be honest and tell you that once you moved home, I had resigned myself to your not coming to church with me for a year or so, and here you came the second week, and again the third. You're learning so much right now, and it can be a lot to take in. God is patient, He'll be there for you."

"But what if I'm not?" Arcineh asked, not even knowing where that came from. "My parents weren't planning to die, and suddenly they were gone."

Sam looked into her eyes and quietly agreed. "You're right. God is sovereign, though. This trip will go just as He has planned. If you know to settle this with God right now, you'd better do it."

"How do I do that?" Arcineh asked, ready to sit there until she got this right.

"You repent. Agree with Him that your sin is separating you from Him and that you want that sin gone. You must believe that can only happen through the death of His Son and accept His gift of salvation. And you must give Him your life. You will no longer be your own. You must understand that. He'll help you through the difficulties, but you cannot come to God on your terms, only His."

"Can I really go from not believing in God at all to seeing that He's everywhere? I mean, I don't know where this came from. I gave Jalaina such a hard time when she talked about God because it seemed that all He ever did was make her feel guilty."

"Your lack of belief, and rejecting Him from your life, are just two of the many sins He's willing to forgive."

"Those *are* sins," Arcineh suddenly said. "All this time my not believing was a sin."

"As was mine."

That aspect was clear to her for the first time. They didn't move the car for more than an hour, but for the first time the things Sam said made sense. Arcineh, overwhelmed by the change in her heart, prayed, her eyes wide open, looking up to tell God how much she needed Him and wanted to be saved.

The relief in saying this, in accepting God's Son and seeing her grandfather's tears, was more than she could handle. She could not stop crying and found relief only when she fell asleep. Sam didn't hurry them out of the gas station parking lot. He had to dry his own tears. But they were still far down the road before Arcineh woke up.

"You've both been through a lot of changes this week," Simon said to Gage and Arcineh at the same time. Sam was also in the pastor's office. "Sam can be a lot of help to you. Listen to him and keep track of your questions. Do you both have Bibles?"

Both Gage and Arcineh nodded; Sam had bought one for her that very day.

"I have some reading I want you to do, and did you tell me that the trial involving your business starts on Monday, Gage?"

"Yes."

"It's a lot to take in right now. Just start reading in Genesis. Start in chapter one and read as much as you have time for. Write down anything that doesn't make sense, and the four of us will get back together and go over it."

Simon had warm handshakes for the men and hugged Arcineh, who had to fight tears over his smile and compassionate voice. They left the church office, a little quiet but excited as well. Gage had come in his own car from work, but before they parted he told Arcineh he would pick her up at 5:30.

"We're still going to your sister's?"

"She's planning on it."

"Have you told her about any of this?"

"No, I think I want to be like Sam and let them notice a change."

Arcineh smiled at him. Gage briefly touched her hand and told her he'd see her that night.

⟨∽⟩

"This is delicious," Arcineh said, not knowing that anyone outside of a restaurant could barbeque ribs this way.

"Luke's specialty," Erika said, smiling at her husband before her eyes went back to Arcineh. She could not believe that this was the woman her brother had brought home. She had snuck into the balcony of the private room at the dance studio and seen her performing with the other women so many times.

"Leave room for dessert," Erika suddenly said, trying not to stare.

"I forgot the ice cream," Luke admitted.

"Oh, Luke." Erika shook her head at him.

"I'll go and get it as soon as we're done. You know everyone will be too full to eat more right now."

Erika rolled her eyes at him, but all was well. A few minutes later, Gage went off with Luke, and Arcineh helped Erika with the dishes. They were almost done before the hostess had the guts to ask her guest about her dancing.

"I thought you seemed familiar," Arcineh said. "You're in Tina's aerobics class, aren't you?"

"Yes, and I've seen you with Windy City. You're very good."

Arcineh waved a hand. "I'm not the hero in that room. I'm the youngest with no husband or children, and they've all been making time for it for years. I'm just privileged to be invited."

"But you've danced for a long time, haven't you?"

"I have, yes. It's about the only exercise I enjoy."

"Can you show me just one move that you guys do?"

"Sure."

Before she could change her mind, Erika had whisked Arcineh into the family room and put on some music with a beat.

"It's the move with the shoulders."

"This one?" Arcineh did a couple of moves, and Erika just about jumped with enthusiasm.

"Yes! I can do the shoulder part, but not with the feet, and I love that move."

"The shoulders are the hardest part," Arcineh said, having Erika stand right beside her. "You can do this."

The music hit a good spot, and Arcineh went into motion, coaching all the while.

"Now lead right here with your right shoulder, left foot back. That's it."

The women were almost synchronized when the men came back, and for a moment they stood and watched. The women did not see Luke head to the stereo. Not until the music turned off did they look around.

Erika was about to complain when the slow sounds of Glenn Miller filled the room, and she ran to her husband in delight. They began to waltz around as Arcineh backed away, feeling shy. Gage would not allow this. He came toward her and took her in his arms. They danced in silence for a while, until Arcineh looked up to find his eyes on her.

"I like your sister," she said.

"I knew you would."

Just looking into his eyes made her emotional.

"All I can do these days is cry," Arcineh whispered.

"It's okay," Gage said, his chin going against her forehead as he pulled her a little closer and continued to dance. Arcineh closed her eyes and let him lead, her heart asking God why it had taken so long to find Him or Gage and then thanking Him it had taken no longer.

"Did she not tell you she has a performance this morning?" Sam asked Gage when he was at the house soon after Arcineh left.

"No."

Sam thought about this. It had been an unsettling week, but it might be more than that.

"You're welcome to ride with me, but you'd better stay slightly scarce in case she's embarrassed by your presence."

Gage was willing to do anything not to miss this. After coffee from Violet, he climbed into Sam's car, and they drove to the hospital. It took a little doing to learn where the performance would take place, but when they arrived it was easy to stay in the back. Many of the staff had gathered, and some children had had to come in their beds. It was standing room only.

Sam and Gage had not been there five minutes when the music, "Me Ol' Bam-Boo" from the musical *Chitty Chitty Bang Bang*, started up. The women were in costume, with hats, bamboo poles, and all. Gage found Arcineh in seconds and could not take his eyes from her. As he'd seen before, dancing seemed to come naturally for her. She smiled at the children when she was in front of them and never missed a beat. There was one dropped pole in the middle of the number, but that was recovered quietly, and the children's cheers and clapping could barely be heard over the applause of the staff.

A couple came out next to dance around to "Toot Sweets," and then the women were all back to do "The Roses of Success." There was no car to work around, and they did more dancing than in the movie, but all was a success.

Gage stood with Sam as the crowd cleared, and when Arcineh spotted them, she came over slowly.

"Hi," she said, looking a little shy.

"That was fun," Sam said. "You look better than ever."

Arcineh made a face. "I can tell I'm not 16 anymore."

"I'm thankful for that," Sam teased her.

It took a little longer for Arcineh to look at Gage. He'd never taken his eyes from her.

"Hi," she finally greeted him, feeling shy all over again.

"Hi. That was well done."

"Thank you. I didn't know you were coming."

"I didn't either since someone didn't invite me."

"Didn't I?" Arcineh tried, but Gage wasn't falling for it.

"There will be a penalty for this," he said. "You can take me to dinner tonight, and I get to pick the restaurant."

Arcineh managed to look longsuffering when in her heart she

was delighted. They had not had five minutes alone since Tuesday, and it felt as though they'd lived a lifetime.

～

"Did you start in Genesis yet?" Gage asked when they had taken seats in the small diner, one of Gage's favorite spots.

"Yes, but I didn't get very far. I kept having to write down questions."

"Like what?"

"Like 'in the beginning.' What beginning? Where does time begin in that verse?"

"That's a good one. My question is about the days. Were they longer than 24 hours at that time?"

"Oh, that's good too."

For a moment they just stared at each other. It felt as though they'd been saved in the nick of time, as though a building or room had been ready to crumble beneath them and they'd been snatched to safety just in time.

"I can't believe all the places God is," Arcineh said quietly. "I just never knew He was all around me."

"It's huge, isn't it?"

"I talked to my cousin today. Well, I guess I cried to her. Neither one of us could manage many words."

"A part of me wants to talk to Luke and Erika," Gage said, "but I feel like I need to know more."

"Do Erika and Luke go to church somewhere?"

"No. They're like I was, having gone to church as children and thinking that belief in God is all you need."

Arcineh sighed. "I have to talk to Jalaina. Even before I understood, I knew that her belief was different from Sam's. At some point, I want to tell her what's happened."

"What does she believe?"

"I don't know exactly, except that it's not very personal."

Their orders were taken in the next few minutes, but the conversation never lagged.

"Are you thinking much about the trial?" Arcineh asked.

"Worrying is a better word. It's so hard to have it completely out of my hands."

"But it's not in the judge's hand, either," Arcineh pointed out.

"That's true. Keep reminding me of that."

They ended up sharing a meal so they would both have room for the fabulous pies under the bakery glass. Arcineh got the key lime pie, but Gage went for chocolate cream. They shared bites and talked until almost ten. Even at that, it didn't feel like long enough.

CHAPTER
Twenty-Three

"Thanks for coming, Sam." Gage welcomed that man to his office on Sunday afternoon. "Stan called. They want to settle out of court."

"When did this come up?"

"I got a phone call as soon as we got home from church. Their lawyers just left. My team is waiting in the conference room for me. I wanted to talk to you."

"What brought this on?"

"My lawyers told them about Arcie's testimony."

"What are you thinking right now?"

"That I want my life back. This whole thing has eaten me alive, first the original deal and then finding out they lied and going through all this litigation. I want to study my Bible and really know it. I want to run my business the way it's meant to be run—no lawyers, no trials. I want to see Arcineh more." Gage gave a short laugh. "I want to court and marry the girl."

"And what do you hope I'll tell you?"

Gage sighed. "I want to make sure I'm doing the right thing as a believer."

"Are you satisfied with their terms?"

"Yes. They won't admit that they were wrong, but they're willing to repay the money and cover my fees. The old Gage would have demanded an admission of guilt, but now I know they'll answer to God, and it's not my problem."

"I would settle," Sam told him. "Like you said, they are in God's hands and you can have your life back."

"Thanks, Sam," the younger man said. "And I'm sorry about calling you down here like this."

"No problem. Shall I let you tell Arcie?"

"No, feel free. Tell her if I can get out of here at a decent time, I'll go to church with you tonight."

Sam went on his way but knew what would happen. Gage was tied up with the lawyers for hours, and they did not hear from him again that day.

∞

"It's amazing news," Arcineh said into the phone. Gage had called her on his way out the door to work on Monday morning.

"It is. I can't tell you how relieved I am. The only downside is how busy the next few days will be, possibly the whole week."

"Will you make it to Sam's party Friday night?"

"Yes, and my lawyers know I want this wrapped up ASAP."

"Good."

"I miss seeing you."

"I miss you too."

"Are you headed to work at the storage units today?"

"For a while, I think, but with the family coming this weekend, I don't want to be an emotional wreck, and that's easy to do with my Aunt Tiffany."

"I remember what she was like. Very interesting."

His tone made Arcineh laugh, a sound Gage loved to hear. They didn't stay on much longer as Gage was getting into traffic, but both looked forward to their next meeting.

∞

Just like old times, Jeremy and Tiffany were coming to town to celebrate Sam's birthday. Austin and Lexa were also coming and bringing their little boy. Quinn and Megan would be staying as well. Arcineh didn't think she would be too tense, but the closer it got, the more anxious she became.

She went to dance class on Thursday night, her head in the clouds, so that even when she got home, showered, and changed, and found Gage watching television with Sam, she looked right through him when she sat down in the room.

"How did it go?" Sam asked.

"Fine," Arcineh said and then remembered Gage. "How is it going with the lawyers?"

"We're done. We finished today. I'm even thinking of taking tomorrow off."

"I think that's a good idea," Sam put in. "It's been a long run for you."

Arcineh watched the men as they talked, but her mind had wandered again. Not until Violet needed Sam to do something in the kitchen did Arcineh come back to earth.

"Come here." Gage patted the sofa cushion next to him, and Arcineh went that way. "Closer," Gage invited, and Arcineh smiled and sat right next to him.

"You're distracted," Gage said.

"Am I? I'm sorry," Arcineh apologized, curling her legs under her so she could put her shoulder into the sofa back and face him. "Tell me all about how it was settled."

Gage gave her the details that the lawyers had covered. "I was given an encouraging word by Stan just before we finished. He said he'd never known someone who grew calmer as things progressed instead of less. I know it was God working in my heart."

"That is encouraging. And you did stay calm. I noticed it several times."

Gage had shifted so he could look into her eyes. With one hand, he took her hand in his. With the other, he brushed down her cheek and chin.

"Why are you distracted?"

"I think because my aunt is coming. She has a profound effect on me, and I haven't seen Austin yet. He's Quinn's brother. We don't have a great history. It's not as bad as Quinn's and mine, but pretty bad."

"When do they come?"

"Tomorrow for the party, and then they leave on Sunday. Sam's other house was bigger. There aren't as many places to hide here."

"You could come next door," Gage invited, and Arcineh smiled.

"We both know that would be a huge mistake."

Gage studied her a moment before saying, "One of these days, Arcineh Bryant, I am going to kiss you for real."

"Promises, promises," she teased, and Gage's eyes narrowed a little.

"Only Sam arriving back here any moment is keeping it from happening right now."

Arcineh didn't laugh or smile about that. She wanted to kiss him as well, and for a moment the tension and attraction between them grew.

They talked a little more, Gage still touching her face, but Sam returned just a few minutes later. They continued to watch television and each other, but the subject of kissing did not come up again.

⟍⟍⟍

"How do you handle your heart with Tiffany and Jeremy?" Arcineh asked Sam on Friday morning.

"I wondered how you were doing with that," Sam said, having just prayed about it. "I remember one very important thing: They're 'died for.' I ask God to save and forgive them and work to trust Him concerning their lives."

"Have there been opportunities to share?"

"Only once with Jeremy. He asked me about my church, but I could tell that he thought I was only growing generous in my old age to get into heaven."

Arcineh laughed a little. His description was funny, and she needed a laugh. But after breakfast she headed back to her room to read her Bible. She didn't get very far before she began to pray, asking God for the very thing her grandfather had mentioned—to remind her that her family was "died for."

ᕦᕤ

"Hi," Arcineh said, suddenly showing up in Gage's garage mid-morning.

"Hi. What are you up to?"

"Oh, just getting out of the house. I was going to ask you to go for a walk when I saw your door up."

Gage stopped and smiled at her, but Arcineh didn't notice. She was too busy looking around, and then at the bike Gage was working on.

"I didn't know you were big into cycling."

"Every chance I get. You?"

Arcineh smiled and slowly shook her head no.

"I would probably kill myself."

"I don't think so. We'll have to go as soon as the weather warms a bit more."

Arcineh didn't argue. She wanted to be with Gage no matter what. However, a small part of her mind did wonder how it would work. She hadn't ridden a bike since she was a child. She didn't even own a bike, but maybe she could ride one of Gage's.

"When does the family arrive?" he asked.

"Probably in a few hours."

"Have you had to work to keep busy?"

"A little. I've been memorizing the books of the New Testament, and that's pretty time-consuming."

"I think I had to do that in Sunday school, maybe in the fifth grade."

"If you were learning about God and the Bible as a child, why didn't you believe in Christ then?"

"We were told we were all good people. I have no memory of ever hearing that God's Son died for me personally and wanted some type of relationship with me, or that He's holy and my sin would separate me from Him forever. I thought I was a good person. My dad thought he was a good person, and so does my sister, so I'm not the only one who missed the truth."

"I've been under the false impression for a long time that a church is a church," Arcineh said.

"It can't be true. The church I grew up in is nothing like our church now."

"We meet with Pastor Simon this week, don't we?"

"For our questions, yes. Is Sam going with us?"

"As far as I know. It might depend on when the family leaves."

Gage was about to say something else when he watched a large Lexus pull into Sam's driveway.

"I think your family is here," Gage told Arcineh, who looked out and saw her Uncle Jeremy emerge from behind the wheel.

"I'd better go," Arcineh said, her face becoming all at once guarded.

"Just a minute," Gage said, wiping his hands on a clean rag and catching her before she could get away. Without hesitation he put his arms around her.

"It's okay," he said, holding her close, Arcineh's arms hugging him right back. "I'll come over in a bit and see if you need rescuing."

"What will you do?" Arcineh put her head back to ask him.

Gage could not resist. He kissed her, ever so softly, and then a bit longer.

Arcineh could barely open her eyes to look at him again.

"That works," she said.

Gage couldn't stop his smile, or the temptation. He kissed her a third time, forcing himself to hold back so she could be on her way.

Arcineh didn't even remember to say goodbye. She floated all the way home.

∾

Oh, Father, please help me, Arcineh prayed not an hour after Tiffany and the family arrived. *I don't know what to do with my aunt. She's so sharp with Quinn and so ready to advise me. I want to run away, and I know I can't.*

"You all right?" Violet asked from behind Arcineh where she stood at the kitchen sink.

"I'm getting there."

Violet came close. "Do you pray at times like this?"

Arcineh turned to look at her. "What made you ask that?"

"I was talking to Sam after you got back, and he said you'd made a big decision and would probably tell me about it sometime."

"I want to tell you, but part of me doesn't have the words. I thought I would understand a little more before I tried."

"Try anyway," Violet said. "Start by telling me why you thought you needed this. You've always been a good girl."

"It started when I knew that Sam had something I didn't have, and

I wanted so much to be with him. After that I began to see myself as God sees me."

"When did you start to believe God was there?"

"When Sam was so changed. It came fast. I almost didn't have time to work it out, but something had gone on in his heart, and when he explained it to me, it was clear that God had been there all along."

Violet looked thoughtful.

"What have you thought about his change?" Arcineh asked.

Violet answered in a voice filled with wonder. "Sam has always been good to me, but a hard man. He liked his way, and even when I had vacation time, he expected me to leave things just so, so he was cared for. I never resented it—it was my job—but then he changed. I began to get days off every week, and when we moved here, he built my apartment over the garage, just the way I wanted it, every detail like I dreamed of.

"And then he gave me six weeks in Europe. He wouldn't take no for an answer. He planned it, and booked it, and even paid for Alice to join me. For a while I thought he was feeling his age and trying to get into heaven, but I don't think that's it. I think this change in him is real.

"And now you. You were always a little sweetheart, but there's been a peace about you in the last few weeks. I don't know what you went through while you were gone, but you've come to some type of peace about your life. I didn't see you get tense until your aunt showed up."

"I love my aunt," Arcineh said, "but I don't know how to respond to her. Things that used to be important to me are still important to her. I somehow thought she would have grown out of that."

"So you pray for her?"

"Yes, I do."

"And for me?"

Arcineh didn't answer until she put an arm around the older woman's shoulders.

"I don't understand all of this, Vi, but God has worked a miracle in my heart. I'm not alone anymore. Why would I want any less for you, the woman who's been my mother and loves me no matter what?"

"You're going to have me bawling." Violet moved away and began to chop carrots.

"But you don't mind, do you?" Arcineh stuck around long enough to ask.

"No, I don't! Now get out of here. I have work to do."

If Arcineh had wanted something to get her mind off Tiffany, God had certainly provided.

∽

Austin had done some growing up, as had Lexa. Their little boy was adorable, and although rather busy, a lot of fun to watch and play with. Arcineh snatched Megan as soon as Quinn arrived, and when Gage showed up he found her settled on the sofa, the baby cuddled close in her arms.

"She's changed a lot," he said, staring at the tiny face.

"She's so sweet," Arcineh cooed, and got a smile in return.

"She's taken with you," Gage said softly, "but then that's easy to understand."

Arcineh smiled into his eyes, loving it when he said things like that.

Quinn, sitting across the room, was about to go and check on her daughter when she noticed the interchange. She thought that if those two didn't get married, it would be a shock. Arcineh had looked tense from time to time, but she hadn't stopped smiling since Gage had walked in the door.

∽

It was with no small amount of emotion that Sam hung his birthday gift from Arcineh. He didn't know when she had time to have it done, but she'd given him a studio portrait of herself. And now today, eleven years to the day since her parents had died, Sam got ready to hang it next to the picture of the three of them, the one they'd given him for his sixtieth birthday.

Sam stood for a long time and stared into his son's face. Did a father ever get over losing a child? He was sure not. And Isabella. She had not had much family, just some distant cousins. Sam still grieved her as well. They had been close. She had been sweet like Arcineh and had made his son the happiest of men.

Sam turned away, knowing that he could do nothing now. His regret was a waste of time. There were still Tiffany, Jeremy, and the next generations.

❧

"Our earth is about 6000 years old," Pastor Simon said, answering Arcineh's question on Sunday evening. "Time as we know it began in Genesis 1:1. When Genesis speaks of six days of creation," he continued, turning to Gage now, "God means just that, six 24-hour days."

Simon answered the rest of their questions, taking all the time they needed. At last the two of them sat back, delighted with what they learned.

"How did it go with the family?" Simon asked Sam before the three of them could leave.

"Not bad. Austin and I had a chance to talk. He was surprised to see Quinn and Arcineh doing so well."

"You didn't tell me that," Arcineh said.

"There wasn't time yesterday, and then it slipped my mind until just now. I'm 71, you know," he teased his granddaughter.

Arcineh laughed, but as soon as they were in the car, she asked about Austin.

"I don't think there is any real hunger," Sam was forced to admit. "But I was proud of you and Quinn and how you're doing."

"Is that kind of pride all right?" Gage asked. He'd just been reading in Proverbs where it was clear that pride was a serious sin.

"I could be sinfully prideful of them, but I wasn't just now. I know that God has worked in their hearts, and that was my way of saying I'm pleased."

"I didn't have talks with anyone," Arcineh put in. "In fact I feel bad because I had to get away from Tiffany a few times."

"She had a rough weekend," Sam said.

"In what way?" Gage asked.

"She told me that she loves her grandchildren but doesn't want to be reminded that she's old enough to be a grandmother. She cried for a long time about it."

Arcineh felt terrible. She had spent time avoiding her and hadn't prayed as she should have. Her aunt was a selfish creature, but Arcineh had not been a whole lot different. Looking out for herself had come very easily.

As Gage drove them home, Arcineh curled up in the backseat and had a long talk with the Lord. There was so much she didn't know, but she was seeing new things all the time. She was thankful, but also very tired.

ᑕᗡ

"I need to ask you something," Arcineh said to Sam when she tracked him down in his bedroom. Gage had gone home, and it was just the two of them. She had been so thankful in the car, but now doubts had started to surface as old memories had come to mind.

"Go ahead."

"Why was Quinn the favorite?"

"I think because she so reminded me of my failure as a parent. It wasn't obvious in Trevor. He found your mother and made a life for himself, but Tiffany married the first man who asked. I'll be honest and tell you that I've been flabbergasted over the years that the marriage lasted. I love and admire your Uncle Jeremy. He's had to learn to live with a lot.

"And then the kids came along. Austin was close to his father and seemed to fare better, but Quinn was as needy as her mother from day one. And Tiffany did not rise to the occasion. She was needy right back, and it made for an amazing amount of stress and pain."

Sam took a breath. "After I became a believer, I apologized to Austin. I told him I was sorry for making him invisible and being so uncaring. He was gracious and kind in his reply, and we've been a bit closer ever since."

Arcineh nodded.

"Why, was it bothering you?"

"I'm sometimes still plagued with doubts. I go from thankfulness to God for saving me to anger that it didn't happen sooner. I sound like a basket case."

"You sound like a newborn," Sam said compassionately. "We've got to grow up."

"You've had those same thoughts?"

Sam had to laugh. "Arcie, you've come to Christ at 22 years of age. I was 69, with more regrets than I could list in a lifetime. And you didn't arrive the moment I believed. At times I was deluded into thinking that if I obeyed, God would reward me with you. He did reward me with you—not because of anything I did but because He's a gracious, mighty God."

Arcineh sighed, knowing it was so true. At the same time, she spotted the picture and went toward it.

"When did you hang this?"

"Yesterday morning when the house was asleep."

Arcineh stared at it, and then at her parents. "It looks nice there. I wouldn't have thought of it."

"Vi spotted it too. She became rather emotional."

"Eleven years." Arcineh's voice was thoughtful. "Half my life."

Sam put an arm around her. "Thank you for coming home."

∽

The phone rang early on Tuesday. Will was calling from the hospital. Jalaina had been in hard labor for an hour and would she come? Arcineh flew into her clothing and raced to be with her friend.

"Where is everyone?" she asked when Will met her in the doorway of the room.

"She wanted it to be a surprise. You're the only one who knows we're here."

"Arcie?" Jalaina suddenly saw her. She'd fallen asleep between contractions.

"I'm right here," she said, going to her friend's side.

"It's so hard," Jalaina gasped. "I didn't realize."

"You can do this. You're going to be a mother today."

"Oh, Arcie, why didn't I send for you hours ago?"

"I'm here now. I don't have a clue what I'm doing, but I'm here now."

This gave Jalaina the giggles, but that didn't last. Another contraction was soon on her. The nurse came in to check a short time later and sent for the doctor. Pushing took longer than Jalaina banked on, but at last, some 90 minutes later, a howling Emilie Marie Schafer was born. She was pink and beautiful, and both Will and Arcineh had tears pouring down their cheeks.

Jalaina held her daughter against her chest, her smile and sigh making Arcineh cry some more. She tried to slip away to give this new family time to themselves, but Jalaina called her right back.

When Will finally took Emilie away to be weighed, measured, and cleaned up, Arcineh came close to her friend's face.

"You did it."

"I did it. Isn't she beautiful?"

"Amazing."

"God has been good to me, Arcie."

"Yes, He has," Arcineh agreed, causing Jalaina's mouth to open. They didn't have a chance to talk. The nurse was back to take care of Jalaina, and the new mother was already giving orders to call everyone, starting with Grandma and Marco, and then Nicky and Libby. It took some doing, but Arcineh was finally on the phone to Sam. He was thrilled with the news, and the two made plans to shop for a gift that very afternoon.

Twenty-Four

Arcineh got home from an especially tough day in the last storage unit to find chaos at the house. It was just past mid-April, and she had not expected the pool work to start so soon. Parking on the street and going in by way of the kitchen, Arcineh found Violet at the stove.

"Did you know about this?"

"Of course I knew about this."

"But you didn't tell me."

"I just do what I'm told," Violet said.

"Since when?" Arcineh teased before making her way to the family room and the patio doors. She looked out at the hole being dug and spotted her grandfather, wrapped against the cool temperatures, enjoying the show from a chaise lounge.

"Surveying your kingdom?" his granddaughter asked.

"No, just thinking that I chose the wrong kind of work. I really want to run that backhoe."

Arcineh had a good laugh over this and pulled up a lounger of her own.

"How did it go?"

"I found this," she said, passing an eight-by-ten photo to him. "I thought Gage might enjoy seeing it, but I'm hoping you can tell me about it first."

"Ah, yes," Sam said, looking at his son with a group of other men, all standing next to bicycles. "This was in college."

"I didn't know he ever rode. I never saw a bike."

"He was too much like me after he graduated—all work and little play. I guess I'm glad he didn't have a bike. You would have seen even less of him."

Arcineh had forgotten about that. Her mother had been home the most and made it such fun that she hadn't always noticed his absence.

"Was it a school team?"

"No, but the young men were all from the university. This man right here," Sam pointed, "was your father's roommate."

Arcineh grew thoughtful. "There aren't a lot of questions you think to ask when you're eleven. I wonder if I even knew my parents."

"In all fairness, Arcineh, that would be their fault. They lived around your world. Do you remember how long it took for you to dance after the accident?"

"A long time."

"Yes. You'd never done it without your mother. She didn't have a life outside of you and Trevor, and because Trevor worked a lot, much of the time it was just you."

Arcineh had to think about this. It was not something she had thought about very much. Gage worked a lot. With the legal business over and the new lineup coming out, he worked late most nights. If they ever got married, would he work just as much, leaving her and their prospective children alone?

"What's going on in that head?"

"What are the right hours for a man to work, especially men like you and Gage who own your own companies?"

"You have to ask the hard ones, don't you?"

Arcineh waited, but Sam didn't answer. His granddaughter didn't press him, but the question stayed on her mind.

⚬ȤȤ⚬

"This is a great photo," Gage said, having studied Arcineh's father for a while, "and comes at a very appropriate time."

"How's that?"

"Come this way," Gage invited, taking Arcineh out her front door and down the sidewalk to his house. He had her stand in the driveway while he ran inside and put the garage door up.

Arcineh had to smile. Gage came out to get her like a kid on Christmas morning. Parked next to his car was his bike, the one he was currently riding. Next to it was a smaller bike, a woman's bike.

"My sister got a new bike for Christmas. This is her old one, and she said you could use it."

"That was sweet of her," Arcineh said.

"Wasn't it? And if you're free, we'll go biking this Saturday. It's supposed to hit 74."

Arcineh had to smile again. He made it sound like a heat wave.

"Am I being laughed at?"

"No," Arcineh lied, working to school her face.

"So you'll go?" he double-checked.

"Yes, but I'm not in shape like you are. Will you remember that?"

"You're in great shape," he argued.

"For dancing," Arcineh tried to tell him, but he was already asking her to sit on the bike so he could adjust the seat and check the pedals.

A day with Gage. Arcineh was looking forward to it already. She only hoped she would be physically up to whatever he had in mind.

∽

"This is the most adorable baby on the planet," Arcineh said, holding two-week-old Emilie in her arms. "How do you get anything done?"

"You can look at this messy apartment and ask that?"

"It looks fine."

"It's picked up, but not dusted or vacuumed. Don't look in the corners."

"Does Will care?"

"No," Jalaina smiled. "He comes in the door looking for one face, and it's not mine."

Arcineh laughed with her friend, and then laughed again when Emilie started. She didn't cry, however, and Arcineh cuddled her close and kissed her downy soft head.

"What changed for you?" Jalaina suddenly asked, and Arcineh looked at her friend, knowing just what she was talking about.

"Seeing Sam. You remember everything I told you—how he favored my cousin? All that is gone. He's working very hard to be close to all of us. And he doesn't fight with his daughter anymore," Arcineh added, "but my Aunt Tiffany hasn't changed a bit."

"So that did what for you?" Jalaina asked, taking her now-fussing daughter and letting her nurse.

"Well, he gives all the credit to God, but he never believed in God. I went to church with him just to see what it was like, and Gage went with us and then Gage had all these questions."

"Did Gage already believe in God?"

"Yes, but not in a personal way like Sam, and Gage wanted that."

"How is it personal?"

"Well, one verse I know about is in John 15. It says, 'You are My friends if you do what I command you.' Jesus says it."

"You know the Bible?"

"Just a few verses, but I'm learning more all the time."

"Could Will and I go with you Sunday?" Jalaina asked.

"Yes. I'd like that."

Jalaina stared at her. "What are the odds that you, an atheist, now know more verses than I do?"

"But you could know them too, Jalaina. I'm sure of it."

"Thanks, Arcie," the new mother said quietly, her eyes still searching Arcineh's, the yearning in her face unmistakable.

Arcineh didn't even know what to pray right then. She just asked God to help them both.

∞

Arcineh read the verses in Genesis 16 a second time, her mind trying to take it all in. Sarai had actually sent her husband to be with another woman in order to have children. Arcineh read about Hagar and Abram and had all she could do not to shake her head.

It was early, but she knew Sam would be up. Bible in hand, she went looking for him and found him in the four-season room, his own Bible open.

"Can I bother you?"

"No bother," he said, looking over the top of his glasses.

"Why would Sarai encourage Abram to take another wife?"

"Because she didn't trust. God had made a promise, one that seemed impossible to her, and so she ran ahead of God's plan, thinking this was the way Abram would bear a son."

"What kind of woman was Sarai to do such a thing?"

"As a matter of fact, Sarah, as she's later called, is very special. That's not to say that she didn't make mistakes, but she was the perfect mate for Abraham, again, a name he came to be called later, and God blessed her repeatedly for her faith."

"He's so forgiving, Sam. I can't believe how much He's willing to forgive."

"It's true, isn't it? Whenever I lose sight of what went on on the cross, I forget what a huge, saving God He is."

Arcineh was quiet as she thought about this. It was almost more than she could take in.

"What time do you go with Gage?" Sam asked.

"Not until 10:00."

"Do you want to read together for a while?"

Arcineh was very pleased with the idea. Sam answered questions as she continued in chapter 16, and then they prayed together. It was a perfect start to the day.

❦

"Are you okay back there?" Gage asked, clearly having the time of his life.

"Yes," she shouted, thinking she could get used to this in a hurry. He had taken them along the lake shore park, and the day was gorgeous. Arcineh, wearing the new Rugby Shades Gage had given her, was having a blast.

Gage had brought a lunch for them, and they would be stopping in an hour to eat. Arcineh could have eaten then—she'd had a small breakfast—but she pressed on. However, some 30 minutes later, when Gage suggested an early lunch, she was all for it.

They sat on a grassy area. It was a bit cool but dry, and Gage trotted out a lovely feast of deli sandwiches, fruit, cheesecake, and plenty of water. They were eating in companionable silence when Gage surprised her with a question.

"Have you ever been overweight?"

"No, why?"

Gage touched a part of her upper arm that extended from the sleeveless top she wore. "These stretch marks."

"Dancing," Arcineh explained. "Years of dancing."

"I didn't know that."

"I guess I don't think too much about them. They're part of dance, and I've been in that world for so long—" Arcineh shrugged, letting the sentence hang, but she had a sudden horrible thought. "Are they gross to you?"

"No," Gage said, his face showing his surprise. "I just didn't realize dancing would do that."

Arcineh brushed at her arm a moment, suddenly wishing her skin were perfect. Just as suddenly, she found her jaw in Gage's hand. With a gentle movement, he brought her eyes to his.

"They're not gross."

Arcineh nodded and relaxed, knowing that pleasing Gage was more important to her all the time. Her grandfather said she was falling in love, and Arcineh knew he had to be right.

"Tell me something," Arcineh said, knowing she had better think about something else before she grabbed this man and kissed him. "What's the biggest change for you, Gage?"

"My thought life. I was pretty distracted by women's bodies, and I wondered if that was always going to be the case, but now I catch myself and know that my thoughts can't go there. It actually feels better not to look, to fight through the temptation."

Arcineh had not expected this.

"In fact," he went on quietly, "that's why you're riding behind me or beside me and not leading."

"That's thoughtful of you," Arcineh said, very impressed that he had planned ahead.

"What about you? What's the biggest change for you?"

"It's probably the lack of fear and resentment. I didn't think I was the type to feel sorry for myself, but I blamed a lot of things on my grandfather and feared being left alone all the time. I still think about those things, and I'm tempted to fear, but there's no panic. I know I'm not alone now."

"The peace is amazing, isn't it? I talked to an old friend on the phone this morning. I tried to tell him about my peaceful heart, but I don't know if he caught it."

"What about Luke and Erika? Any talks there?"

"No, but I've been putting in a lot of hours at work lately, and I haven't had time to see them."

Arcineh didn't comment. He had been working a lot lately, and she didn't know how she felt about that. Pushing it out of her mind, she determined not to let such thoughts ruin their wonderful day.

∽

"Oh, Sam," Arcineh said when she came from the downstairs shower, "I've done it now."

"Come in here and relax," Sam encouraged, leading the way to the four-season room. "I'll see what Violet has."

Arcineh made her way slowly to the comfortable wicker furniture in there. Sitting took an amazing effort, and Arcineh shuddered as her muscles reminded her of the long bike ride.

Violet came with ice and muscle rub. Arcineh sat on the ice for a while, but when she told the older woman where she hurt, they didn't use the muscle rub. Sitting very carefully, and not at all comfortably, Arcineh only hoped she would be on her feet for church in the morning.

∽

"I think Gage is here," Sam told Arcineh about an hour later.

"Oh, no!" Arcineh whispered in a panic. She had taken over the four-season room; climbing the stairs had been too painful. "Don't tell him."

"Why not?"

"Just don't. Just tell him I'm resting, and I'll see him tomorrow."

Arcineh could tell that her grandfather was not happy, but it never once occurred to her that he would tell Gage where she was. When that man showed up, she didn't even want to look at him.

"Too tired for company?" he asked, sitting down across from her.

"No," Arcineh said, her voice not convincing at all, her eyes not meeting his for more than a moment at a time.

"Sore?"

"Yes," Arcineh admitted.

"How sore?"

When Arcineh didn't answer, Gage had another question.

"Why didn't you say something on the ride?"

This was the toughest question of all. Arcineh wanted to be honest, but that was going to be hard.

"What are you doing this evening?" Arcineh suddenly asked. "Big plans?"

Gage laughed. He couldn't help himself.

"You know, you're amazingly smart, with every sign of maturity, but when you don't want to answer a question, you very swiftly turn into a four-year-old, thinking that distraction will work."

Arcineh frowned at him. She didn't care that he was right. It still made her mad.

"Why didn't you say we had gone too far on the ride?" Gage pressed.

"To what end, Gage?" she snapped. "I don't see that much of you as it is, and then you find out that I can't even take a day of bike riding." Well and truly angry now, Arcineh gazed out the window. If she could have walked, she would have stormed out, but the effect would have been lost in all the moaning and groaning that would have had to accompany such an action.

Gage looked at her, debating his next move. He wanted to talk about this, but clearly she was not in the mood. Gage opted for honesty.

"Can we talk, or do you want me to leave? And before you answer," he cut back in, "I'm not going anywhere."

Arcineh frowned at him, her voice tight as she said, "I hurt in places I didn't know existed."

"Then I'll ask again, why didn't you say something?"

"By the time I realized it, the damage was done!"

"And you were afraid I wouldn't ask you again, so you thought you'd keep this quiet," Gage put in, Arcineh's face telling him how closely he'd come to the truth.

Both people let the room get very quiet. Arcineh was on the wicker sofa, her legs stretched out. She had to go to the bathroom but wasn't willing to have Gage see her move. At the moment, it was not a graceful process.

Without warning, Gage began to move furniture. Arcineh watched as the wicker-and-glass coffee table was shifted out of the way and Gage pulled his chair close to the sofa, facing her.

"How sore are you?" he asked gently.

"I can't get upstairs," she admitted.

"Have you taken anything?"

"No. I wasn't hungry, and Violet won't give me ibuprofen without something to eat."

Gage stood. He bent long enough to kiss her forehead and said he'd be right back. When he arrived, he had a glass of milk and ibuprofen tablets in hand. Arcineh took the pills and drank all the milk. She even found the courage to tell Gage she had to be excused. He helped her to her feet and all the way to the powder room door.

From there, they went to the family room and joined Sam. Gage stayed and talked to them for the next two hours. They ended up having a good time, but no one was surprised when Arcineh—who was forced to sleep downstairs—wasn't up to going out the next morning.

"How's the soreness?" Gage asked on Wednesday after work.

"Much better, thank you."

"I have a favor to ask of you."

"Okay."

"Any chance you could work for me at the office for maybe a week or so?"

"Sure, what's going on?"

"Patrice's mother had a heart attack, and she'll be gone for a little while."

"I'm sorry to hear that. Do they think she'll be all right?"

"It's a little iffy right now."

Arcineh nodded, and then remembered something from the past.

"I thought you said one time that it would be too distracting to have me at the office."

To her surprise, Gage didn't laugh when he said, "I probably won't get a thing done."

"Oh, Gage," she said, clearly not believing him. "I was only kidding."

Gage looked at her, his eyes wandering a bit. "I'm not."

Arcineh still didn't believe him, but she was good at her word and presented herself to the fourth floor the next morning. The women had been warned of her arrival and were genuinely pleased to see her.

"How have you been?" Arcineh asked Mallory.

"Doing well, thanks to you."

Arcineh blew that off. She didn't think it was her at all and decided not to waste time getting to work. In little time at all, she was finding out what needed to be done. Things came back to her swiftly, and before she knew it, she was walking down to the second floor to have lunch with Mallory.

The women visited about everything under the sun, including Mallory's boyfriend, who she suspected was getting ready to pop the question. Arcineh loved seeing everyone from the past and had good visits all around. Not until she arrived back on the fourth floor did she doubt her actions. Gage asked to see her, and when she got to his office, he wanted the door shut.

"Where did you eat lunch?" he asked.

"In the cafeteria."

"Why didn't you come and eat with me?"

"I didn't know your company policy on relationships. And I didn't want to assume."

He had come to the front of the desk, sat on it, and stretched his legs out. His arms crossed over his chest, he began in a long-suffering tone, "I behave myself all morning, concentrating on my work, even when you're in the room, telling myself I'll see you at lunch, and then lunchtime comes, and no Arcie."

Arcineh had her hand over her mouth, working not to laugh.

"Oh, yes, it's so funny." His tone had gone sarcastic. "Let's torture the boss with his beautiful girlfriend in the building but not let him get near her."

Arcineh kept her hand over her mouth but still managed to say, "I told you, I didn't want to assume."

"Let me sum it up for you in two words, Miss Bryant: tomorrow—assume."

Arcineh's laugh could be heard in the outer office. Mallory, sitting at Patrice's desk, couldn't wait to tell Victoria that things were progressing quite nicely.

CHAPTER
Twenty-Five

"Okay, sign this," Arcineh directed, placing papers in front of Gage about a week later. "And this letter from a pleased customer just came in. Mallory thought you might want to see it."

"Okay, thank you," Gage said, his eyes already on the letter.

"Oh, and by the way, I signed you up to dance."

"Okay."

Arcineh made her way to the door, but Gage's mind clicked into gear just in time and he beat her there, his hand keeping the portal closed. Arcineh turned to look at him.

"You did what?" Gage asked.

"I signed you up to be my dance partner."

"What kind of dance?" Gage asked, looking as horrified as he felt.

"Mostly waltz and a little bit of swing. You'll do great. It's for a retirement village."

"How will I know what to do?"

"We have four weeks of practice on Thursday nights."

Arcineh smiled at him, and Gage's eyes narrowed.

"This is about the bike ride. You're getting me back."

"Gage," Arcineh replied, managing to sound hurt. "I can't believe you would say that."

Gage's hand dropped off the door, and Arcineh turned the handle to let herself out. Just before she exited, however, she gave Gage an amazingly satisfied smile. Seeing it, that man knew he'd been had.

〜

"You're doing this in high heels?" Gage asked as he watched Arcineh put a black pair on her feet.

"Yes, it's best to practice in what I'll have to wear."

"Speaking of which, what will I be wearing?"

"Black slacks and shoes, a white long-sleeved shirt, and a red tie."

"All from my closet?"

"Not the tie—they have those."

"And you'll be in…"

"A black skirt and white blouse with a small red bow on the pocket."

"Who puts all this together?"

"Mostly Tina. She's very good."

Gage had more questions, but there was no time. The music began, and so did the hard work. He was in good shape, but naturally Arcineh had the edge. To his untrained eye, she never missed a beat. He, on the other hand, thought he messed up constantly. Nevertheless they had a blast, and whether she intended it or not, he was a little bit sore the next day.

〜

"I'm in love with your granddaughter," Gage told Sam on Sunday evening. The older man had deliberately gone next door to talk about the relationship between Gage and Arcineh.

"Does she know that?"

"I haven't said it, but I hope she's catching on."

"To what end, Gage?" Sam asked.

"Marriage, I hope."

Sam didn't comment, and Gage grew concerned.

"What are you thinking about?" he finally asked.

"My past," Sam admitted. "I worked the hours you work, and it cost me much. I don't want that for Arcie."

"What do I do when I'm the owner of the company?"

"I've been thinking about that very thing. And I'll tell you what I would do if I had to do it again. I'd plan to control the workday. I'd hire people who think like I do and understand how productive they must be. If you set the standard, it will work.

"If you're like I was," Sam continued, "you're in on everything, but you don't have to be. Trust the people you hire to get the job done, and then leave them to it. I know there will be times when you're on call or running a bit late, but that can't be the norm. You might even increase production, but if you don't, it's still worth it."

Gage nodded, his mind running with the changes he would have to make. He finally saw the dichotomy within himself as he realized he'd been too hands-off with Patrice and too hands-on with his department heads. It was true—he loved being a part of every aspect of the business, but his people were more than competent.

Sam didn't stay much longer, but he'd given the younger man much to think about. Gage spent the rest of the evening asking God for help and also arguing with Him that it could not be done. He went to bed with very few answers.

⟨∾⟩

"Are you all right?" Arcineh asked on Monday morning.

"Yes, why?"

"You just seem a little quiet."

Gage looked at her. He'd wrestled with Sam's words last night and again this morning, almost forgetting the woman he was *fighting* for. And something else was suddenly clear: Sam had not told her he was coming to see him about their relationship. Gage's heart ached at the thought of not having Sam's blessing, but the man was right. Why would Sam want Arcineh to have a husband who did little but work? It would be horrible for both of them.

"Tell me something," Gage said, not mentioning his conversation with Sam but already forming a plan. "Have you ever played tennis?"

"Just a little in high school with friends," Arcineh answered, her voice confused.

"Perfect."

"Why is that?"

"That's all I've ever played, so if we do that together, we'll be in the same place."

"You're not going to ask me to bike with you again?"

"I am, and I'll dance with you, but tennis will be ours."

Arcineh looked into his eyes and said, "I like you, Gage Sefton."

Gage couldn't help himself. With one hand he gently cupped the side of her face. "I like you too."

The soft kiss he gave her made Arcineh sigh. The sigh made Gage smile, just before he put his arms around her to hold her close. It was a wonderful start to the work week, and to knowing what had to be done.

"Thanks for coming," Gage said to Sam at the end of the workday on Friday.

"You're welcome. What can I do for you?"

"You can take up residence in this building until you figure out where we're wasting time and energy. I want to know what you would do to keep Rugby Shades a viable company without letting it own me."

Sam could have shouted with relief. He had known for a long time that this man was special, but this—this was beyond what he dreamed. Sam knew only God could have done this.

Gage waited, hoping Sam would at least dialog with him about the process. He made him the happiest of men when he asked, "When do you want me to start?"

∞

Arcineh had not forgotten about her conversation with Jalaina, but neither did she expect to see her. They had talked almost four weeks past and not seen each other since, but on a Sunday morning, looking nervous even though Will was at her side, she stood in the foyer of the church building, her face showing relief when Arcineh spotted her. "Hi," she whispered as they hugged. "Are you all right?"

"I think so. Someone just directed us to the nursery. Will Emilie be all right?"

"She'll be fine, but if you want her in with you, that's all right too."

Jalaina looked to Will.

"We're not going to hear what the man is saying if we have Emilie. We might not be all right," he teased his wife a little, "but Em will be fine."

Arcineh loved the smile the two of them shared, and she began to pray. She was a little confused about what God would want in this situation but then remembered what she'd been learning about men leading in the home and church family. As they trooped in to sit with Sam and Gage, Arcineh asked God to save Will Schafer and that Jalaina would follow his lead.

∞

"She's asleep," Arcineh told the men when she got back to the family room. Will had had questions, just as Gage had many weeks before. Sam had invited them over for lunch. Jalaina had listened as long as she could, but the baby needed to be fed, and both had fallen asleep in the rocker in the four-season room.

"I don't know what you said to Jalaina, Arcie," Will said with his wife missing, "but she would not let this go. She's been nagging me to attend your church."

"Did you not want to?" Arcineh asked.

Will shrugged. "I think a church might be a church, but Jalaina wanted it, so we came."

"And now what do you think?" Sam asked.

Will had to smile. "Okay, I heard some things today that were new to me, but I don't know about this sin issue. Why would God create man as a sinner and then cast him off for being that way?"

"If you go back to Genesis, Will," Sam said, fielding the question, "God created a perfect man and woman. They chose to sin."

"That's my point," Will said. "Even Adam and Eve sinned, and they were perfect. How do the rest of us stand a chance, and why would God do that to us?"

"God wants us to make Him our God. He gives us a choice, Will. We can face that we sin and need a Savior and God, or we can live life for ourselves with a god of our own and spend eternity apart from Him."

Will was on the verge of arguing, but in fact he'd been raised to respect the church and God. He sat back and looked at Sam.

"The hard part about God is that it's all His way," Will said.

"That's very astute of you, Will, but allow me to add that it's also the clearest part."

"How so?"

Sam tapped his Bible. "He spells it out for us. He says it's a small gate and a narrow path to finding God and knowing you're saved for all of eternity. It's completely clear in His Word. He's an exacting God, but a clear one."

Will slowly shook his head in wonder. "I can't say I've ever thought of it that way before."

"That's what we call light or truth," Sam continued. "I've just given you some light, and you must decide what you will do with it."

Will didn't hesitate this time. "I think I'll come back next Sunday."

Sam smiled at the younger man before saying, "I can't tell you how glad I am to hear that."

⚬⚬

The employees of Rugby Shades read an email on Monday morning, one from Gage Sefton himself. The email said that a man named Sam Bryant was there to help him, and that changes would be made. He encouraged them to welcome the older man, who might be moving in their midst, and even told some about the meeting they were to attend in the conference room on Tuesday.

The meeting the next day started on time and Gage got right to the point. "The changes might be slow in coming—it might take weeks to adjust—but there will be changes. We will put in hard days, but they will be shorter days," Gage told the fourth floor, his executives, and the design teams. Sam and Arcineh were present as well. "You will know you've worked, but at the end of the day you can go home and forget about Rugby, and that goes for the weekend."

Gage searched the faces of his people. Sam had only been on the job for one day, but he told Gage he could do this. Gage believed in being upfront with his people and had called this meeting for first thing Tuesday morning.

"I would call for questions, but I don't have all the answers right now. I just know that changes will be made in how we do things. I'm not looking to fire anyone, but if you find this is no longer a place you want to work, I will not deny you the reference you deserve because you don't want to work for Rugby."

Gage saw faces relax and knew he'd covered at least one question. "I still love making sunglasses. I still love what we do here. I just want us to do it more effectively. It might even open up opportunities for some of you. We'll have to wait and see.

"Most of you know Sam Bryant, grandfather to Arcie and a successful businessman. As I said in the email, he'll be around for an undetermined time. Answer any questions he might have. Tell him what you do so he can help us. Feel free to ask questions but be patient about the answers. When I know things, I'll communicate them with you." Gage wrapped up the meeting. "That's all I have for now. Thank you for your time."

Folks thanked him and moved on their way. Little by little people went back to their jobs, but naturally there was much speculation about the changes. However, Gage and Sam didn't waste any time. Sam continued his tour of the office. Gage was either with him or working on the business at hand.

⤫

Arcineh woke up with Patrice on her mind and prayed for her. Gage had told her the day before that Patrice's mother was not doing well, and because she was planning to be married in a month, the assistant would not be back to work at all.

Arcineh had agreed to staying on for the time being because Gage was reticent, in light of the changes to come, to add someone new. Arcineh felt discontentment as she got out of bed. She didn't hate the job. It let her see Gage. But it wasn't something she wanted to do for a long time.

What do you want to do for a long time? Arcineh asked herself, but there was no immediate answer. She still wasn't interested in college, and she didn't want to tile. Wondering how she could be so confused when just a short time ago life seemed to be falling into place, Arcineh slipped into the shower and began to pray.

You know what my heart wants. You can see inside of me, she said to the Lord. *I don't know exactly how Gage feels, but I just want to be in his life. And Sam's. I never want to be away from Sam again.*

Arcineh heard herself and stopped. God was not a genie in the lamp that you gave your wishes to. Arcineh scrubbed her hair, wanting to trust God but feeling anxious.

Why do I think that You can't handle things? I keep putting You on my helpless level, and I know that's selling You short. Help me, Lord Jesus. Help me to trust You with all of me. I am a worrier. I never thought I was, but I'm anxious about so many things. Gage calls it distraction, but it's worry. I worry about Will and Jalaina and my future and Sam dying and Gage asking me to marry him.

Arcineh made herself stop. She confessed the anxiety inside of her and finished in the shower. Forcing her mind to remember verses that promised her God was exactly who He said He was, Arcineh slowed down and made herself do the hard work of choosing to trust.

❦

"Did you use sunblock?" Violet asked when she found Arcineh on a raft in the pool on Saturday afternoon. Sam and Gage were working on reconstructing Rugby. Arcineh had been feeling sorry for herself and then remembered there was a pool to enjoy.

"No."

"You're going to burn," Violet warned.

"I never burn," the younger woman countered. "Don't you remember me as a teen? I was black as a berry all summer."

"I remember," Violet said. She'd put her towel down and gone in the shallow end. Arcineh flipped off the mattress. She swam to the shallow end to find Violet getting comfortable on the steps.

"Let me guess," Arcineh teased. "You don't want to get your hair wet."

Violet flicked water at her and laughed, but it wasn't long before she remembered something.

"And what are you doing working on the laundry?" she suddenly demanded.

"I always do my laundry."

"But you did Sam's too. Are you trying to put me out of a job?"

"As if I could," Arcineh argued and then explained, "I didn't have a full load."

"I thought you were going to give your things to me when you didn't have a full load."

"Oh yeah, I forgot about that."

Violet flicked water at her again.

"I'm going off the board," Arcineh announced, starting to climb from the pool.

"You're just trying to get my hair wet," Violet accused her.

Arcineh laughed but didn't actually deny it. Violet's hair did get splashed, but by the time Arcineh reached her side all was forgiven.

"How long will you work for Sam?" Arcineh asked.

"Until one of us dies," Violet said, not sounding the least bit bothered by the idea.

"What will you do if Sam dies first?" Arcineh asked the obvious question as Sam was at least 20 years older.

"He's provided for me," Violet explained.

"I didn't know that."

"*I* didn't know it until a few months ago."

"What has he done?"

"He set up a special account and also included me in his will."

Arcineh stared at her.

"He has changed, Arcie," the older woman said, stuffing her hair under a cap. "You're certainly right about that."

Violet pushed off the edge of the steps just then and began laps.

Clearly she was done talking about Sam, but unless Arcineh completely missed her guess, Violet was not done thinking about it.

⸗⸝⸜

Sunday felt normal. The long hours Sam and Gage had been putting in had felt all wrong to Arcineh, but at last Sunday had arrived and they were in church together. Pastor Simon had started a series on the topic of prayer, and Arcineh was amazed at the things she didn't know. Even understanding that prayer was more than talking to God, that it was agreeing with God, was so new to Arcineh that when the last song was sung, she just sat quietly, working to take it all in.

"Hello." Jalaina and Will were at her pew not five minutes later, Emilie in Will's arms.

"I didn't know you were here," Arcineh said, snapping out of her thoughts and reaching for Emilie.

"We were late and sat in the back."

"Are you free for lunch?" Sam invited.

"Not today. Grandma is expecting us," Will answered.

"She's expecting Emilie," Jalaina corrected. Everyone laughed, but the Schafer family did not rush away. Will sat near Sam and had a few more questions for him. Jalaina listened very carefully to the answers, and Arcineh, watching her, knew in her heart that she was starved for the things Sam shared. The time ran away from them, and they were some of the last people out of the building, but that was all right. Will said they would see them all next week.

Arcineh prayed for them off and on all day, and it was wonderful. She, Sam, and Gage spent the day together, a day full of naps, conversation, and sometimes silence, and one that ended all too soon. Long before Arcineh was ready, Gage was saying goodnight, and she and Sam were headed to their rooms. The workweek was on top of them again.

CHAPTER

Twenty-Six

Sam came home late on Thursday night, calling himself every kind of fool. He thought he would have known better by now, but that was not the case.

The house was dark and quiet, but that didn't change his intent. He had to speak to Arcineh, who was just a little more quiet and withdrawn around the office each day. How could he have forgotten that she would never compete for his or Gage's attention—not with a person and not with a company.

Her bedroom door creaked a little when he opened it, and much as he hated to wake her, Sam left the light on in the hall so he could find his way in.

"Sam?" Arcineh came up on one elbow. "Is something wrong?"

"No, but I have to talk to you."

Arcineh put her light on and squinted against the glare. Sam sat on the edge of the bed while Arcineh pushed against the headboard, her brain fuzzy with sleep.

"I have to apologize," Sam said. "I'm all wrapped up in Rugby, and

I'm taking Gage with me. I just remembered you. I thought I was over that type of behavior, but I'm not."

Arcineh nodded, her face thoughtful.

"Are you all right?" Sam asked.

"Gage missed our dance lesson," she said, her voice sad. "He didn't call, so I know he didn't even remember missing it."

"Oh, honey," Sam began, but Arcineh went on.

"It feels like old times, Sam," Arcineh said, and that was not a positive thing.

"I'm sure it does. I'm sorry," he repeated.

"Maybe I should go away for a while," Arcineh suggested. "I mean, I'll still love Gage and want to be with you, but my expectations will be less if I'm not here."

"No," Sam denied softly. "That's not the way to handle this. We've got to talk to you more and tell you what we're doing and how it's going."

"How much longer, Sam?" Arcineh asked.

"Probably at least a month, maybe more."

Arcineh sighed. "I guess if I know the end is in sight, I can hang in there. I'm not trying to be the center of attention. It just feels like I was the thing that Gage was into for a while, and now he's moved on."

"I can see how you would feel that way, but that's not the case. You've never expected to be the center of attention, and that makes you easy to set aside. I'm sorry."

"You don't have to apologize anymore."

Sam nodded before saying, "Give Gage a few more days. We have nonstop meetings tomorrow, so he might not remember right away about that dance lesson, but he will remember."

"Even if you have to tell him?"

"Yes. I'm part of the reason he's been drawn away. I've thrown myself into this, and he's naturally followed."

The Bryants looked at each other. This was not a conversation they could have had in the past. Painful as it was for Arcineh right now, she knew God was working in each of them.

"Will you be able to get back to sleep?"

"I think so. Is all of this making you tired?"

"A little. At the same time, being back in the business world fires my blood."

Arcineh had to smile at him. He looked just as good as always.

Sam stood and then bent to kiss her cheek. "I love you," he said.

"I love you, Sam."

"Are you going to make it?"

Arcineh nodded, suddenly sure that she was. However, when her grandfather exited, she sat thinking about some things she might do, some outside interests. Right now she was spending a little too much time waiting for others to have time. She thought it might not hurt to do a little more with her life.

❦

"Did you want to see me?" Arcineh asked when she entered the office on Friday.

"Yes. Can you take a memo?"

"A memo?" Arcineh asked from across the room, just holding her smile. "It's a little late in the day, isn't it?"

Gage looked at the clock. "We have five minutes."

"I thought with email, memos were pretty outmoded."

"But if you don't come in and take a memo, how will I have an excuse to chase you around the desk?"

Arcineh smiled but didn't answer. She wanted to laugh with delight—Gage always seemed to have that effect on her—but forced herself not to.

"I've been waiting for years to do that with my secretary," Gage continued, his eyes watchful. "And now she's not just my secretary but the woman I love."

Arcineh stared at him.

"It's not a parlor trick. I'm not trying to distract you into thinking I'm not gone as much as I am. I missed our dance lesson last night, and there is no excuse. But that doesn't change my feelings. I'm in love with you, and this is the real deal for me."

"You just have to get the company under control."

"Yes."

Arcineh stood still, trying to understand her feelings. She loved this man but was afraid too.

"Can you come a little closer?" Gage invited, and Arcineh went to where he was sitting on the front of his desk. She sat next to him, and they looked at each other.

"I am so sorry about last night. I didn't think of it until lunchtime today."

"I understand."

"Do you also understand that I love you?"

"I love you too."

Gage sighed and put an arm around her. "I don't want to lose you."

"I don't want that either, but I'm also not good at flapping around to get someone's attention. And all my doubts began to flood back in."

"Did you think you couldn't call me about the dance lesson?"

"It would only have interrupted whatever you were doing and made you feel guilty."

Gage suddenly looked surprised. "We haven't played tennis, either."

Arcineh slowly shook her head.

"We'll make up for all of this. When things settle down, we'll have the time of our lives. You'll see so much of me, you'll want to run away."

"That's not going to happen," Arcineh said, and the two stopped talking. For a long time they looked into each other's eyes. Gage finally spoke.

"Sometimes I think I started to love you the moment I set eyes on you."

"Even in those funny shoes and skirts?"

"I saw you before that."

"Where?"

"At Blankenship Dance and Aerobics. Erika had just worked out and wanted to stay and watch Windy City. I didn't know who you were, but I was captivated."

"I didn't know that," Arcineh said, her mouth open in surprise.

Gage leaned to kiss that mouth just before someone knocked on the door. It was Sam. They had another meeting. Before Gage let her go he hugged her and reminded her again, this time softly in her ear, that she was loved very much.

❧

"Are you sure?" Jalaina asked, amazed at Arcineh's offer when she arrived at their apartment on Saturday morning.

"Yes, I'm free all day, now go do something fun. I'll keep her happy until you have to nurse again."

Will and Jalaina did not argue. They had not had a day free since Emilie was born. They didn't have a day now—Emilie still needed her mother—but a few hours alone was a gift they were not going to pass up.

After they left, Arcineh and Emilie played for the better part of an hour before Emilie fell sound asleep. Arcineh was not idle. Putting the baby in her cradle in the living room where she could hear every sound she made, Arcineh began to clean. It was not her favorite task, and she didn't get past the kitchen and living room before Emilie woke, but it also did the trick. She didn't think about Gage and Sam until just before Will and Jalaina came back in the door.

❧

Arcineh could not stop crying. Jalaina and Will had stayed after the service on Sunday morning and met with Pastor Simon. The couple had knelt in his office to pray, telling God that they believed on His Son alone. They had come from the church to Sam's to share the good news.

"You have to stop, Arcie," Jalaina begged her friend, her own tears flowing unchecked.

"I can't," Arcineh said. "I'm so thankful for you, Jalaina. You've been the best friend in the world. I've begged God to save you, and now He has."

Will could not stop smiling. He had not known what he was missing and could not stop thanking Sam for all his words and prayers.

"And now I can share with my family," Jalaina said at last. Arcineh nodded, having prayed for Grandma, Marco, Nicky, and Libby so many times.

The Schafers didn't linger, and as soon as they left, Arcineh wished that Gage was home so she could share the news. Things were just starting to come together at Rugby, and Gage had gone on his annual bike ride with friends from college.

Arcineh talked to him in her mind for the rest of the day, and when the phone rang before dinner, she hoped it would be Gage. It was Erika. Gage had fallen from his bike and was in the hospital. Sam and Arcineh rushed to the car and made a beeline for the hospital.

☖

"Erika?" Gage asked from his hospital bed, his eyes still closed. "Are you still in here?"

"Yes."

"Have you gotten ahold of Arcie? I have to talk to her."

"Gage." Arcineh said his name and took his hand when he reached for her. His grip was surprisingly strong, and he was not letting go.

"I didn't know you were here," he said, sounding choked up, his eyes still closed.

"I'm here," she said, sitting as close as the side rails on the bed would allow.

"Don't go."

"I won't."

Arcineh glanced and saw again the helmet on the windowsill. A large dog had darted out without warning and straight into the side of Gage's bike. Gage's head had hit the pavement, a blow that would have likely killed him had he not been wearing that helmet. He also had broken ribs to contend with and multiple abrasions.

Thank You, Lord, Arcineh prayed. *Thank You for sparing him. Help him to recover and to remember Your hand in this. Please use this to make me more aware of how fragile our lives are.*

"Marry me," Gage suddenly said.

Arcineh watched Erika's hand go to her mouth, her eyes flood with tears.

"There you go again, picking those romantic settings," she teased Gage, working not to cry herself.

"What do you mean?"

"Our first real kiss was in your garage, then you told me you loved me in your office, and now you propose in a hospital room."

"You deserve better," he said seriously, his hand still gripping hers.

"I was just teasing."

"Don't go," he said again.

"Don't worry about my leaving. Just get better."

"Okay," Gage agreed on a sigh, his voice sleepy again. Arcineh stayed close, but she knew the very moment he slept; the hand holding hers so tightly had gone completely limp.

∞

Gage woke up early in the hospital, his mind going over the events of the last few days. *You are a saving God,* Gage's heart prayed, still amazed that God had spared him. His head still pained him quite a bit, but he could tell he was going to be all right. *Thank You, Father. Thank You for loving me so much and having a perfect plan.*

All over this hospital, people are sick and even dying, and I know comfort because You are in control. Please save each heart in this place, Lord, Gage continued to pray, remembering the things Simon had been teaching. *Help me to be a light in any way that glorifies You, Lord. Even in pain, help me to keep my mind fixed on You.*

Gage prayed himself back to sleep, a peaceful sleep. When he woke again, the nurse was there with his breakfast. Gage thanked her, asked how she was, and remembered to pray for her as well, so deep was his gratitude that God had brought him to this place.

⚮

Luke and Erika brought Gage home. It had taken some doing. His car had to be retrieved, along with his bike, which was not in the best shape. Luke pulled the car into the driveway, parking alongside a brand new bike with a helmet hanging from the bars. They appeared to be the very image of his old bike and helmet, and Gage got out of the car as fast as his body would allow.

He looked in amazement at the new bike, knowing exactly who had done this but not sure how she had accomplished it. Without further ado, Gage turned for Sam's.

"Oh, no, you don't," Luke said, taking his brother-in-law by the arm and steering him back to his own front door. "The doctor said to take it very easy."

"I have to see Arcie."

"We'll get her over here. Just come in and rest."

But Luke wasn't able to make good on his word. He went next door to get Arcineh but was told she wasn't there. This news received, Gage was on his cell phone seconds later. He had to work very hard on his attitude when he got nothing but her voice mail for the next hour.

∞

Arcineh was on her way home when her phone rang. She almost didn't pick up, but the light changed and she found herself sitting.

"Hello."

"Hello, yourself."

"Gage! Hi! Are they letting you out?"

"I'm home."

"You're home?" This threw Arcineh off. "I didn't think it would be this early."

"Well, I am, and I can't find my girlfriend."

"I'm coming! I was just at Nicky's helping Libby with some wallpaper, but I'm on my way."

"Hurry," Gage said. "Be safe, but hurry."

Arcineh hung up on a laugh and went directly to Gage's. She knocked on the front door but went in when she found it open. Gage was halfway across the foyer, and although he finished the distance rather slowly, he came directly to her and took her in his arms.

"I don't want to hurt you," Arcineh said, her arms moving very carefully.

"Just don't squeeze too hard around my middle."

Arcineh's arms settled around his neck. That done, she looked up at him.

"Did you find your presents?"

"Yes. How did you manage that?"

"Sam and I made phone calls and then ran all over Chicago."

Gage looked down into her face.

"You're amazing."

"I'm glad you think so."

Gage tightened his hold a little, his face growing serious. "I don't want to waste any more time. My accident could have been fatal. We've got Rugby where it needs to be, and I want to get on with my life."

"Okay," Arcineh agreed, not sure what she was supposed to say.

"You didn't answer my question," Gage said.

"What question?"

"The one in the hospital."

Arcineh smiled before saying, "You were in a drug-induced state. I wasn't sure you meant it."

"I meant it."

"In that case, yes, I'll marry you, Gage Sefton."

Gage was done waiting. He claimed Arcineh's lips with his own, all aches and pains from the accident fading away in the sweetness of her embrace.

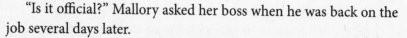

"Is it official?" Mallory asked her boss when he was back on the job several days later.

"Yes. I mean, we haven't set a date, but she said yes."

"Why isn't she wearing a ring?"

Gage stared at his assistant. Why hadn't he thought of this?

"*Is* she wearing a ring?" Mallory asked.

"No, but thank you for saying something. I completely forgot."

Mallory's eyes twinkled at him, but she didn't comment. Gage managed to smile back at her, but his mind was already at work. His acumen at romance had been lacking so far. It was time to pull out the stops. Gage asked not to be disturbed and disappeared into his office to solve this problem.

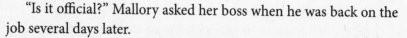

"So how is Margo working out?" Arcineh asked about the new assistant, the one who had made her redundant.

"Very well, liked by all."

"I'm glad. Where are we going, by the way?"

The two were in Gage's car and headed out for the evening. Gage had said it would not be fancy, and since the weather had turned very warm, they were both in shorts.

"I'm in the mood to go to the Shedd," Gage said just before they got close enough for Arcineh to figure it out.

"That's always good news."

"I thought you might say that," Gage said as they parked, praying and working to keep his heartbeat at a normal pace. He had a ring in his pocket and wanted to bring it out at just the right moment.

They started at the Caribbean Reef before slowly making their way toward the Oceanarium. The dolphin show was over, so they sat for a while and looked out at the lake, but eventually Gage took Arcineh's hand and led her to the walkway outside. The sun was setting—streaks of red and orange could be seen in the sky—and Gage slipped an arm around Arcineh and drew her close.

"I think it's time I make this official," he said quietly.

Arcineh looked at him, not sure what he was talking about until she saw the ring he held in two fingers.

"Oh, Gage," she breathed, her heart beginning to thunder as she looked at the large diamond surrounded by sapphires, her favorite stone. "It's so beautiful."

"Then it's perfect for you."

Arcineh watched as he pushed it onto the ring finger of her left hand before throwing her arms around his neck. Gage caught her close, giving her a long kiss before turning her and pointing to the windows of the Soundings Restaurant.

"I think they're ready for us."

Arcineh's mouth opened when she saw whom he'd gathered. Sam, Violet, Jalaina, Will, Quinn, Pastor Simon and his wife, Nicole, Grandma, Marco, Nicky, and Libby were all waving from the window.

Arcineh turned back to Gage and threw her arms around him again. "I'm going to love being married to you."

"Was there ever a doubt?" he asked, his eyes alight with love.

"Not a one," she told him as his lips drew near. "Not a one."

Epilogue

TWELVE YEARS LATER

"Arcineh?" Gage asked sleepily, coming into the kitchen at 2:00 A.M.

"Oh, I'm sorry," she whispered. "Did I wake you?"

"I think so. What are you doing?"

"Are you hiding any white chocolate?"

Gage had to smile. His wife's stomach was so extended she couldn't even reach over the top of the fridge. And as with all of her pregnancies, white chocolate had been the mainstay.

"I think I might have some in the den."

"I already looked."

Gage had to smile again.

"I just need a little," Arcineh said.

"Right now?"

"Yes. Do you think Sam has some?"

"Knowing Sam, he does, but we're not going to wake him."

"I'll run to the store."

"Are you a little tired?" Gage asked, praying for a yes but also thankful he was off work right now.

"A little."

"Come on, I'll rub your back until you fall asleep. And then in the morning," Gage continued, talking when she might have tried a new tack, "I'll head right to Sam's for white chocolate."

Arcineh agreed, knowing it was selfish to do anything else but not sure she would fall back to sleep. She hadn't planned to wake up, but she'd had to use the bathroom, and then the vanilla scented soap had sent her mind off.

"Come on," Gage invited her, his arm going around her.

And he was good at his word. He rubbed his wife's back for almost 30 minutes. It took that long for her to fall off to sleep. Indeed she slept so hard that Gage was back with the white chocolate before she woke. Arcineh found it on the nightstand when her eyes opened.

⁓

"I want you to go," Arcineh said.

Gage stared at his wife, trying to gauge the situation, but then she played the trump card.

"The boys will be so disappointed, and this is Kenny's first year."

"But they'll understand if you're about to go into labor," Gage argued.

"I just saw the doctor. It's going to be ten days at least and probably two weeks."

The boys they were speaking of made an appearance before Gage could say anything else. Ten-year-old Ethan was first. Behind him was three-year-old Kenny and then eight- and seven- year-old Tanner and Derek.

"We're hungry."

"That's a shock," Arcineh teased, reaching for the crackers. "Peanut butter or cheese?"

The answers to that were varied, so Arcineh made a few of each. Even Gage wanted some.

"Not hungry?" he asked his wife.

She looked guilty before admitting, "I ate all four squares of the chocolate."

"Was it good?" Gage asked with amused eyes, reminding Arcineh why this man was so special.

"It was. Thanks for getting it."

"You're welcome. Now, back to the discussion."

Gage drew his wife into the family room, telling the boys to stay put. He sat her down and spoke seriously. "We can postpone this trip."

"Please don't. Even if something starts, you'll have the phone and you're not that far."

"Three hours."

"Things never move that fast."

With a little more discussion, Gage agreed, hoping they were doing the right thing. He did so with some reservation, but he was also very excited. His annual bike trip had turned into a much less taxing trek that the family made each year. Gage didn't know when he'd had such fun. The first year, Ethan and Tanner had been only five and three. They had repeated it ever since, three being the magic age when the boys could join them and not stay with great-grandpa. Arcineh usually went with them, but being eight-and-a-half months pregnant made that out of the question.

Kenny came looking for his mother just then. He tried to climb into her disappearing lap, and Arcineh cuddled him close.

"Are you ready for the bike trip tomorrow?" she asked.

"I want you to come," Kenny said. He'd been a bit clingy lately.

"I want to, but it's not going to work this year. You'll still have a great time."

"Papa says we can pray for you."

"Thank you," Arcineh said, pressing a kiss to his forehead. "I'll pray for you too."

Kenny looked up at her, and Gage had to fight his doubts again. Kenny was reticent, and his wife looked ready to burst. Arcineh looked his way and caught his expression.

"Go," she said softly. "It will be all right."

Gage nodded, and true to his word, they left in the morning.

❧

Jalaina and her two youngest had just left when Arcineh felt a familiar pain. She had gone into false labor twice over the years, so she didn't panic but thought she would check to see if Sam and Violet were at home. Her grandfather came right away, but Violet was out.

"I'm too old for this," he told her, kissing her cheek and taking in the sweat on her brow. She had had a strong contraction that felt like the real thing right after talking to Sam.

"I need your advice," Arcineh said.

"Okay."

"I pressed Gage to go on the bike trip. Do I tell him about it so he has to rush back or just have the baby and hope he understands?"

Sam's look of horror was hysterical.

"You haven't called him yet?"

"No."

Sam began to stand, but Arcineh stopped him.

"I'm not sure yet, Sam. It could be false."

"Get up," he ordered. "We're going to the hospital."

"Why?"

"So they can tell us if this is real."

Arcineh nodded and began to stand. She had just straightened her back when her water broke.

"What's the matter?" Sam asked, his face alarmed.

"My water just broke."

Sam sighed before saying again, "I'm too old for this."

Arcineh laughed as she dialed her husband and then the doctor. She only reached the latter, and much as she hated to do it, left her husband an apologetic message before gathering her things to leave for the hospital.

∽∾

"Any sign of him, Vi?"

"No, sweetheart, but we know he's on his way," Vi said, having just arrived herself.

Arcineh looked up at Violet, who had finally begun to age, and smiled at her.

"What would I do without you?" Arcineh asked.

"Same thing I would do without you—be heartbroken."

Arcineh smiled at her just as another pain hit. She heard Violet praying softly, glad for the reminder that God had a plan and that His plan had included saving Violet just before Ethan was born.

"That was bad," Arcineh gasped. "I feel like I need to push."

"I'll get someone."

Arcineh was right. Just 15 minutes later, the doctor was there and he was coaching Arcineh through the birth. Violet stayed close by. Arcineh could not have said when Gage arrived, but he was suddenly there too.

"I'm sorry," she cried when he kissed her.

"It's all right. I'm here now."

"I'm sorry," she gasped this time, and then desperately had to push. A little boy came into the world just 14 minutes later, and Arcineh had to laugh.

"We already have a name picked out," she said. "I knew it would be a boy."

Gage kissed her and laughed with her. They were looking at their new son, thrilled with his perfect little person, when Arcineh felt another contraction. The doctor was just on his way out when Arcineh gasped.

Ten minutes of mayhem passed before the doctor told his patient she was carrying another baby. Arcineh would have had many questions, but the pains were on her, and she was soon ready to push again.

Another 18 minutes passed this time, and when it was done, Gage openly cried as the nurse put a tiny baby on Arcineh's chest. It was a girl.

ᏉᏇ

"How are you?" Arcineh asked of her sons when they came to visit her in the hospital room. Their answers varied, and Arcineh laughed a little. She finally focused on each one, taking time to hear every word.

"Did you see the babies?" she asked of Ethan first.

He smiled before saying, "They're so small."

"I think you said that about Derek too."

"Probably," Ethan agreed, smiling again when his mother reached to touch his hair.

"How about you, Tanner?"

"Is there going to be a pink room?" he wanted to know.

"Not all pink." Arcineh assured him, wanting to laugh at his doubtful expression. "I think you'll like having a sister."

"I don't know," he said, not afraid to be honest.

"You like me, and I'm a girl."

"That's different," Tanner said before Arcineh turned to Derek.

"What do you think of the babies, Derek?"

"How did the doctor not know?" the astute seven-year-old asked.

"Sometimes they can't tell when there are twins. He was as surprised as I was."

"Did it hurt?" he then asked, more interested in medical matters than any one of his siblings.

"Just a little bit more. Not too bad."

When Derek nodded, seeming satisfied, Arcineh turned to Kenny, who had been sitting quietly in his father's arms.

"Did you see our babies, Kenny?"

That little boy nodded and yawned at the same time.

"How did you like the bike ride?" Arcineh just remembered to ask.

"I wanted you," he said, his eyes getting a bit moist.

"I'll be home tomorrow," she told him.

"With the babies?"

"Yes," Arcineh was pleased to say, so thankful they were doing fine.

"Okay, boys," Gage cut in, seeing that Arcineh was growing fatigued. "Say goodbye to Mom."

The boys who couldn't reach climbed up to kiss her, and Gage handed off Kenny to Ethan before coming close.

"I'll get them home and then I'll be back."

"Okay."

Gage looked into her eyes a moment. "You were amazing today."

"Thank you. I'm just glad you made it."

Gage had to laugh a little. "I won't be talked into going without you again."

Arcineh had to laugh with him, not wanting him to leave for even an hour and thinking that he was right—she would never talk him into leaving without her again.

ᎧᏧᎧ

A week later Arcineh found Gage in the nursery. The boys were all asleep. She had already prayed over them, thinking that Gage had retired for the night. Planning to pray at the twins' cribside, she found Gage staring down into the crib they had fashioned to hold two babies, Keith Joseph and Jalaina Violet. Arcineh came up behind him, her arms going around his middle.

"I can't get over it," he said softly, staring down at the tiny forms God had given them.

"They're so little." Arcineh laughed softly.

"And she was hiding," Gage said, his smile huge. "The girl my wife has waited for was hiding from us."

Gage's arms went around Arcineh as she looked up into his face.

"Thank you," Gage said.

"For what?"

"For being you." Gage kissed her brow. "For being the mother you are." He kissed her cheek. "And for being my girl."

Arcineh sighed when Gage finally found her mouth.

"I knew it would be fun being married to you."

Gage's pleased laugh came softly to her ear just before he kissed her again.

About the Author

LORI WICK is a
multifaceted author of Christian fiction.
As comfortable writing period stories
as she is penning contemporary works,
Lori's books (5 million in print)
vary widely in location and time period.
Lori's faithful fans consistenly put her series
and standalone works on the bestseller lists.
Lori and her husband, Bob,
live with their swifly growing family
in the Midwest.

Books by Lori Wick

A Place Called Home Series
A Place Called Home
A Song for Silas
The Long Road Home
A Gathering of Memories

The Californians
Whatever Tomorrow Brings
As Time Goes By
Sean Donovan
Donovan's Daughter

Kensington Chronicles
The Hawk and the Jewel
Wings of the Morning
Who Brings Forth the Wind
The Knight and the Dove

Rocky Mountain Memories
Where the Wild Rose Blooms
Whispers of Moonlight
To Know Her by Name
Promise Me Tomorrow

The Yellow Rose Trilogy
Every Little Thing About You
A Texas Sky
City Girl

English Garden Series
The Proposal
The Rescue
The Visitor
The Pursuit

The Tucker Mills Trilogy
Moonlight on the Millpond
Just Above a Whisper
Leave a Candle Burning

Contemporary Fiction
Sophie's Heart
Pretense
The Princess
Bamboo & Lace
Every Storm
White Chocolate Moments

To learn more about books by Lori Wick
or to read sample chapters, log on to our website:

www.harvesthousepublishers.com

HARVEST HOUSE PUBLISHERS

EUGENE, OREGON